Reading
BOROUGH C

2002

Author: MARSHALL Michael
Title:

Class no.

To avoid overdue charges please return this book to a
Reading library on or before the last date stamped above.
If not required by another reader, it may be renewed by
personal visit, telephone, post, email, or via our website.

THE
STRAW
MEN

Writing as Michael Marshall Smith

Only Forward
Spares
One of Us

Stories

What You Make It

MICHAEL
MARSHALL

THE
STRAW
MEN

HarperCollins*Publishers*

This novel is entirely a work of fiction.
The names, characters and incidents portrayed
in it are the work of the author's imagination.
Any resemblance to actual persons, living or dead,
events or localities is entirely coincidental.

HarperCollins*Publishers*
77–85 Fulham Palace Road,
Hammersmith, London W6 8JB

www.fireandwater.com

Published by HarperCollins*Publishers* 2002
1 3 5 7 9 8 6 4 2

Copyright © Michael Marshall Smith 2002

The Author asserts the moral right to
be identified as the author of this work

A catalogue record for this book
is available from the British Library

Hardback ISBN 0 00 225601 0
Trade Paperback ISBN 0 00 715186 1

Typeset in Minion and Din by
Palimpsest Book Production Limited, Polmont, Stirlingshire

Printed and bound in Great Britain by
Clays Ltd, St Ives plc

For
Jane Johnson

Acknowledgements

Thanks to Doug Winter, for using a phrase that set my mind rolling; to Susan Allison, Chris Smith, and Jim Rickards for getting it to roll far enough, and also to Linda Shaughnessy, Bob Bookman, Jonny Geller, and David and Margaret Smith for their comments; to Nicholas Royle, Howard Ely, Conrad Williams, Stephen Jones, and Adam Simon for support during this and other processes.

Love as always to my family, with special thanks to Paula – for helping me see the cracks in the wall I was banging my head against, and being there when I stopped.

The Straw Men

We are too late for gods
and too early for Being.
Being's poem,
Just begun, is man.
Martin Heidegger
Language, Truth, Thought
Translated by Albert Hofstadter

Palmerston, Pennsylvania

Palmerston is not a big town, nor one that can convincingly be said to be at the top of its game. It's just there, like a mark on the sidewalk. Like all towns, it has a past and once had a future, but in this case that future turned out to involve little but getting dustier and more sedate, nudged ever further from the through lines of history: a stiff old faucet at the end of an increasingly rusty pipe, that someday is going to leak so badly that no water makes it to the end at all.

The town sits on the Allegheny River, in the shade of muscular hills, and has more trees than you could shake a stick at unless you had a lot of time and were unusually demented. The railroad used to pass close by, just the other side of the river, but in the mid 70s the station was closed and most of the track lifted up. Little remains of it now apart from the memory and a half-hearted museum, which not even the schoolkids visit much any more. Every now and then a few tourists will wander in, peer with bemused indifference at grim photographs of the long-dead, and then elect to get back in the car and make time. Though it's been thirty years, long-term residents (and in Palmerston, they're all long-term, and vaguely proud of it) still feel the absence of the railroad, like an amputated limb that itches from time to time. For some there were petitions and town meetings, bumper stickers and fundraisers; for others the change came quietly, numbly accepted as part of history's entropic progress in some other direction. Were the town a little bigger and more boisterous, the overgrown track might make a good place to buy drugs or get mugged. In Palmerston it's used mainly by earnest parents to trek children down at weekends, for pointing at birds and trees; and equally earnestly, a few years down the line, for those same kids to get each other pregnant in order to exchange one style of confinement for another.

The town is built around a T junction, the shape of the letter obscured by side streets that seem unsure of their purpose. The upright is littered with gas stations, a car wash, a video store, two small motels and a minimart with a rack of cheap CDs of the Marshall Tucker Band's Greatest Hits. An old wooden church stands at the intersection with the cross stroke, paint peeling now, but still picturesque against a cold blue sky. The right fork takes you up into the hills towards New York State and the Great Lakes.

If you take a left, as you would if you were heading west on Route 6 to go look at the Allegheny reservoir – and that's pretty much the only reason that you'd be passing through – you get onto Main Street. Here you find a few banks and stores, the windows of the former mirrored and anonymous; those of the latter in need of cleaning, and framing antiques of limited worth. Something about the desultory arrangement of the displays suggests that the objects will have plenty more time to accrue value *in situ*. There are two small movie houses, one of which tried to show art movies ten years ago and was rewarded by attendances so low that it closed in a fit of pique and never reopened; the other still steadfastly toeing the party line of popular culture, hawking unrealizable dreams to

2

popcorn junkies. On the southern side of the street, in a large plot all by itself, sits a beautiful Victorian house. It has lain empty for some years, and though most of the windows are intact, it's peeling a good deal worse than the church and some of the boards are beginning to slip.

If you're hungry, chances are you'll find yourself in the McDonald's a little further up the street, just along from the Railway Museum. Most people do. Palmerston isn't a bad place. It's peaceful, and the people are friendly. It's a pleasant part of the world, low on crime and close by the Susquehannock State Forest. You could be born, raise kids, and die there, without feeling you'd been especially short-changed by fate.

There just isn't much to do in between.

At lunchtime on Wednesday, 30th October 1991, the McD's was crowded. Most of the tables were already occupied, and four lines straggled out from the counter. Two little girls, four and six years old and out for a treat with their mother, clamoured vehemently for Chicken McNuggets. Everyone else gazed at the menu boards with the reverence they deserved.

There were three non-locals present, a red-letter day for Palmerston's tourist industry. One was a middle-aged man wearing a suit, sitting by himself at a table in the corner. His name was Pete Harris, and he was driving back to Chicago after a long sales trip that had been largely disappointing. The Victorian house's Italianate tower was just visible from his seat and he was considering the house as he chewed, finding it astounding that no one had bothered to reclaim the property and fix it up.

The other two were a couple of English tourists, by coincidence sitting at the next table. Mark and Suzy Campbell had skipped breakfast to do a couple hundred miles in the morning and were more than ready for some food. They'd been hoping for a picturesque diner, but after a slow trawl through town they'd settled on the burger den by default. Munching their sandwiches in a defensive huddle, they were at first alarmed and then mildly pleased to find that they had sat next to a local who talked. His name was Trent, and he was tall, in his forties, and had a good deal of copper-coloured hair. On hearing that they were a few days into a coast-to-coast drive, he nodded with distant approval – as if being told of a practice he could understand but had no desire to undertake himself, like collecting matchbooks, or rockclimbing, or having a job. He was familiar with England as a concept, and gathered that it had a whole lot of history and a thriving rock music industry, both of which he was in favour of.

In the end the conversation petered out, running aground in the shallows of shared experience. Suzy was a little disappointed, having enjoyed the encounter. Mark was preoccupied, wanting to do some shopping. In the hotel they'd stayed at the night before, the bartender had spent some time trawling the radio waves in search of something to play very loudly. He'd accidentally wandered across a classical station, and for a brief, wonderful moment, a snatch of the *Goldberg Variations* had floated across the bar. Mark had pictured the radio station as just one guy holed up in the mountains someplace, the door barred against hordes armed to the teeth with Garth Brooks records. The Bach had remained in Mark's head through the following hours of syrupy ballads contrasting the fragility of marriage and the steadfastness of dogs, and he wanted to buy a CD and play it in the car. Palmerston didn't have a classical music store.

Trent was soon joined by a gaggle of floppy and unattractive teenage boys, and as Suzy eavesdropped it emerged that he was engaged in convincing the youths to help him move a huge pile of dirt outside his trailer, down by the old railroad line. It was never established why the dirt was there, nor why it now needed to be moved somewhere else. The boys were, not unnaturally, interested in some kind of payment for this work, and this was offered in the form of a case of beer. As none were within three years of legally being able to buy alcohol, the proposition was readily accepted. While they waited for Trent to finish wading through his burgers,

4

they lurked like a crew of disreputable seagulls, trading the affectionate insults and unrealistic suggestions which are the key discourse of boys. During this it became clear that despite the surfing-related T-shirts in which most were clad, not a single one had ever surfed, most had not been out of state, and only one had even seen the sea.

Overhearing this, the Campbells realized how extraordinary it was that they were – on a whim conceived one drunken evening in a pub six thousand miles away – driving the entire breadth of someone else's vast country. They became both flushed with pride and utterly overawed with the magnitude of the undertaking, and sipped their coffees meditatively, taking perhaps five or six minutes longer than they normally would have allowed. Without this delay, they'd have been out the door by 12.50. Even with it, they'd have been on the road by 12.56 at the latest. By then Suzy would have been ready for a cigarette, which the signs on the walls forbade through curt, easy-to-read sentences and internationally recognizable iconography. Pete Harris was in no real hurry, and would have been there anyway: still gazing at the house on a plot by itself, wondering vaguely how much it might cost, knowing that even if he could rustle up the money, his wife would have earmarked it for something else.

At 12.53 a woman shouted in the middle of the restaurant.

It was a brief, emphatic utterance, conveying nothing except urgency. People moved unconsciously out of the way, creating a clearing in the central aisle. It became evident that two men – one in his late teens, the other mid-twenties, both wearing long coats – were the focus of the woman's concern. The older man had short fair hair, the younger's was darker and rather longer. It was soon also clear that they were carrying semi-automatic rifles.

The light in the room seemed suddenly very bright, sounds abnormally clear and dry, as if some cushioning ether had been swept away. When you're sitting in a McDonald's on a weekday

5

lunchtime with your coffee just approaching a drinkable temperature, and you realize that night has fallen out of a clear blue sky, time slips into a slow moment of lucidity. Like the long second before the impact of a car crash, this hiatus is not there to help you. It's not an escape route, or a gift from God, and it is not enough to do anything in except take the chance to greet death and wonder what took it so long.

One of Trent's crew of slackers had just time to say 'Billy?' in a tone of goofy bafflement, and then the two men started shooting.

They stood in the central aisle and fired calmly and quickly, the stocks of the rifles securely anchored in their shoulders. As the first casualty jerked backward, an expression of wordless surprise on her face, the gunmen moved on: intently, earnestly, as if seeking to demonstrate to some higher authority that they were worthy of this task, and carrying it out to the best of their ability.

After about another second, and two more deaths, everyone in the restaurant suddenly fought their way up out of bewilderment. Time hit the ground running, and the screaming started. They tried to flee, or hide, or to pull other people in front of them. Some made a break for the doors, but the guns turned as one and took down the deserters efficiently. Their line of fire swept past the out-of-towners, and Mark Campbell took a direct shot in the back of the head at about the same instant his wife's face was spread over a spiderweb of cracks in the plate-glass window that halted both of the bullets' progress. Trent died furiously soon afterwards, halfway to his feet on a doomed mission to throw himself at the gunmen. Few were sufficiently self-possessed to even consider such positive action, and those that did died quickly. The two guns swivelled as if pulled on the same string, and the action heroes discovered that while passive smoking may be bad for you, passive bullet use will take you down quicker.

Most people just tried to run. To get away. The vice-president of Bedloe Insurance tried, as did his exasperatingly inefficient assistant. Twelve schoolchildren tried. They all tried together, and got in one another's way. Many found that their feet were tangled amidst the bodies of the injured, and died awkwardly, dislocating knees and hips as they fell. Those whose way was unobstructed were shot down as they fled, crashing into tables and walls and the serving counter, behind which the remaining living server was curled in a tight ball, all too aware that she lay in a pool of her own urine. From where she lay she could see the twitching feet of Duane Hillman, the young man with whom she'd most recently walked the line of the railroad. He had been sweet, and offered to use a condom. As she knew that he'd not only been shot but had fallen while holding a tray of hot oil, she wasn't inclined to look at him. She was hoping instead that if she looked at nothing at all, and made herself small, maybe everything would be all right. A stray bullet later cut directly through the counter and into her spine.

There were those who didn't even try to escape, but held their positions, eyes wide, souls already departed before shells tumbled through their lungs, groins and stomachs. At least one of them, recently diagnosed with the same cancer that had slowly killed her father, did not view this turn of events in an entirely negative light: although the fact of the matter is that the young doctor at the hospital, whom she did not trust largely because he looked a little like the villain on her favourite TV show, would have been able to save her had she lived and taken his advice.

The other statue people had no such reason for equanimity. They were simply unable to move until the choice was no longer theirs to make.

In a room full of victims, murderers look like gods. The men kept shooting, with occasional changes of direction, rifles turning together to rain fire on an unexpected corner of the room. They reloaded a number of times, though never at the same moment. They were very efficient. Neither said anything throughout the entire incident.

Of the fifty-nine people in the McDonald's that lunchtime, only thirty-one heard the deadened report of the final shot. Twelve of

7

those were dead before dark, bringing the toll to forty. Among those who lived was the girl behind the counter, who never walked again and became an alcoholic before finding God and then losing him once more. One of the little girls also survived. She was fostered out to an aunt in Iowa, and went on to live a life of relative peace. One of Trent's friends made it, and four years later was a coast guard on Laguna Beach.

Pete Harris also survived. By rights he should have died early, in the first sweep of gunfire down the left side of the restaurant, but Suzy Campbell's body had crashed on top of him just as he tried to slip under his table. Her weight caused him to slew off his seat and crunch head-first to the ground. They were joined moments later by Suzy's husband, who was already dead. Neither of the Campbells' faces would have been recognizable from their passports (both carefully stowed in their jacket pockets, in case somebody broke into the car while they ate), but the clothes the couple were wearing – some carefully packed back in England, others frugally acquired at a Gap sale in Boston's Back Bay area – were virtually unblemished. Barely a brush-down would have been needed and they could have walked out the door, climbed back in their hire car, and driven on up the road. Perhaps in some better reality that was allowed to happen, and Mark found the *Goldberg Variations* by happy chance at a town up the way, and they drove the rest of the day along a long straight road between trees with leaves that seemed lit from within: riding the crests and dips of the highway as it took them into afternoon and then evening, never noticing that they rode alone.

In this world they merely saved the life of another human being, as Pete Harris lay frozen beneath them, stunned into immobility by the contact of his head with the tiled floor. All around him were limbs, and all he could see was chaos and death: all he could feel was the whistling of his cuts and a cold ache in his head that developed into a concussion so severe that some days he felt as if it never went away. A young staff nurse, who seemed to regard him with superstitious awe because he had survived when almost everyone else had died, spent the night in the hospital in Pipersville keeping him awake, when he would have much preferred to have slept.

But that was later, as was the heart attack in 1995 that achieved what the bullets had not. He never tried to find out if the Victorian house was for sale. He just worked until he dropped.

Above the measured *snap* of gunfire and the coughs and screams of the dying, the distant sound of approaching sirens became evident. The gunmen fired for perhaps another twenty seconds, clearing a small pocket by the counter where the mother and her girls had found temporary respite. Then they stopped.

They looked around the room, faces betraying no reaction to what they'd done. The younger of the two – the boy called Billy – took a step back, and shut his eyes. The other man shot him point-blank in the face. While Billy's body still languidly spasmed on the floor, the man squatted to wash his hands in the blood. He stood again to write something on the glass door, working calmly, in big dripping letters, then surveyed the room once more, calmly, at his ease. He didn't even glance at the cop cars hurtling up Main, far too late to influence an event that would finally put Palmerston back on the map.

Then, when he was good and ready, the man jumped through the shattered window behind the Campbells' bodies and disappeared: escaping, it was believed, along the track of the old railroad line. He was never apprehended. No one was ever able to give a clear description of his face, and in time it was as if he slipped out of the event and into shadow. The blame ended up being wholly Billy's: a young boy who had only been doing what he was told, by a man he'd thought was a new friend.

When he heard the sound of the police cars pulling up outside, Pete Harris tried to sit up, tried to gather the strength to push the Campbells' bodies off. He failed, but succeeded in raising his head far enough to see what had been written in blood on the doors.

The letters had dripped, and his eyesight was clouded by a white light in his head, but the words were clear enough. They said 'The Straw Men'.

Eleven years passed.

Part 1

Of the hill, not on the hill . . .
Frank Lloyd Wright,
on the architecture of Taliesin

Chapter 1

The funeral was a nice affair, in that it was well-attended and people dressed appropriately and nobody stood up at any point and said 'You realize this means they're dead.' It was held in a church on the edge of town. I had no idea what denomination it might be, still less why it should have been stipulated in the instructions left with Harold Davids. So far as I'd known, my parents had no religious views save a kind of amiable atheism and the unspoken belief that if God did exist he probably drove a nice car, most likely of American manufacture.

Organization for the event had been efficiently undertaken by Davids's office, leaving me with little to do except wait to turn up. I spent most of the two days in the lounge of the Best Western. I knew I should go up to the house, but I couldn't face it. I read most of a bad novel and leafed through a large number of hotel-style magazines, without learning anything except that you can pay an awful lot of money for a watch. Early each morning I left the hotel, intending to walk along the main street, but got no further than the parking lot. I knew what was on offer along the shopping drag of Dyersburg, Montana, and I was in the market for neither ski gear nor 'art'. I ate in the hotel restaurant in the evenings, had room-service sandwiches delivered to the bar at lunch. All meals were accompanied by fries whose texture suggested that a number of industrial processes had intervened between the soil and my plate. It was impossible not to have fries. I discussed the matter on two occasions with the waitresses, but relented in the face of mounting panic in their eyes.

After the preacher had explained to everyone why death was not the complete downer it might at first appear, we filed out of the church. I was sorry to leave. It had felt safe in there. Outside it was very cold, and the air was crisp and silent. Behind the graveyard rose the foothills of the Gallatin range, the peaks in the distance muted, as if painted on glass. Two side-by-side plots had been prepared. There were about fifteen people on hand to witness the burial. Davids was there, and someone who appeared to be his assistant. Mary stood close to me, white hair strictly pulled back in a bun, her lined face battered smooth with the cold. A couple of the others I thought I vaguely recognized.

More words were said by the priest, comforting lies in which to swaddle these events. Possibly they made a difference to some of the mourners. I could barely hear them, concentrating as I was on stopping my head from exploding. Then a couple of men — whose job it was, who did this kind of thing every week — efficiently lowered the coffins into the ground. Ropes were gently fed through their hands, and the coffins came to measured rest six feet below the flat plain on which the living still stood. A few more sentences of balm were offered, but muttered quickly now — as if the church recognized that the time to make its pitch was running out. You can't put people in wooden boxes under the ground without the audience realizing that something very amiss is afoot.

A final quiet pronouncement, and that was that. It was done. Nothing would ever happen to Donald and Beth Hopkins again. Nothing that bore thinking about, at least.

Some of the mourners lingered for a moment, aimless now. Then I was alone. I stood there as two people. One whose throat was locked into fiery stone, and who could not imagine ever moving again; another who was aware of his iconic stature beside the graves, and also that, a little distance away, people were driving past in cars and listening to the Dixie Chicks and worrying vaguely about money. Both sides of me found the other ridiculous.

I knew that I couldn't stand there for ever. They wouldn't expect me to. It would make no sense, would change nothing, and it really was very cold. When I finally looked up I saw Mary was also still present, standing only a few feet away. Her eyes were dry, harsh with a knowledge that such a fate would be hers before very long and that it was neither a laughing nor a crying matter. I pursed my lips, and she reached out and laid her hand on my arm. Neither of us said anything for a while.

When she'd called me, three days before, I had been sitting on the deck of a nice, small hotel on De la Vina in Santa Barbara. I was temporarily unemployed, or unemployed again, and using my scant savings on an undeserved vacation. I was sitting with a good bottle of local merlot in front of me, and efficiently making it go away. It wasn't the first of the evening, and so when my cellular rang I was inclined to let the message service pick it up. But when I glanced at the phone I saw who the caller was.

I hit the TALK button. 'Hey,' I said.

'Ward,' she replied. And then nothing.

Finally I heard a sound down the line. The noise was soft, glutinous. 'Mary?' I asked quickly. 'Are you okay?'

'Oh, Ward,' she said, her voice sounding cracked and very old. I sat up straight in my seat then, in the vain hope that faux readiness, last-minute rigour, would somehow limit the weight with which this hammer was going to fall.

15

'What is it?'

'Ward, you'd better come here.'

In the end I got her to tell me. A car crash in the centre of Dyersburg. Both dead on arrival.

I'd known immediately it would be something like that, I suppose. If it hadn't involved both of them then it wouldn't be Mary on the phone. But even now, as I stood with her in the graveyard looking down upon their coffins, I was unable to truly understand a sentence framing their death with its full weight. I also could not now return the call that my mother had left on my machine, a week before. I just hadn't gotten round to it. I hadn't expected them to be erased from the surface of the earth without warning, and put below it, down where they couldn't hear me.

Abruptly I realized that I didn't want to be standing near their bodies any more. I took a step back from the graves. Mary dug in the pocket of her coat and brought out something attached to a small cardboard label. A set of keys.

'I put out the trash this morning,' she said, 'and took a few things out of the refrigerator. Milk and such. Don't want them smelling it up. Everything else I just left.'

I nodded, staring at the keys. I didn't have any of my own. No need. They'd been in, on the few occasions I'd visited. I realized that this was the first time I'd ever seen Mary somewhere other than my parents' kitchen or living room. It was like that with my folks. You went to their house, not the other way round. They tended to form a centre. Had tended to.

'They spoke of you, you know. Often.'

I nodded again, though I wasn't sure I believed her. For much of the last decade my parents hadn't even known where I was, and anything they had to say concerned a younger man, an only child who'd once grown up and lived with them in a different state. It wasn't that we hadn't loved each other. We had, in our ways. I just hadn't given them much to talk about, had checked none of the boxes that make parents prone to brag to friends and neighbours.

16

No wife, no kids, no job to speak of. I realized Mary was still holding her hand out, and I took the keys from her.

'How long will you stay?' she asked.

'It depends how long things take. Maybe a week. Possibly less.'

'You know where I am,' she said. 'You don't have to be a stranger, just because.'

'I won't,' I said quickly, smiling awkwardly. I wished I had a sibling who could have been having this conversation for me. Someone responsible and socially skilled.

She smiled back, but distantly, as if she already knew this was not the way things worked.

'Goodbye, Ward,' she said, and then set off up the slope. At seventy she was a little older than my parents, and walked awkwardly. She was a lifelong Dyersburg resident, an ex-nurse, and more than that I didn't know.

I saw that Davids was standing by his car on the other side of the cemetery, killing time with his assistant but evidently waiting for me. He had the air of someone ready and willing to be brisk and efficient, to tidy loose ends.

I glanced back once more at the graves, and then walked heavily down the path to face the administrative tasks created by the loss of my entire family.

Davids had brought most of the paperwork in his car, and took me to lunch to deal with it. I don't know whether this ended up being any less unpleasant than doing it in his office would have been, but I appreciated the courtesy from a man who knew me barely at all. We ate in historical downtown Dyersburg, at a place called Auntie's Pantry. The interior had been slavishly designed to resemble a multi-level log cabin, the furniture hand-hewn by elves. The menu offered a chilling variety of organic soups and home-made breads, accompanied by salads largely predicated upon bean sprouts. I know I'm out of step, but I don't regard bean sprouts as food. They don't even *look* edible. They look like pallid, mutant grubs. The only worse

17

thing is cous cous, of which there was also plenty on offer. I don't know of any aunt on this planet who eats that kind of shit, but both staff and patrons seemed about as happy as could be. Almost maniacally so.

After a brief and somewhat stilted wait we scored a seat by the front window. This annoyed a spruce young family behind us, who'd had their eye on the table and didn't understand how being first in line entitled you to certain benefits. The woman outlined her dissatisfaction to the waitress, loudly observing that the table had space for four people and we were only two. Normally this kind of thing brings out the very best in me, particularly if my foes are all wearing identical navy blue fleeces, but right then the well was dry. The husband was no competition, but the two children were blond and solemn and looked like a pair of judging angels. I didn't want to get on their bad side. The waitress, who was of the genus of tan, pretty but rather hefty young women who flock to places like Dyersburg for the winter sports, elected not to get involved, instead staring brightly at a patch of the floor approximately equidistant between the two sets of combatants.

Davids glanced briefly across at the matriarch. He's of my parents' age, tall and gaunt with a good-sized beak, and looks like the guy who God calls on when he really wants Hell to rain down. He opened his briefcase and drew out a lot of documents, making no effort to conceal the kind of event they pertained to. He laid them out in front of him in a businesslike way, picked up the menu, and started to read it. By the time I'd finished watching him do these things, the family was all studiously looking elsewhere. I picked up my own menu, and tried to imagine why what it said was of interest to me.

Davids was my parents' attorney, and had been since they'd met him after moving from Northern California. I'd spoken to him on a couple of previous occasions, Christmas or Thanksgiving drinks at their house, but in my mind he was now simply one of a number of people with whom my acquaintance was about to draw to an abrupt close. This bred a curious mixture of distance and a desire

18

to prolong the contact, which I was unable to translate into much in the way of conversation.

Thankfully, Davids took the lead as soon as the bowls of butternut and lichen soup arrived. He recapped the circumstances of my parents' death, which in the absence of witnesses boiled down to a single fact. At approximately 11:05 on the previous Friday evening, after visiting friends to play bridge, their car had been involved in a head-on collision at the intersection of Benton and Ryle Streets. The other vehicle was a stationary car, parked by the side of the road. The post-mortem revealed blood-alcohol levels consistent with maybe half a bottle of wine in my father, who had been the passenger, and a lot of cranberry juice in my mother. The road had been icy, the junction wasn't too well lit, and another accident had taken place at the same spot just last year. That was that. It was just one of those things, unless I wanted to get involved in a fruitless civil litigation, which I didn't. There was nothing else to say.

Then Davids got down to business, which meant getting me to sign a large number of pieces of paper, thereby accepting ownership of the house and its contents, a few pieces of undeveloped land, and my father's stock portfolio. A legion of tax matters pertaining to all of this were efficiently explained to me and then dispatched with further signatures. The IRS stuff went in one ear and out the other, and I gave none of the papers more than a cursory glance. My father had evidently trusted Davids, and Hopkins Senior hadn't been a man to cast his respect around willy-nilly. Good enough for Dad was good enough for me.

I was listening with less than half of my attention by the end of it, and actually enjoying the soup – now that I'd improved the recipe by adding a good deal of salt and pepper. I was watching the spoonfuls as they came up toward my mouth, savouring the taste in a studious, considered way, encouraging the flavour to occupy as much of my mind as possible. I only resurfaced when Davids mentioned UnRealty.

He explained that my father's business, through which he had successfully sold high-priced real estate, was being shut down. The value of its remaining assets would be forwarded to any account I cared to nominate, just as soon as the process was complete.

'He wound up UnRealty?' I asked, lifting my head to look at the lawyer. 'When?'

'No.' Davids shook his head, wiping round his bowl with a piece of bread. 'He gave instructions that this should take place upon his death.'

'Regardless of what I might have to say?'

He glanced out of the window, and rubbed his hands together in an economical little motion that dislodged a few crumbs from his fingers. 'He was quite clear on the matter.'

My soup had suddenly gone cold, and tasted like liquidized pond weed. I pushed the bowl away. I understood now why Davids had insisted that we go through the papers today, rather than in the period before the funeral. I collected up my copies of the papers and shoved them into the envelope Davids had provided.

'Is that it?' My voice was quiet and clipped.

'I think so. I'm sorry to have put you through this, Ward, but it's better to get it over with.'

He pulled a wallet from his jacket and glared at the check, as if not only distrusting the addition but taking a dim view of the waitress's handwriting. His thumb hesitated over a charge card, pulled out some cash instead. I logged this as him electing not to allot the cost of lunch as a business expense.

'You've been very kind,' I said. Davids dismissed this with a flip of his hand, and tipped exactly ten percent.

We rose and left the restaurant, weaving between the tables of chatting tourists. I meant to look away as we passed the table occupied by the nuclear army in blue fleece, but then suddenly they were in front of me. Mother and father were bickering mildly about where to stay in Yellowstone; the little boy meanwhile was using his spoon and soup to approximate the effect of an asteroid landing in the

Pacific. His sister was sitting with a plastic beaker clutched in both hands, contentedly staring at nothing in particular. As I passed she looked up at me, and smiled as if seeing a large dog. It was probably a cute smile, but for a moment I felt like removing it.

Outside we stood together for a moment, watching well-heeled women roving up and down College Street in hungry packs, charge cards on stun.

Eventually Davids thrust his hands in the pockets of his coat. 'You'll be leaving soon, I imagine. If there's anything I can do in the meantime, please be in touch. I can't raise the dead, of course, but on other things I might be able to help.'

We shook hands, and he walked rather quickly away up the street, his face carefully blank. And only then did I realize, unforgivably late, that Davids had not just been my father's attorney, but had also become his friend, and that I might not have been the only person who'd found the morning difficult.

I walked back to the hotel with my hands clenched, and by nine I was very drunk. I had the first boilermaker in both hands before the hotel doors had shut behind me. I knew as I took the first swallow that it was a mistake. I knew it all the way home, had known it in the cemetery and from the moment I'd woken that morning. I wasn't falling off some painfully-scaled wagon, rejecting my higher power and committing myself to waking up in Geneva with two wives and the word 'Spatula' tattooed on my forehead. But getting drunk was like having a one-night stand because your partner had been unfaithful to you: an act that could achieve nothing except pain, meanwhile diminishing a moral high ground which, for once in your life, you were actually entitled to. The problem was, there didn't seem to be any other intelligent response to the situation.

At first I perched at the bar, but after a while I moved to one of the booths by the long window. A large pre-emptive tip had ensured that I didn't have to wait, or indeed move, in order to keep my glasses full. A beer, then a Scotch. A beer, then a Scotch. A solid and efficient way of getting drunk, and the smooth-faced barman kept them coming like I'd asked.

I pulled the documents out of Davids's manila envelope and spread them in front of me, my mind fixated on one point in particular.

In all the time I was growing up, I was aware of one thing about my father. He was a businessman. That was what he did and who he was. He was *Homo sapiens businessmaniens*. He got up in the morning and shoved off to do business, and he came back in the evening having by-God done some. My parents never talked about their early life, and rarely about anything of consequence, but I knew about UnRealty. He'd worked for a number of years at a local firm, then one night took my mother out for a fine dinner and told her he was going it alone. He actually used those words, apparently, as if appearing in an advertisement for bank loans. He had talked to a few people, made some contacts, engaged in all the textbook corporate heroics that entitled you some day to stand at the bar of a country club and say 'I did it my way'. It can't have been easy, but my father had a certain force of will. Car mechanics and plumbers, meter maids and check-in clerks, all took one look and elected not to fuck him around. When he walked into a restaurant, the word went round the staff that it was time to stand up straight and stop spitting in the soup. His company, and its history, was the most real thing I understood about him.

And yet, in his will, he had stipulated that UnRealty be wound up. Instead of leaving it to his son to make the decision, he had calmly imploded twenty years' work.

As soon as Davids had told me this, I knew it could only mean one thing. My parents hadn't wanted me to take over the business. In many ways this was explicable. I have sold many, many things, shifted many and varied commodities, but never an expensive house. I knew about them, however. Did I ever. I knew about *Unique Homes* magazine, about the DuPont Registry and *Christie's Great Estates*. I knew about conservation easements and dude ranches, was familiar with the value of old-world craftsmanship, views of the 15th fairway,

22

end-of-the-road privacy where serenity abounds. I couldn't help but be. It had seeped into my blood. I even did two years of an architecture degree, before I sidestepped out of college via an unfortunate incident and into a different line of work. And yet he either hadn't wanted me, or hadn't trusted me, to take over the business. The more I thought about it, the more hurt I got.

I kept drinking, to see if things got any better. They didn't. I kept drinking anyway. The bar remained quiet throughout the early part of the evening. Then at ten o'clock there was a sudden influx of men and women in suits, sprung from some ball-breaking corporate flipchart-fest. They milled about in the centre of the bar, networking rabidly, excited as children at the prospect of going berserk and having a couple of Lite beers. By this stage my brain felt very heavy and cold. The noise started loud and got worse, as if I was surrounded by people shovelling pebbles.

I held my ground in my booth, glaring virulently at the invaders. A couple of the men rakishly removed their jackets. One fellow even loosened his tie. Underlings sidled up to their bosses and hung about like sandpipers, pecking for Brownie points. I'd cope. I'd weather the storm. These people might know how to run spreadsheets and asset-strip, but if it came to a bar endurance test, they were wearing water wings. I was confident. I was in the zone. I was also, in retrospect, even more drunk than I realized.

Three men came in the door. They stopped, looked around.

The next thing I knew there was screaming, and the suits were diving for cover. At first I felt frightened, and then I realized it was me they were running from.

I was swaying in the middle of the floor, clothes wet from upturned beer. I had a gun in my hands and was pointing it straight at the men in the doorway, barking a long, incoherent series of contradictory instructions at them. They looked scared out of their wits. This was probably because when a man points a gun at you, you want to do what he asks. But it's difficult when you can't make out what he's saying.

Eventually I stopped shouting. The men in the door briefly became six, then resolved into three again. The room was quiet around me, but my heart felt like it was going to melt down. Everybody waited for things to either get better or worse.

'Sorry,' I muttered. 'Misunderstanding.'

I put the gun back in my jacket, swept the papers up off the table, and lurched out. I got halfway across the lobby before I fell over, taking a table, a large vase and a hundred bucks' worth of flowers down with me.

At three o'clock in the morning, frigid with iced water, I was lying on my back on the bed in my room.

I had been talked to by both the hotel management and the local police, who'd been understanding, while insisting I relinquish the gun for the duration of my stay. I let the funeral carry the day. I do have a licence to carry a concealed weapon, which surprised them. But they observed, reasonably enough, that the licence doesn't say I can wave it around in bars. The papers from Davids's office, the ones that announced I now had 1.8 million dollars cash, were carefully laid out on the heater to dry. I was no longer angry at anybody. The fact that my father's last will and testament now smelled of spilt beer seemed to effectively make his point.

After a while I rolled over, picked up the phone, and dialled a number. The phone rang six times, and then an answering machine kicked in. A voice I knew better than my own said that Mr and Mrs Hopkins were sorry they couldn't answer the phone, but that I should leave a message. They'd get back to me.

Chapter 2

At ten o'clock the next morning I stood, pale and penitent, at the end of my parents' driveway. I was wearing a clean shirt. I had eaten some breakfast. I had apologized to everyone I could find in the hotel, right down to the guy who cleaned the pool. I was amazed that I hadn't spent the night in a cell. I felt like shit.

The house sat near the end of a narrow and hilly road on the mountainside of Dyersburg's main residential area. I'd been a little surprised by it when they moved. The lot was decent-sized, about half an acre, with a couple of old trees shading the side of the house. Properties of similar size bordered it, home to nice late Victorians, that no one looked too obsessed about painting. A neat hedge marked the edge of both sides of the property. Mary lived in the next house up, and she wasn't anything like wealthy. A college professor and his post-grad wife had recently moved in on the other side. I think my dad actually sold them the house. Again, decent people – but unlikely to bathe in champagne. The house itself was a two-storey, with a graceful wraparound porch, a workshop in the cellar and a garage round the back. It was, without question, a nice-looking and well-appointed house in a good neighbourhood. Someone wanted to set you up there, you wouldn't complain. But neither would *Homes of the Rich and Famous* be doing a showcase special anytime soon.

I waved across the fence in case Mary happened to be looking out the window, and walked slowly up the path. It felt as if I was approaching an impostor. My parents' real house, the one I'd grown up in, lay a long time in the past and a thousand miles west. I'd never been back to Hunter's Rock since they moved, but I could remember that house like the back of my hand. The arrangement of its rooms would probably always define my understanding of domestic space. The one in front of me was like a second wife, taken too late in life to have a relationship with the children that extended beyond distant cordiality.

A galvanized trashcan stood to one side of the door, the lid raised by the full bag inside. There were no newspapers on the porch. I assumed Davids had seen to that. The right thing to do, but it made the house look as if it already had a dust sheet over it. I pulled the unfamiliar keys from my pocket and unlocked the door.

It was so quiet inside that the house seemed to throb. I picked up the few pieces of mail, junk for the most part, and put them on the side table. Then I wandered for a while, walking from room to room, looking at things. The rooms felt like preview galleries for some strange yard sale, each object coming from a different home and priced well below its value. Even the things that went together – the books in my father's study, my mother's collection of 1930s English pottery, neatly arrayed on the antique pine dresser in the sitting room – seemed hermetically sealed from my touch and from time. I had no idea what to do with these things. Put them in boxes and store them somewhere to gather dust? Sell them, keep the money, or give it to some worthy cause? Live within this tableau, knowing that in the objects' minds I would never have anything more than a second-hand regard for them?

The only thing that seemed to make any kind of sense was leaving everything as it was, walking out of the house and never coming back. This wasn't my life. It wasn't anybody's, not any more. Apart from the single wedding picture in the hall, there weren't even any photographs. There never had been in our family.

In the end I wound up back in the sitting room. This faced down the garden toward the road, and had big, wide windows that transformed the cold light outside into warmth. There was a couch and armchair, in matching genteel prints. A compact little widescreen television, on a stand fronted with smoked glass. Also my father's chair, a battered warhorse in green fabric and dark wood, the only piece of furniture in the room that they'd brought from the previous house. A new biography of Frank Lloyd Wright was on the coffee table, my father's place marked with a receipt from Denford's Market. Eight days previously one of them had bought a variety of cold cuts, a carrot cake (fancy), five large bottles of mineral water, some low-fat milk and a bottle of vitamins. Most of these must have been amongst the fridge contents that Mary had thrown away. The mineral water was maybe still around, along with the vitamins. Perhaps I'd have some later.

In the meantime I sat in my father's chair. I ran my hands along the worn grain of the armrests, then laid them in my lap and looked down the garden.

And for a long time, in savage bursts, I cried.

Much later, I remembered an evening from long ago. I would have been seventeen, back when we lived in California. It was Friday night, and I was due to meet the guys at a bar out on a back road just outside town. Lazy Ed's was one of those shoebox-with-a-parking-lot beer dens that look like they've been designed by Mormons to make drinking seem not just un-Godly but drab and sad and deadend hopeless. Ed realized that he wasn't in a position to be picky, and as we were never any trouble and kept feeding quarters into the pool table and juke box – Blondie, Bowie and good old Bruce Stringbean, back in the glory days of Molly Ringwald and Mondrian colours – our juvie custom was fine by him.

My mother was out, gone to a crony of hers to do whatever it is women do when there aren't any men around to clutter up the place and look bored and not listen with sufficient gravity to stories about people they've never met, and who anyway sound kind of dull, if their troubles are anything to judge by. At six o'clock Dad and I were sitting at the big table in the kitchen, eating some lasagne she'd left in the fridge, and avoiding the salad. My mind was on other things. I have no idea what. I can no more get back inside the head of my seventeen-year-old self than I could that of a tribesman in Borneo.

It was a while before I'd realized Dad had finished, and was watching me. I looked back at him. 'What?' I said, affably enough.

He pushed his plate back. 'Going out tonight?'

I nodded slowly, full of teenage bafflement, and got back to shovelling food into my head.

I should have understood right away what he was asking. But I didn't get it, in the same way I didn't get why there remained a small pile of salad on his otherwise spotless plate. I didn't want that green shit, so I didn't take any. He didn't want it either, but he took some – even though Mom wasn't there to see. I can understand now that the pile in the bowl had to get smaller, or when she got back she'd go on about how we weren't eating right. Simply dumping some of it straight in the trash would have seemed dishonest, whereas if it spent some time on a plate – went, in effect, *via* his meal – then it was okay. But back then, it seemed inexplicably stupid.

I finished up, and found that Dad was still sitting there. This was unlike him. Usually, once a food event was over, he was all business. Get the plates in the washer. Take the garbage out. Get the coffee on. Get on to the next thing. Chop fucking chop.

'So what are you going to do? Watch the tube?' I asked, making an effort. It felt very grown up.

He stood and took his plate over to the side. There was a pause, and then he said: 'I was wondering.'

28

This didn't sound very interesting. 'Wondering what?'

'Whether you'd play a couple of frames with an old guy.'

I stared at his back. The tone of his inquiry was greatly at odds with his usual confidence, especially the mawkish attempt at self-deprecation. I found it hard to believe he thought I'd take the deception seriously. He wasn't old. He jogged. He whipped younger men at tennis and golf. He was, furthermore, the last person in the world I could imagine playing pool. He just didn't fit the type. If you drew a Venn diagram with circles for 'People who looked like they played pool', 'People who looked like they might' and 'People who looked like they wouldn't, but maybe did', then he would have been on a different sheet of paper altogether. He was dressed that night, as he so often was, in a neatly pressed pair of sandy chinos and a fresh white linen shirt, neither of them from anywhere as mass-market as The Gap. He was tall and tan with silvering dark hair and had the kind of bone structure that makes people want to vote for you. He looked like he should be leaning on the rail of a good-length boat off Palm Beach or Jupiter Island, talking about art. Most likely about some art he was trying to sell you. I, on the other hand, was fair and skinny and wearing regulation black Levi's and a black T-shirt. Both looked like they'd been used to make fine adjustments to the insides of car engines. They probably smelled that way, too. Dad would have smelled the way he always did, which I wasn't aware of then but can summon up now as clearly as if he was standing behind me: a dry, clean, correct smell, like neatly stacked firewood.

'You want to come play pool?' I asked, checking that I hadn't lost my mind.

He shrugged. 'Your mother's out. There's nothing on the box.'

'You got nothing salted away on tape?' This was inconceivable. Dad had a relationship with the VCR like some fathers had with a favoured old hound, and racks of neatly labelled tapes on the shelves in his study. I'd do exactly the same now, of course, if I lived any-where in particular. I'd have them stamped with bar codes if I had the time. But back then it was the thing about him that most strongly put me in mind of fascist police states.

He didn't answer. I cleared the scraps off my own plate, thoughtlessly making a good job of it because I was at an age when showing my love for my mother was difficult, and ensuring her precious dishwasher didn't get clogged with shit was something I could do without anyone realizing I was doing it, including myself. I didn't want Dad to come out to the bar. It was that simple. I had a routine for going out. I enjoyed the drive. It was *me* time. Plus the guys were going to find it weird. It *was* weird, for fuck's sake. My friend Dave would likely be stoned out of his gourd when he arrived, and might freak out there and then if he saw me standing with a representative of all that was authoritarian and straight-backed and wrinkly.

I looked across at him, wondering how to put this. The plates were stowed. The remaining salad was back in the fridge. He'd wiped the counter down. If a team of forensic scientists happened to swoop mid-evening and tried to find evidence of any food-eating activity, they'd be right out of luck. It annoyed the hell out of me. But when he folded the cloth and looped it over the handle on the oven, I had my first ever intimation of what I would feel in earnest, nearly twenty years later, on the day I sat wet-faced in his chair in an empty house in Dyersburg. A realization that his presence was not unavoidable or a given; that one day there would be too much salad in the bowl and cloths that remained unfolded.

'Yeah, whatever,' I said.

I quickly started to freak about how the other guys were going to react, and hustled us out of the house forty minutes early. I figured this might give us as much as an hour before we had to deal with anyone else, as the other guys were always late.

We drove out to Ed's, Dad sitting in the passenger seat and not saying much. When I drew up outside the bar he peered out the windshield. 'This is where you go?'

I said it was, a little defensively. He grunted. On the way across the lot it occurred to me that turning up with my dad was going to bring into focus any doubts Ed might be entertaining about my age, but it was too late to turn back. It wasn't like we looked very similar. Maybe he'd think Dad was some older guy I knew. Like a senator, or something.

Inside was nearly empty. A couple old farts I didn't know were hunkered down over a table in the corner. The place never really stuttered into life until late, and it was a precarious form of vitality, the kind that two consecutive bad choices on the jukebox could kill stone dead. As we stood at the counter waiting for Ed to make his own good time out of the back, Dad leaned back against the bar and looked around. There wasn't a great deal to see. Battered stools, venerable dust, a pool table, interior twilight and neon. I didn't want him to like it. Ed came out eventually, grinned when he saw me. Usually I'd drink my first beer sitting gassing with him, and probably he was anticipating this was going to happen tonight.

But then he caught sight of Dad, and stopped. Not like he'd run into a wall or anything, but he hesitated, and his smile faded, to be replaced by an expression I couldn't interpret. Dad wasn't the usual kind of guy who spent time in that bar, and I guess Ed was wondering what kind of bizarre map-reading error had brought him there. Dad turned to look at him, and nodded. Ed nodded back.

I really wanted this over with. 'My dad,' I said.

Ed nodded once more, and another great male social interaction ground to a close.

I asked for two beers. As I waited I watched my father as he walked over to the pool table. As a kid I'd got used to the fact that people would come up to him in stores and start talking to him, assuming he was the manager and the only person who could sort out whatever trivia they were spiralling up into psychodrama. Being able to look equally at home in a scummy bar was kind of a trick, and I felt a flicker of respect for him. It was a very specific and limited type of regard, the kind you allow someone who displays a quality you think you might one day aspire to, but it was there all the same.

I joined him at the table, and after that the bonding session went rapidly downhill. I won all three games. They were long, slow games. It wasn't that he was so terrible, but every shot he played was five percent out, and I had the run of the table. We didn't talk much. We just leant down, took our shots, endured the misses. After the second game slouched to a conclusion he went and bought himself another beer while I racked the balls up. I'd been kind of hoping he'd stick at one, so I still had most of mine left. Then we played the last game, which was a little better, but still basically excruciating. At the end of it he put his cue back in the rack.

'That it?' I asked, trying to sound nonchalant. I was so relieved I took the risk of holding up another quarter.

He shook his head. 'Not giving you much of a challenge.'

'So – aren't you going to say "Hey kid, you're good," or something like that?'

'No,' he said, mildly. 'Because you're not.'

I stared at him, stricken as a five-year-old. 'Yeah, well,' I eventually managed. 'Thanks for the ego-boost.'

'It's a game.' He shrugged. 'What bothers me is not that you're no good. It's that it doesn't bother you.'

'What?' I said, incredulous. 'You read that in some motivational management textbook? Drop a zinger at the right moment and your kid ends up chairman of the board?'

Mildly: 'Ward, don't be an asshole.'

'You're the asshole,' I snarled. 'You assumed I'd be no good and you'd be able to come out here and beat me even though you can't play *at all*.'

He stood for a moment, hands in the pockets of his chinos, and looked at me. It was a strange look, cool and appraising, but not empty of love. Then he smiled.

'Whatever,' he said. And he left, and I guess he walked home.

I turned back to the table, grabbed my beer and drank the rest of it in one swallow. Then I tried to smack one of his remaining balls down the end pocket and missed by a mile. At that moment I really, really hated him.

I stormed over to the bar to find Ed already had a beer waiting for me. I reached for money, but he shook his head. He'd never done that before. I sat down on a stool, didn't say anything for a few minutes.

Gradually we started talking about other things: Ed's views on local politics and feminism – he was somewhat critical of both – and a hide he was thinking of lashing together out in the woods. I didn't see Ed ever having a huge impact on the first two subjects, or getting it together to build the hide, but I listened anyway. By the time Dave wandered in I could more or less pretend that it was just business as usual.

It was an okay night. We talked, we drank, we lied. We played pool not very well. At the end I walked out to the car, and stopped when I saw a note had been pushed under one of the wipers. It was in my father's handwriting, but much smaller than usual.

'If you can't read this the first time,' it said, 'get a ride. I'll drive you out here tomorrow to pick up the car.'

I screwed the note up and hurled it away, but I drove home carefully. When I got back Mom was in bed. There was a light in Dad's study but the door was shut, so I just went upstairs.

I got up once, in the late morning, and made a cup of instant coffee. Apart from that I sat until mid-afternoon, until the sun moved across the sky and started to come directly through the window and into my eyes. This broke the spell I'd been in, and I got out of the chair knowing I'd never sit there again. It wasn't comfortable, for a start. The cushion was threadbare and lumpy, and after a couple of straight hours on it, my ass hurt. I walked back to the kitchen, rinsed my cup out, left it upside down on the side to dry. Then I changed my mind, wiped it, and put it back in the cupboard. I folded the cloth and looped it over the handle on the oven.

I stood irresolute in the hallway, wondering what to do next. Part of me believed that the filial thing to do would be to check out of the hotel and come stay here for the night. The rest of me didn't want to. Really did not want to. I wanted bright lights and a burger, a beer, someone who'd talk to me about something other than death.

Suddenly irritable and sad, I stalked back into the sitting room to retrieve my phone from the coffee table. My lower back ached, probably from sitting in that lousy chair.

The chair. Maybe it was because the light was different; the sun had moved around the yard since the morning, creating new shadows. More likely, a few hours of tears had simply cleared my head a little. Either way, now that I was looking at it, the seat cushion looked a little odd. Slowly slipping the Nokia into my pocket, I frowned at the chair. The cushion, which was an integral part of it, definitely bulged up in the centre. I reached out experimentally, prodded it. It felt a little hard.

Maybe he'd had it reupholstered, or refilled with something. Rocks, perhaps. I straightened up, ready to forget it and leave the house. My hangover was beginning to bloom. Then something else caught my attention.

There's a proper way of placing objects in relation to each other, especially if those objects are large. Some people don't see this. They'll just throw the furniture down any old how, or all against the walls, or at right angles, or so everyone can see the TV. My father always made sure stuff was placed just so, and then got riled if anybody moved it. And my father's chair wasn't in the right place. It wasn't off by much, and I don't think anybody else would have noticed it. It was too square on to the other furniture, and seemed to stand too much out on its own. It just didn't look right.

I squatted down in front of it, examined the line where the cushion was attached to the body of the seat. A strip of braid covered the join. It was worn and frayed. I grabbed one end of it and pulled. It came away easily, revealing an opening that looked like it once had been stitched.

I slipped my hand inside. My fingers navigated through some kind of dry, squishy stuff, probably cut-up chunks of foam. In the middle they found a solid object. I pulled it out.

It was a book. A paperback novel, a new-looking copy of a blockbuster thriller, the kind of thing my mother might pick up on a whim at the checkout, and skim through in an afternoon. It didn't look read. The spine was unbent, and my mother was no stickler for keeping books in pristine condition. It didn't make any sense. It couldn't have gotten in the chair by accident.

I flicked through the pages. In the middle of the book there was a small piece of paper. I pulled it out. It was a note, just one line, written in my father's handwriting.

'Ward,' it said: 'We're not dead.'

Chapter 3

A stream in southern Vermont, the water clear and cold, hurrying over a bed of pale boulders between the steep banks of a valley up in the Green Mountains. The sky seems to start a few bare feet above the trees, a sheet of spun sugar frozen grey in fading light. The leaves on the ground, broken bulbs of stained-glass colours, are covered with a patchy dusting of snow. On either side of the stream, connected by a pair of old stone bridges fifty yards apart, lies the small village of Pimonta. There are perhaps twenty houses all told, though nearly a dozen of these appear solely for summer use or abandoned altogether. Next to one squats the hulk of a very old Buick, its oxidized shell now the colour of a thundercloud. A few vehicles sit in other driveways, rugged types suggesting their owners are the owners of several children and at least one dog. It is very quiet, apart from the noise of the stream, which has been flowing for so long that its clamour is more of a colour than a sound. Smoke slips sluggishly out of a few chimneys, including those of the Pimonta

Inn, a refined bed-and-breakfast that backs onto the river and which is almost full in this last week of the foliage season.

A man stands on one of the bridges, leaning against the wall and looking down at the tumbling water. His name is John Zandt. He is a little under six feet tall and wearing a thick coat against the cold. The coat accentuates his shape, which is compact and broad-shouldered. He looks like a man who could carry a pair of suitcases a long way or hit someone extremely hard. Both are true. His hair is short and dark, his features harsh but well-arranged. There is a two-day growth of stubble on his chin and cheeks. He has stayed for the last week at the Pimonta Inn, living in a suite consisting of a bedroom, a bathroom and a small sitting room with a wood fire, all of which is expensively comfortable in an unkempt country style. He has spent the days walking in the mountains and valleys in the area, avoiding the marked trails, with their straggles of brightly clad hikers fretting about bears. Sometimes he has found the vestiges of old homesteads, now little more than piles of dark wood strewn amongst the undergrowth. There are no echoes to be heard, no matter how long you stand and listen, and places that were once by a path have become uncharted again. The roads found different routes, turning some spots into destinations and leaving others as wilderness, perhaps for ever.

Zandt likes to sit in these places a while, considering how it might have been. Then he starts walking again, walking until he is tired and it is time to return to the inn. In the evenings he has sat in its cosy sitting area, politely avoiding conversation with other guests and the establishment's proprietors. The books in the small library speak of ossification and contentment. Perhaps forty people have nodded at him in the last couple of weeks, without learning his name or being able to describe him in any detail.

After the evening meal, which has generally been excellent if slow in coming, he has returned to his suite, built a fire, and stayed up as long as he can bear it. He has been dreaming a great deal recently. Sometimes the dreams are of Los Angeles, of a life that is gone for good and therefore cannot be escaped. In the past he has tried both alcohol and heroin, but found neither of much help even in great excess. These days he simply wakes and lies on his back, waiting for morning, thinking of emptiness. He has never tried to kill himself. It is not in his nature. If it was, he would already be dead.

Now, as he leans on the wall of the bridge in the fading light, he is considering what to do next. He has money, some of it the remnants of a summer of hard manual work. He thinks that it is perhaps time for him to get back in the saddle, and head to a city. Maybe somewhere down South, though he has found that he likes the cold and the dark forests. His motivation is hampered by the fact that he has no special need for more cash, or any desire to do anything with that he already has. Also that after a life spent amongst buildings, they have suddenly stopped having any meaning to him. Empty roads and unbounded spaces seem to have more resonance than whatever lies on either side.

He looks up when he hears the sound of a car approaching from along the road from the north. After a while its headlights, used earlier in the afternoon than is the local custom, peer up over the hill. Soon the car follows them down into the village, past the small general store and videotape library. It is a Lexus, very black and new. It stops smoothly outside the inn.

The car makes a ticking sound as the engine cools. Nobody gets out for a few moments. Zandt watches it until he is sure that the shapes inside are looking at him. His own car, something cheap and foreign he bought off a bleak lot in Nebraska, is sitting in front of the outbuilding that holds his room and several others. The keys to the car are in his pocket, but he cannot get to it without taking himself closer to the Lexus. He could turn, walk across the bridge and between the houses on the other side, head up into the hills, but he does not have a mind to. He should, he knows, have paid cash for his lodging. That is his usual practice. But when he arrived he had none, and it was late. Withdrawing some from an ATM in the nearest town would have left just as clear a sign. The time to avoid this confrontation, whatever it may hold, is two weeks past. He merely looks down again at the water below, and waits.

Over at the car, the passenger door opens and a woman climbs out. She has medium-length dark hair, wears a dark green suit, and is of average height. Her face is striking, meaning that you will either find her plain or beautiful. Most people put their money on the former, which is fine by her. Her silence on the journey has already irritated Agent Fielding, who first met her three hours previously – and who, had he not been tasked with driving her down to Pimonta, could have been home several hours by now. Fielding still has no idea why he has been dragged all this way, which is just as well, because it could only barely be classified as official business. He is simply doing what he is told, a much-underrated skill.

The woman closes the door with a soft *clunk* that she knows the man at the bridge can hear. He doesn't move, or even look up, until she has walked down past the inn, past the boarded-up premises of a defunct local potter, and onto the bridge.

She walks to within a few yards of him and then stops, feeling slightly absurd and rather cold.

'Hello, Nina,' he says, still without looking.

'Very cool,' she replies. 'I'm impressed.'

He turns. 'Nice suit. Very Dana Scully.'

'These days we all want to look that way. Even some of the guys.'

'Who's in the car?'

'Local agent. From Burlington. Nice man gave me a lift.'

'How did you find me?'

'Credit card.'

'Right,' he says. 'Long way to come.'

'You're worth it.'

He looks sceptically at a woman he had once thought striking, and now finds plain once more.

'So what do you want? It's cold. I'm getting hungry. I'd be sur-prised if we have anything to say to each other.'

For just a moment she looks beautiful again, and hurt. Then, as if none of this meant anything to her, or ever had, 'It's happened again,' she says. 'Thought you'd want to know.'

She turns on her heel and walks back up toward the car. The engine is running before she opens the door, and within two minutes the valley is empty and quiet again, leaving just a man on a bridge, his mouth slightly open, his face pale.

He caught up with her twenty miles south, driving hard down narrow mountain roads and slinging the car around every bend. Southern Vermont isn't designed for speed, and the car twice started to plane on ice patches. Zandt noticed neither this nor the handful of local drivers who had just time to register his approach before he was behind them, gaining speed, leaving their cars rocking in his wake. At Wilmington he hit a junction. The Lexus wasn't visible in either direction. He reasoned that she'd be heading for the nearest place where she could get airlifted back to civilization, and took the left turn up Route 9 for Keene, just over the state line in New Hampshire.

He made better time on the wider road, and soon began to see the Lexus's distinctive tail lights in the distance ahead, flickering through trees on a kink in the road, or blinking off the other side of a dip. He eventually caught it on a straight patch just south of Hardsboro, where the road passed by a cold, flat lake that looked like a mirror reflecting a sky full of shadows.

He flashed his headlights. There was no response. He pulled closer, flashed again. This time the Lexus picked up a little speed. Zandt accelerated, pressing hard, and saw Nina turn and clock his face through the back window. She spoke to the driver, who didn't slow.

Zandt floored the pedal and pulled out from behind, roared forward until he was just ahead, then angled in and braked the car hard. He was out of the door before the engine had died, and so was Fielding, hand already coming back out of his jacket.

'Put it away,' Zandt suggested.

'Fuck you.' The agent held the gun in both hands. Meanwhile Nina climbed out of the other side of the car, stepping carefully to avoid the mud. 'I'm telling you,' Fielding said evenly. 'Back off.'

'It's okay,' Nina said. 'Shit. There go the shoes.'

'Fuck it is. He tried to force us off the road.'

'He probably just wanted to talk. It can get lonely out here.'

'He can talk to my dick,' Fielding said. 'You – put your hands on the car.'

Zandt remained where he was until Nina made it round the front of the Lexus and onto the road.

'Are you sure it's him?' he said.

'You think I'd come all this way otherwise?'

'I never understood a single thing you did. At any stage. Just answer the question.'

'Will you just get your hands the fuck on the hood of the car?' Fielding shouted. There was the soft, mechanical sound of a safety being flicked off.

Zandt and Nina turned to look at him. The agent was full-on furious. Nina glanced up the road, where a large white Ford that shrieked 'rental' was headed toward them, driving slowly so the inhabitants could get a good view of the lake in what remained of the light.

'Easy,' she suggested. 'You want to explain a friendly-fire incident to your SAC?'

Fielding glanced over his shoulder. Saw the car pull over into a vantage point, about a hundred yards away. He lowered the gun. 'You going to tell me what the hell is going on?'

Nina shook her head curtly, then turned back to Zandt. 'I'm sure, John.'

'So why are you here instead of there?'

She shrugged, a habitual motion. 'Actually, I don't know. Shouldn't be, and I most certainly shouldn't be talking to you. You want to walk on me, or shall we go someplace and talk?'

Zandt looked away, across at the flat surface of the lake. Parts of it were black, others a frozen grey. On the other side was a little clearing and a wooden holiday home, with plenty of cords of wood stacked up against the side. The structure didn't look prepackaged or catalogue-bought: more like someone, or two someones, had sat for many evenings somewhere hectic and sketched it out on pads brought home from the office, desperate for some other story to be in. Not for the first time, Zandt wished he was someone else. Maybe the guy living in that house. Or one of the tourists up the way, who were now standing in a clump by the water and looking across at the trees, their brightly coloured anoraks making them look like a small herd of traffic lights.

Eventually he nodded. Nina walked across to Fielding, and spoke to him for a while. Within a minute, the agent's gun was back where it should be. By the time Zandt turned away from the lake Fielding was back in the car, face composed.

Nina waited for Zandt at his car, a large file under her arm. 'I told him I'd be going with you,' she said.

As Nina got in his car, Zandt stepped over to the Lexus. Fielding looked up at him through the window with an unreadable expression, and started the engine. Then he pressed a button and wound the window down.

'Guess I'll let it go, this time,' he said.

Zandt smiled. It was a thin smile, and bore little resemblance to anything caused by merriment. 'There is only this time.'

Fielding cocked his head. 'And that's supposed to mean what?'

'That if we meet again and you pull a gun on me, some pretty lake is going to have little scraps of Fed floating in it. And I don't give a shit if it fucks up the ecosystem.'

Zandt turned away, leaving the agent open-mouthed.

Then Fielding reversed rapidly, kicking a shower of grit into the air. He gunned the engine and sped past, pausing only to lean across to display the middle finger of his right hand.

When Zandt got into his car he saw Nina was sitting watching, arms folded and one eyebrow raised.

'Your people skills just keep on getting better,' she said. 'Maybe you should teach a course or something. Write a book. I'm serious. It's a gift. Don't fight it, share it. Be everything you can be.'

'Nina, shut up.'

He drove in silence back up to Pimonta. Nina sat with the file on her lap. By the time they got back to the village it was dark, and a few more residents' cars had appeared. Lights were on in many of the windows. He parked up in front of the inn, turned off the engine. He made no move to open his door, so Nina stayed as she was.

'Do you still want to eat?' she asked, eventually.

The car was getting cold. Two couples had already wandered past the car, on their way to the main building, their faces round with the contented prospect of food.

He stirred, as if returning from a long distance. 'Up to you.'

She tried for cheerful: 'I'm easy.'

'Not out here you're not. Supper's six-thirty until nine. We eat now or in the morning. Breakfast's seven until eight. And small.'

'What – there's nowhere you can get a burger in between? Or this place can't lay on a sandwich a little later?'

Zandt turned his head, and this time his smile looked almost real. 'You're not from around here, are you?'

'No, thank God. Neither are you. Where we come from you can eat when you want. You hand over money and they give you food. It's modern and convenient. Or have you been in the country so long you've forgotten?'

He didn't answer. Abruptly she dropped the file in the foot well and opened the door. 'Wait here,' she said.

Zandt waited, watching out of the windshield as she marched purposefully toward the main building. The hunger he'd felt after the day's walking was long gone. He felt chilled, inside and out. He was unaccustomed to dealing with someone who knew him, and felt awkward, his thoughts and feelings out of sync. He had spent a long time on the move, as background texture: the man at the

43

counter who was due for a refill; the guy who was working out the back for a couple days; someone at a wind-swept gas station, staring at nothing over the top of his car as he filled it up, and who then pulled back out onto the road and was soon gone. For long periods he had thought of almost nothing at all, aided by a complete absence of any hooks into his past existence. Nina's presence changed that. He wished he had moved on a day earlier, that she had arrived to find him gone. But Zandt knew more about her doggedness than most people, and knew she would have kept on going once she'd set her mind to find him.

He looked at the file lying in the foot well. It was thick. He felt no desire to touch it, still less to see what was inside. Most of it he knew too well already. The rest would be more of the same. The feelings it inspired were a rank mixture of numbness and horror, razor blades wrapped in cotton wool.

He heard the sound of a door closing, and looked up to see Nina walking back from the main part of the inn. She was carrying something in one hand. He got out of the car. It was much colder now, the sky leaden. Snow.

'Jesus,' she said, her breath clouding around her face. 'You weren't kidding. Food on a need-to-eat basis only. I got this though.' She held up a bottle of Irish whiskey. 'Said it was needed in evidence.'

'I don't really drink any more,' he said.

'I do,' she said. 'You can sit and watch.' She opened the door and retrieved the file. Zandt caught her checking its position on the floor, as if to see whether he'd taken a look in her absence.

'Nina, why are you here?'

'Come to save you,' she said. 'Welcome you back into the world.'

'And if I don't want to come back?'

'You're already back. You just don't know it yet.'

'What's that supposed to mean?'

'John, it's colder than a nun's pants out here. Let's get inside. I'm sure you can do your new thousand-yard-stare just as effectively under a roof.'

He was surprised into a grunt of laughter. 'That's kind of rude, isn't it?'

She shrugged. 'You know the rules. You sleep with a woman, she's got the right to be superior to you for the rest of your life.'

'Even if she started it? And ended it?'

'You fought tooth and nail on neither occasion, as I recall. Which of these rustic barns is your current abode?'

He nodded toward his building and she marched off. After a moment in which he considered and rejected the notion of getting back in the car and driving away, he followed.

45

Chapter 4

He built a fire while she sat in one of the threadbare armchairs, her feet on the coffee table. He was aware of her assaying the surroundings in the lamplight: the tastefully worn rugs, shabby chic furniture, paintings only a hotelier could love. The floorboards were painted creamy white, and a spray of local flowers sat perkily in a vase a few inches from Nina's feet.

'So what time's Martha Stewart dropping by?'

'Just as soon as you've gone,' he said, heading to the bathroom for glasses. 'Me and her, it's like an animal thing.'

Nina smiled, and watched the kindling in the grate. The fire clicked and crackled, pleased to be wakened, ready to consume. It seemed like a long time since she'd seen a real fire. It reminded her of childhood vacations, and made her shiver.

When Zandt returned she screwed the cap off the bottle and poured two measures. He stood a moment longer, as if still unwilling to commit himself to joining her, but then took the other chair. The room slowly began to warm.

She held the tooth glass up to her lips with both hands, and looked at him across it. 'So, John – how've you been?'

He sat, staring straight ahead, and didn't look at her.

'Just tell me,' he said.

Three days previously, a girl called Sarah Becker had been sitting on a bench on 3rd Street Promenade in Santa Monica, California. She was listening to a minidisc, on a player she'd received for her fourteenth birthday. She had printed out a neat little label on the computer at home, and her name and address were stuck to the back of the player, fixed with invisible tape to prevent the ink from wearing off. While she'd hated to compromise the machine's sleek brushed chrome, she disliked the idea of losing it even more. When the player was found, it emerged that the album she'd been listening to was *Generation Terrorists*, by a British band called the Manic Street Preachers. Except, as Sarah knew, you called them The Manics. The band wasn't big at her school, which was one of the reasons she listened to them. Everybody else mooned over feisty pop princesses and insipid boy bands, or else bobbed their heads while some hip-hop yahoo bellowed last year's slang over someone else's tune from the safety of a walled compound in Malibu. Sarah preferred music that sounded as if, somewhere down the line, someone had meant something by it. She supposed it was her age. At fourteen, you weren't a kid any more. Not these days, and not by a long shot. Not in LA. Not here in 2002. It was taking a while for her parents to come up to speed, but even they knew it was so. In their own ways they were getting used to the idea, like Neanderthals warily watching the first Cro-Magnons coming whistling over the rise.

At the end where she was sitting, by the fountain opposite the Barnes and Noble, the Promenade was pretty empty by this time in the evening. A few people came and went from the bookstore, and you could see others through the two-storey plate-glass window: leafing intently through magazines and books, geeking out over computer specs or scouring for magic spells in screen-writing manuals. Her family had gone on a two-week vacation to London, England, the year before, and she'd been baffled at the indigenous bookstores. They were utterly weird. They just had, like, books. No café, no magazines, no washrooms even. Just rows and rows of books. People picked them up, bought them, then went away again. Her mom had seemed to believe this was cool in some way, but Sarah thought it was one of the few things she'd seen about England that really sucked. Eventually they'd found a big new Borders, and she'd fallen upon it, discovering The Manics at one of the listening posts. British bands were cool. The Manics were especially cool. London was cool in general. That was that.

She sat, head nodding in approval as the singer loudly proclaimed himself a 'damned dog', and watched down the Promenade. Down the other end of the three-block pedestrianized zone was mainly restaurants. Her father had dropped her off twenty minutes before, and would be coming to pick her up at nine sharp – a once-monthly occurrence. She was supposed to be meeting her friend Sian at the Broadway Deli. They were ladies who dined. The supper club had been the brainchild of Sian's mom, who was adapting to her daughter's adolescence by throwing open all the doors she could find, for fear that leaving the wrong one closed might ruin their special relationship. Sarah's mother had gone along with it pretty easily: partly because everyone tended to go along with Monica Williams, but also because Zoë Becker was sufficiently in contact with her younger self to realize how much she'd have liked to have done the same at her age. Sarah's father had occasional right of veto, however, and for a long, bad moment she thought he was going to exercise it. A few months prior there had been a spate of gang-related killings, part of the seasonal undertow of corporate restructuring in the crack industry. But eventually, after proposing and reaching agreement on a battery of precautionary measures – including dropping and picking her up at closely defined times and places, demonstration of a fully-charged cellular battery, and a recitation of the key common-sense means of avoiding the chaotic intrusion of the fates – he'd agreed. It was now part of the social calendar.

Problem was, when they'd pulled up this evening, Sian hadn't been standing on the corner. Michael Becker craned his neck, peering up and down the street.

'So where is the legendary Ms Williams?' he muttered, fingers drumming on the wheel. Something was bitched with the series he was developing on the Warner lot, and he was big-time stressed: heavy calm spiked with jumpiness. Sarah wasn't sure exactly what the problem was, but knew her father's credo that there were an infinite number of ways for things to go wrong in The Business, and only one way of them going right. She had seen proposals and drafts for the show's pilot episode, and he'd even picked her brains over a few things, gauging her reaction as part of the potential target audience. Actually, and to her slight surprise, Sarah had thought the series sounded pretty cool. Better than *Buffy* or *Angel*, in fact. She privately thought Buffy herself was kind of a pain, and that the older English guy didn't sound half as much like Hugh Grant as he seemed to think. Or look enough like him, either. The heroine in *Dark Shift* was more self-contained, less showy, and less prone to whining. She was also, though Sarah didn't realize this, loosely based on Michael Becker's daughter.

'There she is,' Sarah had said, pointing up the way.

Her father frowned. 'I don't see her.'

'Yeah, look – up under that streetlight, outside Hennessy and Ingels.'

At that moment some asshole blared his horn behind them, and her father swung his head to glare ominously out of the back windshield. He almost never got angry within the family, but he could sometimes lay it on the outside world. Sarah knew, having recently covered it in school, that this was a pecking order thing, hierarchy being established in the asphalt jungle – but she was privately nervous that one of these days her dad would choose to assert his will with the wrong naked ape. He didn't seem to realize that fathers could antagonize the fates, too, or that age made little difference to the vehemence of their retribution.

She opened the door and hopped out. 'I'll run over,' she said. 'It's fine.' Michael Becker watched tight-mouthed as the impatient guy in the LeBaron pulled out around them.

Then he turned, and his face changed. For a moment he didn't look like he had story arcs and demographics running behind his eyes, as if he saw the world through a grid of beat lists and foreign residuals. He just looked tired, in need of some hot caffeine, and like her dad.

'See you later,' Sarah said, with a wink. 'Have a heart attack on the way home.'

He looked at his watch. 'Haven't got the time. Maybe a little prostate trouble instead. Nine o'clock?'

'On the dot. I'm always early. It's you who's late.'

'As if. Nokkon, little lady.'

'Nokkon, Dad.' She shut the door and watched him pull back into traffic. He waved at her, a little salute, and then he was gone: swallowed back into an interior world, at the mercy of people who bought words by the yard and never knew what they wanted until it was already in syndication. As she watched him disappear, Sarah knew one thing for sure – The Business wasn't getting her for a sweetheart.

Sian hadn't been under the lamppost, of course. Sarah had only pretended, to help her father on his way, so he could get home and back to work. She continued to not be there for another ten minutes, and then Sarah's phone rang.

It was Sian. She was currently standing by her mom's car on Sunset, and just about annoyed enough to spit. Sarah could hear Sian's mother in the background, imperiously letting off steam at some hapless mechanic, who'd probably seen mother and daughter in distress and developed visions of his own real-life porno film. Sarah hoped he now realized that not only was this *not* going to happen, but if he didn't get the car fixed pronto he'd be a dead man.

Either way, Sian wasn't going to make it. Which left Sarah in a quandary. Her father wouldn't be home yet, and when he pulled into the drive he'd be a vortex of bullet points and plot fixes, maybe already on the phone to his partner, Charles Wang, conjuring ways to pull the project back into the comfort zone. There was some big deal breakfast meeting with the studio the next morning, a make-or-break powwow over decaf and cholesterol-free omelettes. She knew her father dreaded that kind of meeting most of all, because he never ate breakfast and hated having to pretend he did, toying with toast to avoid fiddling with the silverware. She didn't want him to get any more stressed than he already was, and her younger sister, Melanie, would be providing plenty of background noise by herself.

So then she realized – she didn't actually have to call at all. She had a little under two hours, and then he'd be back. The Promenade was wall-to-wall browsing opportunities, most of them still open for business. She could get a Frappuccino and just hang. Wander round Anthropologie, on the lookout for gift ideas. Check the listening posts in B&N, in case they'd finally racked up something new. Even go sit in the Deli, and have a Cobb salad by herself. Basically, bottom line, simply make sure she was at the right place at the right time, and then – depending on what kind of mood he was in – either reveal that Sian hadn't showed, or pretend everything had gone as usual.

She dialled Sian to make sure that this plan wouldn't be undermined by Mrs Williams calling her mom. She couldn't get through, which probably meant the car was up and running again and out of radio contact in a canyon. Sarah was confident that if her mother had been contacted then she'd know all about it already. Helicopters would be circling overhead, Bruce Willis being lowered down toward her on a rope.

She left a message for Sian, then walked over and went into Starbucks. It had occurred to her that if she did go to the Deli she could have whatever she wanted, rather than ordering the Cobb salad because that's what they always did, dieting twenty years before they needed to. She could have, of all things, a burger. A huge great big burger, rare, with cheese. And fries.

She was thinking that maybe this was what it was like to be a grown-up, and that it could work out kind of interesting.

She'd come to the end of her Frap, and The Manics had bellowed their last this time round, when she saw a tall guy come out of the bookstore. He ambled a few yards, then stopped and peered up at the sky. It wasn't yet dark, but it was getting past twilight. He reached into his pocket, pulled out a pack of cigarettes and struggled to extricate one from the packet while juggling what was evidently a heavy bag of books. This went on for quite a few moments, the man completely unaware of Sarah's amused scrutiny. She was thinking that in his position she might try putting the bag down, but this obviously hadn't occurred to him.

Eventually, exasperated, he walked over to the fountain and stuck the bag down on the edge. Once he'd got the cigarette lit he put his hands on his hips, looking down the way, before glancing at her.

'Hello,' he said. His voice was soft and cheerful.

Now that he was closer she thought he was probably about forty, maybe a little less. She wasn't sure how she knew this, as there was a lamp behind his head and his face was slightly difficult to see. He just had that kind of older guy thing.

'Say that again.'

He said: 'Er, hello?'

She nodded sagely. 'You're English.'

'Oh God. Is it that obvious?'

'Well, like, you have an English *accent*.'

'Oh. Of course.' He took another drag of his cigarette, and then looked at the bench. 'Do you mind if I join you?'

Sarah shrugged. Shrugging was good. It didn't say yes, it didn't say no. Whatever. The bench was plenty wide. She was salad-bound within seconds anyway. Or burger-bound. Still undecided.

The man sat. He was wearing a pair of corduroys, not especially

52

new, but a light jacket that looked well-made. He had big, neat hands. His fair hair had been dyed a stronger blond, but expensively, and his face worked pretty well. Like a hip science teacher, or maybe social studies. The kind that probably wouldn't sleep with a student, but could if he wanted.

'So are you an actor, or something?'

'Oh no. Nothing as grand as that. Just a tourist.'

'How long are you here for?'

'A couple of weeks.' He reached in his pocket and pulled out a small object, made of shiny chrome. He flipped the top off and revealed it to be a small portable ashtray.

Sarah watched this with great interest. 'The English smoke a lot, don't they.'

'We do,' said the man, who wasn't English. He stubbed out his cigarette and slipped the ashtray back in his pocket. 'We are not afraid.'

They chatted for a little while. Sarah reminisced about London. The man was able to join in convincingly, as he had returned from the country only two days before. He did not reveal that the Barnes and Noble bag he was carrying was full of books he had owned for some years, nor that he had spent a full hour in the bookstore sitting in the Politics and Economics section, his face averted from the other customers, watching out of the window for Sarah to arrive. He instead asked for suggestions for what else he should see in the city. He listed the parts of Los Angeles he had already visited, a selection of the usual tourist traps.

Sarah, who took her responsibilities seriously, suggested the La Brea tar pit, Rodeo Drive, and the Watts Tower, which she felt would give a good span of where LA had come from, and where it was going. Plus, she thought privately, on Rodeo he could replace his corduroys with something a little more *bon marché*, as Sian – who'd vacationed in Antibes last year – was fond of saying.

Then the man went quiet for a moment. Sarah was thinking that it was time for her to windowshop her way down to dinner. She was gathering herself to say good night, when he turned and looked at her.

'You're very pretty,' he said.

This might or might not be true – Sarah's opinion was currently fiercely divided on the subject – but it was without question straight out of the 'Watch out, a wacko' box of conversational sallies.

'Thanks,' she said, bright-eyed with deflection. For a moment the evening seemed a little cooler, then steadied as she took control. 'Anyway, nice talking to you.'

'I'm sorry,' he said, quickly. 'That's rather an odd thing to say, I know. It's just that you remind me of my own daughter. She's about your age.'

'Right,' Sarah said. 'Cool.'

'She's back in Blighty,' the man went on, as if he hadn't heard her. 'With her mother. Looking forward to seeing them again, don't you know. Top hole. Gor blimey. Princess Di, God rest 'er soul.'

His eyes flicked away from her then, took a quick glance around. Sarah assumed he was embarrassed. In reality he was estimating that in about twenty seconds all paths would converge to convenience him, the lines of sight all elsewhere. He was good at judging this kind of thing, at telling when he would be in vision, of seeing the small steps that would take him back out of sight. It was one of his special skills. He shifted a few inches closer to the girl, who stood up.

'Anyway,' Sarah said. 'I got to go.'

The man laughed, as he felt the lines fall into place. He grabbed Sarah's hand and tugged it with surprising force. She squawked quietly and fell back onto the bench, too shocked to resist.

'Let go,' she said, fighting to stay calm. The ground seemed to be falling away, a vertiginous, fluid feeling. She felt as if she had been caught cheating, or stealing.

'Pretty girl.' He gripped her hand more tightly. 'A keeper.'

'Please, let go of me.'

'Oh shut up,' he muttered, all pretence of an English accent gone.

54

'You ludicrous little slut.' His fist jack-hammered up in a compact, short-armed punch, smashing straight into her face.

Sarah's head jerked back, her eyes wide open and stunned. Oh no, she thought, the interior voice quiet and dismayed. Oh no.

'Take a look, Sarah,' the man said, his voice low and urgent. 'Look at all the lucky people. The people who aren't you.'

He nodded down the Promenade. Only a block down, the street was crowded. People going in and out of stores, taking exploratory looks at restaurant menus. Around Sarah and the man there was nobody to be seen.

'Once there was just bush here, do you realize that? Ragged coast-line, rocks, shells. A few tracks in the sand. If you're quiet you can hear the way that it was, before any of this shit was here.'

Blinking against her watering eyes, Sarah tried to work out what he was getting at. Maybe there was something she could do, some unexpected final question in this test, some way of scraping a pass. 'But people *don't* see,' he continued. 'They don't even look. Blind. Wilfully blind. Trapped in the machine.'

He grabbed her hair, turned her face so she could see into the Barnes and Noble. There were plenty of people in there, too. Reading. Standing. Chatting. Why would you look outside, when you're in a bookstore at night? Even if you did, would you see more than a couple of dark figures on a bench? Why would that seem exceptional?

'I should do you here and now,' the man said, in a tone of quiet indignation. 'Just to show it could be done. That nobody really cares. When you're surrounded by people you don't know all the time, how can you tell what's wrong? In five square miles of disease, who cares what happens to one little virus? Only me.'

Sarah realized there was going to be no get-out-of-this-free question, not now or ever, and gathered herself to scream. The man felt her chest expand, and his hand quickly looped over her face. Two fingers grabbed her upper lip from above, tugging it hard. The scream never made it out of her throat. Sarah tried to struggle, but the hand held her in position, coupled with the weight of his arm, pressing down on her head.

'Nobody watching,' the man assured her, with the same hateful calm. 'I made it this way. I can walk where nobody sees.'

Indistinct noises came out of the girl's mouth, as she tried to say something. He seemed to understand.

'No they're not,' he said. 'They're not on their way. They're at home. Mommy's a Jackson Pollock in the kitchen. Daddy's in the garden, with little sister. Both naked. They make an interesting tableau. Some might even consider it obscene.'

In fact, Sarah's mom and Melanie were watching a *Simpsons* rerun at that moment. It was, as Zoë Becker would always remember, the episode where George Bush moves into Springfield. Michael Becker was typing furiously in his den, having found, he fervently hoped, a way of making everything all right. If he could just fix the opening ten minutes, and find a way of selling the idea that some of the characters *had* to be older than teenagers, then everything would be okay. Failing that, fuck it, he'd just make them all teenagers – and reinstate all the fucking pans down the front of the high school, the way Wang wanted it. A few miles away, Sian Williams had just picked up Sarah's message, and was feeling a little envious of her friend's Out Alone adventure.

'If you keep wriggling,' the man said, 'I'll pull your teeth out. I will. I promise. Not easy, but it's worth it. It's really a very unusual sound.'

Sarah went completely still, and for a moment neither of them moved. The man seemed to take a pleasure in sitting that way, the girl's mouth pulled up to a point of screaming pain, as if they were sharing a private moment in the middle of a busy street.

Then he sighed, like a man reluctantly putting aside an absorbing magazine. He stood, pulling Sarah up with him. Her minidisc player slipped to the floor with a brittle clatter. The man glanced at it, and let it lie.

'Goodbye and good night, good people,' he said, in the general direction of the other end of the street. 'You'll all rot in hell, and I'd love to lead you there.' His right arm rotated around Sarah's head until his hand was clamped firmly over her mouth. With his other hand he picked up the bag of books. 'But I have a date, and we must go.'

Then, with quick, long strides, he dragged Sarah across the street and into an alley where his car was parked. She had no choice but to accompany him. He was tall and very strong.

He threw open the back door, then grabbed her hair again and peered closely into her face. The close presence of his face scared all useful thought out of her head.

'Come, my dear,' he said. 'Our carriage awaits.' Then he head-butted her just above the eyes.

As Sarah's knees buckled, her last thought was matter-of-fact. In her bedside table was a notebook in which she had written down many thoughts. Some of the most recent were about sex: breathless musings on a part of life she had not yet experienced, but knew was coming her way. Most were transcriptions of things Sian had told her, but she'd used her own imagination too, plus what she'd gleaned from TV and movies and a not-too-gross magazine she'd found under the Pier.

The notebook was hidden, but not very well. When she was dead, her mother and father would find it, and they would know she had brought this evening upon herself.

Nina was unaware of much of this, but this was the event she described. When she had told what she knew, she topped her glass up. Zandt's remained untouched.

'Four witnesses put Sarah Becker on the bench between 7.12 and 7.31. Their descriptions of the man with her range from "Nondescript, maybe tall", to "Shit, I don't know", via "Well, he was, like, a guy". We don't even have an age or colour that I'd take to the bank, though we got two hits with white and blond. Two say he was wearing a long coat, another said a sport jacket. Nobody saw them

57

leave, despite the fact that the bench is within yards of a zillion people. If the man spent any time in the bookstore before accosting her, then nobody noticed him. Another witness describes seeing a car of undetermined colour and model in the nearest side street. It's possible that a trashcan may have been placed to obscure the number plate – which is pretty slick, though does require more confidence than God. Anybody could have just moved the can, and he was illegally parked. The car was gone by 8.15.

'The girl's father arrived at the south end of the Promenade at 9.07. He parked up in the usual place, waited. When neither his daughter nor Sian Williams appeared after a few minutes, he went into the restaurant. The staff told him they hadn't served a table who matched his description, though they did have a no-show in the name of Williams. He called the other girl's mother and found that the dinner had been cancelled at the last moment due to a problem with the Williamses' car. The car's been checked, but we can't get a firm opinion on whether it was tampered with.

'Michael Becker demanded to speak to the girl herself and was eventually told Sarah had left a message saying she didn't want to bother her dad, and that she was going to just kill time and wait for the usual pickup. He searched up and down the street without finding any sign of his daughter. Finally he made it up to the far end and after checking in the Barnes and Noble he spotted a Sony minidisc player lying partially obscured under the bench. His daughter's ownership of this device was certain, both through a label she had affixed and because he had bought it for her. The disc in the machine was some album by her favourite band. She has a poster of them on her bedroom wall. Becker then called the sheriff's department, the LAPD, and also his agent, somewhat bizarrely. He seems to have thought that she would have more pull with the cops than he did. He called his wife, and told her to stay where she was in case their daughter arrived home by cab.

'The whole area was searched. Nothing. There are no prints on the player apart from the girl's. There are about a hundred cigarette butts around the bench, but we don't even know if the perpetrator smoked. One of the witnesses said he thought he might have done, so some poor fucker in a lab is currently trying for DNA off a whole bag of them.'

'The father isn't a suspect.'

'Not in this universe. They were very close, in the right ways. Still, for a couple of days that's what people were wondering. But no. We don't think it's him, and the timings don't work at all. We've also eliminated his partner, a Charles Wang. He was in New York.'

Zandt slowly raised his glass, emptied it, lowered it again. He knew there was more. 'And then?'

Nina pulled her feet off the table, reached over to pick the file up off the floor. Inside, in addition to a large number of copied documents, was a thin package wrapped in brown paper. What she pulled out, however, was a photograph.

'This arrived at the Becker residence late the following afternoon. Some time between half past four and six o'clock. It was discovered lying on the path.' She handed it to Zandt.

The picture showed a girl's sweater, pale lilac, neatly folded into a square. What looked like ribbed ribbon had been tied around the sweater into a bow.

'It's been tied up with plaited hair. Sarah's was long enough for it to be hers, and it's the right colour. Forensics has taken samples off her hairbrush, and will have confirmation very soon.'

Zandt noticed that his glass had been refilled. He drank. The whiskey stung in the dryness of his mouth, and made him nauseous. His head felt as if it were a balloon, blown up slightly too much, floating a couple of inches above his neck.

'The Upright Man,' he said.

'Well,' Nina said, judiciously, 'we've checked with the families of the victims two and three years ago, and every officer who was involved in those investigations. We're pretty convinced that the nature of the parcels he left on those occasions has remained secret. It could still be a copycat. I doubt it. But I have an all-media scan in operation, including the Internet, for any use of the phrases "Delivery Boy" or "Upright Man".'

'The Internet?'

'Yeah,' she said. 'Kind of a computer thing. It's all the rage.'

'It's him,' Zandt said. Only he was fully aware of the irony inherent in his confidence.

She looked at him, and then reached reluctantly back into the file. This time the photograph showed the sweater after it had been carefully unwrapped and laid out flat. Sarah's name was embroidered on the front, not fancily, but in neat block letters.

'The hair used for the name is of a dark brown. It is much drier than the hair that we believe to be Sarah's, suggesting that it was cut some time ago.'

She stopped then, and waited while Zandt slowly reached into his pocket. He pulled out a pack of Marlboros and a matchbook. He had not smoked since they had been in the room. There was no ashtray. His hands, as he pulled a cigarette out, were almost steady. He did not look at her, but only at the match as he struck it: regarding it with fixed concentration, as if it were something unfamiliar to him, but whose purpose he had divined through intuition. It took three attempts before it flared, but the match could have been damp.

'I made sure the dark brown hair was tested first.' She took a deep breath. 'It's a match, John. It's Karen's hair.'

She left him alone for a while, went and stood outside in the cold and listened to the darkness. Muted laughter drifted across from the main building, and through the window she could see couples of varying ages, bundled up in sensible sweaters, plotting tomorrow's adventures in hiking. A door was open on the other side of the building and through it she could hear the clatter of plates being cleaned by someone who didn't own them. Something small rustled in the undergrowth on the other side of the road, but nothing came of it.

When she returned, Zandt was sitting exactly as she'd left him, though he had a new cigarette. He didn't look up at her.

She put a few more pieces of wood on the fire, inexpertly, unable to remember whether you piled them on top or placed them round the sides. She sat in the chair and poured herself another drink. Then sat up with him through the night.

Chapter 5

By late afternoon I'd had conversations with the police and the hospital, and before that with my parents' neighbours on either side. Each of these had been carefully judged.

I called the cops from the house, and was put through to an Officer Spurling – thankfully not one of the men who'd interviewed me after the incident in the hotel bar. Spurling and his partner had been first on the scene of my parents' accident, alerted through a call from a passing motorist. Officers Spurling and McGregor remained on the scene until the ambulance and fire service arrived, and assisted in the removal of the bodies from the car. They followed the ambulance to the hospital, and Spurling had been present when Donald and Elizabeth Hopkins had been pronounced dead on arrival. The deceased had been identified by their driver's licenses, with subsequent confirmation from Harold Davids (attorney) and Mary Richards (neighbour) within two hours.

Officer Spurling was sympathetic to my desire to establish the circumstances of my parents' death. He provided me with the name of the relevant doctor at the hospital, and suggested I look into counselling. I took him to mean receiving some, rather than as a career. I thanked him for his time, and he wished me the very best. I ended the call hoping I didn't run into him when I went to the station to retrieve my gun, though chances were he already knew all about it. The counselling suggestion hadn't sounded entirely uninflected.

Tracking down the doctor was a good deal more difficult. She wasn't on duty when I called the hospital, and the length of time it took to elicit this information, via a succession of conversations with harried nurses and other disembodied and bad-tempered voices, suggested that I'd be lucky to get her on the phone when she arrived. The ER was there for the living. Once you were dead you were merely an unwelcome reminder, and out of their hands.

I drove over and spent a very quiet hour waiting there. Dr Michaels eventually deigned to come out of her bunker and talk to me. She was in her late twenties, studiously harassed, and awfully pleased with herself. After ruthlessly patronizing me for a few moments she confirmed what I'd already been told. Major head and upper body trauma. Dead as dead could be. If that was all, could I excuse her. She was very grown up now, and had patients to see. I was more than happy to relinquish her company, and tempted to help her along her way with a brisk shove.

I walked back out of the hospital. The light was gone, a fall evening come early. A few cars were parked randomly around the lot, made monochromatic and anonymous by high overhead lamps. A young woman stood smoking and crying quietly, some distance away.

I considered what to do next. After finding the note, I'd sat on the coffee table for quite some time. Neither the light-headedness nor the crawling sensation in my stomach went away. A search through the rest of the book showed that it was empty. There was no question that the note was in my father's handwriting.

'Ward,' it said, in writing that was in no way different from what

I would expect, neither too large nor too small, not forced or notice-ably faint: 'We're not dead.' My father had written this on a piece of paper, slipped it into a book, and then stashed it inside his old chair, taking care to replace the braid that covered the join. A note denying their death had been placed in a position where it would come to light only if they were dead. Why else would I be in the house alone? What would I be doing in his chair? The positioning of the note suggested that whoever had placed it believed that, in the circumstances that next led me to be in the house, I would sit in the old chair – despite knowing it was the least comfortable in the room. As it happened, they'd been right. I had sat there, and for some time. It made sense that I would do so if they were dead, or that I would at least look at it, maybe run my hand over the fabric for a moment. It was exactly the kind of thing a grieving son might be expected to do.

But, and this was the point that kept jabbing away at me, this implied that some time before their deaths one or both of them had spent time thinking about what would be likely to happen after they died. They had considered the situation in detail, and made judgments on my likely behaviour. Why? Why would they be thinking of death? It was bizarre. It made no sense.

Assuming they were actually dead.

The idea that the last few days had been a farce, that my parents weren't dead after all, was a difficult one to face head-on. Part of my heart leapt at the idea, the part that had awakened me at some stage in every night since the phone call from Mary. Even if I hadn't cared for them, and had only wished for a chance to bawl them out about UnRealty, I wanted my parents back. But when your flesh is damaged the body gets to work within seconds. White blood cells flood into the area, repairing and patching, throwing up every sandbag they have. The body protects itself, and the same happens in the mind. It occurs sluggishly and imperfectly, a bad job done by indifferent craftsmen, but within minutes an accretion of defence mechanisms starts to form around the trauma, blunting its edges, eventually sealing it away inside scar tissue. Like a sliver of glass buried deep in a cut, the event will never go away, and often a movement will cause it to nudge a nerve ending and burn like fire for a while. However much it hurts when that happens, the last thing you want to do is take a knife and reopen the wound.

I left the house, locking up carefully, and went next door to Mary's. She seemed both pleased and surprised to see me, and dealt coffee and cake in dangerous quantities. Feeling underhanded and unworthy of her kindness, I established in roundabout ways that my parents had seemed their normal selves in the days and weeks leading up to the accident, and that – as Officer Spurling later confirmed – Mary had identified the bodies. I knew this already. She'd told me on the phone, as I sat bonelessly in Santa Barbara. I just needed to hear it again. I could have visited the bodies at the undertakers myself, of course, instead of sitting in the hotel for two days. I hadn't, which now made me feel ashamed. I'd told myself at the time that it was important to remember them as they had been, rather than as two lengths of damaged putty. There was truth in that. But also I had been afraid, bothered by the idea, and simply unwilling.

After I left Mary I went round to the other neighbours. A young woman opened the door almost instantly, startling me. She was confident and healthy-looking, and wearing generously paint-spattered clothes. The hallway behind her was half finished in a shade I considered ill-advised. I introduced myself and explained what had happened to their neighbours. She was already aware of events, as I'd known she would be. She expressed her condolences and we chatted for a moment. At no point did anything in her manner suggest that the accident hadn't come as a surprise, what with one or both of the Hopkins being evidently off their heads. That was that.

I called the cops, and then went to the hospital. As I stood in the parking lot after talking to the doctor, I decided that three confirmations were enough. My parents were dead. Only a fool would follow this line of inquiry any further. I could talk to Davids the next day if I wished – I'd missed him at his office, and left a message – but I knew anything he told me would lead to the same conclusion. The note wasn't what it purported to be. It wasn't a get-out-of-grief card. It didn't undo what had happened.

But there had to be a reason for it, even if that reason turned out to be only that one of them had not been completely sane. The note's existence meant something, and I found that I needed to know what that was.

I searched in the garage, and then my father's workshop in the cellar of the house. I felt I should be looking for something in particular, but didn't know what, so I just poked around. Drills, routers, other handyman kit of obscure purpose. Nails and screws in a wide variety of sizes, neatly sorted. Numerous scraps of wood, rendered purposeless and inexplicable by his death. Nothing seemed obviously out of place, all was arranged with the tidiness and rigour I would have expected. If external order can be taken as an index of state of mind, my father had been the same as ever.

I went back up into the house and did the downstairs first. The kitchen and utility room, the sitting room, my father's den, the dining room, and the section of the porch that at some time in the past had been glassed in and turned into a sunroom. Here I was more thorough. I looked beneath every cushion, under the rugs, and behind every piece of furniture. I looked inside the cabinet, under the television, and found nothing except technology and a couple of DVDs. I took everything out of the cupboards in the kitchen, looked in the oven and the larder. I picked up and shook every book I found, whether on the bookcases in the hallway, or filed, in my mother's idiosyncratic way, among the dried pasta. There were a lot of books. It took a long time. Especially my father's study, off the half-landing, which was where I looked first. I dug through the drawers of his desk, on every shelf, and dipped into each hanging file in the oak cabinet. I even turned on his computer and took a cursory trawl through a few files, though this felt unwelcome and invasive. I wouldn't want anyone who loved me sifting through the contents of my laptop. They'd be likely to dig me up and set fire to me. It soon became obvious that it would take far too long to read everything on the machine, and that it would very likely turn out to be nothing but invoices and workaday correspondence. I left the machine on, with the idea of coming back to it if all else failed, but my father wasn't a computer buff. I didn't think he'd leave a further message anywhere he couldn't touch with his hands.

Before long I was beginning to feel worn out. Not with the physical effort, which was negligible, but the emotional undertow. Thoroughly upending my parents' lives brought them back even more vehemently, especially the trivial things. A framed photocopy of the contract for the first house UnRealty had sold, capped by a logo that I now realized looked a little hand-drawn. By my mother, probably. A scrapbook of recipes for childhood meals, including a lasagne I could smell just by reading the ingredients.

I took a break and spent fifteen minutes sitting in the kitchen, drinking their mineral water. I tried once again to put myself in their position, to think what might be an obvious second step. Assuming they'd left the note in the chair to attract my attention, it made sense that any further note or clue would also be in a place that had resonance. I couldn't think where that would be. I'd turned everything over. There was nothing there.

The upstairs of the house proved just as much of a bust. I looked under the bed in their room, searched all the drawers. After a deep breath, I went through the contents of the wardrobes, paying special attention to those I recognized – my father's old jackets, my mother's battered ex-handbags. I found a few things – receipts, ticket stubs, a handful of loose change – nothing that seemed to mean anything. I lingered over a collection of old ties, neatly boxed in the back of my father's side of the closet. I'd never seen most of them.

I even looked under the roof, pulling myself up into it via a small trapdoor in the ceiling of the upstairs hallway. My father had got as far as stringing a light up, but no further. There was nothing in the attic space but dust and two empty suitcases.

In the end I went downstairs, and back to my father's chair. It was early evening. I had found nothing, and I was beginning to feel stupid. Perhaps I was just trying to flay a nonexistent order out of chaos. I sat in my father's chair, and read the note once again. It meant neither more nor less, however many times you read it.

As I raised my eyes, they fell once more on the television. The chair was aligned perfectly with it, and a thought occurred to me. If I'd been right in thinking that it looked a little out of place, then perhaps its position wasn't just to help draw my attention to the cushion – but to redirect my gaze to another area entirely.

I got up and opened the glass doors that hid the storage space underneath the television. I found exactly what I had previously. A VCR, a DVD player, and two DVDs: old movies. Nothing else.

No tapes. That was odd.

In the whole of the house I'd found no videotapes. There were two shelves of DVDs in the study, and a further one in the second bedroom. But not a single videotape.

My father was a semiprofessional tube watcher. For as long as I could remember, there'd been tapes lying around the house. So where were they now?

I quickly strode back to his study. No tapes in there either, even though there was a second VCR stowed on a low shelf. I didn't bother to search the drawers or the cabinet again. There'd been none there. There had been none anywhere in the house or the shop or garage either. I tried to think back to the Thanksgiving before last, when I'd deigned to stop by for twenty-four hours. I couldn't specifically remember seeing tapes around. I couldn't remember *not* seeing them. I'd been pretty drunk most of the time.

It could be that my father had embraced DVD as the dawn of a long-awaited new age in home entertainment, declared the videotape dead, and held a bonfire in the garden. I didn't think so. Dyersburg doubtless had a dump somewhere, but I couldn't see that scenario either. Even if he'd found as the years went on that there was less and less he wanted to watch, he wasn't going to throw all the old favourites away. I started to wonder whether creating an absence of something unremarkable might be a subtle way of attracting the attention of someone who knew you well, who had an understanding of the things that should be in your environment.

Either that, or I was losing objectivity, running too far and fast with a meaningless ball. I'd already searched the house. It didn't matter that I now had an idea – however spurious – of what to look for. I already hadn't found it. I was getting hungry, and also angry. If there had been something they had thought I needed telling, why the subterfuge? Why not just tell me on the phone? Leave a letter with Davids? Send an email? It made no sense.

But I knew by then that when I left the house, it would be for good. It was better to be sure. You want that scar tissue as tough as it can be.

I turned the outside lights on and went and had a look around the porch. None of the boards in the decking was loose, and I couldn't see how there could be much of a crawl space underneath. There was a large wooden box around one side, but a tiring couple of minutes established it held nothing but firewood and spiders. I walked down the couple of steps to the yard, took a few paces back, and stared irritably up at the house.

Chimney, horizontal boards, windowpanes. The upper rooms. Their bedroom. The guest room.

I went back inside. As I passed my father's study, something caught the corner of my eye. I stopped, took a pace back, and looked in, not certain what I had seen. I got it after a second or two: the VCR.

Like an idiot, I hadn't actually looked inside either of the tape machines. I checked the one in the living room first. It was empty. Then I walked into the study, bent down and peered at the machine until I found the Eject button. I pressed it and there was an irritable whirring sound, but nothing happened. Then I realized this was because there was black duct tape across the slot.

As a warning not to put a tape in, or to prevent my father from doing so accidentally? Hardly – if the machine was screwed, he'd just replace it.

I tried pulling the tape off, but it was of a strength sufficient to bond planets together. I got my knife out of my jacket pocket. It has two blades. One is large and sharp and designed for cutting things. The other is a screwdriver. It's surprising how often you need one right after the other. I flipped the sharp blade out and sliced through the centre of the tape.

There was something inside the slot. I cut and pulled at the remaining obstruction until the Eject button worked. The machine whirred aggressively, and popped its slot.

It ejected a videotape, a standard VHS. I took it out and stared at it for a long time.

As I was slowly straightening up, my father called from the stairs.

'Ward? Is that you?' he said.

After a moment of light-headed shock, my body tried to move quickly toward a safe place it evidently believed existed somewhere else. It wanted to be some other place altogether. It didn't know where. Perhaps Alabama. It tried every direction at once, to be on the safe side.

I leapt backward, dropping the tape and coming close to sprawling full-length on the floor. I snatched the tape up from the ground and stuffed it in my pocket, doing so barely consciously, feeling caught and guilty and in danger. Footsteps made their way up the last few stairs, paused for a moment, and then headed toward the study door. I didn't want to see who made them.

It hadn't been my father, of course. Just a voice that wasn't entirely dissimilar, coming out of nowhere in a quiet house. The person I saw on the landing was Harold Davids, looking old and nervous and bad-tempered.

'Goodness,' he said. 'You scared the life out of me.'

I breathed out like a cough. 'Tell me about it.'

70

Davids's eyes drifted down to my hands, and I realized that I was still holding my knife. I flipped the blade back in, started to drop it in my pocket, realized the tape was there.

'What are you doing here?' I asked, trying to sound polite.

'I got your message from this afternoon,' he said, slowly raising his eyes back up to look at my face. 'I called the hotel. You weren't in your room, so I wondered if you might be here.'

'I didn't hear the doorbell.'

'The front door was ajar,' he said, somewhat testily. 'I became concerned that someone might have heard the house was unoccupied, and broken in.'

'No,' I said. 'It's just me.'

'So I see. I shall consider the crisis over.' He raised a good-humoured eyebrow, and my heartbeat slowly returned to normal.

Back in the hall he asked why I'd called. I said it was nothing, a minor point in the will's legalese that I'd subsequently puzzled out for myself. He nodded distantly and wandered through into the sitting room.

'Such a lovely room,' he said, after a moment. 'I shall miss it. I'll stop by every now and then, if I may, for any residual mail.'

'Great.' I didn't bear him any ill will, but I didn't want to spend any more time in the house. I went back up to my father's study to turn off the computer. I'd noticed earlier that he had a ffiz! drive, and on impulse I dumped a backup onto the disk in the machine.

By the time I'd turned it all off and gone back out, Davids was standing at the front door, looking brisk once again.

I walked with him down the path. He seemed in no hurry to get back to his business, and asked about my plans for the house. I told him I didn't know whether I'd be keeping or selling it, and accepted the implied offer of his services in either event. We stood by his big black car for a further five minutes, talking about something or other. I think he might have been giving me restaurant recommendations. I wasn't feeling hungry any more.

In the end he lowered himself into the driver's seat and strapped in with the thoroughness of a man who had no intention of dying, ever. He took a last look up at the dark shape of the house, and then nodded gravely at me. I suspected that something between us had changed, and wondered whether Davids had filed for later consideration the question of what Don Hopkins's son might be doing with a knife that was so clearly not ornamental.

I waited until he was safely round the corner, and then ran to my car and drove the other way.

Chapter 6

A small amount of money and only a little flattery got me a VCR in my room. Either the hotel was better than I'd thought, or my stunt in the bar had convinced the management that I was a guest whose needs were worth meeting. I waited with increasing impatience while a monumentally stupid youth made a mess of a very simple cabling job, and then shooed him out.

I took the tape from my pocket, and carefully inspected it. There was no writing on it anywhere. From the amount of videotape on the spool, it looked like it would run to about fifteen or twenty minutes, half an hour at the most.

I waited until my room-service coffee arrived. I wanted my environment just so. Eventually it came, still fairly warm. Miraculously, there were no fries with it.

I put the tape in the machine.

*   *   *

Four seconds of data hash, the white noise of null information.

Then the sound of wind, and a view of a high mountain pasture. In the distance, a postcard view of snow-covered peaks across a range – seen too briefly to identify. The foreground was a gentle slope covered in snow, cut off by a stern-looking building: no obvious coffee shop, or ski-wear emporium. There was no one around, no cars in the small lot. Out of season. The camera panned to show another administrative-looking structure, and severe grey clouds above. This view was held for a few seconds, the sound of a sleeve flapping in the wind discernible in the background.

Cut to an interior. The camera was held low, as if covertly, and the scene only lasted a few seconds. I rewound, paused the clearest image. It wasn't the world's best VCR, and the frozen picture jumped a little, but I could make out the public area of what looked like a ski lodge, with a cathedral ceiling. A long desk ran along one side, presumably the reception, but currently deserted. There was a large painting on the wall behind it, the usual easy nonsense by some overpaid and under-talented fraud. I could see the left-hand side of a towering fireplace, constructed out of river rock. An ornamental fire generated well-behaved ambience in the bottom. Nut-brown leather armchairs were carefully arranged around low coffee tables, each featuring a heavily varnished wooden sculpture celebrating the sentimentally revered wildlife of the old West: an eagle, a bear, a Native American – none of whom survived the old West in any great numbers.

I flipped the tape off pause and, on second viewing, saw that someone had been about to enter the area just before the scene cut. There was a shadow along the wall of a corridor leading off the top of the space, the sound of footsteps on stone.

Then a final exterior, back out in the parking lot. A little time must have passed since the first shot – assuming it had even been taken on the same day. The wind had dropped and the sky was a clear and savage blue. A medium shot of the stern building, which I assumed must have been the one we were just inside. A number of figures stood in the snow in front of it. There were perhaps seven or eight of them, though it was difficult to tell because they were all dressed in dark clothing, and standing close together, as if in conversation. No faces were visible, and all I could hear was the wind – except for right at the end, when whoever was holding the camera said something, a short sentence. I listened to it three times. It remained inaudible.

Then, as one of the figures seemed to start to turn toward the camera, the screen cut back to white noise.

I paused the tape, stared at the screen as it jumped and fretted. I didn't know what to make of what I'd seen. It wasn't what I'd expected. From the quality of the image, it looked like the footage had been obtained using a digital camcorder. I hadn't seen anything like that in the house. The video could have been shot pretty much anywhere in the mid- to Northern Rockies, Idaho, Utah, or Colorado: but it made sense for it to be somewhere in Montana, and probably nearby. I knew the kind of place it showed. Compounds for the rich, the country's most beautiful areas carved into private homesites so the wealthy could slide down mountains without fear of bumping into anyone of average income. Some had gated security, most didn't even need it. Put one foot over the border and you knew whether you were welcome. Anyone thinking of burglary would slink right back out, stung to their very core.

My parents probably knew people in the area who'd got themselves a home with ski-in, ski-out convenience. My father might even have sold it to them. So what?

I restarted the tape.

Real noise. Music, shouting, loud conversation. A face, blurred and very close up, laughing uproariously. It fell across the frame to reveal a bar in the throes of a boisterous good time. A long counter ran down one side of the room, ranks of bottles and a mirror behind. Men and women stood in droves around it, bellowing at each other, at the barmen, up at the ceiling. Most looked young, others were clearly in middle age. Everybody seemed to be smoking, and the murky yellow lighting was hazed with clouds. The walls were plastered with posters in rainbow colours or stark black-and-white. A jukebox was working overtime in the background, cranked up so loud it was distorting out both its speakers and the microphone and I couldn't even tell what the song was.

It was obvious this scene was much older than the first on the tape. Not only did the video look like it had been converted from 8mm film, but the clothes the people were wearing – unless this had been some kind of laboriously authentic retro party – said this was an evening back in the early '70s. Terrible colours, terrible jeans, terrible hair. A look that said being 'tidy' had been judged and found wanting. My reaction was probably about the same as their parents' must have been: Who *are* these aliens? What do they want? And are they *blind*?

The camera swept and bobbed through the bar, with a verve that suggested the operator was either under the influence of hallucinogenic drugs or very drunk indeed. At one point the picture pitched forward alarmingly, as if he or she had nearly fallen over. This was followed by a loud and prolonged belch, which degenerated into a violent coughing fit, the camera meanwhile held down so that it showed a patch of beer-slicked floor. Then it whipped back upward, and careered off into the fray as if fixed to a bumper car. My eyebrows crawled slowly up my head in bemused embarrassment, as I tried to get my head round the idea that it might be my father operating the camera. A few people waved or hooted as it moved past them, but no one called out a name.

Then the camera swerved abruptly round a corner, revealing an extension to the main bar area with people standing and sitting all around the sides. In the middle was a pool table. Some guy was hunkered down on the other side to take a shot. He was large and had a big nose and his face was almost totally obscured with hair and moustache and sideburns. He looked like a bear with the mange.

Behind him wobbled a blonde woman with long hair, leaning on a cue as if it was the only thing holding her up. She was trying very hard to focus on the game, a frown of concentration on her face, but it looked like the world was getting away from her. Her partner didn't seem like he was having a much easier time of it, and was taking a very long while lining up for his shot. Closer to the camera, on the near side of the table, was another couple, both holding pool cues. They had their backs to the camera and an arm round each other. Both had long brown hair. The girl wore a big white blouse and a long skirt in dark purples shot with green; the man sported bell-bottoms in tatty denim and an afghan waistcoat that looked only recently tamed.

The blonde girl looked up from the table and caught sight of the camera. She let out a whoop, and pointed at it with great vigour but extreme vagueness, as if she was selecting between three different images and kept forgetting which one she'd settled for. The pool player glanced up, rolled his eyes, got back to his shot. The brown-haired couple turned round, and I realized that my earlier embarrassment had been misplaced.

It wasn't my father running the camera. I could tell this because the brown-haired couple were my parents.

As I stared at the image open-mouthed, my father grinned a crooked grin and flipped his middle finger at the camera. My mother stuck her tongue out. The camera abruptly swept away from them to the pool player, as he finally made his shot. He missed by a country mile.

I paused, rewound.

My parents turned. My father grinned, and flipped the bird. My mother stuck her tongue out.

I paused again. I stared.

My mother never really got large, but she got comfortable, and moved with the sedate grace of a liner being pulled by a tug. The person I saw on screen weighed about one hundred twenty pounds, and they were distributed very well. Without even realizing what I

77

was thinking, I knew that if I'd walked into a bar and saw her looking like that and standing with another guy, then a fight would have broken out. This was someone you'd turn caveman to stand next to. Not that my father looked incapable of holding his own: he was a little heavier than I remembered him ever being, but he moved easily and with great economy. He could have been an actor. The pair of them looked fit and healthy and lustrous. They looked like real, living people, a couple that had sex. Most of all they looked young. They looked so astonishingly *young*.

The scene lasted about another five minutes. Nothing in particular happened, except that I got to see my father playing pool, back when he'd have looked at me as I am now and seen an older man. And he could play. He could really play. When the bear man missed his shot and reeled back from the table, my father turned from the camera and bent over the green. He didn't bother to go round to find the easiest shot: he just took the one in front of him and fired it off. It went down. He started moving then, prowling round the table, glancing with the intent nonchalance you see in people who expect to pot the balls, who've come to the table with that in mind. The next shot went home, too, rolled a foot down a cushion, and the one after that – as if the ball had been snapped back into the pocket on a piece of elastic. My mother cheered and slapped my father on the ass. He made an ambitious reversed double into the centre pocket and then sunk the black from halfway down the table, turning away before it was even down. Game over, man.

He winked at the bearlike guy, who rolled his eyes again. Just as the bear was used to the camera wielder being an asshole, he was clearly also accustomed to being trashed by my father at pool. This was business as usual. These were people who knew each other very well.

Nothing in particular happened, except that my mother began dancing with the blonde girl. Then she started doing a kind of side-to-side ragdoll thing, arms and legs turning in different directions, fingers clicking. I'd seen this done in films, on television, by professional dancers. But I'd never really seen it properly until I saw my mother doing it, rattling along to the music, mouth half-open and eyes half-shut.

You go girl, I found myself thinking. You really did go.

Nothing in particular happened, except while the bear was laboriously resetting the table I saw my father sit back on a stool and slug back a few swallows of beer. My mother – still dancing – winked at him, and he winked back, and I realized they weren't quite as drunk as everyone else in the room. They were having a fine old time, but they had jobs and when Monday morning came they'd be able to do them. Come to think of it, my father must already have been a realtor, despite the weekend afghan and scraggy T-shirt. The extra few pounds actually kind of suited him. He had a breadth of shoulder that could accommodate the weight and look powerful rather than fat. Much more and he could have been heading for out-of-shape, but for the time being he merely looked like someone you'd be careful not to bang into if he was heading across the floor carrying a tray of beers. I could tell that the weight must have been a fairly recent acquisition, however, and that he wasn't comfortable with it. Every now and then he rolled his shoulders back, ostensibly out of a desire to remove kinks from leaning down to rocket balls around the table. But also, I suspected, to make sure his shoulders were held square. Later he'd discovered jogging, and the gym, and never looked this way again. But on the tape of that evening I saw him do something: it was trivial, and innocuous, but as I sat in the hotel room in Dyersburg and watched it a small sound escaped from my mouth, like I'd been gently punched in the stomach.

As he lit a cigarette – and I'd never known that he'd once smoked – he absently lifted the patch of T-shirt lying over his midriff, and let it fall again – so it hung a little better over what was only a pretty small belly. I rewound, played it again. And then again, leaning forward, squinting against the grain in the background of the video. The movement was unmistakable. I've done it myself. In all the time I knew my father, I don't think I ever saw him do something that

79

naked, a thing so explicable and personal. It was the act of a man who was aware of his body, and a perceived flaw in it, even in the midst of a rocking evening. It was an adjustment he'd made before, but which was not yet habitual enough to be a tic. Even more than the T-shirt itself, the pitchers of beer and the vibrant good cheer, my mother's dancing and the fact that my father could evidently once wield a pool cue with the best of them, that little movement made it inconceivable that they were now dead.

The table was finally set up for play again, and my father got up and prepared to break, squaring up like the cue ball was going to receive a whack it'd remember the rest of its spherical little life. The scene stopped abruptly right at that moment, as if a reel of film had run out.

Before I could hit pause again, it had cut directly to something else.

A different interior. A house. A living room. Dark, lit with candles. The picture quality was murky, the film stock not coping well with the low light. Music on quietly in the background, and this time I recognized it as coming from the soundtrack to *Hair*. A herd of wine bottles stood on the floor in varying states of emptiness, and there were several overflowing ashtrays.

My mother was half-reclining on a low couch, singing along, singing an early morning singing song. The bear-guy's head was more or less on her lap, and he was rolling a joint on his chest.

'Put the sodomy one on again,' he slurred. 'Put it on.'

The camera panned smoothly to the side, showing another man lying facedown on the ground. The blonde girl was sitting behind him, tending a neat row of candles in saucers that had been laid on the guy's back. He had evidently been comatose long enough to count as furniture, and my guess was he was the man who'd been operating the camera in the bar. The girl was inclining slowly and unpredictably from the waist, staying upright by pure force of will. Now there was less going on around her, it was obvious she was older than she had at first appeared. Not in her teens, but late

80

twenties, maybe even thirty – and a little old to be part of this scene. I realized that if I was watching the very early '70s, then my parents had to be around the same age.

Which meant that I'd already been born.

'Put it on,' the bear insisted, and the camera jerked back to him, swinging in close to his face. 'Put it on.'

'No,' said a voice very close to the microphone, laughing, confirming that it was now my father who was running the camera. He was making a better job of it than passed-out man had done. 'We've played that song like a million times.'

'That's cause it's cool,' the bear said, nodding vigorously. 'It's, like, what it says is . . . aw, shit.' The camera pulled back to show that he'd dropped the joint. He looked bereft. '*Shit*. Now I got to start again. I been rolling that fucker all my life, man. I've been rolling it since before I was *born*. Fucking Thomas Jefferson started that fucker off, left it to me in his will. Said I could finish the joint or have Monticello. I said fuck the building, I want the spliff. All my life I've been rolling it, like a good and faithful servant. And now it's gone.'

'Gone,' intoned the blonde girl. She started giggling.

Without missing a beat of 'Good Morning Starshine', my mother reached forward and took the gear from the bear's fumbling paws. She held the paper expertly in one hand, levelled the tobacco with an index finger, reached for the dope.

'Roll 'em, Beth,' crowed the bear, much cheered by this turn of events. 'Roll 'em, roll 'em, roll 'em.' The camera zoomed in on the joint, then back out again. It was already nearly done.

By this stage my eyebrows were raised so high they were hovering over my head. My mother had just rolled a joint.

'Put it on,' the bear wheedled. 'Put on the sodomy song. Come on Don, big Don man the Don, put it on Don, put it *on*.' In the background my mother kept singing.

The camera swerved and started walking out of the room, and into a hallway. A pile of coats lay on the floor where they'd been dropped. I saw that there was a kitchen off to the left, and a flight of stairs on the right. It was our old house, the one in Hunter's Rock. Every aspect of the furnishing and décor was different from the way I remembered it, but the spaces were the same.

I watched, wide-eyed, as the camera walked across the hall and then started up the stairs. For a moment there was little more than swirling darkness, and from downstairs the muffled sound of bear-guy bellowing. 'Sodomy . . . fellatio . . . cunnilingus . . . pederasty . . .' without any attempt to approximate a tune.

My father made it to the upper landing, paused a moment, muttered something under his breath. Then started forward again, and I realized with a lurch where he was going. It was quiet below now, and all I could hear was his breathing and the quiet swish of his feet on the carpet as he pushed open the door to my room.

At first it was dark, but gradually enough light seeped in from the landing to show my bed against the wall, and me sleeping in it. I must have been about five. All you could see was the top of my head, a patch of cheek where the light struck it. A little of one shoulder, in dark pyjamas. The wall was a kind of mottled green colour, and the carpet brown, as they always had been.

He stood there a full two minutes, not saying or doing anything. Just holding the camera, and watching me sleep.

I sat and watched, too, barely breathing.

The quality of the ambient sound on the tape changed after a while, as if a different song had started downstairs. Then there was a soft noise, could have been footsteps on carpet. They stopped, and I knew, knew without seeing or hearing anything to confirm it, that my mother was now standing next to my father.

The camera stayed on the boy in the bed, on me, for a few moments longer. Then it moved, slowly, panning round to the left. At first I assumed they were leaving, but then I realized the camera was being pivoted, turned to face the other way.

It turned a hundred and eighty degrees, and stopped.

My parents were looking directly into the lens. Their faces filled the frame: not crowded together, just side by side. Neither looked drunk or stoned. They seemed to be looking right at me.

'Hello, Ward,' my mother said, softly. 'I wonder how old you are now.'

She glanced over the camera, presumably at the sleeping shape in the bed. 'I wonder how old you are,' she repeated, and there was something in her voice that was sad and off-key.

My father was still looking into the camera. He was maybe five, six years younger than I am now. He, too, spoke quietly, but without a great deal of affection in his eyes.

'And I wonder what you've become.'

White noise. Someone clanked past my hotel room with a trolley.

I didn't pause the tape. I couldn't move.

The last scene was from 8mm, too, but the colours were more faded, washed out, pale surfaces bleached to pure light. Dark hairlines and spots popped and flickered all over the screen, making movements behind them feel measured and distanced.

A blaze of hazy yellow sunshine through a big window. Outside, trees rushing past, leaves blurred into sound. The steady beat of a train, and some other quiet noise I couldn't place.

My mother's face, younger still. Hair shorter, and black with lacquer. Looking out of the window at the passing countryside. She turned her head, looked at the camera. Her eyes seemed far away. She smiled faintly. The camera was slowly lowered.

Abrupt cut to a wide city street. I couldn't tell where it might be, and my attention was caught by the shapes and colours of the cars parked by the sides of the road, and the clothes worn by the few passers-by. The cars had panache, the suits didn't, the dresses were on the short side. I didn't know enough about such things to date it on the dime, but I guessed we were now back in the late '60s.

The camera moved forward at an even walking pace. Every now and then the back of my mother's head wandered into the left side of the frame, as if my father was slightly behind her and to the right.

It wasn't obvious what he was supposed to be recording. It wasn't an especially interesting street. There was what looked like a department store on the right, and a small square on the left. There were leaves on the trees, but they looked tired. He kept the camera high, panning neither up nor down nor to the sides. They made no attempt to point anything out, or to communicate with each other. After a while they crossed a road and then turned off down a cross street.

Cut to a different street again. This was a little narrower, as if further from the centre of town. They seemed to be walking up a steep hill. My mother was in front of the camera, seen from the shoulders up. She stopped.

'What about here?' she said, turning. She was wearing sunglasses now, businesslike. The camera hesitated for a moment, and wobbled, as if my father had taken his eye from the lens to look around him.

His voice: 'A little further.'

Onwards they walked, for perhaps another minute. Then stopped again. The camera panned round, giving a tantalizingly quick panorama of what seemed to be the top of a rise in the middle of a hilly city, tall buildings either side of the street. Signs at ground level declared the presence of grocery stores and cheap restaurants, but the windows above looked like those of apartments. People stood outside the stores, assaying produce, wearing hats; others walked in and out of the stores. A busy neighbourhood, coming up for lunchtime.

Mother looked back at the camera and nodded. It was her call. She made it, reluctantly.

Cut to later in the day. A slightly different view, but the top of the same hill. Where before it had been morning light, now the shadows were longer. Late afternoon, and the streets were nearly empty. My mother was standing with her arms down by her sides. An odd gurgling sound came from somewhere out of shot, and I realized it was similar to the noise I'd heard on the train.

There was a little movement of the camera, as if my father had reached out to touch something. Then my mother moved forward a little way, or he stepped back. A harsh release of breath from my father.

And then, thirty-five years later, from me.

My mother was holding the hands of two very young children, one on either side. They looked to be the same age, and were dressed to match, though one wore a blue top, the other yellow. They appeared little more than a year old, perhaps eighteen months, and tottered unsteadily on their feet.

The camera zoomed in on them. One's hair was cut short, the other slightly longer. The faces were identical.

The camera pulled back out. My mother let go of the hand of one of the children. The one with the longer hair and yellow top, a little green satchel. She squatted next to the other child.

'Say goodbye,' she said. The child in blue looked at her dubiously, uncomprehending. 'Say goodbye, Ward.'

The two children looked at one another. Then the one with the short hair, the child that must have been me, glanced back at his mother for reassurance. She took my hand, and lifted it up.

'Say goodbye.'

She made my hand wave, then took me in her arms and stood up. The other child looked up at my mother then, smiled, held his or her arms to be lifted, too. I couldn't tell, not for sure, what sex it might be.

My mother started walking down the street.

She walked at an even pace, not hurrying, but not looking back. The camera stayed on the other child, even as my father walked away after my mother down the hill. They left it standing there.

The child got further and further away, silent at the crest of the rise. It never even cried: at least, not until we were too far away for the sound to be heard.

Then the camera turned a corner and it was gone.

*   *   *

The image cut back to white noise, and this time nothing came afterwards. Within a minute the tape turned itself off, leaving me staring at my reflection in the screen.

I fumbled for the remote, rewound, paused. Stared at the frozen image of a child, left standing at the top of a hill, my hands held up over my mouth.

Chapter 7

The slot opened. A dim light shone down from above.

'Hello, my dear,' the man said. 'I'm back.'

Sarah could not see his face. From the sound of his voice, it appeared he was sitting on the floor just behind her head.

'Hello,' she said, her voice as steady as she could make it. She wanted to shrink away from him, put just an extra inch of distance between them, but couldn't move even that much. She fought to remain calm, to keep to her plan of sounding as if she didn't care. 'How are you today? Still insane, I guess.'

The man laughed quietly. 'You're not going to make me angry.'

'Who wants you angry?'

'So why do you say these things?'

'My mom and dad are going to be worried sick. I'm scared. I may not be that polite.'

'I understand.'

He was silent then, for a long time. Sarah waited.

Perhaps five minutes later, she saw a hand reaching out over her face. It held a glass of water. Without warning, he slowly tipped it. She got her mouth open in time, and drank as much as she could. The hand disappeared again.

'Is that it?' she said. Her mouth felt strange, clean and wet. The water had tasted the way she had always expected wine to, from the way grown-ups made such a big deal of it and rolled it around in their mouths like it was the best thing they had ever tasted. In fact, in her experience, wine generally tasted like something was wrong with it.

'What else were you expecting?'

'You want me to stay alive, then you're going to have to give me something more than water.'

'Why do you think I want you alive?'

'Because otherwise you would have killed me right off and have me sitting naked someplace where you could look at me and jack off.'

'That's not a very nice thing to say.'

'I refer you to my earlier comments. I'm not feeling very nice, and you're a sicko, so I don't have to be.'

'I'm not a sicko, Sarah.'

'No? How would you define yourself? Unusual?'

He laughed again, delightedly. 'Oh certainly.'

'Unusual like Ted fucking Bundy.'

'Ted Bundy was an idiot,' the man said. All humour had vanished from his voice. 'A grandstanding fool and a fake.'

'Okay,' she said, trying to placate him, though privately she thought he now sounded pompous as well as insane. 'I'm sorry. I'm not a big fan of his either. You're much better. So do I get some food or what?'

'Later, perhaps.'

'Great. I'll look forward to it. Cut it up small, so I can catch it.'

'Good night, Sarah.'

When she heard him standing, her pretend calm fled. The plan hadn't worked. At all. He knew she was frightened.

'*Please* don't put the lid back on. I can't move anyway.'

'I'm afraid I have to,' the man said.

'Please . . .'

It was replaced, and Sarah was in darkness again.

She heard his footsteps receding, a door shutting quietly, and then all was silent once more.

She licked frantically around her mouth, collecting as much of the remaining moisture as she could. Now that the initial shock of it was gone, she realized the water tasted different from the stuff she was used to at home. It must be from a different supply, which meant she had to be a long way from home. Like when you went on vacation. That was something, at least, something that she knew. The more she knew, the better.

Then she realized that maybe it was mineral water, something from a bottle, in which case the taste didn't mean anything. It could just be a different brand. That didn't matter. It was still worth thinking about. The more ideas she had, the better. Like the fact that when she'd mentioned her parents, the man hadn't said again how he'd killed them. When he'd captured her he'd been very keen to talk about what he'd done to them. Maybe it meant something. Hopefully it meant that they were still alive, and he'd only said the other things to frighten her.

Maybe not. Sarah lay in the darkness, her hands clenched into fists, and tried not to scream.

Part 2

Few people can be happy unless they
hate some other person, nation or creed.
Bertrand Russell

Chapter 8

The flight got in to Los Angeles at 22.05. Nina had nothing except her handbag and the file, and Zandt could carry all he owned with one hand and not look lopsided. There was a car waiting for them. Nothing sleek and official. Just a cab Nina had booked from the plane, to drop him in Santa Monica and then take her home.

Lights and signs in the darkness, half-seen faces, the rustle and honk of life on just another of those evenings in a city whose heart never seems to be quite where you are, but is always round a corner, or down that street, or the other side of hulking buildings in some new club whose glory nights will be over before you've even heard of it. Between there and here are a clutch of cheap hotels, dusty liquor stores, car lots selling vehicles of dubious provenance. A tatty herd of people waiting on street corners with nothing very positive in mind, in a veldt of concrete bunkers housing businesses that will swallow countless hollow lives without ever being quoted on NASDAQ. Gradually the change to residential streets, and then into

Venice. From the outside, on the right streets, Venice can look like it's trying to claw itself back upmarket. Some of the property is expensive, in a crappy International style. Every now and then you'll see a tattered piece of 1950s signage, something exuberant that harks back to flash bulbs and frozen glamour. Most have been torn down now, replaced by brutal information boards stamped out in Helvetica, the official typeface of purgatory. Helvetica isn't designed to make you feel anything good, to promise adventure or gladden the heart. Helvetica is for telling you that profits are down, that the photocopier needs servicing and by the way, you've been fired.

Finally, Santa Monica. Nicer houses, small offices, places to get Japanese food and the London *Times*. The sea, with a pier that was born in sepia but knows those days are over. The Palisades up above, busy Ocean Avenue, then the first line of hotels and restaurants. The sense, from somewhere, that this suburb had once been a town. Perhaps it's the sea that makes it feel that way, that gives an impression that this community is here for a reason. In places it still is, still feels as if it has a relationship to its environment that goes beyond simply having flattened it. Stores and cafés and places to be, places to walk into and to buy from. You could live there and understand where you were, as the Becker family had until recently. It's not a real place, but then so little of Los Angeles is real, and the parts that are real are the places you don't want to be. Real is for people with guns and hangovers. Real is what you want to avoid. LA believes itself full of magic, and sometimes can even feel that way, but much of this is a mutually agreed upon sleight of hand. You can stand in one place and believe that one day you'll be a movie star – stand somewhere else, and you'll believe that you'll soon be dead. You know that what you see is a trick, but still you want to believe. You can buy maps that tell you where the stars live, but not where to stand to become one: all you can do is walk the lots and prop up the bars, hoping that luck will come find you. LA is a city that has taken Fate to its heart, has bought her many drinks and scribbled her phone number down after long evenings making eyes: but to call Fate a harsh mistress is giving her the benefit of very many doubts. Fate is more like a malevolent little starlet on a downhill cocaine slide, doing a slightly good deed once a week just in case someone important is watching. Fate doesn't always have your best interests in mind. Fate just doesn't give a shit.

'Good to be back?' Nina asked. Zandt grunted.

The cab dropped him at The Fountain, a ten-storey tower of faded yellow stucco on Ocean, standing between the junctions where Wilshire and Santa Monica deliver people to the sea. The building has an Art Deco mien that makes it look a little classier than it is. Originally expensive apartments, it spent a while as a hotel before being converted back to short-term rentals again. The pool around the back was filled in, creating a large and somehow pointless seating area that is seldom used: despite the lanai, the plants, and the shaded chairs, it's too obvious that something's missing. The lobby was familiar to Zandt from a homicide he had worked back in 1993: a minor European actor and a young prostitute, a roleplay that got out of hand. The actor walked, of course. Zandt couldn't remember which room it had been. It certainly wasn't the suite he was given, which was large and well-furnished and had a good view of the sea. He dropped his bag in the living area, looked quietly around at the kitchenette. Empty cupboards, very little dust. He wasn't hungry, and found it hard to imagine cooking anything. The Fountain didn't have a bar or restaurant or room service. It wasn't a destination, which is why he had chosen it as a place to stay. That, and its position.

He left the suite and went back down in the elevator, stood outside the building for a while. Nina had been taken off in the cab, and they were due to meet late the next morning. She'd already called the Bureau's Westwood branch from the plane, and previously from Pimonta, but presumably she had to show her face in the office once in a while. Something made him wait a moment, however, watching the cars parked along the street. He wouldn't put it past Nina to have gone round the block, then come back to watch what he did. Not because he was any kind of expert. Just so she knew. Nina liked knowing things.

After five minutes he walked along to the corner, hung a right onto Arizona, and walked the couple of blocks to 3rd Street Promenade. Arizona Avenue was the street on which Michael Becker had dropped his daughter the night she had disappeared.

He turned left and walked up the west side of the Promenade, heading up to the end where Sarah Becker had last been seen. It was coming up for eleven, much later than the time the girl had been abducted. Virtually all of the stores were shut. The street performers and musicians had long packed up for the night, even the Frank Sinatra impersonator who put in longer hours than most. That didn't matter. Without the presence of the abductor and the victim, the circumstances are irreproducible.

He kept half an eye on the other people walking up and down. Killers often come back, especially those for whom murder is something more than a momentary expedience. They revisit and rewind so they can watch the memory one more time. He didn't expect to notice anyone in particular, but he kept watch anyway. When he passed the side street Nina had mentioned in her description, the place where a car had been seen parked illegally, he stood and looked down it for a while. Not trying to see anything. Just being there.

'Waiting for someone?'

Zandt turned to see a young man, slim and pretty. Mid-teens, eighteen at the most. 'No,' he said.

The boy smiled. 'You sure? I think you are. I wonder if you're waiting for me.'

'I'm not,' Zandt said. 'But someone will be. Not tonight, not here, but somewhere along the line.'

The smile faded. 'You a cop?'

'No. Just telling you the way it is. Go find yourself a date someplace light.'

He went into Starbucks and bought a coffee. He got it to go and went back out to sit on the bench from which Sarah had been abducted. The boy had gone.

You might think that such an event would leave a resonance. It doesn't. The human mind is organized to recognize faces. Its understanding of space is more tenuous. With appearance, it's simple: the more people who know your face, the more famous you are. We don't have to search for credentials. You're not a stranger, but instead part of our extended family: strong brothers and pretty sisters, kind parents, fake relatives to help us forget that our social groups have contracted down to nothing. With places, it's a case of knowing what events this space has played a stage to. But when that's stripped aside, when you've sat for long enough, you don't feel anything at all. You go back to the place as it was before anything happened there, to the way it was on that night. This is as near as you can come to going back in time, to *before*, to being able to hold a knife as it was when it came from the kitchen drawer, before it had been slicked with blood; when potential was all it had.

He sat on the bench until it was just any place, and then he sat there some more.

In his time as a homicide detective, Zandt had dealt with an unusual number of serial killers. As a rule such matters are handled by the FBI. They have the Behavioral Science lab in Quantico, their Profiling Procedures, the Jodie Fosters and David Duchovnys with the suits and neat haircuts. Like the killers themselves, the Feds seem a cut above the usual. But in eight years Zandt, a lowly mortal, a homicide cop, had found himself involved in several sets of killings that had eventually turned out to be the handiwork of someone who might be termed a serial killer. Two of those men had been apprehended, and Zandt had played a significant role in both cases. He had a feel for it, and this was recognized. The first case concerned a man from Venice Beach responsible for the murder of four elderly women, and Zandt's involvement had been accidental. On the second investigation he was working from the start with the FBI, which is how he had met Nina Baynam.

Over the summer of 1995 the remains of four young black boys were found half-buried in different areas of the city. The method of dismemberment, along with the leaving of a videotape with each victim, was enough to declare the killings the work of the same person. Each of the victims had been abducted from junk zips, and three were already acquainted with drugs and street prostitution. The first two deaths were largely ignored by the general population, dismissed as part of society's tidal culling of the underclass. It was only with repetition that the murders began to fight their way up out of random noise into story. The videotapes left with the bodies contained between one and two hours of roughly edited camcorder footage that made it clear how unpleasant the victims' last days had been. Each tape had a cover that featured a picture of the boy, his name, and the word 'Showreel'.

The papers dubbed the killer 'The Casting Agent', which everyone agreed was very droll. Everyone apart from the parents, that is, but as their grief was embarrassing evidence of the underlying reality of these theatrical events, it was ignored except when required to hype public interest. The relatives were merely the audience to these deeds, not actors, and it's the actor we like best. Someone we can get to know, a face back-lit through the papers and television. We want a personality. A star.

Zandt worked the case of the first boy, and after the second victim the FBI became involved. Nina was a young agent with experience, having worked a long bad case in Texas and Louisiana the year before. Between them, through a combination of Zandt's intuition and legwork, Nina's analysis of the placings of the bodies, and a break relating to the fact that the perpetrator had registered the camcorder used to make the videos, the killer was found. He was a thirty-one-year-old white male, employed as a graphic designer on the fringes of the music video industry, previously a child extra in long-forgotten movies. In a series of interviews with Zandt he admitted the crimes, providing corollary information and revealing the whereabouts of his talismans, the right hand of each of the victims – which had been squeezed into jars previously holding the product of a prominent instant coffee manufacturer. He eventually led the police to the bodies of two earlier victims, experiments in killing during which he had developed his technique. He placed the blame for his behaviour on having been molested on set as a child, an allegation which fit nicely with the public's desire for a beginning and a middle for every tale. The truth of the claim proved impossible to establish, and the end of the story was provided when the killer was sliced across the throat with a sharpened spoon by another inmate while awaiting trial. The food chain has victims at both ends: even rapists and murderers need someone to look down on, and kid killers will do nicely. Ultimately The Casting Agent's story became immortal and endless, celebrated in one moderately successful hack book and innumerable Web sites. A piece of buggy video editing shareware called CastingAgent enjoyed a brief notoriety, as did a store in Atlanta that offered a couch, in a deep splotchy red, which it called The Casting Couch.

The investigation lasted thirteen weeks. For the last eight of those, John and Nina were sleeping with each other. The affair ended soon after the apprehension of the suspect. Nina had done much of the initial encouragement. Then she stopped doing so, and it came to an end. Zandt never spoke of it to his wife, with whom he had a relationship that was in general cordial and successful, but that had been going through an arid patch. He wanted to lose neither her nor their daughter, and was largely relieved when the affair ended.

He and Nina met occasionally for lunch over the next five years, while Zandt worked the usual slate of gang slayings, family feuds, and bullet-holed John Does found in alleyways gasping like landed fish and pronounced DOA to general apathy. Some he solved; some he didn't. So it goes. Nina worked a well-publicized double murder in Yellowstone, a series of disappearances upstate and one more in Oregon, all of which remained unsolved and ongoing. Out in the real world, beyond the curtain of death and misdemeanour that law enforcers live behind, business continued as usual. Bosnia imploded; the President got in trouble with his cigars; we discovered the joys of email and *Frasier*, of Playstations and Sheryl Crow.

Then, on December 12th 1999, a teenage girl disappeared in Los Angeles. Josie Ferris, age sixteen, had been celebrating a friend's birthday over a burger at the Hard Rock Café on Beverly Boulevard. At 9.45 a.m., having said goodbye on the pavement outside the restaurant, she walked alone down toward Ma Maison. She was intending to catch a cab from outside the hotel. Beverly Boulevard is not a back road or an alley. It is a wide and well-travelled street, and on this evening both the forecourt of the hotel and the foyer of the Beverly Center Mall opposite were busy. Nonetheless, somewhere along that three-hundred-yard stretch, she vanished.

Josie's failure to return home was reported to the police by 12.50 a.m. On receiving what they considered to be a response of insufficient alacrity, her parents turned up in person to fill out the forms. Mr and Mrs Ferris were possessed of forceful demeanours, and the police were soon taking the incident more seriously, at least while the parents were within earshot. Sadly this made no difference. Their daughter was never seen alive again.

Two days later a sweater was left outside their house. The name Josie had been stitched into the front, using what was subsequently demonstrated to be the girl's own hair. The sweater had been a sixteenth birthday present from the girl's best friend, who had sewn the letters 'FFE' onto the sleeve: Friends For Ever. They had been. Eternity had merely turned out to be short. There was no demand for money with the garment. The police started taking the situation very seriously indeed, regardless of who was around to overhear. A task force was set up, coordinated through the FBI's local SAC, Charles Monroe. The news of the garment's delivery was eventually released to the press, but not the way in which it had been altered. A month later, no headway of any kind had been made in tracing the missing teenager.

In late January and early March of 2000, two other girls went missing. Elyse LeBlanc and Annette Mattison failed to return from the cinema and a friend's house respectively. Both resembled Josie Ferris in trivial ways – they were of a similar age (fifteen and sixteen) and wore their hair long. The LeBlancs and Mattisons were comfortably well-off, and their daughters were attractive and of above-average intelligence. This was not enough to suggest a firm link between the three disappearances, occurring as they did in widely spread parts of the city.

The arrival of two more sweaters was, however. Again, they were delivered to the family homes, in broad daylight, and again they featured the girl's name embroidered on the front with their own hair. No further communication was received. The seriousness of the situation led the FBI to keep the second and third disappearances quiet. Most serial kidnappers sought to hide the fact of their abductions. The selection of girls whose absence would be spotted immediately, and the further highlighting of the event through the delivery of the parcels, suggested they were dealing with an unusual individual. One who wanted attention right now.

They denied him it.

A week after the disappearance of Annette Mattison, the clothed body of a young woman was found by picnickers in Griffith Park. Though bald, badly burned and deteriorated through the activities of local wildlife, the body was quickly identified through recent dental work and a distinctive piece of jewellery. It was Elyse LeBlanc. It was estimated that she had been dead for approximately half of the period since her abduction, though only recently moved to the location at which she was found. She was discovered to have suffered a number of minor head traumas prior to death, though none had led to her demise. Although the body was immediately forwarded to the federal lab in Washington, no physical evidence of the killer was gained from her clothes or remains. A search of the remainder of the park by local police and the FBI evidence team from Sacramento failed to discover

101

either Josie Ferris's or Annette Mattison's body in whole or in part.

The press embargo was dropped. A call for witnesses garnered nothing more than the usual hoaxes, lunatics, and misinformation. Parents arranged for their teenage daughters to travel in groups.

Josie's body turned up ten days later. It was found lying in bushes by the side of a road in Laurel Canyon, in a similar state to that of the LeBlanc girl. Unlike the previous victim, there was evidence of a period of gross sexual abuse.

By then the killer had a nickname. The media called him The Delivery Boy. This had been suggested unofficially by Special Agent Monroe, who believed that by minimizing him in this way, reducing his status by using the word 'boy', some kind of investigative advantage might be gained. That someone who had managed to snatch three bright and worldly young women from busy streets, murder them, and dump their bodies in public places, all without being seen or leaving a single piece of evidence, would be somehow thrown by this taunt.

That he might get all offended, and just go right to pieces.

Nina had disagreed. For this and other reasons she had been discussing the case with John Zandt, despite the fact that he was not involved in the official investigation. They'd worked together well on The Casting Agent case. She wanted to know what he thought.

Zandt proffered his views, but without much enthusiasm. Nina worked these cases with an intensity and zeal that he found he could no longer match. His marriage was back on firm ground, and his daughter had grown, transforming from a child into a young person, consolidating their family. She had her mother's hair, a rich, almost auburn, dark brown – but her father's eyes, brown flecked with green. She played music too loud and her room was a mess and she spent too long on the Net and smelled of cigarette smoke every now and then. There were arguments. But she went grocery shopping with her mother, even though it was super-boring, because she knew

Jennifer enjoyed having her along. She would mainly listen to her father when he talked, and stifle any yawn that came. Her parents didn't know she had smoked dope on several occasions, tried coke, and once stolen a pair of quite expensive earrings. If they had, they'd have grounded her ass to kingdom come but otherwise wouldn't have been too worried. All of this was within the acceptable range of errant behaviour in her place and time.

As much as anything, Zandt had simply grown a little older, and wanted to spend no longer than necessary thinking about the dark things the world could bring into being. He got on with his job, and then he went home and got on with his life. After two earlier investigations into the deeds of multiple murderers, he'd lost interest in the workings of their minds. It was something you could only take so much of before you started feeling sick inside.

Once you got behind the glamour of their celebrity, Zandt knew that serial killers were not the way they were portrayed in the movies: charming geniuses, slick with evil, charismatic crusaders of a bloody art. They were more like drunkards or the slightly mad. Impossible to talk to, or to get sense out of, sealed off from the world behind a viewpoint that could never be expressed or made accessible to those who lived outside it. They came in all shapes, sizes, and types. Some were monstrous, others were fairly decent individuals – aside, that is, from the propensity to kill other people and ruin the lives of those who had loved them. Jeffrey Dahmer had initially made every effort not to yield to urges that he knew placed his desires well outside normal life. He failed, big-time. He did not ask for clemency when caught, did not play games with the police, did nothing except admit his guilt and express sorrow at what he had done. Within the confines of being a murderous sociopath, he behaved as well as he could. The fact remained that he had ended the lives of at least sixteen young men in circumstances almost too horrendous to believe.

Other killers basked in their notoriety, bartered for publicity or privileges through manipulation of the media and police, toying with the grief of the people from whom they had amputated something irreplaceable. They revelled in what they had done, in their rich secrets. They devoured the newspaper coverage of their trials, profoundly content that they had finally achieved the attention they had always felt they deserved. This did not necessarily make them worse. It simply made them different. Ted Bundy. The Casting Agent. John Wayne Gacy. Philippe Gomez. The Yorkshire Ripper. Andrei Chikatilo. Some were better looking, some were more efficient; some intelligent, some border-line or even demonstrably subnormal. Some came across like regular guys; others you would have thought could have been spotted as wackos from across a busy street. None were special humans or touched with evil except in the most superficial sense. All were simply men with a craving to take the lives of other people, to augment their sexual experience with the torture and degradation of others. They were not demons. They were just men – and women, very occasionally – who did unacceptable things, as a factor of neurotic obsession. It was not a binary of good or evil, but a spectrum also inhabited by people who had to check their locks ten times at night, or who could not rest until the kitchen was tidy after each meal. Serial killers were not chilling in and of themselves. The chill was in the realization that it is possible to be human without feeling as other humans do.

Zandt knew the factors that could produce a serial killer. A violent and domineering mother, an abusive or weak father. Early and conflictive sexual experience, especially with parents, siblings, or animals. Being a native of America, the former Soviet Union, or Germany, areas that produce multiple murderers out of all proportion to their populations. Exposure to dead bodies at a formative age. Head injuries, or juvenile heavy metal poisoning – the elements, not the music. A trigger event, something that caused the potential to be actualized. None were necessary or sufficient conditions, merely part of a syndrome that sometimes provided a soil dark enough to yield a sickly flower of urges: an anxious, neurotic and violent individual who could not live as others did. The shadow in our streets. The bogeyman.

He'd seen enough of them. He didn't want to know any more. In his private thoughts, he always referred to The Casting Agent as just that: The Casting Agent. He went to some trouble not to think of him by his real name, but to assign to him the same cartoonish unreality that the killer had evidently believed his victims to possess. If he had been unable to credit the six young boys with the dignity of their individuality, then Zandt felt it was the least he could do to consign The Casting Agent to the same fate.

In the meantime he worked the usual drug-, love-, and profit-related murders. He drank with colleagues, listened to Nina talk about her attempts to connect Josie Ferris, Elyse LeBlanc, and Annette Mattison's disappearances. He had dinner with his wife, drove his daughter places, went to the gym.

On May 15th 2000, Karen Zandt left school at the end of the day. She didn't come home.

At first her parents assumed the best. Then the worst. A sweater was delivered three endless weeks later.

Zandt called Nina. She arrived very quickly with two colleagues. The parcel was unwrapped. This time there was no name embroidered on the sweater inside, and it was not Karen's sweater. Hers had been peach in colour; this was black.

There was a note tucked into it, laser-printed in Courier on a paper stock used in offices and homes across the country.

```
Mr Zandt,
A 'delivery'. You'll have to wait for the
rest.
I have seen thy affliction and the work
of thine hands, and rebuked thee.

The Upright Man
```

*　　*　　*

105

A month after that, the body of Annette Mattison was found in a canyon in the Hollywood Hills. Same condition as Elyse LeBlanc, same lack of forensic evidence. No other girls were abducted, at least none whose disappearance was subsequently marked by the delivery of a garment.

No other bodies were ever found.

After two hours the Promenade was nearly deserted. Barnes and Noble and Starbucks were shut. People shuffled past the bench periodically, winos on their way to the Palisades for the night, pulling neat little trolleys with their belongings. They saw a man who sat with his hands lying open by his sides, eyes staring straight down the street. No one pulled over to ask for money. They steered clear.

Eventually Zandt stood up and dropped his empty cup in the trash. He realized that he could have gone into the bookstore and established what points within it could have given The Upright Man a vantage from which to watch for Sarah Becker. Though there was no physical evidence for this, Zandt believed he staked out his victims carefully before striking. A few didn't, most did. It could have been that Karen had been a special case; The Upright Man making a point. Zandt didn't think so. The girls were too similar, the disappearances too immaculately wrought.

Barnes and Noble could wait, possibly for ever. He had allowed Nina to convince him to come back. He had wanted to believe that this time it would be different, that he would be able to do more than run around the city, chasing his tail, shouting in the night, never finding the man who had taken his daughter from him. Who had taken Zandt's life in the palm of his hidden, rabid hand, and crushed it to death. Tonight he didn't believe it any more.

He walked back to The Fountain, picking up a few groceries on the way. The lobby of the apartment building was empty, with nobody behind the desk. There was no Muzak, and little reason to believe that there was anyone apart from him inside. The elevator

106

ascended slowly and fitfully, letting him know that its was a difficult task.

While he waited for water to boil he stood and watched the television, as CNN did its best to reduce the world's complexity to bullet points a businessman could parrot over lunch. After a few minutes it cut back to a breaking story. A middle-aged man had walked down the high street of a small town in England, late in the morning. He'd had a rifle, with which he'd killed eight adults and wounded fourteen others.

Nobody knew why.

Chapter 9

I was sitting in the passenger seat of my car with the door open. It was just after eight in the morning. I had a latte in one hand, and a cigarette in the other. My eyes were wide and dry and I was already regretting the cigarette. I used to smoke. I smoked a lot, for a long time. Then I gave it up. But during the night, which I had spent driving slowly and aimlessly down unlit roads as if trying to find the exit from an endless system of tunnels, I'd come to believe that smoking was the only thing that was going to help. Once you've smoked for a while, there are situations where you're always going to feel something's missing if you don't have a tube of burning leaves in your hand. Without a cigarette you feel friendless and clueless and alone.

I was parked on the main street of Red Lodge, a small town maybe a hundred and twenty miles southeast of Dyersburg. I was sitting in the car because the shop where I'd bought the coffee – a spick-and-span little place where the staff wore aprons and dimply little smiles – was adamant in its resistance to the tobacco arts. The quality of coffee a place sells these days is in inverse proportion to the likelihood of them letting you have a cigarette while you're drinking it. The latte was extremely good: they had smokers' heads stuffed and hung on the wall. I'd bad-temperedly taken my coffee to go, and watched through the windshield as Red Lodge gradually came to life. People walked to and fro, opened up little stores selling stuff you buy to prove you've been on vacation. Some guys arrived with pots of paint and started making a house on the other side of the street look more lovely. A few tourists appeared, bundled up in ski wear to the point where they were almost spherical.

I got halfway through a second cigarette, winced, and threw it outside on the ground. It wasn't helping. It was just something to feel guilty about. Plus I gather it's bad for you. Knowing that my willpower is about as weak as the light from the farthest star on a cloudy night, I grabbed the pack off the dash and tossed it toward a trashcan, which was nailed to a nearby pole and emblazoned with wholesome civic slogans. The pack went in without even touching the rim. No one was there to see it. They never are. It must be weird, being a professional basketball player. People are there to see it when you get them in.

I hadn't checked out of the hotel. I'd just taken the video out of the machine and left the room. I was probably thinking of going to the bar, but this time even my withered sense of propriety had deemed this an inappropriate response. Instead I'd found myself walking outside to the car, getting in, and driving away. I drove slowly around Dyersburg, twice crossing the place where my parents' car had been totalled. The video sat on the passenger seat beside me. The second time I went over the crossing I glanced at it, as if this would help in some way. It didn't, and only made me shiver, a frigid little spasm too small for anyone else to see.

After a while I achieved escape velocity and left town. I wasn't working from the map, merely following the roads and making turns when it occurred to me to do so.

I eventually found my way onto I 90 as the sky was beginning to lighten. I realized I needed coffee, or something, and took the turn that led me to Red Lodge at about the time things were beginning to open up.

I felt hollow and light-headed. Hungry, perhaps, though it was difficult to tell. My mind was worn smooth, as if it had thrashed for too long and too hard in the wrong gear.

There was no question that it was my parents in the oldest two passages on the tape. There seemed little reason to doubt that it had been my father holding the camera in the first, most recent, section. The three scenes, either individually or together, were evidently supposed to convey meaning. Why else put them on the tape? I found it difficult to even think about the last scene, the one in which it appeared that a child had been abandoned on a city street. My first overwhelming sense, that the child was an unknown sibling of the same age, was still my holding position. Everything about my mother's body language, and the way we'd been dressed, had implied it. Either the child was my twin, or they wanted me to believe that this had been the case. The latter seemed ridiculous. But was I really to credit that I once had a sister or brother, and that he or she had been abandoned somewhere? That we, as a family, had travelled away from home – a point I believed to have been deliberately made through the snippet of a train journey at the beginning of the scene – and left the child somewhere? And that my father had filmed the scene? There could only have been one reason for this: an awareness that one day they might want me to know what had happened, and a realization that nothing short of film would convince me. I had rerun the segment in my mind throughout the night, trying to read it differently. I couldn't, and in the end what stuck with me most was the matter-of-factness of the event. They had looked for the right place to leave the child, rejecting one, and then moving a little further up the street. They had chosen somewhere that looked well-populated, where the businesses and homes on the other side of the street suggested that the child would not remain unnoticed for long. Somehow this made it worse, not better. It made it seem more considered, more deliberate, more real. They hadn't been killing the child. Just getting rid of it. They'd planned how they'd do it, and then gone ahead and done it.

The middle scene was less extraordinary. Once you got past the strangeness of the glimpse it yielded into the pasts of people I now realized I had never really understood, for the most part it recorded what was merely a social evening. I hadn't recognized any of the other people in the film, but that wasn't surprising. Your group of friends alters as you get older. You change, you move. People who once seemed indispensable gradually become first less crucial and then merely names on a Christmas-card list. Finally one year you grumpily observe that you haven't seen such and such in over a decade, the cards stop, and the friendship is severed except in memory, a few catchphrases and a handful of half-forgotten shared experiences. It lies dormant until the very end, when you wish that you had kept in touch, if for no other reason than it would just be nice to hear a voice whose owner knew you when you were young, who understands that your coffin-ready wilt is a joke of recent vintage and not everything you have ever been.

The kicker was the way they had addressed the camera. The things they had said. As if they'd known or believed that I'd watch it someday. If I'd been in their position, I'd have striven for a perkier tone. 'Hi, son, how're you doing? Love from us, way back when.' My mother hadn't sounded this way at all. She'd sounded sad, resigned. The last line of my father's chimed most sharply in my head: 'I wonder what you've become.' What kind of thing was that to say, when the person you were talking to was only five or six years old, and sleeping at the time in the same room? This seemed to fit in some way with the closing down of UnRealty: a profound distrust of someone who was their son. I'm not especially proud of my life, but regardless of what I may or may not have become, I have not yet abandoned a baby on a city street, and filmed the event for posterity.

I had no memory of my father ever owning or using a home movie camera. I certainly had no recollection of watching such films. Why bother filming your family if you're not going to all sit around some evening and watch, laughing at hairstyles and clothes and pointing out how much everyone has grown in height or waist size? If he'd once been someone who filmed such things, why did he stop? Where were the films?

Which left only the first scene, the one shot on video, much more recently. Because of its very brevity and lack of identifiable meaning, this was the segment that seemed to provide the key. When my father had edited together this little bombshell, he must have tacked this non-event on the front for a reason. He'd said something at the end, the short phrase that the wind had obscured. I needed to know what it said. Maybe it would be a way into understanding the tape's purpose. Maybe not. But at least I would then have all of the evidence.

I shut the car door and got out my phone. I needed help, and so I called Bobby.

Five hours later I was back at my hotel. In the meantime I'd been to Billings, one of Montana's few stabs at a decent-sized town. In accordance with advice, and contrary to my expectations, it had proved to have a copy shop where I could do what I required. As a result I had a new DVD-ROM in my pocket.

As I walked through the lobby I remembered that I'd only booked for a couple of days after the funeral, and stopped by the desk to extend. The girl nodded absently, not taking her eyes off a television tuned to a global news channel. The newscaster was rehashing the scant details that had so far emerged in the mass killing in England, which I'd heard about on the radio on the way out to Billings. It didn't seem like they'd found out anything new. They were repeating the same stuff over and over, like a ritual, breathing

112

it into myth. The guy had barricaded himself somewhere for a couple hours, then killed himself. Probably at this very moment his house was being torn apart by the cops, trying to find some explanation, somebody or something to blame.

'Terrible thing,' I said, mainly to check if I had genuinely caught the receptionist's attention. Hospitality boards in the lobby indicated that the hotel would be hosting a comprehensive slate of corporate brainstorms and deep-thinks over the rest of the week, and I didn't want to suddenly find myself without a room.

She didn't respond immediately, and I was about to try again when I noticed that she was crying. Her eyes were full, and one tear had escaped to run nearly invisibly down one cheek.

'Are you okay?' I asked, surprised.

She turned her head toward me as if dreaming, nodded slowly. 'Extra two days. Room 304. That's fine, sir.'

'Great. Are you all right?'

She quickly wiped the back of one hand across her cheek. 'Oh, yes,' she said. 'It's just sad.'

Then she turned back to the television again.

I watched her as I stood in the elevator, waiting for the doors to close. The lobby was deserted. She was still staring at the screen, motionless, as if looking out of a window. She couldn't have been more caught up in this event — which had taken place thousands of miles away in a country she'd probably never even visited — if she'd lost a relative of her own in it. I wish I could say that it exacted the same degree of unthinking empathy from me, but it didn't. It wasn't that I didn't care, more that I couldn't get the feeling to sink to my heart out of my head. It wasn't like the World Trade Center, something vile and astonishing within our own borders, happening to people who'd saved coins of the same currency in their piggy-banks when they were children. I knew intellectually that shouldn't make a difference, but it seemed to. I didn't know these people.

When I was inside my room I got my laptop out of the wardrobe, put it down on the table, and fired her up. While I waited, I got the

DVD-ROM out of my pocket. My father's videotape was hidden in the tyre well of the rental car. What I had on the disk was a digitized version of it. When the PowerBook had gone through its wake-up routine – a shower, slurp of coffee, quick read of the newspaper, whatever the hell else it is that takes it so long – I stuck the cartridge in the slot in the side. It appeared as a disk on the desktop. The video had been saved onto it as four very large MPEG files. It had been too long to digitize at full resolution and still fit on one disk: so, while I was at one of the workstations in the Billings copy shop with no one hovering over me, I ripped the first and last sections down at high resolution, together with the portion of the middle section that had taken place at my parents' house. The long section in the bar I'd laid down at a lower frame rate. It still took a while. The whole shebang barely fit on the eighteen-gig disk.

First I tried using CastingAgent, an old piece of editing share-ware that is buggy as shit but sometimes lets you do things other software won't. It crashed so conclusively I had to hard boot the computer. So then I reverted to standard stuff, and got the movie playing on the screen.

I spooled forward to the end of the first section, the one taken somewhere up in the mountains, and took a clipping of the last ten seconds. I saved this to the hard disk. Then I used MPEGSplit to axe out the video portion of the file, leaving me with just the audio track. I knew what the picture showed: a group of people wearing black coats, standing in a loose group. What I wanted to know was what had been said by the cameraman.

I saved the file, swapped out of the video software, and launched a professional battery of sound-processing applications – SoundStage, SFXlab, AudioMelt Pro. For the next half-hour I jiggered the track, trying different filters to see what they brought up. Increasing the amplitude just made it sound worse, but louder; scattershot down-sampling and noise reduction made it muddier. The best I could tell was that it was two or three words.

So then I got serious, and took another audio clip from the section

114

of the tape just before the dialogue. I analysed the frequencies of the background wind, then set up a band-pass filter. I ran this on the other section of the tape, and it started to sound clearer. A little more refining and slowly the noises began to coalesce into words. *Un craunen? Vren ouwnen?* When I'd done all I could, I got some headphones out of the laptop bag and put them on. I set the track to loop and closed my eyes.

After about forty times through I got it. 'The Straw Men.'

I stopped the loop; took the headphones off. I was pretty sure that was it. The Straw Men. Problem was, it was meaningless. Sounded like an indie rock band – though I doubted that the people on the tape had earned a living through under-produced caterwauling. The members of bands don't live together in ski resorts. They build themselves mock-Tudor mansions on opposite sides of the planet, and only meet up when they're being paid. All I'd done was add another layer of inexplicability to what was captured on the tape. I watched the video again, running it off the DVD just in case the different format helped me to notice something new. Nothing struck me.

I sat in the chair for a while, staring into space, feeling the night catching up with me. Every now and then I heard the sound of someone walking past my door in the corridor, and from outside came the occasional swish of cars or floating fragments of distant conversations between people I didn't know and would never meet. None of this meant anything to me either.

At just after six my cell phone rang, jerking me out of half-sleep. I picked it up blearily.

'Yo,' said a voice. In the background there was the sound of other voices, and muffled music. 'Ward, it's Bobby.'

'My man,' I said, rubbing my eyes. 'Thanks for the tip. Place in Billings worked out just fine.'

'Cool,' he said. 'But that's not why I'm calling. I'm in some place, what the fuck, the Sacagawea I think it's called. Kind of a bar thing. Kind of. On the big main street. Huge-ass great sign.'

Suddenly I was awake. 'You're in Dyersburg?'

'Sure am. Flew in.'

'Why the hell did you do that?'

'Well, thing is, after you called, I was kind of bored. Picked up on something you said, did a little poking around.'

'Poking around in what?'

'Some stuff. Ward, get your butt down here. Got a beer sitting waiting for you. I got something to tell, my friend, and I'm not doing it over the phone.'

'Why?' I was already packing up the computer.

'Because it's going to freak you out.'

Chapter 10

The Sacagawea is a large motel on the main drag. It has a huge multicoloured neon sign that can be seen from about half a mile in either direction, drawing the unwary like a magnet. I'd stayed there for about ten minutes once, the first time I'd come to visit my parents. The room I was given was a museum-standard tableau of cheap '60s design and had carpets like an unloved dog. At first I thought this was kind of funky, until I looked closer and realized it simply hadn't been redecorated since around the time I was born. On discovering there was no room service I checked the hell out again. I won't stay in a hotel without room service. I just won't stand for it.

The lobby was small and damp and smelt strongly of chlorine, presumably because of the tiny swimming pool in the next room. The wizened old twonk behind the reception desk directed me upstairs, doing so without recourse to speech but with a curious look. When I got to the bar I could see why. It wasn't humming with life. There was a service island in the middle, a lone waitress, and a rank of archaic slot machines over on the side with equally superannuated people placidly feeding coins into them. As a species, we really know how to live. A long bank of large windows at the front of the room gave a view over the parking lot and the drizzle of traffic tootling up and down the street. A few couples were dotted around the room, talking loudly, as if in the hope this would goose the room into having something approaching atmosphere. It wasn't working.

Sitting at a table up against the window was Bobby Nygard.

'What the fuck is this Sacagawea shit?' was the first thing he said.

I sat down opposite. 'Sacagawea was the name of the Amerind maiden who hung with Lewis and Clark. Helped them work deals with the locals, not get killed, that kind of thing. The expedition passed by not far from here, on the way to the Bitterroot Mountains.'

'Thank you, professor. But are you allowed to say "maiden" these days? Isn't it kind of sexist or something?'

'Probably,' I said. 'And you know what? I don't give a shit. It's better than "squaw" anyhow.'

'Is it, though? Maybe not. Maybe it's like "nigger". Assumed as a badge of pride. Absorption of the terms of the oppressor.'

'Be that as it may, Bobby. It's good to see you.'

He winked, and we touched glasses. Bobby looked pretty much the same as he ever had, though I hadn't met him face-to-face in two years. A little shorter than me, a little broader. Cropped hair, a face that always seemed slightly flushed, and the general air of someone you could take a baseball bat to without him being overly bothered. Used to be in the Forces, and sometimes still seems as if he is – though not the kind of army you see in the news.

After we'd taken a drink, Bobby set his glass back on the table and looked around the room. 'Kind of a shithole, I'd say.'

'So why are you here?'

'Fucking great sign outside. Got me in its tractor beam. Why? There a better hotel in town?'

118

'No, I mean why did you come to Dyersburg?'

'I'll come to that. Meantime, how you doing? Sorry about your loss, man.'

Suddenly, maybe because I was sitting with someone I counted as a friend, the death of my parents hit me again. Hit me hard, and unexpectedly, as I knew it probably would every now and then for the rest of my life, regardless of what they had done. I started to say something, but didn't. I just felt too tired and confused and sad. Bobby clinked his glass against mine once more, and we drank. He let a silence settle for a while, then changed the subject.

'So. What are you doing these days? You never said.'

'Not much,' I said.

He raised an eyebrow. 'Not much as in "Don't ask"?'

'No. Just nothing worth talking about. There may be a job or two I haven't tried yet, but I doubt they'll be much different. Seems that I'd always rather be working something on the side, and employers still don't understand what a key role that is in a modern economy.'

'Timidity and commercial short-sightedness,' he nodded, flagging for another couple beers. 'Ain't that always the way.'

After the waitress, who was young and depressed-looking, got us our drinks, we chatted for a while. That former employment I mentioned was with the CIA. I worked for them for nine years, which is how I met Bobby. We got along immediately. Most of the time I was in the field, though by the end I was doing a lot of media surveillance. I left when the Agency introduced annual lie detector tests a few years back. Lot of people left the service then, indignant at the implied distrust after they'd put themselves on the line for their country. Me, I got out because I'd done some things. Not terrible things, I should add. Just the kind of things they put you in prison for. The CIA may not be the world's most straightforward organization, but they prefer their employees to avoid actual felonies most of the time. I'd used a few contacts to make a little money, bled a little cash out from between the cracks. There were some incidents. A guy got killed. That was all.

119

Though he now lived in Arizona, Bobby still worked for the Company on and off, and was in contact with a few old mutual friends. Two of them were now working to infiltrate militia groups, and hearing this made me glad all over again that I'd left the firm. That's not the kind of work you want to get into. Not if you value your life. One of these guys, a skinny nutcase called Johnny Claire, was actually living in one of the groups, a collection of ineffectively socialized gun fanatics holed up in a forest in Oklahoma. Better him than me, though Johnny was weird enough to hold his own in any company.

'Okay,' Bobby said, when armed with another beer, 'are you now going to explain how come you're out here in the sticks and suddenly conceive of a need to digitize some home-video footage?'

'Maybe,' I said, admiring the way he was pumping me without revealing what was on his own mind. A trick of the trade, now evidently habitual. When we met he was spending a lot of time in interrogation rooms with citizens of Middle Eastern countries. They all talked in the end. From that he'd sidestepped into surveillance. 'Not definitely. And *certainly* not until you finally reveal why you hopped on a plane and flew across three states to buy me a beer.'

'Okay,' he said. 'Okay. Let me ask you something first. Where were you born?'

'Bobby . . .'

'Just tell me, Ward.'

'You know where I was born. County Hospital, Hunter's Rock, California.' The place name rolled off my tongue as easily as my name would have done. It's one of the first things you learn.

'Indeed. I remember you telling me. You got all upset about the fact that nobody uses the apostrophe in "Hunter's" any more.'

'It pisses me off.'

'Right. It's a scandal. Now. When we spoke earlier today you told me about your folks, and you said something about the video having something to do with your childhood. So there I am, when we've done talking. I've got nothing to do. I'm surrounded by computers and I've surfed the Web all I can bear and I've already had my handjob for the day.'

'Nice thought,' I said. 'I'm hoping that wasn't while you were on the phone to me.'

'Keep hoping,' he said, with a sly little smile. 'So I think, what the hey, maybe I'll poke around in Ward's life a little.'

I stared at him, knowing that he was my friend and that this was okay, but still feeling like he'd intruded.

'I know, I know,' he said, holding up a placating hand. 'I was bored, what can I tell you? I'm sorry. So anyway, I get the computers buzzing and hit a few databases. I should say straight away that I didn't find anything I didn't know about already. Held for questioning over a few matters over the years, blah, released through lack of evidence. Plus a witness who recanted. And the one who disappeared. The drug-dealing bust in the Big Apple in 1985, quashed when you agreed to inform on a certain student group at Columbia.'

'They were assholes,' I said, defensively. 'Racist assholes. Plus one of them was sleeping with my girlfriend.'

'Come on, man. You already told me about it and I don't give a shit either way. You hadn't done that, you wouldn't have wound up in the Agency and I wouldn't know you, which I'd regard as a bad thing. Like I say, either there's nothing in the files that I don't already know about, or you've got it hidden well. Real well. Kind of like to know which, just as a matter of interest.'

'Not telling,' I said. 'A guy's got to have some secrets.'

'Well, Ward, you got them. I'll give you that much.'

'Meaning?'

'After an hour or so I'm kind of annoyed not to have turned anything up, so I come down to checking stuff in Hunter's Rock – and I said that with an apostrophe. Got the street address of your parents' house, plus when they moved in and out. They took up residence there on July 9th 1956, which I believe was a Monday. Paid their taxes, did their thing. Your father earned a wage at Golson Realty, mother worked part-time in a store. Little over a decade later you were born there. Right?'

'Right,' I said, wondering where this was going. He shook his head.

'Wrong. The County Hospital in Hunter's Rock has no record of a Ward Hopkins having been born on that date.'

The world seemed to take a little sidestep. 'Excuse me?'

'There is also no such record at the General in Bonville, or at the James B. Nolan, or at any other hospital within a two-hundred-mile radius.'

'There wouldn't be. I was born in the County. In Hunter's.'

He shook his head again, firmly. 'No, you weren't.'

'Are you *sure*?'

'Not only am I sure, but I checked five years either side, just in case you'd misled people on your age for some reason, like vanity or not being able to count. No Ward Hopkins. No Hopkins under any name. I don't know where you were born, my friend, but it sure as hell wasn't Hunter's Rock or its environs.'

I opened my mouth. Shut it again.

'Maybe it's no big deal,' he said, and then looked at me shrewdly. 'But has this got any bearing on your digitizing needs?'

'Play it again,' he said.

'I honestly don't think I can bear to, Bobby.'

He looked up at me. He was sitting in one of the hotel room's two chairs, hunched over my laptop. I'd just played him the MPEGs, and strongly believed I'd seen them enough times for one day. Perhaps for one lifetime. 'Trust me. What you see the first time is all there is.'

'Okay. So play me the audio file.'

I reached across, navigated to the file and double-clicked it.

He listened to the filtered version a few times, then stopped it himself. He nodded. 'Sounds like "The Straw Men" all right. And you got no idea what that might mean?'

'Only in the sense of "surrogate", which doesn't seem to go any-where. You?'

He reached for his glass. We were in possession of a half-bottle of Jack Daniel's by then. 'Only other thing I can think of is straw purchases.'

I nodded, thought about it. He was referring to the process by which those who shouldn't be able to buy guns – either through youth, previous convictions, or lack of a licence – are able to get hold of them. What you do is go in the gun store with a friend who has the requisite qualities. You negotiate with the dealer, find what you want. When the time comes to pay, then your friend – the straw purchaser – is the one who actually hands over the cash, who makes the buy. Of course the dealer isn't supposed to let this happen, when he knows it's you who's going to wind up having the gun, but a lot of them will. A sale is a sale. Once you're out of his store, what does he care what you're going to do? As long as you don't go around and shoot his mother he isn't likely to give a damn. There are, of course, a great many honest and upstanding people who sell guns. But there are also many who feel in their hearts that every American, every man jack of us and the little ladies, too, should be equipped with a firearm at birth. Who are at ease with the fact that these small, heavy pieces of machinery are a simple means by which to halt someone's life, who trust that guns are morally uninflected and that it's only their users who have the power to make them bad. Users with black skins, mainly, or no-good white trash punks on drugs who we don't serve in this gun store, no way.

'You think that's it?'

'Seems unlikely,' he admitted. 'Though there's been a thing about them in the last couple of years. The Feds and a few cities have been trying to crack down, targeting dealers who are too blatant about letting people get away with it. Huge percentage of inner-city guns get onto the streets that way, via guys who buy in bulk and then sell them to corner boys. Couple of test cases pending, and I think one of them actually went through a year ago. Can't remember how it played. But either way I don't get how it relates to your folks.'

'Nor me,' I agreed. 'Far as I know, my father never owned a weapon. I don't remember him ever coming down hard on the subject either way, but those in favour tend to have a well-stocked gun cabinet. Plus I just don't see it.'

'You looked it up?'

'Looked it up where? The Big Book of Short Sentences?'

He rolled his eyes. 'On the Net, of course.'

'Christ, no.' I like the Internet. Really, I do. Any time I need a piece of crap shareware or I want to find out the weather in Bogota or to look at a picture of a woman and a mule, I'm the first guy to get the modem humming. But as a source of information, it sucks. You got a billion pieces of data, struggling to be heard and seen and downloaded, and anything I want to know seems to get trampled underfoot in the crowd. Somehow, whenever I'm looking for something in particular, I get 404s right across the board.

'You're a fucking Luddite, Ward.' He was already plugging in the phone cable. I left him to get on with it, wishing I hadn't thrown away the cigarettes earlier in the day.

Five minutes later he shook his head. 'I get nothing with the major search sites, nothing with the minor ones, nothing with a bunch of specialized Netcrawlers I happen to know about including some you need robust security clearance for.'

'That's the Web for you. The deaf and dumb oracle with amnesia.' I made no effort to sound like I hadn't told him so.

'Doesn't mean there's nothing there. It just means that if the term does appear on a site, then it's one that isn't known to the search engines.'

'Bobby, there's no reason to believe anything will be out there. Not every single thing that ever happened is typed up there yet. Plus, it's just a sentence. Three words. You leave a bunch of monkeys for long enough, one of them will type it a lot sooner than they'll get around to Macbeth. But it doesn't mean he's going to whip up some HTML and sling it on a server with some banner ads and a hit counter – and even if he did, why should it have anything to do with what's on the tape?'

'You got anything better to do?'

'Yes,' I said, firmly. 'The bottle's running low and I'm tired and need a lot more to drink.'

'We'll do that after.'

'After what? You already found out there's nothing there.'

Bobby rapped his fingernails on the table for a while, squinting at the curtains. I could almost hear his brain humming. I was bored and the whiskey was making my brain feel heavy and cold. Too much new information in the last two days was making me want to forget everything I knew.

'There must be something else in the house,' he said eventually. 'Something you missed.'

'Only if it was hidden in a fucking lightbulb. I tossed the place. There's nothing else there.'

'Everything changes when you know what you're looking for,' he said. 'You thought you were looking for another note. So that's what you looked for. That's the grid you had. You only happened to think about video by chance.'

'No,' I said. 'I thought about it because the house had been set up that way. I think my father had gone to some trouble to . . .'

I tailed off. Got up, rummaged in the laptop bag.

'What?'

'I backed up his hard disk onto a ffiz! cart. It's the one thing I haven't really checked.'

I sat back down in the chair next to Bobby and slotted the tiny cartridge in the machine. Soon as it was mounted I got a Find Slip onscreen and typed in 'straw men'. Hit return. The machine chirped and whizzed for a while.

NO MATCHING ITEMS FOUND.

I tried it with 'straw' only. Same result.

'Well, that's that,' I said. 'The bar beckons.' I stood, expecting him to join me. Instead he started doing something with another Find Slip. 'What are you doing now?'

'Getting Find to index the contents of all the text files on the disk,' he said. 'If this straw thing is some big deal, it would make sense that there'd be no file by that name. You'd want to be less obvious about it. But it might appear *inside* one of the files.'

It was a reasonable point, so I waited. The ffiz! has a fast access time, and the process only took a couple of minutes.

Then it told us: the text was still nowhere to be found.

Bobby swore. 'Why the hell didn't he just leave a letter or something, just telling you whatever the fuck he wanted to say?'

'I already asked myself that question a billion times and the answer is that I don't know. Let's go.'

He still didn't get up. 'Look,' I said. 'I know you're doing this for me, and I'm grateful. But in the last twenty-four hours I've discovered either that my parents were insane and that I once had a twin or they were *really* insane and pretended I had. I've had nothing to eat in days. I stupidly had a cigarette this morning and now I want about a hundred more and it's taking all my mental energy to resist. I'm done here. I'm going to the bar.'

He turned his head toward me, but his eyes were far away. I'd seen that look in him before. It meant he couldn't even really hear what I was saying, and wouldn't until he'd run his course.

'I'll see you there,' I said, and left.

Chapter 11

I remember feeling proud of something when I was young – the fact that mosquitoes didn't bite me. If we went on holiday to the right kind of area, or I went on a school trip at the wrong time of year, I discovered that most people found themselves covered in little red bumps that itched like hell – no matter how much they futzed around with creams and sprays and nets. I didn't. I'd get maybe one bite, on the ankle. Kind of a strange thing to be proud of, you might think, but you know how it is when you're young. Once you come to realize that you're not the centre of all creation, you're so keen to find some concrete way of differentiating yourself that just about anything will do. I was the boy who didn't get bitten by insects. Take note, ladies and gentlemen, and have a little respect: there goes No-Bite Boy, the Mosquito-Free Kid. Then, one day when I was in my late twenties, I realized I'd got it wrong. Chances were that I got bitten just as much as everybody else. The only difference was that I didn't have as strong an allergic reaction, so I didn't get the bumps. I was still 'special' – though by then I was old enough to realize this wasn't any great distinction to have, and also to be more concerned with hoping that I wasn't actually so different from other people – but not in the way I'd thought. I got bitten like the rest of you, and No-Bite Boy was vanquished there and then.

As I sat there in the bar and waited for Bobby, this memory was hard to dislodge. My family, my life, was something I suddenly didn't understand. It was as if I'd noticed that I saw the same buildings in the background of my life, wherever I was, and had finally begun to wonder if it was a film set. As a matter of fact, I *did* generally see the same buildings. Since the Agency, I had never really gotten a mainstream existence on track, and seeing Bobby had made me realize this far more acutely than ever before. I did a little bit of this, and a little bit of that; some of this had been illegal, and some of that had been violent. Most of it was hard for me to even remember. It blurred. I lived in motels and restaurants and regional airports, talking to strangers, reading signs written to people in general and never meant just for me. All around me seemed to be people whose lives had content, who looked like the folks you see on television. Contextualized. Part of a story with the usual beats. Mine seemed to have none. The 'this is where you came from' section had just been abruptly scrapped, leaving an undisclosed number of empty pages.

My barman was on duty, and once again proved an able and efficient ally. He got over the whole 'previous incident' aspect of our reunion by bringing it up right away.

'Going to get your gun out later?'

'Not if you give me some peanuts.'

He got me some. He was a good barman, I decided. The place was free of corporate androids, and the only other guests were a very old foursome in the corner. They'd looked up at me grimly when I came in. I didn't blame them. When I get to their age, I'll resent young people, too. I resent them already, in fact, the slim

128

little fresh-faced assholes. I don't find it surprising that super-old people are so odd and grumpy. Half their friends are dead, they feel like shit most of the time, and the next major event in their lives is going to be their last. They don't even have the salve of believing that going to the gym is going to make things better, that they'll meet someone cute in the small hours of a Friday night or that their career is going to suddenly steer into an upturn and they'll wind up married to a movie star. They're out the other side of all that, onto a flat, grey plain of aches and bad eyesight, of feeling the cold in their bones and having little to do except watch their children and grandchildren go right ahead and make all the mistakes they warned them about. I don't blame them being a little out of sorts. I'm just surprised more oldsters don't take to the streets in packs, swearing and raising hell and getting drunk. With demographics going the way they are, maybe that's going to be the next big thing. Gangs of octogenarians, taking drugs and running amok. Though walking amok is more likely, I guess – with maybe an hour of dozing amok in the afternoon.

After a while the group in the corner seemed to accept that I wasn't going to start playing a new-fangled musical instrument or challenging conventional sexual mores. They got on with their business, and I got on with mine: we co-existed, two species warily sharing the same watering hole.

Nearly two hours later, Bobby came striding in. He caught sight of me slumped in my booth, signalled to the barman for two more of whatever I was drinking, and came over to join me.

'How shit-faced are you?' He had an odd look on his face.

'On a scale of one to ten,' I said breezily, 'I'd have to give myself an F.'

'Good,' he said. 'I've found something. Kind of.'

Suddenly feeling tense, I sat up and saw that he was holding a small sheaf of paper.

'Got reception to let me use their printer,' he said. 'Where the hell are the drinks?'

At that moment the barman appeared with them. 'Any more nuts?' he asked.

'Oh no,' I said. 'Just the two of us.' Then I laughed for quite a long time. I'm pretty sure I was laughing. The barman went away. Bobby waited patiently for me to get a grip. It took a while. I think that for just a moment I was on the verge of losing it.

'Okay,' I said eventually. 'Shoot.'

'First thing is I had another look on the Net. Still no record of the Straw Men as an actual thing, but I found encyclopaedia references to other meanings of the term "straw man", – something about guys who in the last century would stand outside courts with straw in their shoes – didn't really understand that part – indicating they'd give false testimony for money. And another reference regarding lack of conscience – I guess a straw versus flesh thing.'

'In other words, dummy guys in illegalities,' I said. 'As discussed. So what?'

'Then I looked right through the disk,' he said, ignoring me. 'Ran a low-level media scan, checked for hidden files, partitions, the works. Nothing. Then I looked through the software, of which there ain't much.'

'Dad wasn't a nerd,' I said. 'That's why I didn't bother to look through the computer in the house.'

'Right. But he did use the Net.'

I shrugged. 'Email, occasionally. Plus he had a site for his business, though someone else maintained it. I used to go look at it once in a while.' It had seemed easier, somehow, than calling them on the phone. Since I'd dropped out of college, they'd never really known what I was doing. They certainly didn't know the reason I hadn't finished the course, or who I'd gone on to work for. My parents never gave the impression of being political people, but they'd been there in the 1960s, as the video I'd found made more than clear. You were there in the Summer of Stupid Pants, then you took certain attitudes on board. Finding their son was working for the CIA would not have gone down big. I'd hidden this from them, not realizing this meant I was hiding everything else. Of course that now seemed a little bizarre, given what they'd been withholding from me.

Bobby shook his head. 'He had Explorer and Navigator on his disk, and he obviously used both a great deal. Huge cache, and about a zillion bookmarks in each.'

'For what kind of thing?'

'You name it. Reference. Online stores. Sports.'

'No porn?'

He smiled. 'No.'

'Thank God for that.'

'I went through every single one. Even the ones that seemed like nothing, just in case he'd covered up by re-naming the bookmark to cover what the link actually led to.'

'You're sneaky,' I said. 'I always said so.'

'So was your father. He had renamed one, in fact, hidden in a folder of a hundred and sixty bookmarks for what I can only regard as the dullest facets of the realty business. It was called "Recently sold Mizner/Intercoastal lots". Mean anything to you?'

'Addison Mizner was an estate architect in the 1920s and '30s. Built a bunch of prestige property in Miami, Palm Beach. Italian villa-style. Very sought-after and outlandishly expensive.'

'You know some wacky stuff. Okay. But the link didn't lead to a site to do with land or houses. It led to a blank page. So I thought shit, dead end. Took me a few minutes to realize that actually the page was covered with a transparent graphic that had a hidden image map. When I worked that out I got through to another set of pages, with some pretty odd links.'

'Odd how?'

He shook his head. 'Just odd. Looked like the usual home pages, complete with excessive detail, bad punctuation and rancid colour use, but all the material seemed very anodyne. There was just something hinky about them, almost as if they were fakes.'

'Why would someone put up fake home pages?'

'Well,' he said, 'that's what I wondered. I followed most of the links down into dead ends and 404s. But the line kept on going, through pages of links – and on each page only one of the links seemed to lead more than a couple of pages away. Then I started hitting passwords. At first, easy Java stuff that I could hack myself, using a few goodies I found stashed on your disk. Incidentally, you need more RAM. Fucker crashed on me about five times. Then – hope you don't mind, there's a few long-distance calls on your room – I got some help from specialist friends. I had to get down to wedge tracing and UNIX backdoors and shit. Someone who really knew what they were doing had set up a lot of obfuscation.'

'But what's the point?' I said. 'Surely anyone could just bookmark the end site, whatever it is, and go straight there the next time. Why screw around setting up a paper trail when the whole point of the Web is nonlinear access?'

'My guess is that the destination address changes regularly,' Bobby said. 'Anyway, finally I got through to the end.'

'And what was there?'

'Nothing.'

I stared at him. 'Say again?'

'Nothing. There was nothing there.'

'Bobby,' I said, 'that's a shit story. It sucks. What do you mean, "nothing"?'

He shoved the sheaf of papers toward me. The top sheet was blank apart from a short sentence centred in the middle of the page. It said: WE RISE.

'That's all there was,' he said. 'A couple of hours' worth of subterfuge to hide a page with no links and just two words. The other sheets are just printouts of the route I took to get there, along with some of the hacks required. Plus I got the IP address of the final page and did a trace on it.'

Most Web addresses are known by a format that, while often not exactly something that trips off the tongue, can at least be understood as words. In fact, the Internet's computers regard them as

132

purely numerical addresses – 118.152.1.54, for example. By using this more basic form of address you can track the page down to a rough geographical location. 'So where was it?'

'Alaska,' he said.

'Whereabouts? Anchorage?'

He shook his head. 'That's it. Just Alaska. Then Paris. Then Germany. Then California.'

'What are you talking about?'

'It moved. Kept blipping all over the place, and I don't think it was ever really in any of those places at all. It was ghosted. I'm not King Nerd, but I know what I'm doing and I've never seen anything quite like it. I've got a couple of friends looking into it, but either way, something weird is going down.'

'No shit.'

'Not just what's happening to you. This kind of thing is my job. I need to know how they're doing it. And who they are.' He took a long pull on his drink, and looked at me seriously. 'What about you? What are you going to do now? Aside from more drinking.'

'There's three sections on the tape. I can't do anything about the last one, about finding . . . the other child.' I'd been intending to say 'my twin', but shied away at the last moment. 'I don't know what city it was, and it's over thirty years ago anyhow. He or she could be anywhere in the world. Or dead. The second section doesn't seem to lead anywhere. So I'm going to go looking for the place in the mountains.'

'Sound thinking,' he said. 'And I'm going to help you.'

'Bobby . . .'

He shook his head. 'Don't be an asshole, Ward. Your parents didn't die in any accident. You know that.'

I guess I did, and had done for a little while, though I hadn't really allowed the thought to settle, to say it to myself in words.

Bobby did it for me. 'They were murdered,' he said.

Chapter 12

Nina sat in the yard with Zoë Becker. The night was cool and she wished she'd accepted the tea she had been absently offered. Zandt had already spoken with the woman, and stood in her daughter's room, and was now inside with her husband. Neither Becker had seemed surprised to find two investigators on their doorstep, even this late in the evening. Their lives were already too far divorced from what they were prepared to accept as reality. The two women talked fitfully for a while, but soon lapsed into silence. Zoë was watching her foot as it jogged up and down at the end of her crossed leg. That at least was the direction in which her eyes were directed. Nina doubted she was seeing anything at all, but rather floating in a void in which the movement of her foot was as meaningful an event as any other. She was glad of the silence, because she knew the only thing the woman would want to talk about. Was her daughter still alive? Did Nina think they would ever get her back? Or would there, in this house that Zoë had spent so much time getting just so, now always be a room whose emptiness and silence would darken until it was a black crystal at the centre of their lives? On the wall of this room was a poster for a band that none of the rest of them had ever heard except by accident. So what was the point of it now?

Nina had no answer to this question or others like it, and when the woman appeared about to speak she looked up with dread. Instead she found that Zoë had started to cry, exhausted tears that seemed neither the beginning of anything nor its end. Nina didn't reach out for her. Some people would accept comfort from strangers, and some would not. Mrs Becker was one of the latter.

Instead she leaned back in her chair, and looked across through the French doors to the sitting room. Michael Becker was perched on the edge of an armchair. Zandt was standing behind the couch. Nina had spent the entire day with Zandt without hearing more than five sentences that did not relate to the case. They had walked the ground of the disappearance early in the day, before the shopping crowds gathered. They had visited Sarah Becker's school, so that Zandt could see how it fit into its environment. He had observed the sight lines and access points, the places where someone might wait, looking for someone to love. He spent a long while over it, as if believing there was some new view he might chance upon that would enable him to glimpse a man's shadow in the daylight. He had been irritable when they left.

They had not visited any of the families from The Upright Man's previous murders. They had the files of the original interviews, and it was very unlikely there would be anything new to be learned. Nina knew he held their interviews in his head, and could have told the families things they had themselves forgotten. Talking to them could only confuse matters. She also privately believed that if Zandt was able to lead them closer to the killer, it would be little to do with something he had learned, and much more to do with something he felt.

Nina had another reason for keeping Zandt away from the

families. She did not want any of the relatives stirred up enough that they might call the police or the Bureau to check how the investigation was going. No one knew she had reinvolved John Zandt in the case again. If anyone found out, all hell would break loose. This time it wouldn't just be disciplinary: it would be the end of her career. Allowing him to talk to the Beckers was a risk she had to take. The parents had seen so many police and Bureau men since the disappearance that it was unlikely they would remember one in particular, or mention him to someone else. Or so she hoped. She also hoped that whatever the men were talking about, it might spark something in Zandt's mind.

And that he would tell her about it if it did.

'I'll go through it again if you want.'

Michael Becker had already recounted his movements twice, responding quickly and concisely to questions. Zandt knew that the man had nothing helpful to tell him. He had also gathered that, in the weeks leading up to the disappearance, Becker had been so involved in his work that he would have noticed very little about the outside world. He shook his head.

Becker abruptly looked down at the floor and put his head in his hands. 'Don't you have *anything* else to ask? There must be something else. There has to be something.'

'There's no magic question. Or if there is, I don't know what it might be.'

Becker looked up. This was not the kind of thing the other policemen had said to him. 'Do you think she's still alive?'

'Yes,' Zandt said.

Becker was surprised by the confidence he saw in the policeman's face. 'Everyone else is acting as if she's dead,' he said. 'They don't say it. But they think it.'

'They're wrong. For the time being.'

'Why?' The man's voice was dry, the breathing wrong, the sound of a man caught wanting to believe.

'When a killer of this type disposes of a victim, he usually hides the body and does what he can to obfuscate its identity. Partly just to make it harder for the police. But also because many of these people are seeking to hide their activities from themselves. The three previous victims were found in open ground, wearing the remains of their own clothes and still with their personal effects. This man isn't hiding from anybody. He wanted us to know who they were, and that he had finished with them. Finishing implies a period in which he requires them to be alive.'

'Requires them . . .?'

'Only one of the previous victims was sexually abused. Apart from minor head injuries, the others showed no abuse apart from the shaving of their heads.'

'And their murder, of course.'

Zandt shook his head. 'Murder is not abuse in this kind of situation. Murder is what ends the abuse. Forensics can only show so much, but it suggests that all of the girls were alive for over a week after their abductions.'

'A week,' the man said, bleakly. 'It's been five days already.'

There was a pause before Zandt answered. During the interview, his eyes had covered most corners of the room, but now he saw something he hadn't noticed before. A small pile of schoolbooks, on a side table. They were too advanced to belong to the younger daughter. He became conscious that the other man was looking at him. 'I'm aware of that.'

'You sounded like you had another reason.'

'I just don't believe he will have killed her yet.'

Becker laughed harshly. 'Don't "believe"? That's it? Oh right. That's very reassuring.'

'It's not my job to reassure you.'

'No,' Becker said, face blank. 'I suppose not.' There was silence for a few moments. And then he added: 'These things really happen, don't they?'

Zandt knew what he meant. That certain events, of a kind that most people just watch or read about, can actually happen. Things like sudden death, and divorce, and spinal injuries; like suicide, and drug addiction, and fading grey people standing in a circle looking down at you muttering 'The driver never stopped'. They happen. They're as real as happiness, marriage and the feel of the sun on your back, and they fade far more slowly. You may not get back the life you had before. You may not be one of the lucky ones. It may just go on and on and on.

'Yes they do,' he said. Unseen by the other man, he touched the cover of one of the schoolbooks. Ran his finger over its rough surface.

'What chance do you think we have of getting her back?'

The question was asked simply, with a steady voice, and Zandt admired him for it. He turned away from the table.

'You should assume that you have none at all.'

Becker looked shocked, and tried to say something. Nothing came out.

'A hundred people are killed by men like this every year,' Zandt said. 'Probably more. In this country alone. Almost none of the killers are ever caught. We make a big fuss when we do, as if we've put the tiger back in his cage. But we haven't. A new one is born every month. The few we catch are unlucky, or stupid, or have been driven to the point where they start making mistakes. The majority are never caught. These men are not aberrations. They are part of who we are. It's like anything else. Survival of the most fit. The cleverest.'

'Is The Delivery Boy clever?'

'That's not his name.'

'That's what the papers called him before. And the cops.'

'He's called The Upright Man. By himself. Yes, he's clever. That may be what causes him to fall. He's very keen for us to admire him. On the other hand . . .'

'He may just not get caught, and unless you find him we're never going to see Sarah again.'

'If you see her again,' Zandt said, replacing his pad and pen in an inside pocket, 'it will be a gift from the gods, and you should see it as such. None of you will ever be the same. That need not be a bad thing. But it's true.'

Becker stood. Zandt didn't think he'd ever seen a man who looked both so tired and incapable of sleep. Unknown to him, Michael Becker was thinking the same thing of him.

'But you'll keep trying?'

'I'll do everything I can,' he said. 'If I can find him, then I will.'

'Then why tell me to assume the worst?'

But his wife came in through the French doors, with the FBI agent just behind, and the policeman did not say anything more.

Nina thanked the Beckers for their time, and promised to keep them up to date. She also managed to imply that their visit had been a formality, without direct relevance to the course of the investigation.

Michael Becker watched as they walked away down the path. He did not shut the door when they were out of sight, but stood a moment looking out at the night. Behind him he heard the sound of Zoë going upstairs to check on Melanie. He doubted his second daughter would be asleep. The nightmares of a year ago were returning, and he could not blame her. What little sleep he managed was an enemy to him, too. He knew she still used the spell he had written, and the knowledge filled him with horror. Irony was no protection, whatever he and Sarah and the directors of modern horror films might think. In a land of blood and bones, irony doesn't cut it. He remembered discussing night fears with Sarah, several years before. She had always been a questioning child, and asked why people were afraid of the dark. He told her it was a leftover from when we were more primitive, and slept out in the open or in caves, and wild animals might come and kill us in the night.

Sarah had looked dubious. 'But that's an *awfully* long time ago,' she'd said. She'd thought for a little while, before adding, with a ten-year-old's perfect certainty: 'No. We must be frightened of something else.'

Michael believed now she was right. It's not monsters we're afraid of. Monsters were only a comforting fantasy. We know what our own kind is capable of. What we're frightened of is ourselves.

He closed the door eventually and walked into the kitchen. Here he made a pot of coffee, something that had become a ritual for this part of the evening. He would carry it into the sitting room on a tray, along with two cups and a jug of warm milk. Perhaps a cookie or two, which was all Zoë seemed willing to eat. They would sit in front of whatever the television had to offer, waiting for time to pass. Old films were best. Something from another time, from before Sarah had been born and any of this could be true. Sometimes they would talk a little. Usually not. Zoë would have the phone close by.

As he took two cups from the new dresser – old pine, imported from England after their recent trip – Michael thought back on the things the policeman had said, holding each sentence up for consideration. He realized that, for the first time since the disappearance, he felt a small thread of something that must be hope. It would be gone by the morning, but he welcomed its temporary respite. He felt it because he believed he knew what had been said between the lines, that what the policeman had said was less important than what he had not.

The female investigator had shown identification, but the man had never been named. With the dedication of someone who believed in the magic of articulation, that naming and containing events in words could subdue them, Michael Becker had read as much as he could concerning the previous crimes of the man who had taken his daughter. He had been on the Internet, and found copies of the news pieces, even sought out a copy of the supermarket hackbook on unsolved crimes. He had done this at the expense of, among other things, his work. He hadn't touched *Dark Shift* since the night of the disappearance. He privately thought it was unlikely he ever would, though his partner was as yet unaware of this, and kept frantically rescheduling the meeting with the studio. Wang had money, and his contacts appeared inexhaustible. He was plugged into the city in a way Michael could never hope to be. He'd survive.

Through his research Michael had learned, or been reminded, that in addition to the LeBlanc girl and Josie Ferris and Annette Mattison, another young woman had disappeared at around the same time. This girl had been the daughter of a policeman who had been involved in the apprehension of two previous serial killers. There had been speculation, of a quiet kind, that she had been targeted as a taunt, a punishment for her father's successes. He had become involved in the investigation of her disappearance, against the advice of the FBI, and at least one newspaper had implied that he was believed to be making concrete progress where they were manifestly failing. Then he had simply dropped out of sight. The policeman's name had been John Zandt. The Delivery Boy, as Michael Becker had reason to know, had not been apprehended. A retrospective published a year after the disappearances had reported that a Mrs Jennifer Zandt had returned to Florida to be close to her family. The journalist had been unable to discover what had happened to the detective.

Michael thought that tonight, whatever was on television, he and his wife should talk. He would tell her what he believed concerning the man who had come to see them, and he would suggest that when the other policemen and women came to visit, the well-meaning people with whom they now shared a horrible familiarity, they should not mention this evening's visit.

And something else. Though his faith in words had been deeply shaken, he clung to the belief that words and names were to reality what pillars and architecture were to space. They humanized it. Just as DNA took the random chemicals and turned them into something recognizable, language could take inexplicable phenomena and tame them into situations about which something could be said, and thus about which something could be done.

141

He would no longer think of The Delivery Boy. He would call him The Upright Man. But in the meantime he would assume the worst. The policeman was right. More than that, Michael Becker realized that it was what Sarah would want.

Nokkon Wud be damned. If the fates demanded this level of tribute, then they could go fuck themselves.

They were sitting outside the Smorgas Board, a combination café and surfer hangout about eight yards down the street from where the Becker girl had been abducted. They had been for an hour, and the place was near to closing. The only other customers were a young couple hunkered around a table a couple of yards away, list-lessly sipping something out of big cups.

'Are you thinking, or just watching?'

Zandt didn't respond immediately. He sat beside Nina, observing the street. He had barely moved. His coffee was cold. He had only smoked one cigarette, and most of that had burned away unno-ticed. His attention was focused entirely elsewhere. Nina was reminded of a hunter, though not necessarily a human one. An animal that was prepared and able to sit, to wait, for as long as it took, without boredom, rage or pain to distract it.

'They don't all come back,' she said, irritably.

'I know,' he said, immediately. 'I'm not watching.'

'Bullshit.' She laughed. 'It's either that or you've had a seizure.'

He surprised her by smiling. 'I'm thinking.'

She folded her arms. 'Care to share?'

'I'm thinking what a waste of time this is, and wondering why you brought me here.'

Nina realized it hadn't really been a smile. 'Because I thought you might be able to help,' she said. She shifted uncomfortably in her seat. 'John, what is this? You know why. Because you helped me before. Because I value your advice.'

He smiled again, and this time she actually shivered.

'What did I achieve last time?'

'I don't know,' she admitted. 'Tell me. What happened?'

'You know what happened.'

'No, I don't,' she said, suddenly angry. 'All I know is that you told me that you were getting somewhere. And you started getting secretive and not telling me anything, despite the fact that up until then you'd relied upon me to feed you stuff out of the Bureau. Stuff you wouldn't have gotten otherwise because you'd been specifically barred from taking part in the investigation by your own department. I did you a favour and you cut me out.'

'You did me no favours,' Zandt said. 'You did what you thought would do you the most good.'

'Oh, fuck you, John,' she snapped. The two slackers at the far table jerked upright, like puppets whose master had suddenly woken up. Heavy vibes.

She lowered her voice and spoke fast. 'If that's what you really think of me, then why don't you just walk away, go back to fucking Vermont. It's going to snow hard there real soon. You could just bury yourself in it.'

'You're telling me that you helped me out of consideration for my family?'

'Yes, of course. What the hell else?'

'Despite the fact you'd helped me be unfaithful to my wife.'

'That's pathetic. Don't blame me for what your dick did.'

She glared at him. Zandt stared back. There was silence for a moment, and then she abruptly let her eyes drop.

He laughed, briefly. 'That supposed to make me think I'm in control?'

'What?' She silently cursed herself.

'Looking away. Kind of an animal kingdom thing. Male ego massaged by a sign of submission. Now I'm back to being king of the hill, I'll do what you want again?'

'You've gotten really paranoid, John,' she said, though of course he'd been right. She realized she spent too much of her time with fools. 'I just don't want to argue with you.'

143

'What do you think the deal with the hair is?' he said.

She frowned, thrown by the sudden switch. 'What hair?'

'The Upright Man. Why cut the hair off?'

'Well, for the sweaters. So he could embroider the names.'

Zandt shook his head, lit a cigarette. 'You don't need a whole head for that. All of the girls had long hair. But when they're found, it's all been cut off. Why?'

'To dehumanize them. To make it easier to kill them.'

'Could be,' he said. 'That's what we all assumed back then. But I wonder.'

'Are you going to tell me what you *do* think?'

'I'm wondering if it was a punishment.'

Nina considered this. 'For what?'

'I don't know. But I think this man took these girls, a very particular type of girl, on purpose. I think he had something in mind for them, and each of them failed to come up to scratch in some way. And as a punishment for that, he took something he thought would be of paramount importance to them.'

He took a drink of his coffee, seeming not to care that it was cold. 'You know what they did to collaborators in France, at the end of the Second World War?'

'Of course. Women who were thought to have accepted their German invaders too wholeheartedly were paraded down the street with their hair shorn off. A proud moment for our species.' She shrugged. 'I can maybe see the punishment thing, but I don't see what global conflict has to do with it. These girls hadn't fraternized with anyone.'

'Maybe not.' Zandt seemed to have lost interest in the subject. He was sitting back in his chair and gazing vaguely across the patio. One of the slackers accidentally caught his eye. Zandt didn't look away. The slacker did, rapidly. He made a signal to his friend, evidently suggesting this might be a good time to go wax their boards. They got up and sloped off into the night.

Zandt seemed satisfied with this.

Nina tried to haul his concentration back. 'So where does that lead?'

'Possibly nowhere,' he said, grinding out his cigarette. 'I just didn't think hard enough about it last time. Then I was hung up on the method he'd used to find them. How the intersection of their lives had come about. Now it strikes me as curious. How they failed. What he really wanted them for.'

Nina didn't say anything, hoping there would be some more. But when he did speak, it wasn't about the case.

'Why did you stop sleeping with me?'

Caught again, she hesitated. 'We stopped sleeping with each other.'

'No.' He shook his head. 'That's not the way it was.'

'I don't know, John. It just happened. You didn't seem especially hurt at the time.'

'Just kind of accepted it, didn't I.'

'What are you getting at? You don't accept it now?'

'Of course I do. It was a long time ago. I'm just asking questions that I haven't before. Once you start doing that, you find they pop up all over the place.'

She didn't really know what to say to that. 'So what do you want to do next?'

'I want you to go,' he said. 'I want you to go home and leave me alone.'

Nina stood. 'Suit yourself. You got my number. Call me if you decide to get off your butt and do something.'

He turned his head slowly, and looked her directly in the eyes. 'Do you want to know what happened? Last time?'

She stopped, looked at him. His face was cold and distant. 'Yes,' she said.

'I found him.'

Nina felt the hairs on the back of her neck rise. 'Found who?'

'I tracked him for two weeks. In the end I went to his house. I'd seen him watching other girls. I couldn't leave it any longer.'

She didn't know whether to sit or keep standing. 'What happened?'

145

'He denied it. But I knew it was him, and now he knew I'd made him. He was the man, but I had no proof, and he would have run. I stayed with him two days. He wouldn't tell me where she was.'

'John, don't tell me this.'

'I killed him.'

Nina stared at him, and knew it was the truth. She opened her mouth, shut it again.

'And then two days later the sweater and the note arrived.'

He looked suddenly very tired, and turned away. When he spoke again, his voice was flat. 'I got the wrong guy. It's up to you what you do with the information.'

She walked away, across the Promenade. She willed herself not to look back at him, and instead concentrated on the tops of the palm trees nodding in the faint breeze, a couple of blocks away.

But when she reached the corner she did stop, and turn. He'd vanished. She waited for a moment, chewing her lip, but he didn't reappear. Slowly she started walking.

Something had changed. Until tonight Zandt had seemed malleable, but sitting with him in the café had been an uncomfortable experience. She realized it wasn't a hunter that he had reminded her of, but a boxer, glimpsed on camera in the period an hour before the actual fight. The time when the show business was put to one side, and the fighter seemed to move off into a realm of his own, a place where he stopped meeting people's eyes and became absorbed into his archetype. Other people might bet on the outcome, put on monkey suits, get high on corporate hospitality. The rest would crap on about how boxing should be banned, cocooned in lives from which nobody wanted an escape route, any escape route. For the guys in the ring, it was different. They did it for the money, but not only for that. They did it because that was what they did. They weren't looking for a way out. They were looking for a way in, a road back to some place they sensed inside themselves.

The parents had been a mistake. Zandt had access to little enough real information as it was, and was already questioning what she wanted of him. The only new investigative material could come from the Beckers. She'd had to let him talk to them. But she'd known as soon as she came back from the garden that this had opened doors that would have been better kept shut.

She didn't need this. She'd never wanted a hunter, or a killer. She believed the only thing that would draw The Upright Man into the open was a man he wanted to dominate.

She wanted bait.

Chapter 13

The man sat in his chair, in the centre of the living room. The room was large and stuck out from the front of the house, with windows on three walls. Two sides were protected by a stand of trees; the other looked down on a sloping, terraced lawn. This afternoon all of the curtains were drawn, heavy drapes that allowed not the slightest suggestion of the outside to penetrate. Sometimes the man had them shut, sometimes he left them open. He was entirely unpredictable in this regard.

The chair was positioned with its back to the door into the room. He liked the way this made him feel. It generated a mild tension, the sensation of being unprotected. Someone could, in theory, sneak up behind him and bash him over the head. That person would have to overcome the comprehensive security systems, but the point still held. It showed how in control of his environment he was. He had no fear of the outside world. From an early age he had been forced to make his way in it, to help himself. But he liked his interior spaces to be just so.

His face was smooth and unlined, the result of assiduous use of moisturizer and other skin foods. His eyes were sharp and clear. His hands were lightly tanned, the nails trimmed. He was entirely naked. The chair was at a slight angle to the polished floorboards that traversed the room in orderly rows. A very hot cup of black coffee sat on a small table beside the chair, next to a saucer filled with tiny glass beads. A thin publication lay nearby. The cup was placed so that just less than half of its base protruded past the edge of the surface. The chair was old, covered in battered leather. By rights it should have a copy of *The New York Times* folded on one of the arms, and a flunky hovering just behind, ready to dispense sandwiches with the crusts cut off. One entire bookcase he had decorated by crosshatching it with green, blue and red pens, each stroke of the pen no longer than three millimetres, until an overall effect of subtly mottled black had been achieved. It had required seventeen pens, and taken several weeks. A fine Arts and Crafts bureau on the other side of the room was entirely covered by very small glued-on photographs of Madonna, all cut from magazines and none later than her Material Girl incarnation, after which the man had lost interest in her. He had covered the result with a number of coats of dark varnish, until it looked as though the piece was covered in nothing more than an unusual walnut veneer. As with the bookcase, only very close inspection would reveal how the effect was obtained.

His current project involved the small occasional table by his chair, which he was covering with the glass beads. The beads were about one millimetre in diameter, and came in four colours: red, blue, yellow, and green. Genetic colours. Gluing them in position took a great deal of care, not least because they were not placed at random but in a long and complex pattern, which was at least partly speculative. When the table was done he was going to cover it with several coats of thick black lacquer, until all but the faintest hint of texture was removed. It would occur to no one to wonder what was beneath the surface, in the same way that no one would realize that one, and only one, of the floorboards in the house had been constructed from a very large number of wooden matchsticks and then sanded and varnished until it exactly resembled the others. The collecting of the matches had taken the man over six months. Each had, so far as he had been able to ensure, been struck by a different person. He believed deeply in individuality, in its crucial importance to humanity. These days everyone watched the same television shows, read the same glossy magazines, and was press-ganged by the media into dutifully lining up to watch the same ludicrous movies. They stopped smoking because they were told to by people who meanwhile crammed themselves with fat. For the comfort and convenience of others. They lived their lives by rules designed by these others, by people they had never even met. They lived on the surface, in an MTV and CNN world of the last five minutes. Now was all. They had no understanding of 'then', but wallowed in a perpetual present.

The publication on the table was a recent academic paper, which had arrived in the mail that morning. He had seen a synopsis of it online and ordered a copy of the full text for closer inspection. Though its subject was quite specialized, he was more than capable of comprehending it fully. He had spent many years reading carefully in the subjects that interested him: genetics, anthropology, prehistoric culture. Although his schooling had finished very early, he was intelligent, and he had learned a lot from life. His life, and other people's. The things they said, *in extremis*. There was often a lot of truth to be found there, once you got beyond the pleading, and the body spoke without interference from the mind.

Before reading it he stood up, walked a short distance from the chair, and did three sets of push-ups. One set with his palms flat on the floor and hands shoulder-distance apart. One set with palms flat again, but hands wide apart. A final set with hands back close together, but closed like fists, knuckles on the floor. A hundred of each, with a short break in between.

He barely broke a sweat. He was pleased.

Sarah Becker heard the muffled sound of the man's measured exertions below her, but spent no time trying to work out what the noise might mean. She didn't want to know. She didn't know what time it was, and wasn't inclined to know that either. Her internal clock told her it was probably day, maybe afternoon. In some ways that was worse than it being night. Bad things happened at night. It was to be expected. People were scared of the dark because when it was dark it was night, and when it was night things sometimes came to get you. That was the way of the world. Daytime was supposed to be better. Daytime was when you went to school, and had lunch, and the sky was blue and everything was pretty much safe so long as you stayed out of places where people were poor. If daytime wasn't going to be safe, then she didn't want to think about it. She didn't want to know.

If she craned her neck upward, she could just touch her forehead against the top of the space she inhabited. It was utterly dark. She was lying on her back, and able to move her hands and feet about two inches in any direction. She had been in this position for a long time, which she estimated to be at least four days, maybe six. She remembered nothing from the period between being on 3rd Street Promenade and finding herself lying flat on her back, with a narrow window in front of her face. After a few moments she had realized she could see the ceiling of a room, and that the window was a hole in a floor, beneath which she lay in a space only very slightly larger than her own body. The window in the floor was approximately five inches tall by four wide, and reached from just above her eyebrows to just below her mouth.

She had started screaming, and after a while someone had entered the room. He whispered some things to her. She had screamed a little more, and he had placed a small panel in the hole in the floor.

She had heard the sound of his footsteps going away, and only one thing had happened since. Sarah had woken from a doze in what had felt like night to find that the panel above her face had been removed again. The room above was nearly dark, but she could make out the head of someone watching her. She tried to talk to the man, to plead, to offer, but he said nothing. After a while she stopped, and started crying instead. The man's hand came into view, holding a beaker. He tipped water out of this onto her face. At first she tried to turn her head away but then, realizing how thirsty she was, she opened her mouth and swallowed as much as she could. Afterwards the man replaced the panel and went away.

Some indeterminate period of time later he had returned, and they had their conversation about Ted Bundy. This time she drank the water.

Over time she had found her mind becoming clearer, as whatever drug she had been given slowly worked its way out of her system. The downside of this was that her initial feeling of floating inconsequence was harder to maintain. She had tried to push up the panel with her nose and tongue, straining her neck up as far as it would go, but its position had been carefully judged and it was impossible to move in this manner. Like the space itself, it had been immaculately designed for someone of her size, almost as if it had been made in preparation for her and her alone. Sarah was physically fit, a good rollerblader, and stronger than most girls of her size. She had nevertheless been unable to make any impression on the space that held her, and had stopped trying. Her father often said that the problems in many people's lives were caused by the energy they wasted trying to change that which couldn't be changed. She was not yet old enough to understand exactly what he meant by that, but on a literal level she took the point. She hadn't eaten in what seemed like for ever. Until it became clear that a source of additional energy was going to be provided, it made no sense to waste what she had. Struggling was stupid. So she lay still, and thought about Nokkon Wud.

Mr Wud was something that she and her father had invented. At least, they *thought* they'd invented him. He had come about, indirectly, through Sarah's mother. Zoë Becker believed in many things. Well, maybe not believed in, as such, but wasn't going to take any chances where they were concerned. Astrology? Well, yes, of course it's nonsense, but there's no harm in knowing what it says and it's surprising how often it seems to be very accurate. Feng shui? Just common sense, of course, but windchimes look pretty and make a nice sound so why not have them anyway? And if a certain type of bird happens to fly across your path, which *some* people might think could be unlucky, then there are rhymes to say and small hand gestures to make which surely can't do any harm.

As often within families, Zoë had inherited her superstitions from her grandmother, rather than her mother, a hardheaded ex-publisher who believed primarily in jogging. Michael Becker had no truck with such spells and signs, and neither did his daughter. Mr Wud had come about as a private joke between them, a response to the superstition that most drove Michael Becker up the wall. Whenever anyone in the family said anything that could – to even the very mildest of degrees – be said to be tempting fate, then Zoë Becker would immediately follow it by saying 'Knock on wood,' as swiftly and unconsciously as you might say 'Bless you' after someone sneezes. If someone said 'I'll never end up like that,' she'd say 'Knock on wood' and rap the table with her knuckles. If they said 'My father's in good health,' she would say it – increasingly quietly, as she became aware that her husband found the habit wildly irritating – but she would say it. She would even say it, and this was the kind of occasion that made her husband want to gnaw chunks out of the piano, if someone said something like, 'I've never broken my leg.' Michael Becker would point out that this was a factual statement, and not flipping the bird at the fates. It was merely a recital of a true condition of the world, and hedging it off with a superstitious mantra was ridiculous. You wouldn't, he'd patiently observe, say 'Two plus two equals four – knock on wood,' and so why use the expression after any other kind of fact? It was an explicable habit, and borderline bearable, when used after a statement that showed hubris in the face of the world's potential to hurt. But if it was just a goddamned *fact* . . .

Zoë would listen to this, as she had many times before. She would then point out that it was a well-established tradition in many parts of the world – in England and Australia, for example, where they would say 'Touch wood' in similar circumstances – and that there might be some basis to it because trees had power, and anyway it didn't do any harm. And Michael would nod, walk quietly out of the room, and go gnaw chunks out of the piano.

Sarah sided with her father on the subject, and over the years they'd developed the character of Nokkon Wud, an evil sprite, probably Scandinavian in nature, whose sole job was to listen for people challenging the fates by rashly making factual observations. He would then swoop invisibly into their homes in the dead of night, and give their lives a stir for the worse. You'd better not feel lucky when Nokkon was around, because he'd know, and punish you for it.

Over the years this had evolved into their parting routine, in which they genially wished some ill upon each other so that Nokkon would hear and know he wasn't required in their lives. It had also proved useful when Sarah's sister, Melanie, had started having nightmares a year back. At Sarah's suggestion, Michael had told her this was Nokkon Wud at work, flying past the bed, sniffing out for people to harm. All Melanie had to do was recite a little rhyme – which her father spent a long time writing, with more redrafts than most of the scripts through which he earned his living – and Nokkon Wud would know that he wasn't needed there and go bother someone else. Melanie tried this solution, dubiously at first, but was soon saying it before she went to bed every night – and in time the bad dreams went away and it mattered less whether her cupboard doors were sealed absolutely tight. Her mother didn't really approve of the joke, and never personally invoked him, but would sometimes smile when Nokkon was mentioned. He explained things about the world, and was now enshrined in *Dark Shift* as one of the recurrent minor demons ganging up on the heroine. Her father's partner had questioned the idea, with much questioning of skill sets and back story, but Michael kept it in anyhow.

As Sarah lay beneath the floorboards in a house inhabited by a madman, she was wondering if her mother hadn't been right after all. Maybe there was such a monster, such a spirit. And maybe he had known they had been mocking him, had been too complacent. And maybe this had made him angry. And maybe it was he who had come for her, and he came in darkness to see her now because he had no face beneath the mask he had shown to capture her.

Sarah lay still, her eyes open wide.

The paper, which was entitled 'The Krüniger Plot and Mittel-Baxter Society', detailed an archaeological investigation that had recently taken place in an area of Germany with which the man was unfamiliar. He had found it in his atlas, and established it was too distant from any of his contacts for them to be able to provide any on-the-spot observations, and so he was restricted to the information in the paper.

A graveyard had been discovered not far from the remains of a Neolithic settlement. Carbon dating of the skeletons, together with corollary evidence from personal items found within some of the graves, had allowed the site to be dated to the latter part of the eighth millennium B.C. Ten thousand years ago. The man sat for a while, savouring the thought, summoning up an image of this cross-section of time. Before any now-recognizable language had been spoken, long before even the Pyramids had been built – unless one believed the claims of the New Age archaeologists with their selective evidence-gathering and flimsy projections – these people had lived and died and been laid in the earth, had made love and eaten and shat their waste on the ground. The man sipped a little of his coffee, being careful to replace the cup on the side table so that it was only just balanced. Then he read on.

There were twenty-five sets of remains. Women of up to young middle age, children, a few men in their late teens or early twenties, and one man of more advanced years. Thorough appendices detailed the condition of each of the skeletons, and outlined the techniques that had been used both to age them and establish the dietary and environmental conditions within which they had lived. The authors of the paper remarked how the skeletons had been laid in a grid, an organized system of burial observed in no other sites in that part of Europe at the time. They provided diagrams demonstrating how the orientation of the grid was in accordance with what was understood of the period's interest in the summer and winter solstices, thankfully avoiding a digression into primitive astronomy. They instead produced a series of arguments to show that this arrangement provided further evidence for a proposition to which they had been committed for some years: that this particular area of Germany had been host to a hybridized form of social organization that they termed Mittel-Baxter Society (for such were the authors' names), a sporadic and localized culture of very minor academic interest and negligible long-term significance.

The man read the paper carefully to the end, and then worked steadily through the appendices. After reading the reports on the skeletons of the other deceased, nodding occasionally at what he regarded as perfectly well-argued conclusions, he came to the section regarding the older man who had been found at the site. The position of his skeleton – at the exact centre of a five-by-five grid – suggested that he had been the first to be buried in this plot, and the authors argued compellingly that this implied that the man had been a person of importance within the nearby village. It was also deduced that he had been born in a different part of the country, as bilateral pitting in the interior of his eye sockets – a condition known as *cribra orbitalia* – suggested that his diet had been deficient in iron for much of his life. The amount of iron in vegetation is determined by the geological qualities of the soil in which it grows, and its absorption affected by the amount of lead present: people from different areas will therefore show marked variations in the condition. Cross sections taken from the man's teeth, and subsequent analysis of the levels of lead and strontium isotopes, had enabled them to link him to an area over two hundred and fifty miles away. In an aside it was observed that a lesion on his skull bore witness to a blow to the head that had not proved fatal – as the damage it had caused to the bone tissue was long-healed prior to the man's eventual demise. They speculated that this might have been a result of a battle or struggle for power, and that this proved he had lived a long and vibrant life. A man who, the authors provokingly speculated, might even have been personally responsible for bringing Mittel-Baxter culture into a previously uncivilized and backwoods area, and whose local significance had been enshrined in the manner of his burial.

The man read this section for a second time, and then closed the paper on his lap. He was very pleased. This was the best yet, much better and far, far older than even the seven ancient burials discovered together high on the Nazca plain at Cahuachi, each with fossilized excrement in their mouths. He felt pity for Mittel and Baxter, though he supposed it unlikely that the full stupidity of their conclusions would ever be brought to light. Perhaps the paper might even help maintain their tenure at the godforsaken midwestern university for which they toiled. He could, he supposed, get in touch with them and put them in the picture. He doubted that he would be believed, however, even though the truth of the matter was there for those who had eyes to see. Archaeologists were worse than most when it came to judging evidence on the basis of their pre-existing suppositions. It didn't matter whether they were flair players like Hancock and Baigent, or journeymen like Klaus Mittel and George Baxter: they all saw what they wanted to see. The traditionalists could only ever see ceremonial walkways, the New Agers their alien landing strips – however absurd each idea was in individual

157

circumstances. Some of the time each was correct, but they'd never know when – because in their minds they were right all the time. Only if you were prepared to examine the evidence dispassionately could you reliably divine the truth.

The skull lesion most certainly denoted a head injury, though one that had been far more significant than Mittel and Baxter realized – a childhood injury profound enough to wake a portion of the brain that in most men remained regrettably dormant. The evidence of *cribra orbitalia* was likewise not merely of import with regard to geographical positioning. It was indeed often related to iron deficiency, and sometimes anaemia of a congenital or haemolytic type, but it could also have a far more interesting genesis. Excessive exposure to lead could cause the condition. This, the man knew, wasn't 'poisoning' at all, but a gift that could combine with other factors and lead to alterations on a genetic level, changes that woke suppressed parts of the human genome and allowed them to become manifest.

It was not Mittel and Baxter's misinterpretation of the forensic evidence that was most at fault, however, but their inability to judge the true nature of the site. The man in the centre of the cemetery grid had not died first. Of course not. He had died last. In his own time, and by his own hand.

At the centre of his creation.

Chapter 14

The realtor leaned forward on his elbows, opened his little mouth, and spoke.

'And what kind of bracket would you be looking to purchase into? Please be frank. I appreciate that these are early days in our relationship, Mr, uh, Lautner, the dawn of our search for a potential home – but I'm going to come right out and say it'll promote our settling into a mutually beneficial mode if I know exactly how much you're hoping to realize into real estate at this time.'

He sat back in his chair and squinted knowingly at me, evidently pleased to have laid his cards on the table. There was to be no pulling the wool over this guy's eyes, I gathered wearily. If I only had eight dollars and change to spend, or was maybe hoping to barter with shiny stones, he intended to know right away. He was middle-aged and skinny with red hair, and his name – scarcely credibly – appeared to be Chip Farling. I'd already talked to several very similar people, and my tolerance was getting lower and lower.

'I'd like to cap it around six,' I said, briskly. 'For the time being. Something special, I may go higher.'

He beamed. 'That would be cash in full?'

'Yes it would.' I smiled back.

Chip's head bobbed, and his neat little hands moved a couple of pieces of paper around on his desk. 'Good,' he said, still nodding. 'Excellent. That gives us something to play with.'

Then he pointed a finger at me. I frowned, but soon realized this was merely a prelude to his next action, which involved putting his hand up to his chin and rubbing it while staring shrewdly into the middle distance. This I understood to mean he was thinking.

After nearly half a minute of this, he refocused. 'Okay. Let's get to work.'

He bounced up from the desk and walked briskly to the other end of the office, clicking his fingers. I sighed into my coffee, and prepared to wait.

I'd gone to UnRealty first, of course. It was shut. A notice on the door thanked people for their patronage and explained that the business was being wound up on account of the death of its owner. It stopped short of adding that his heir being an asshole had been an additional factor. I leaned close to the window and peered in. It doesn't matter if the desks and filing cabinets remain, if the computers sit in place and a year planner from the local print shop still hangs on the wall, vacation time firmly plotted by the office anal retentive – you can tell at a glance whether the business has air in its lungs. UnRealty didn't. I'd known it would be that way, but the sight still stopped me short. I realized I hadn't tried to work out whether the discoveries of the last forty-eight hours made my father's actions over UnRealty any more explicable. I couldn't make the thought go anywhere.

So I moved my body instead, and took myself around all the realtors I could find on foot. A rough index of a small community's status can be taken from the number of real-estate businesses on its streets. In Cowlick, Kansas, you're going to have to look real hard.

160

Everyone wants to get out, not in, their only proviso being that it not be through the medium of their death. Preferably. Somewhere of moderate wealth you'll find one or maybe two offices, mixed in amongst the other businesses by the process of commercial Brownian motion. In a place like Dyersburg you can't move for realtors. Even more than the scarves and the galleries and little restaurants, what that kind of town is selling is an idea: the notion that you could live this way all year round, that you could be one of the people who carve off a piece of the good stuff and put a sturdy fence round it; that you, too, could sit in a custom-built log home with cathedral ceilings and feel at one with God and his angels. All over America, the rich are carving out their hidey-holes. Ranches that used to support cattle or simply beauty are being bought up and subdivided into twenty-acre home sites where you can rejoice in stunning views and neighbours who are absolutely just like you. I'm not dissing this. I want one of these views, I want one of those lives, held in the palm of the mountains in one of the most beautiful landscapes in the world. I just don't want what comes with it. The golf. The part-share in a Lear jet. The cigar humidors. The bland, screamingly serene androids who live in these country clubs and lodges: bluff men with leather tans and firm handshakes, women with their steely eyes and surgery-tight cheeks; conversations that are one part greed, two parts self-satisfaction, and three parts eerie silence. I think it would drive me insane.

After a little while Chip reappeared, clutching a handful of prospectuses and two videotapes. 'Mr Lautner?' he breathed. 'It's time to find the dream.'

I dutifully watched the tapes, taking care to make occasional grunts or moues of interest. Neither had anything that resembled what I was looking for. Then I leafed through the brochures, which featured faux wooden lodges interior-decorated by some cowboy on drugs, or gleaming white boxes of such Modernist sterility they looked like they'd been discovered on the moon. The only thing that varied, and that not by much, was the hilariousness of the prices. It had been this way with each of the previous realtors. I was on the verge of dutifully asking for Chip's card and leaving, maybe calling Bobby to check how he was getting on with his task, when hidden amongst the glossies I found a single piece of paper.

'The Halls,' it said, in an attractive typeface. 'For people who want more than a home.'

It went on, in three paragraphs of curious restraint, to describe a small development up in the Gallatin range. Ski-in, ski-out convenience, naturally. End-of-the-road seclusion, of course. A two-hundred-acre tract of highlands, fashioned into a community of such ineffable perfection that Zeus himself probably bought a town house off plan – and yet the copy wasn't trying very hard to sell. There weren't even any pictures, or a price, which piqued my interest further.

I picked up one of the other brochures more or less at random, just making sure it was expensive.

'Like to take a look at this one,' I said.

Chip checked, nodded delightedly. 'It's a peach,' he said.

'And while we're in the area,' I added, as if an afterthought, 'let's check this place out too.'

I shoved the single piece of paper across the desk at him. He glanced at it, then folded his hands together and looked at me.

'With The Halls, Mr Lautner,' he said, judiciously, 'exclusivity is very much the name of the game. We would be looking at very high-end, in monetary terms. Six million would no longer suffice. By quite some margin.'

I gave him my best and richest smile.

'Like I said. Show me something special.'

An hour later I was listening to Chip talk about golf. Listening again. Still listening. Would, I was beginning to fear, always be listening. Early in the drive, before we were even out of Dyersburg, he'd quizzed me on my own commitment to the game. I'd rashly admitted I didn't play, though luckily stopped short of adding, 'Why on earth would I, for the love of God?' He stared at me for so long, with a look of such stunned incomprehension, that I said I was intending to take the sport up just as soon as I was settled – that this ambition was, in fact, foremost among my reasons for seeking a property of this type. He'd nodded slowly at this, and then taken it upon himself to give me a crash course on everything there was to know about the game. I reckoned I could bear about another fifteen minutes, and then I'd just have to kill him stone dead.

I'd already endured being shown the house in Big Sky, with its Sub-Zero appliances and Honduran maple flooring and fireplace handcrafted by some moron out of big pebbles. In the end I simply shook my head. Chip clapped me encouragingly on the shoulder – we were well on the way to best buddies by now – and we trooped back to the car. We drove back down to the main road and followed it further into the mountains, Chip giving me the lowdown on what he perceived to be two tiny flaws in Tiger Woods's game – both of which he considered to be related to racial temperament. The sky, which had been clear in the early morning, was now the same colour as the road. The Gallatin River, cold and fast, ran along the left. On the other side was a narrow band of valley, filled with trees. The mountains rose steeply on either side, a notch up into the Rockies. You travel far enough down this way you come up out onto a high plain and then swing east into Yellowstone Park, the caldera of a dormant supervolcano that last erupted six hundred thousand years ago. Molten rock has been gathering in the hollows underneath it since then, and my father told me one time that local legend speaks of a faint buzzing noise on the shores of Yellowstone Lake – the sound of pressure slowly building deep in the rock. Apparently the whole lot could go off again any day, plunging us right back into the Stone Age, which would be a bummer. The way I felt after an hour with Chip, I believed I was capable of triggering it just with the crackling coming from my head.

Twenty miles down the road, Chip pulled over to the right, apropos of nothing as far as I could tell. He hopped out of the car and hurried over to the fence, where I realized there was a small and unassuming gate. This surprised me. Big Sky, in common with most such places, had a huge great entrance, fashioned from trees that had already been sizeable when the Farlings were as yet unheard-of in the area. This gate looked like it led to nothing more than a service road. Chip leaned close to the right-hand side, and I saw his lips move. I realized that an intercom had been built into the post. He straightened and waited for a moment, peering into the sky. A few drops of rain had begun to fall. Then he turned back, listened to something, and walked back to the car.

By the time he was strapped back in, the gate had opened. Chip drove through, and it shut again immediately behind us. He steered us along a track beyond, two patchy lines where the grass had been flattened. He drove carefully, but I was still bounced around. I winced. 'Kind of a rustic thing, is it?'

He smiled. 'You'll see.'

The track continued for maybe a quarter of a mile, cutting at an angle away from the main road and toward a dense stand of trees. As we rounded them, the surface abruptly changed. From two worn lines in the scrub it switched to narrow but immaculate blacktop. I turned quickly in my seat, and saw that the main road was now invisible, obscured behind the trees.

'Cunning,' I said.

'Nothing is left to chance at The Halls,' Chip intoned. 'Those who choose to make their homes there can count on the very highest standards of privacy.'

The path turned back away from the river, winding behind an outcrop to follow a steep course up a gully, curving further and further around to remain obscured from the main road. Within a few minutes it was hard to believe that the highway had ever existed. Somebody had put genuine thought into The Halls. I was mildly impressed. 'How long has this place been here?'

'Development started seven years ago,' Chip said, peering through the windshield against the rain. 'Just a shame you're not going to see it in better weather. You get a good snowfall up here, you're going to think you've died and gone to heaven.'

'Have you sold many?'

'Not a one. There's only ten home sites, and they're in no hurry to fill the last few. Be honest with you, their leaflet does them no favours. I've told them they should have some pictures on it.'

We were approaching the top of a rise now, having climbed at least five hundred feet in a long series of zigzags.

'None of the other realtors I talked to seemed to know about it.'

Chip shook his head. 'It's our exclusive. Leastways, it is now.'

He winked at me, and for just a second I got a glimpse of the man Mr Farling might be when he shut his door behind him at night. I turned away, suddenly sure that it had been a good decision not to introduce myself by my real name. I got the feeling that Chip might have recognized the name Hopkins sooner than he would that of a dead Los Angeles architect, however many movies the latter's buildings had been in.

A gate now became visible, as we turned a final bend. It was made not of wood, but of very large pieces of mountain rock, and sat on the top of a small rise, so that what lay beyond was not visible. As we drew closer, I saw that the words 'The Halls' had been hand-carved into it, in the same typeface they'd used on their sales sheet.

'This is it,' Chip chirped, superfluously.

On the other side of the rise the road turned sharply left. I got an impression of a range of higher peaks half a mile away, but this was obscured by another bank of trees. Behind them was a fence that stretched off in both directions. The fence was very high, hiding everything that lay beyond. The rain was coming on harder, and the sky looked black fit to burst.

'The course is over the other side,' Chip said, switching seamlessly onto autopilot. 'Nine hole, Nicklaus *pere et fils* design, *bien sur*. As they say – who can beat a pair of Jacks? Naturally it's under cover at this time of year, and who needs it – with the Thunder Fall and Lost Creek runs barely minutes away? Imagine the convenience of world-class outdoor facilities, only a short drive from homes to delight the most discerning and sophisticated buyer.'

Indeed, I thought. And imagine me poking a finger up your nose.

'This is the entrance compound right here,' Chip said. A clump of low wooden buildings became visible, looming out of the murk. 'Club room, non-smoking bar, and a fine restaurant.'

'Have you eaten there?'

'No. But I gather it's, uh, extremely fine.'

He pulled the car over to park in a space to one side of the entrance to the building, alongside a row of very expensive cars. We got out, and he led me to the door. I tried to look around, to get a sense of the rest of the development, but the visibility was shot and we were moving quickly because of the rain now drumming down onto every horizontal surface.

'Fucking rain,' Chip muttered quietly. He noticed my surprise and shrugged apologetically. 'Sorry. Realtor's worst enemy.'

'What – worse than Hispanic neighbours?'

He laughed uproariously, clapped me on the back, and shepherded me through the door.

Inside, all was calm. To the left stretched a kind of club room, leather chairs around dark wood tables. It was empty. Down the end was a window, which on any other day would have afforded a doubtless stunning view. Today it was just a grey rectangle. To the right was a large fireplace, in which a well-behaved fire crackled. Very quietly in the background was the sound of Beethoven, one of the Sonatas for Violin and Piano. The reception desk was a smooth line of good wood, and on the wall behind it hung a piece of 'art'. As we stood, waiting for someone to respond to the buzzer Chip had rung, I reached inside my jacket and pressed a button on my cell phone. Assuming there was service out here, Bobby's phone would ring. We'd arranged that I'd do this if I'd found what I was looking for.

I had.

*   *   *

166

The induction process took half an hour. A slim and attractive woman of early middle age, augmented by many, many dollars' worth of hairstyling, sat us in the lounge and explained the glories The Halls had to offer. She was dressed in an immaculate grey suit and had bright little blue eyes and good skin, so I guess everything she said had to be true. She didn't give her name, which I thought was odd. In American commercial discourse we always give our designation: straight off, right at the top along with the handshake. A token of engagement. You know my name, so I can only want the best for you. There's no way I'm going to rip you off – what, me, your friend?

At the heart of The Halls, Ms No-Name explained, was a desire to reproduce the traditional ideals of 'community' – only better. Staff were on hand at all times to assist in any matter, however arcane. The residents apparently thought of them as friends – presumably that special kind of friend who has to do whatever you tell them, no matter what time it is or how boring and arduous the task. The restaurant's chef had previously worked at a glamour trough in Los Angeles even I had heard of, and residents could have meals delivered to their homes between the hours of 9.00 a.m. and midnight. Their wine cellars, she assured me, beggared belief. All houses were automated up to the hilt, with cable Internet access as standard. In addition to the much-vaunted golf club, there was a health club and a dining club and several others I didn't bother to commit to memory. Membership of each of these was mandatory for residents and came in at around a half-million dollars. Per year. Each. Throughout all this I was aware of Chip nodding vigorously beside me, as if unable to believe what a good deal this all was. I sipped my hundredth cup of coffee of the day – at The Halls, at least it was good – and tried not to blanch.

She concluded by observing that there were only three homes still available within the community, priced at between eleven point five and fourteen million dollars – barkingly expensive even by luxury real-estate standards. She rounded off with a heartwarming paean to the joys of residence that I could see Chip mentally taking notes from.

'Cool,' I said, when this eventually drew to a measured close. I put my cup down. 'So let's go have a look.'

The woman stared politely at me. 'Of course that's not possible.'

'I've been wet before,' I reassured her. 'Many times. I even went swimming once.'

'The weather is immaterial. We don't allow viewing of The Halls until a demonstration of appropriateness has taken place.' She glanced at Chip, who was looking carefully blank.

'Appropriateness,' I said.

'Financial and otherwise.'

I raised my eyebrows, smiled pleasantly. 'What?'

'What's being said, if I might intrude,' Chip said, 'is that, as we discussed on the way here, The Halls maintains a very . . .'

'I heard,' I said. 'So I'm to understand, Ms . . .?' I left a gap, but she didn't fill in her name. This woman was in no hurry to be my friend. 'I'm to *understand* that I can't get further than this room until I've jumped through some hoops you've set up to determine whether I'm suitable.'

'Correct.' She smiled brightly at me, as if at a child who had finally understood, after long and painful effort, how the relative positions of the big and little hands could be used to divine how long it was until bedtime. 'As Mr Farling should have made clear.'

'And what form would these demonstrations take?'

The woman reached into a folder and drew out a piece of paper. Placing it in front of me, she said:

'The placing of the cost in full of your proposed purchase, along with sufficient funds to cover club memberships for five years, in an escrow account. No mortgage or other part-payment options are entertained. The granting of access to your accountant or other agreed-upon representative for the purpose of establishing a general financial impression. A meeting by yourself with the full board of the community, which consists of the managing agents and a representative from each of the occupied properties, with a subsequent follow-up in subcommittee should this be required. Your nomination of two significant individuals – and by "significant" we mean that they should be so within our society at large – to whom the board may make reference with regard to your past and present situation. Assuming that all of the above proceeds smoothly, then you will be welcomed onto the property to be introduced to the finer points of the development, and to make your selection.'

'You've got to be kidding.'

'I assure you that I am not.'

I tried for bluster. 'Do you have any idea who I am?'

'No.' She smiled, turning her lips into a thin line resembling a recently healed scar. 'Which is precisely the point.'

I was dimly aware that the receptionist, a young man who had spent a great deal of time in the gym, was watching us. I held the woman's gaze for a moment, and then smiled back.

'Excellent,' I said.

After a moment's hesitation, she frowned. 'Excuse me?'

'This is exactly what I hoped for. Mr Farling has evidently divined my needs accurately.' My voice was now a little clipped, presumably to be in keeping with my shifted persona. 'Someone in my position requires certain assurances, and I'm pleased to say that you have afforded them.'

Ms No-Name began to look friendly again. 'We are in understanding?'

'Perfectly so. Might I be permitted to see plans of the available properties?'

'Of course.' She went back to her folder and pulled out two bundles. She unfolded these across the table and I scanned them quickly. They were detailed and well-annotated. What I saw interested me more than I'd expected.

'Intriguing,' I said. 'I'm sorry not to be able to examine them in the flesh on this occasion, but this is certainly enough to maintain my interest.' I started to refold the plans, then realized that a man as rich as I was supposed to be would let someone else handle such a menial task. Instead I stood up. The abruptness of this caught both of them unawares, and they hurried to follow. I thrust my hand out to the woman, and shook hers firmly.

'Thank you for your time,' I said, as if I was already thinking of other matters. 'I assume that any further questions I might have should be directed through Mr Farling?'

'That is the usual way. Might I ask how you heard of The Halls?'

I hesitated for a moment, as it occurred to me that admitting I'd just seen a piece of paper might sound weak.

'Friends,' I said. She nodded, almost imperceptibly. Good answer.

I bowed my head and walked out across the lobby, not waiting for Chip. Outside I stood under the awning for a moment, watching the rain come down. Even if I'd felt like braving it, I could now see that the buildings had been arranged in such a way that no glimpse of the community was possible from the outside. Chip hadn't been kidding about the privacy.

He emerged soon afterward and walked me across to the car. As I climbed in I noticed that another vehicle had just come in the gate and was heading quickly down the drive. It was large and black, some kind of all-terrain monster. It sloshed in an arc around the small lot and pulled up twenty feet away.

I took as long as I could to open the door, climb in, and get into my seat, even leaving one of my feet outside to prolong the operation. As I strapped myself in a man emerged from the building we had just left. He was about my height, with blond hair, and walked purposefully, head down. He didn't look at us at any point, and I got an impression of strong features but no more. As he walked toward the car, a man hopped out of the driver's seat and went round to open the back of the vehicle. With his back to us, the other man hefted a bag into it. The bag was large, and a kind of petrol blue colour. It had a paper customs strap around the handle, but I couldn't see the letters. Both men climbed into the car.

By then Chip had our own vehicle started. He reversed carefully out, headed up the drive, and we left The Halls behind.

Chip was quiet for most of the journey back into town. I got the feeling that he might have been grilled by No-Name after I'd left, and was berating himself for not being able to adequately answer her questions. Like who I was, and where I was from. Even I knew that these were the first things a realtor should find out from a potential customer, the amino acids of the transaction genome. My father used to say, in his rare expansive moments, that the way into a man's pocket is with his own hand: by which he meant ensuring that you know enough about him to approach him in the way to which he's most accustomed.

Chip did ask me what I thought of what I'd seen. I told him the Big Sky property was of no interest, especially after seeing what The Halls had to offer. He didn't seem surprised. I asked how many other people he'd shown up there. The answer was eight, in the past three years. All had gone through the procedures required by the management. None had been offered the opportunity to buy.

I stared at him. 'These people put fifteen, twenty million in an account, opened up their affairs, and *still* they didn't get in? They actually want to sell these houses, or what?'

'Exclusivity, Mr Lautner. That's the name of the game.' He glanced at me, to check he had my full attention. 'We're living in a strange world, and that's a fact. We've got the most beautiful country on the planet, the most hard-working folks, and yet we live cheek by jowl with people you wouldn't want in the same hemisphere. There's a historical dimension. We opened the doors too wide, and we shut them too late. We said "Come on, everybody, join us – we need warm bodies. Got us plenty of land to fill" – but we didn't spend enough time making sure we got the right *kind* of bodies. Didn't think clearly enough about the future. That's the reason why people like yourself come out West. To get away from the cities, from the hordes, to get in amongst their own folk. To get back to real ways of living. I'm not talking about race, though that does play a part. I'm talking about attitude. About quality. About people who are meant to be with each other, and people who aren't. That's why folks come to a place like Dyersburg. It's a kind of filter, and most of the time it works pretty good – but still you wind up with some people who just don't meet the grade. Students. Ski bums. White trash out by the freeway. People who don't understand. What are you going to do? Can't stop folks moving out here – it's a free country. Nothing you can do but look after your own.'

'And how do you do that?'

'You make the mesh of your filter a whole lot finer. You find some like-minded people, and you build yourself a king-sized wall.'

'That's what The Halls is?'

'One way of looking at it. But mainly, of course, a unique home-making opportunity.'

'You had the money, would you move in up there?'

He laughed, a short bitter sound. 'Yes, sir, I surely would. Meantime, I'll just work for my commission.'

We drove down out of the hills and onto the small high plain. By the time we got back to Dyersburg it was full dark, and the rain had begun to slacken a little. Chip parked up outside his office, and turned to me.

'So.' He grinned. 'What's your next move? Want to think about what you've seen, or can I bring you in to the office, maybe show you a few more options for tomorrow?'

'Wanted to ask you a question,' I said, looking through the wind-shield. The pavement was deserted.

'Shoot.' He looked tired but game. My mother always used to say that real estate wasn't a business for people who wanted to keep predictable hours.

'You said you just got the exclusive on The Halls. So there used to be another firm looking after it?'

'That's right.' He looked confused. 'What of it?'

'They ever get any sales that you know of?'

172

'No, sir. They didn't even have the account very long.'

'So how come they're not still representing it?'

'Guy died, business got wound up. Can't sell homes if you're dead.'

I nodded, feeling very quiet inside. 'How much would your commission be on one of those places? A fair sum, I'd imagine?'

'Quite a piece,' he allowed, carefully.

I let a pause settle. 'Enough to kill someone for?'

'*What?*'

'You heard me.' I wasn't smiling any more.

'I don't know what you're talking about. You think ... what? What the hell are you saying?'

There was something about his denial I didn't like, and you'd be amazed, and saddened, if you knew how good people are at lying, in even the most difficult circumstances. I'd waited. I'd been good. Now I was fed up with playing games.

I grabbed the back of Chip's head and yanked it forward, smacking his forehead hard into the steering wheel. I angled this so that the hard plastic caught him dead on the bridge of the nose. Then I wrenched his head back.

'I'm going to ask you a question,' I said, pulling his head forward to smack it into the steering column again. He made a quiet moaning sound as I held it there. 'This time, I need to believe your answer. I need to know you're telling me the truth, and you have just this one opportunity to convince me. Otherwise I'll kill you. Understand?'

I could feel his fevered nod. I pulled him back up by the hair once more. His nose was bleeding, and there was a livid welt across his forehead. His eyes were very wide.

'Did you kill Don Hopkins?'

He shook his head. Shook it, and kept shaking it, with the frantic and jerky movements of a child. I watched this for a while. I've dealt with many liars in my time, have been one myself for long periods. I have a good eye for it.

Chip hadn't killed my father. At least, not personally.

'Okay,' I said, before he broke his own neck. 'But I think you know something about what happened to him. Here's the deal. I want you to take a message. You going to do that for me?'

He nodded. Blinked.

'Tell the Nazis up in the mountains that someone is taking an interest in them. Tell them that I don't believe my parents died by accident, and that I will exact payment for what happened. Got that?'

He nodded again. I let go of his head, opened the door, and climbed out into the rain.

When I was standing outside I leaned down and looked at him. His mouth was downturned with fear and shock, blood running down his chin.

I turned away with my hands shaking, and went to find someone human.

Chapter 15

Bobby was leaning against the counter in my parents' house, sipping a glass of mineral water. He glanced up when I walked in, watched me stand and drip on the floor. It had rained virtually the entire time I had been walking.

'What have you done?' he asked mildly.

'Nothing.'

'Right,' he said, eventually. I took the glass and drank the remainder of the water in one swallow. Only when it was gone did I remember it had come from my parents' last shopping list.

'Is there any more of that?'

'A little,' he said.

'Don't drink it.' I put the glass on the counter and sat down at the table. As an afterthought I took my coat off, almost as if I'd heard a voice warning me that I'd catch my death. Through the window I could see that Mary's sitting-room light was on. I hoped she didn't find out I was still in town. It would have looked rude that I hadn't dropped by. Then I realized that I was sitting in a house with several lights on and a car outside, and so she probably knew already. I wasn't thinking very clearly.

Bobby waited, arms folded.

'So,' I asked. 'How was your day?'

'Come on, Ward,' he said irritably.

I shook my head. He shrugged and let it go. 'I checked out the scene of the accident. Given the position of the car they ran into, it's entirely conceivable your mother could have simply screwed up the turn. It's kind of sharp, it was dark, and it was pretty misty by all accounts.'

'Right,' I said, wearily. 'And she had only been driving for, like, forty years. Probably never come across a sharp turn before, never crossed that junction in all the time they'd been living here. I guess the cranberry juice and the mist was just all too much for her. I see it all now. It's a miracle the car didn't flip clean over the first row of buildings and bounce all the way to the sea.'

Bobby ignored me. 'There was a small gas station kitty-corner to the crash site, and a video rental a little further along the way. It goes without saying that neither of the guys I talked to were there the night of the accident. The video store is an independent run by two brothers. The one I talked to was certain that his brother hadn't known anything about it until he saw a police car arriving.'

'He didn't hear the sound of one heavy metal object running into another, think maybe something might be afoot?'

'You know what these places are like. Big old TV hung from the ceiling, John Woo movie playing ear-bleeding loud, guy behind the counter getting through the evening with beer and a joint the size of a burrito. Chances are you could have cracked him over the head with a hammer and he'd've barely blinked. So I went over to the gas station, and the guy gave me his manager's number. I called him and got the address of the guy on duty at the time.'

'Telling him what?'

'That I was assisting the police with their inquiries.'

'Great,' I said. 'That's going to get the local PD right up my ass.'

'Ward, who fucking cares?'

'I'm not Agency any more, Bobby. Out here in the real world, the cops can do things to you.'

Bobby flipped a hand, indicating this was a negligible concern. 'So I visited him. I confirmed that he saw nothing either. He heard a noise, but thought it was maybe someone dicking around at the back of the station. Dithered about calling the cops, and by the time he realized there'd been an accident outside and the station was safe, the police were already on the scene.'

'Okay,' I said. I hadn't expected anything to come of Bobby looking into the crash, but he'd been insistent. 'So what else?'

'So then, as agreed, I came here and looked around.'

'Find anything?'

He shook his head. 'Nope. Absolutely nothing.'

'I told you.'

'You did,' he snapped. 'You're not only handsome, Ward, you're always right. Man, I wish I was gay. I'd look no further. You're the best. So now you tell *me* something.'

'The place in the first scene of the video is called The Halls, and it's up a gully off the Gallatin Valley. You have to be really very rich to join, and they won't even let you *see* the houses until you've proved you're good enough.'

'The Halls? What kind of a name is that?'

I breathed out heavily. 'I don't know. Maybe they're thinking of Valhalla. Maybe they believe they're gods. That much money, maybe they are.'

'You're sure it's the one?'

'There's no question. The lobby was exactly the same as the one from the video, right down to the artwork. It's the place. And they are very, very tight about letting people join.'

'So how come you didn't put a call through?'

'I did. Must be there's no signal out there. I did it with the phone in my pocket, so I couldn't tell.'

'What was it like?'

'Just swell. I didn't see any of the residents, except one guy briefly at the end and I didn't get a good look at him either. Basically if you've got the money and don't want to be bothered by standard-issue earthlings, then this is the place for you. I got a peek at the house plans, though, and these are not your average trophy homes. They got someone pretty good on the case, someone who had something specific in mind.'

'Like what?'

I took a pen from my pocket and sketched. 'Exploded layout. Main living spaces elevated over the terrain. Central fireplaces withdrawn to internal room edges. Stained glass on the windows opposite the fires, and in skylights over corridors. Hanging eaves, horizontal banding of windows, conspicuous terraces.'

Bobby peered at the drawing. 'So? I tell you, my friend, that just sounds like a regular house to me.'

'Lot of this has been incorporated into standard design now,' I agreed. 'But the way it was put together in these drawings was textbook Frank Lloyd Wright.'

'So maybe they hired him.'

'Unlikely. Unless they hired a medium, too.'

'So they got someone who designs like him. There must be hundreds. Big deal.'

'Probably. But this kind of stuff isn't fashionable these days, never has been for this kind of development. Usually it's oil baron staircases, master bedroom suites, and look-at-me aren't-I-rich.'

'Sounds great.'

'But artificial. In the beginning, the places where we lived were sculpted from natural environments, not constructed from scratch. That's why so much modern architecture feels barren: it makes no organic use of the site. Wright's houses were different. The entrance route is made complicated to symbolize a retreat to a known safe haven, and the fireplace is withdrawn into the centre of the structure to take the place of a fire in a deep cave. Spaces within the house flow to allow internal prospect as an ultimate defence, additionally suggesting the adaptation of a naturally created space. External windows are banded so the sight lines reveal the outside without compromising the inside. Stained glass evokes a wall of vegetation that the inhabitants can see through, but which presents a wall from without. Humans feel most comfortable when they've got both prospect and refuge – when they've got a good view of the terrain they inhabit, but also feel protected and hidden. That's what his patterns provide.'

Bobby stared at me. 'You're an unusual man.'

I shrugged, embarrassed. 'I listened in class. My point is, you find me another development in the world looks like this, I'll kiss your ass.'

'Tempting, but I'm just going to take your word for it.'

'It's probably one of the reasons they don't let people see the houses beforehand. It's not what they'd usually lay out their millions for. Which means they have to have some other reason for making them that way.'

'So the developer's a Wright nut. Or they hired an architect who listened in class, too. I don't see how this leads anywhere, and I'd really like you to tell me what happened at the end.'

'I lost it with the realtor.'

'On site?'

I shook my head. 'Give me some credit. Back in town. There was no one around.'

'Is he dead?' The question was businesslike.

'Christ, no.'

'Why did you do this?'

'I didn't like him. Plus there used to be two firms looking after The Halls. Now there's only one.'

Bobby nodded, slowly. 'Your dad's firm being the one no longer on the case.'

'You're a bright guy.'

'I also take it, from the fact we're not discussing a homicide, that you don't think this realtor killed your folks. Despite the financial incentive.'

I shook my head. 'Not personally. But he's in bed with people who did. Why else is there footage of this place on the tape?'

Suddenly I was on my feet, walking quickly out of the kitchen. As I passed through the hall something tugged at me, but I couldn't work out what, so kept on going. Bobby followed me into the sitting room, where I went over to the coffee table.

I picked up the book lying there, and waved it at him.

'A book about the aforementioned great architect,' he said. 'So what? Your dad was a realtor. They're into houses. And an old guy. Old dudes really dig biographies. It's that and the Discovery Channel that keeps them going.'

'Bobby . . .'

'Okay,' he conceded. 'It's an interesting coincidence. Sort of.'

I wandered back out into the hallway and then came to a halt again. I felt like I had an engine of activity inside me, turning over, ready to run – but having no idea what direction to go in. 'You tossed this place hard?'

'I took carpet up, I went under floorboards, I went in the roof and shone a flashlight in the tank. I looked inside the phones. There's nothing else here. Of course – I can't tell what might be missing.'

'Me neither,' I said. 'I didn't come here enough. The only thing I noticed was the videos.' I frowned. 'Wait a second. When I was here the other day I put the mail here. Now it's gone.' I looked up at him, suddenly sure I was onto something.

'Relax, detective. A couple hours ago an old guy picked it up. Beaky, said he used to be your folks' lawyer. I let him in, explained I was a friend of yours. He was cool about it, though he did look like he wanted to check how many spoons I'd stolen.'

'Harold Davids,' I said. 'He said he'd keep coming by.'

Bobby smiled. 'Ward, you got enough weirdness going on without looking for it. Stop being so paranoid.'

We heard a loud shattering sound from the sitting room. We started moving, but not quickly enough.

*   *   *

It's not so much a sound as a feeling of immense pressure, and as shocking as being a child smashed across the face by someone who's never hit you before. If you're close enough to an explosion, what you're mainly aware of is the thud of your head and chest, an impact that turns any noise into a deep sensation, a feeling that the world itself has been knocked out of its path. The sound itself seems secondary, as if you're hearing it days afterward.

It seemed like I hit the wall immediately, hard, and smacked face-first into a row of pictures. As I hit the ground, my head full of white light and surrounded by falling glass, there was another, quieter explosion, and then I was hauling Bobby off the floor and toward the remains of the front door.

We careered down the path together, slipping and falling on the wet flagstones. There was another detonation behind us, much louder than the first. This time I heard the whistle and fizz of things flying around me, the *whupp-a* of air compressed and released. Bobby kept scrabbling forward, using his hands to keep us moving. I screwed up his efforts by turning to look back at the house, and we tangled and ended up skidding flat on our backs on the wet grass. The whole of the outer wall of the sitting room was gone, and the interior was already beginning to burn. I couldn't take my eyes off it. When you see a house on fire it's like watching the burning effigy of someone's soul, like seeing the grave work of worms writ sixty feet tall.

By the time I'd pushed myself up Bobby already had his phone out and was walking away, looking over the fence. I took a few paces back toward the house. Maybe I thought I could go back in and put the fire out. Or that I should save some things. I don't know. I just felt there ought to be something that I could do.

There was another small detonation, and I heard things break deep inside the house. The heat was building rapidly. The rain had slackened into a faint drizzle, and I remember feeling that this was about typical. It had rained hard all afternoon. Why not now?

Bobby ran back over to me, snapping his phone shut. He had a small cut on his forehead, which was dripping blood.

'They're on their way,' he said.

I couldn't imagine who he would be talking about. 'Who are?'

'The fire brigade. Let's go.'

'I can't go,' I said. 'That's their house.'

'No,' he said firmly, 'it's a crime scene.'

When we reached my car he walked quickly all around the vehicle, looking carefully at the ground. Then he went down on hands and knees in the mud and peered up underneath. He got back up, rubbed his hands, then unlocked the door. He squatted down and looked under the driver's seat, then popped the hood, walked round the front, and looked at the engine.

'Okay,' he said. 'We'll take the chance.'

He closed the hood and walked back to the driver's side. He stuck the keys in the ignition, winced at me, and turned his hand. The engine started, and nothing exploded. Bobby breathed out heavily, patted the top of the car.

'But we didn't hear anything,' I said. 'No car.'

'Not surprised,' he said, and his voice was a little shaky with relief. 'Area like this it's easier to lose yourself in backyards than on the road. I'd stash a car downhill and come the last quarter mile on foot. Though if it had been me, we wouldn't be having this conversation. You hear the way it kept futzing after the first explosion? Someone put it together in a hurry and screwed up.'

'What difference? Surely the first blast takes the whole lot up?'

'The sections got blown apart by the ignition charge. Someone tried to put together a real mother, and it blew itself apart before it could go off properly.'

'If we'd been in the sitting room, it would have been enough.' I abruptly rubbed my face with my hands. 'I guess Chip delivered the message.'

'Sure looks like it.'

'In which case . . .' I looked at my watch. 'They put this whole thing together in just over an hour, including someone getting down here.' I noticed I was bleeding briskly from a gash on the back of my hand, and wiped my jacket over it.

'Like I said. They rushed it.'

'They may screw up on the details, but they're definitely on the case, wouldn't you say?' In the distance I could now hear the sound of approaching sirens, and across the road I saw front doors opening.

'They bombed my parents' house,' I said, incredulously, turning to look at it once more. 'Like, with a *bomb*.'

The burning house looked bizarre, a point of utter wrongness amongst a street of perfect little dwellings. I turned to look at Mary's house across the hedge. A few lights were on, and the front door was open.

'You're dealing with Grade-A cocksuckers,' Bobby agreed, slapping the top of the car again. 'And now let's leave.'

But by then I was running, slipping and careering down toward the gate. I heard Bobby swear and start after me. Near the end of the path I thrashed my way straight through the hedge and into Mary's front yard. I'd barely made it into her property before Bobby grabbed my shoulder and spun me round.

I shrugged him off, tried to keep walking up the yard. He reached for me again, but faltered when he saw what I'd seen, and then he was moving faster than me.

She was lying half on the porch, her head and shoulders tipped downward onto the steps, one arm thrown out by her side. At first I thought maybe a heart attack, until I saw the blood all over her, the pool already turning sluggish on the weathered wood. Bobby dropped to one knee beside her, supporting her head.

'Mary,' I said. 'Oh, Jesus Christ.'

Between us we pulled her gently round so that she was lying level. Her breathing was ragged. Enough light was thrown by the fire next door to make the lines in her face look like canyons. Bobby was searching through the folds of her clothing, finding hole after hole, trying to stanch blood that didn't seem to be flowing as fast as it

183

should. She coughed, and a slug of something dark glotted up into her mouth.

Before this I had only ever seen an old woman, one of those people who clutter up the lanes of supermarkets and stand waiting for buses, who know or care about what gift people are supposed to give on which anniversary, who look papery and cold and as if they can never have been any other way. People who can never have been drunk, or clambered over forbidden fences, or moved, giggling, so that someone else gets stuck with the wet patch in the bed. Dry old sticks who you cannot credit with having loved someone, not someone alive anyhow, not someone who wasn't just a memory, whose resting place was now decorated with fading flowers that only she remembered to bring. Now I saw someone else. Someone she'd once been and presumably remained, beneath the patina of failing cells and dry skin and wrinkle canyons and grey hair curled and cut short. Behind the disguise the years had conferred, behind the mistaken assumption that because of her age she had never been, and wasn't still, somebody real.

And then her throat clicked, and a full bladder voided, the smell warm and acrid. Her eyes seemed to go from moist to dry in an instant, as if fast-forwarded. Perhaps it was the coldness of the air, but it looked as if she'd been pulled away in front of our eyes, and pulled away fast.

Bobby looked slowly up at me. I stared back. I didn't have anything to say.

'What happened?' I asked. It was the first thing I had been able to say in ten minutes. 'What the *hell* happened back there?'

Bobby was peering hard through the windshield, whipping his head back and forth to look up side roads as we sped past them. All were early-evening quiet. Mary's body was two miles behind us now, still lying on her porch. It would receive medical attention there faster than we could have got it to a hospital, and anyway it was dead without hope of reprieve. Both Bobby and I knew that.

He shrugged. 'She got in the way. Like I said, someone came in over the yards. She heard something, came out. So they emptied half a gun into her. I'm sorry, man.'

'Someone comes down here to blow me up, bringing a gun with a silencer just in case. A harmless old lady gets in the way and they whack her. Just like that.'

'These people are serious, Ward, and they really don't like you at all.'

He yanked the car round a sharp left and then we were back down in the main part of town. A fire truck flashed past us along the main drag, heading in very much the wrong direction to get to the house.

'Where the fuck is he going?'

A car behind us honked. Bobby and I turned as one and a guy in a pickup indicated that the lights had changed and maybe we'd like to move. Bobby pulled out, and headed down the road after the fire truck.

'The truck's going the wrong way, Bobby.'

'I told them the address just as you told me. It was good enough to get me there.'

'But why the . . .' I stopped. We could both now see the orange light up ahead.

Bobby abruptly pulled over, without signalling. We got another stern honk from the oldster in the pickup, who turned to stare heavily at us as he passed. Neither of us really paid him much mind. We could see now that the Best Western, or at least a small part of it, was on fire. I stared at it in frank disbelief, wondering how Dyersburg had suddenly come to reside within one of the circles of Hell.

'Get closer,' I said, faintly.

He drove slowly, and after a block left the main drag to come around at the hotel along a side street. We stopped at the top, putting us about a hundred yards from the hotel. From here we could see that the fire was relatively small, only affecting a forty-yard stretch of one wing. The hotel would survive to host another convention. Four fire trucks were already in attendance, and a fifth joined them as we watched. The other end of the street was already thronged with people, and more were walking quickly past the car, hurrying to get a better view of the excitement. Half of the town's police force appeared to be in attendance.

'That start round about where your room was?'

I didn't even answer. I felt sick. For some reason attacking the hotel felt like more of a personal wound than the house had done. I wondered if my neighbours had been in, the people in the rooms around me.

'Ward, this message you sent them,' Bobby said, 'what exactly did you *say*?'

'This is ridiculous,' I said. 'This is completely out of hand.' Then: 'What about the house? What are they . . .'

'They've probably got someone up there already. Other neighbours will have called it in. And before you even get around to wondering, your stuff is safe.'

'What stuff?'

'Well, not your clothes. Look in the back.' I turned and saw my laptop bag in the backseat of the car.

'Never assume you've got refuge,' he said, tapping his fingers on the steering wheel, and watching the fire. 'I'm a prospect man myself. Keep what you need within reach. I think now would be a good time to blow Dodge.'

I wanted to go up into the hills and kill someone. Bobby read my mind, and shook his head firmly. 'Once this fire is under control they're going to find which room went up first. Chances are they'll have taken more time and made it look halfway credible. But add it to the house and you're going to leap straight to Dyersburg's Most Wanted.'

'In what fucking sense? I didn't do anything.'

'There an insurance policy on your folks' house?'

'Yes.'

'Big one?'

I sighed. 'Probably. I didn't listen. And then they'll find Mary and some bright cop will decide to dust her down just in case. That much blood, they may get some latents. Your prints on file, Bobby?'

'You know they are.'

'Mine, too. You're right. It's time to leave.'

Twenty minutes later we were at Dyersburg airport.

Chapter 16

Zandt reached Beverly Boulevard at nine in the evening. He was exhausted, and his feet hurt a good deal. He was also drunk.

At 3.00 a.m. he'd stood outside the cinema where Elyse LeBlanc had last been seen. Cinemas look strange at that time, as do stores and restaurants. In the small hours they seem odd and arbitrary and edificial – as if we are explorers who have missed, by a bare decade or two, whatever civilization brought them into being. A few hours later he watched the house where Annette Mattison spent her last evening with a friend. He recognized the woman who came out at seven o'clock, dressed in a business suit, on her way to the television mines. Zandt had interviewed Gloria Neiden on more than one occasion. She had aged a great deal in the past two years. He wondered if she was still in touch with Frances Mattison. Their daughters had visited with each other many times, and always walked the three short blocks home. It was the usual arrangement. They lived, after all, in a very nice neighbourhood, up in Dale Lawns,

90210 – and surely one of the reasons why you paid seven figures for a house was so that you could walk under the stars after dark. Zandt suspected that the relationship between the two mothers would have become strained, if not altogether dead. When Zoë Becker had mentioned Monica Williams, her voice acquired a colourless tone – though the latter could hardly be held responsible for Sarah's electing to wait out the time until her father came to pick her up. Their small community had failed. When this happens, you ask what it's for, and look for someone to blame. The people within the walls are closest.

Zandt turned away as Mrs Neiden's car swished past. It was possible she would recognize him, and to have watched for longer would have made him feel unwelcomely like another man, the one who had stood outside her house, perhaps in the same spot, two years before.

He walked on. By late morning he had been in Griffith Park, at the place where Elyse's body had been found. There was nothing to mark the space, though for a while there had been flowers and he found the remains of a broken glass jar. He stood there for a long time, looking out over the hazy city, at the places where a million people worked and slept and lied, turning rank in the urban field.

It was soon after this that he first went into a bar. And, a little later, into another. He kept walking in between and afterward, but more slowly, feeling his sense of purpose bag around the seams. He had walked these routes many times. All they had brought him was blood and breakage. He could still hear the voices that had propelled him to his feet when Nina left, the cries of the missing – but obscured by daylight and rationality they were too faint to lead him anywhere. His shirt became untucked, and when he passed other pedestrians he was aware of their scrutiny. It's claimed that you can tell the police, especially a policeman, by his eyes, a gaze that measures and assays, that judges from a position of suspicion and strength. Zandt wondered if you could also tell someone who was not a cop any more, by the look of emasculation, of having turned away. He had known this city once, known it from inside. He had walked the streets as one to whom the residents turned in times of chaos. A part of the immune system. Now he lived without this sanction. He was no longer identified, was without fame or its equivalent in function. He was just a man on the street in a city where very few people walk – and where those who did regarded him with caution. It was a habitat as real as any steppe or shaded valley, no more different to the countryside than Death Valley was to Vermont, or Kansas to the bottom of the sea. The only distinction was in the people, the smog-stained and battle-weary. All the people.

By late afternoon he had stood, weaving slightly now, by the side of a side road in Laurel Canyon. The bushes that had once grown there had been uprooted and replaced with a stretch of pavement perhaps a couple of feet longer than Annette's body. By now he was quite drunk, but not so that he didn't spot the person watching him from the safety of the nice house across the road.

Within a few minutes a man emerged from the house. He was wearing jogging pants, a pale grey vest. He looked very healthy.

'Can I help you?'

'No,' Zandt said. He tried a smile, but the man wasn't having any of it. Had Zandt seen the result of his attempt, he probably wouldn't have blamed him.

The man sniffed. 'Are you drunk?'

'I'm just standing here a moment. Go back inside. I'll be gone soon.'

'What is it, anyway?' The man turned slightly, revealing that he was holding a phone in the hand behind his back.

Zandt looked at him. 'What?'

'That pavement thing. Why's it there? It's useless.'

'Somebody died there. Or was found there, dead.'

The man's face became more open. 'You knew them?'

'Not until she was dead.'

'So what do you care? What was she – a working girl?'

Zandt's throat constricted. Death's sliding scale, as if whores and

190

addicts and young black men were little more than unwanted pets, as if they had never run laughing to the return of a parent, or said a first word, or spent long nights wondering what their stocking would hold.

The man took a hurried step back. 'I'll call the cops,' he warned.

'They'd be too late. Maybe you'd rate one more slab of pavement, but I wouldn't bet on it.'

Zandt turned and walked away, leaving the man no different and no wiser.

When he finally reached Beverly Boulevard he went past the Hard Rock Café, tucking in his shirt and straightening his jacket, pulling his shoulders back. He walked into the Ma Maison hotel without incident, steered right and straight to the gents in the bar. A splash of water and no one but a barman could tell he didn't belong. He went back out into the bar and sat at a low table where he could see the street. After the miles of walking, the softness of the couch made him feel like he was sitting on a cloud. A pleasant young man promised to bring him a drink.

While he waited, Zandt looked out at the road where Josie Ferris had disappeared. It was not quite the last scene that related to the crimes, but he was unwilling to go and stand by the school Karen had attended, or outside the house where his family had once lived. And there was no point going back to that other, final place. It was a place he had created. Though it had a bearing, it couldn't help him now. It had not helped him then. Standing above the dead body of the man he had killed had done nothing but prove the fineness of the distinctions we turn into laws.

Jennifer had known what he had done. He told her, two days later, when the sweater had arrived. It had not been the death of them, not at first. She'd understood his actions, condoned every-thing except the mistake. They tried to hold it together. They failed. His position had been untenable. Either he bore the horror of Karen's disappearance and remained strong for his wife, while feeling like he was going to break apart into small sharp pieces: or he could reveal the pain he was in. When he did so he lost the male claim to strength without gaining any foothold on the high ground of revealed trauma that was the preserve of women. It was her job to express the outrage; it was his to withstand it.

He decided he could no longer pretend to be a policeman at around the same time that she decided to go back to her parents. Someone had stolen their golden egg, and the goose that laid it had died.

Now, when he looked back, he believed he had been most in the wrong. It was his rigidity that had enabled the fault lines to form. She would have let him be weak for a spell. Women are often wiser when it comes to understanding which rules can be allowed to bend. Relationships require flexibility, particularly in times of high stress, those periods when they feel like a desperate pact against a world of unbearable darkness. Strong pairings will fight to retain an equilibrium, regardless of short-term changes in balance. Though it was a double-edged consolation, this realization had enabled him to stay alive. Sometimes the key to regaining one's life is looking back at a terrible situation and realizing that you were partly to blame. Before you see this, you feel wronged, hurt – and cannot find any peace. But 'It's unfair' is the cry of a child, of someone who does not realize that causal relationships act in two directions. When you come to understand that you were also at fault, the pain slowly fades away. Once you realize that you made your own bed, it becomes easier to lie in it, however hard and soiled it may be.

When his Budweiser arrived he nursed it a while, ostensibly looking out of the window. In reality he was, as he had been all day, trying to see a set of facts differently. In a crime where there was no evidence to speak of, the best you could do was try new ways of fitting the information together. Most crimes, in their essence, boiled down to a single sentence. Fingerprints and an affair and a hastily concealed knife and debts and an exploded alibi; these were the business of the courts, requisites for tidying away. The true crime, in all its glory, boiled down to this: people killed each other. Husbands killed their wives. Women killed their menfolk, too, and parents their children, and children their parents, and strangers other strangers. People took things they didn't own. People set fire to places, for money, or because there were people inside. When each manifestation had been tucked away into its judicial drawer, the truth still remained at large. You could take any two people and put the word 'killed' between them.

Zandt had been able to make no headway in trying to work out what The Upright Man might want from his victims. Why they were being punished. Had they failed him by not loving him, not responding to his advances? Had they been too frightened, or not frightened enough? Had they failed by breaking, by not showing some of the strength he looked for and wished to steal?

He noticed that he'd finished his beer, and twisted in his seat, looking for the young waiter. There was no sign of him, though the other people dotted around the lounge seemed to have recently been served. He watched them for a while. Strangers, drinking alcohol to feel more comfortable. To sand off the edges of anxiety. Everybody did. Americans – except for a brief experiment that led to an explosion of crime never seen before or since. The Germans and French, heartily. The Russians, with melancholy seriousness. The English, too, beery maniacs. They spent their hours in bars and pubs and at home, making everything blurred. They needed the fizzing mask, the glue.

Eventually a man appeared. He was dressed in black with a white shirt, exactly as the previous barman had been – but ten years older and considerably less sunny in demeanour. Whereas the younger man's hopes of selling a screenplay or shouting 'Cut!' were probably still fresh, this man appeared on the edge of a curdled acceptance that Hollywood's actresses would continue to survive without his good loving. He regarded Zandt suspiciously, waiter radar telling him that this was a man who was neither resident in the hotel nor waiting to meet anyone in particular.

'Same again, sir?' Said with an inclined head, a gesture of cordial irony: we both understand that Sir is not of the type one prefers, is moreover somewhat drunk, and not clad to an adequate standard.

'Where's the other guy?'

'Other "guy", sir?'

'The waiter who served me before.'

'Shift change. Don't worry. It'll be the same beer.'

As the waiter walked off, languidly, bouncing his tray on his knee, Zandt briefly considered shooting him. As a lesson to all the other waiters who somehow managed to suggest that the people paying their wages were scum. A long-overdue wake-up call. Perhaps word would get out to the store assistants, too, even the ones on Rodeo Drive. Zandt could still, would always, remember an incident that had taken place one anniversary afternoon six or seven years before. An occasion when he had taken his wife to an expensive store to buy a blouse, and they had left soon afterwards; Jennifer awkwardly clutching a bag, Zandt shaking with unexpressed fury. She had seldom worn the shirt. It was stained by how small she had been made to feel while buying it.

The memory made him feel far worse than he had before. He was sliding one of the remaining pieces of stationery closer, intending to make notes on something – anything – when suddenly he paused. He could see the waiter, standing behind the counter in the next section of the bar, pouring out his beer.

It was a Budweiser. Same as he'd had last time. That was to be expected. The previous waiter would have left a chit showing how much he owed, what he had been served so far.

An indication of what he wanted, in other words.

Of what his preferences were.

When the waiter arrived with the beer, he found an empty seat and a ten-dollar bill.

Chapter 17

The house was high up in the Malibu hills. It was small, and unusual, arranged as a series of rooms like a tiny motel. To get from one living area to the next you went outside and walked along a covered path, re-entering the building via another outer door. It stood on the edge of a cliff and was approached down a steep and twisting lane that was inadequately lit. It wasn't somewhere you'd find yourself by accident. It was cheap to rent, despite its position, because it was on unstable ground and one step away from being condemned. The combined living room and kitchen area, which was large and glass-sided and easily the best feature, had a crack across the centre of its concrete floor. You could get most of a fist down into it, and the sides differed in height by over two inches. Outside, on the landward side of the lot, was a small swimming pool. It was empty, the pipes having been melted in a brushfire years before she'd come to live there. It took a certain courage to sleep at night.

Nina had spent the evening on the patio, at the rear of the house, her back against the wall and legs splayed out in front of her. Usually the view was of the ocean, with just a few trees and bushes before the land shaded sharply away. No other houses were visible. Tonight the sea was invisible, too, obscured behind a mist that seemed to start at the ends of her feet. It was sometimes this way, and she wondered if she didn't prefer it. A place on the edge of being, in which anything could happen. She had meant to bring a glass of wine out with her, but forgot. Once she had sat down she seemed becalmed, unable to summon the will to go back in and confront the refrigerator.

She had spent the day looking for Zandt. He had not been at the hotel, nor on the Promenade, or anywhere else she had tried. Early evening she had driven all the way out to sit and watch the house where he had once lived. Other people owned it now, and he had not appeared. She had driven home again. So all she could do was sit. The living room behind her was lined with bookshelves filled with texts and papers and notes. She did not wish to look at any of them. She didn't want to talk to anyone in the Bureau. Her position there was not as it had been before. The Upright Man had side-lined her career – not because of their failure to apprehend him, though that had not helped. Rather because she had continued to leak information to a policeman who had been ordered not to inter-fere after the disappearance of his daughter. Agents had lost their jobs for far less. She had managed to keep hers, but things were dif-ferent now. Once she'd had Monroe's ear, had been a comer. Now their relationship felt stretched and tired.

She felt alone, and afraid. Her fear was unconnected with the loneliness. She was used to solitude and did not mind it, despite a nature that yearned for something else. She had ended the affair with Zandt for one reason only. The more she came to care about him, the less she had felt willing to destroy the life he already had. The fact that it had been destroyed anyway had made it impossible to explain this fact to him when he asked. Not impossible, perhaps: sentences could have been framed to convey the information. But somewhere within them might have been something that betrayed her. Betrayed the fact that, two weeks after Karen's disappearance, she had witnessed a thought that had floated unbidden across the back of her mind. That if this thing had been going to happen, the destruction of this family, she might as well have been the one to do it.

There had been other men in the meantime, though not many, and there would presumably be more. Finding men was no real problem, at least the ones you had little desire to keep. It was more the despair that ground her down, the endless procession of terrible events. If this was what we were like, then perhaps there was nothing to be done. If you looked at what our species did to its own kind and to other animals, you had to ask if we didn't deserve whatever we had coming to us, whatever autonemesis we brought merrily into being; if the rough beasts that slouched towards Bethlehem were anything more than our own prodigal children, coming home.

At about nine-thirty she stood up and went back inside. As she opened the fridge, which held nothing except a half-drunk bottle of wine, she kept half an eye on the small television on the counter. More coverage of the killings in England, though with the sound turned down she could not tell what was being said, or revealed, or alleged. Some dismal facts or other, some new reason to feel sad.

She shut the door again, the bottle untouched, and leaned for a moment with her face against its cool surface.

She looked up when she heard a sound from outside. After a moment the noise resolved into the sound of tyres on the gravel of the road. She walked quickly across the room, stepping over the crack, and got a gun from her bag.

The car came to a halt outside, and she heard a muffled conversation. Then the sound of a door slamming shut, and the noise of tyres again, reversing back up the drive. Footsteps, and a knock on the door. Hand behind her back, she went to open it.

Zandt stood outside. He looked breathless, and a little drunk.

'Where the hell have you been?'

'All over.' He walked into the room, stopped, and looked around. 'I love what you've done with the place.'

'I haven't done anything to it.'

'That's what I mean. It looks exactly the same.'

'Not every chick is obsessed with interior decoration.'

'Yeah, they are. I think you must be a man in disguise.'

'Damn. You got me.' She stood with arms folded. 'What do you want?'

'Just to tell you I killed the right man after all.'

By the time she came out onto the patio with the bottle, he had already started talking.

'The problem was that we couldn't work it like other cases. It didn't respond to normal investigative procedure. When people disappear you trace back through the contacts, work it down. You talk to the families, their friends, the people in their environments. You're looking for an intersection. A bar they went to at different times on different nights. Memberships to the same gym. A friend of a friend of a friend. Some point of confluence that says these people are linked by something other than now being dead. By something before, something that *led* to their deaths. With The Upright Man we had multiple disappearances but only superficial similarities. Same sex, same age, more or less. All pretty. So what? There's boys sitting in rooms all over the city praying for girls like this. Women, come to that. It's a consensual desire, not psychopathology. Apart from the long hair. That's the only thing that can be pointed at, the only preference – along with the fact the girls came from families where money isn't a big issue. They're not runaways, they're not junkies. Which just means that what he did was more difficult, because girls like this are harder to steal. It's not a lead.'

He paused. Nina waited. He wasn't looking at her. He didn't even seem aware of her presence. He stood on the very edge of the patio.

From the doorway his outline looked indistinct. When he started again, he spoke more slowly.

'A man is looking for something. He has an anxiety, something that can only be resolved through a certain course of action, which he has become aware of through accident or trial and error. He hasn't allowed it to happen for a while. He's been good. He hasn't done the bad thing. He's kept himself to himself, and not done anyone any harm. He's never going to do it again. He's not weak – he doesn't need it. Not now, maybe not ever. Maybe he's never going to do it again. Maybe he can leave it behind. Maybe it's over.

'But gradually . . . it stops being okay. It starts getting harder. His concentration goes. He finds he can't function. He can't focus on his job, his family, his life. He's getting tense. Ideas start recurring, patterns of fantasy. He's becoming anxious, and what makes it worse is that he knows what is causing it. He knows the only thing that is going to resolve it. He begins to revisit old campaigns in his head, but they don't help. He may find it difficult to remember them in any detail. They don't diminish the way he's feeling now. It's yesterday's news. You can't resolve a current anxiety through something that has already happened: last year's good times do not combat this week's misery. He needs something in front of him, something he hasn't done yet. Not even the talismans help, the things he kept, the proof that he's done it before. All they do is remind him that it's possible. He needs to do it so much and knows that he can't live without it – and in any event, no matter how hard he tries, he's already done it and there can never be any real peace or any hope of forgiveness. His life is tainted and he can't go back.

'And so, accidentally, almost, he starts looking again. He may tell himself that this is all he is doing. Looking. That he is more in control now. That this time he will only look, not take. But he will start looking again, and once he has taken this step there can be only one outcome. He will forget how bad he felt last time, as the memory of a hangover will not stop you drinking next Friday night. He may have done it so many times that he no longer feels bad about it even in prospect. It may be the only thing that has meaning to him. He will go to a place he's been before, or somewhere like it. He will have a plan by now. This is a dangerous business, and he will have developed ways of reducing the risk. This is where the intersections come into play, because the intersections are the man, and lie at the heart of his paths. They come from the places where he feels safe, where he wanders as himself. Some will think of it as a hunting ground. Others will just think of it as somewhere they blend in, or where nobody watches, where they're invisible. Where he is not weak, but has power; where he is not part of the crowd, but above it. His hidden places, the ones where people come to find him, where the thing he is looking for walks in out of the evening and into a night he has planned for them. He will watch for a while, and then finally one night, when the girl turns as she walks down the street, she will see someone behind her and then it will all be over until it's time to clean up and feel sick and promise God or whoever you think listens that he will never, ever do it again.'

'And that's how you found him,' Nina prompted.

'No. We found nothing that tied all the girls together. We never came close to finding the man because we could never work out where he'd first seen the girls. That's why, when Karen disappeared, I ended up falling back on the places the girls had been taken from. They were the only sites we knew were linked to the killer. It was all I had left. There's no link. No way of finding one. Except . . . last time he did come back. He came back to visit a site, and I thought it was to relive what had happened there. And once I'd seen him at two of them, I believed he was the man. And so I tracked him, and I found him.'

'But then,' Nina said, choosing her words carefully, 'you discovered that he wasn't the man after all.'

'Wrong. The man I killed *was* the man who abducted some of the girls.'

'Are you saying the one now is a copycat?'

'No. I'm saying I killed the waiter, not the man who ordered the beer.'

'I don't understand.'

'The man who sent the parcels was different from the one who abducted the girls.'

Nina stared at him. 'The Upright Man decides he needs a girl, and he just puts in an order? And then this guy just goes out and snatches them to order? Like a fucking pizza delivery?'

'That's why no more girls disappeared after Karen, even though someone delivered the package. The man who abducted them was gone. The killer was still alive.'

'But serial killers don't work that way. Okay, there's been a few who worked in pairs. Leonard Lake and Charles Ng. John and Richard Darrow. The Wests, depending how you look at it. But nothing like this.'

'Not until now,' he agreed. 'But we live in a changing world, where everything is bigger, brighter and better. Convenient. On-demand.'

'Then how come there were no links between all of the girls? The abductor must have had a standard MO, like you said. We should have been able to find it.'

'If it was the same man each time.'

Nina just looked at him, and blinked. 'There were *two* abductors?'

'Maybe more. Why not?'

'Because, John, because The Upright Man has only taken one potential victim in the last two years. Sarah Becker.'

'Who says it's just him?' He picked up the wine bottle, found it was empty. 'You must have some more wine somewhere.'

Nina followed him as he walked back into the house. He opened the fridge, stared with disbelief at its emptiness.

'John, I don't have anything more to drink. What do you mean, who says it's just him?'

'How many serial killers you got working in California at this time?'

'At least seven, maybe as many as eleven. Depends how you define . . .'

'Exactly. And those are the ones you know about. In one state, and a state that comes way down the rankings. Call it a hundred and fifty nationwide, and say ten to fifteen of them can afford twenty thousand a pop. Maybe more. Maybe a lot more. That's a client base. A big one. You could get a fucking *bank loan* on the back of that business plan.'

'Even if you're right, which frankly remains to be proved, how does this help us find Sarah Becker?'

'It doesn't,' he admitted, and his nervous energy abruptly disappeared. He rubbed his forehead with his fingers, hard. 'I assume the Feds are still running down any lines leading from the family?'

Nina nodded.

'Well,' he said, sounding tired and defeated. 'Then I guess we just wait.' He was watching the mute television. They were still doing a wrap-up of recent mass murders, background to the high street massacre in England. 'Have you been following this?'

'I've tried not to,' she said. They stood in the kitchen and watched it together awhile. There was no real news. They still didn't know why the man might have done it. A search of his house had turned up some generic hate literature, another gun, a computer full of porn, and a very bad painting of a number of dark figures against a white background, like wraiths in front of snow.

None of it was judged to be important.

Chapter 18

'You have to give me something more than water,' Sarah had said.

Her voice sounded weak, even to herself. She had repeated this sentence many times. It had become the first thing she said every time the lid was removed.

'Don't you like the water?'

'I like the water. Thank you for the water. But I need something more. You have to give me something more than water.'

'What do you want?'

'I need food. Something to eat.' She coughed. She seemed to be coughing a lot now, and when she did it made her feel nauseous.

'We eat too much these days,' the man said. 'Far too much. It's killed for us and grown by the ton and then delivered to our door and we sit like pigs at the trough. We're not even hunters any more. Just scavengers. Hyenas with coupons who pick through the shrink-wrapped leavings of people we've never even met.'

'If you say so. But I have to eat.'

'I have to eat I have to eat I have to eat,' the man chanted. He seemed to like the sound the words made, and continued repeating the sentences for some minutes.

Then he was silent for a while, before observing: 'Once we would go for days without food. We were lean.'

'Right, the Great Depression. Dust Bowl years, blah.'

The man laughed. 'That was yesterday and of no interest to us. I meant before the invasion.'

'The invasion?' Sarah asked – thinking: Okay, here we get to it. Little green men. The Russians. The Jews. Whatever. She coughed violently again, and for a moment everything went white in front of her eyes, and when he answered his voice sounded as if it was coming from a long way off or as if he was using one of those things like Cher did when she sang 'Believe'.

'Yes, invasion. What else would you call it?' he asked.

She swallowed, screwed her eyes shut and then opened them again. 'I wouldn't call it anything. I'm too hungry.'

'You can't have any food.'

Something in the man's voice made her suddenly very afraid. He didn't sound like he meant she just couldn't have any today. He sounded like he meant she couldn't have any, period. In a surprisingly short time she had adapted to her current circumstances, aided by an increasing sense of dislocation. But the threat of nothing to eat, ever, was enough to momentarily jog her completely back to reality.

'Look,' she said, voice unsteady now, 'you must want something from me. There must be some reason you are doing this. Please just get on with what you want and either kill me or give me some food. *I have to have something to eat.*'

'Open your mouth.'

She did so eagerly, saliva immediately flooding into her mouth. For a moment nothing happened, and then a hand appeared. It wasn't holding anything that looked like food, but only a small piece of white paper. The hand pressed it to her tongue briefly, and then withdrew. Sarah started to cry.

204

The man said nothing for a while, and then tutted. 'No change,' he said. 'Stubborn little genome.' The piece of white paper fluttered down into the hole to lie beside her. 'You haven't really learned anything, have you?'

She sniffed. 'You haven't told me anything.'

'I'm beginning to wonder about you,' he said. 'I thought you were different. That you might change. I came for you personally. I had plans for us. But now I'm wondering if you'll do after all.'

'Oh yes? Why's that?'

'You're lazy and spoiled and not coming on very well.'

'Yeah? Well you're a wacko.'

'And you're a silly little bitch.'

'Fuck you,' she said. 'You're a fucking nutcase and I'm going to escape and smash your head in.'

She kept her mouth shut as he poured the water.

He hadn't come back for a long time.

Chapter 19

We got to Hunter's Rock at three o'clock in the morning, after a short flight and a long drive. When we landed in Oregon I drove down the highway over the state line, and then along roads that I recalled from long ago – feeling as if I were retracing the steps of an explorer I'd only read about, rather than revisiting old ground of my own. Gradually we began to pass places I had known better, and it got harder. I chose routes that I would not have taken for directness. I think Bobby realized. He didn't say anything.

Eventually we stopped at an old motel I didn't recognize, twenty miles out of town. I had been all for sleeping in the car, but Bobby, ever practical, pointed out we'd do a better day's work if we got a few hours in a bed. We walked over and banged on the door to the office. After a pretty long time a man in a T-shirt and pyjamas emerged, and was frank in expressing his dissatisfaction at our presence. We allowed that the hour was late, but suggested that now he was awake he might as well turn a buck by giving us a twin room.

He took a long look at us. 'You a couple of perverts?'

We looked back at him, and he evidently decided that worse than renting to two potential homosexuals was the prospect of having those same homosexuals beat the living crap out of him in the middle of the night. He handed me a key.

Bobby lay down on one of the beds and went straight to sleep. I tried to do the same, but couldn't get it to stick. Eventually I got back up and left the room. I bought a pack of cigarettes from the machine and went out to the centre of the old court, where a rusty fence surrounded the remains of a swimming pool. I pulled a battered chair up to one end and sat there in the darkness. There was no light apart from the dusty pink of the VACANCY sign over the office, a smudge of moon, some glints off peeling hard surfaces. I got out the gun Bobby had given me and looked at it for a while. It didn't have much of interest to say, so I put it back in my jacket.

Instead I stared at the shadows of the empty pool, wondering how long it had been empty. Quite a time, by its appearance: the sides were cracked and the six inches of sludge at the bottom looked as if it could have provided the forum for the first emergence of life. Once it had been full of cool water, and families would have gratefully dispatched their children to it, glad of the relief after a long drive. The sign for the motel, faded and unloved though it was, dated it to the late fifties. I could picture the way life had been then, but only as still images: snapshots of the glory years, the colours slightly off and everything frozen in an advertisement for the kind of life we've always been promised is inevitable. A backyard of sweetness and light, cookouts and firm handshakes, of hard work and true love and fair play. The way life is supposed to be. Instead we wander about, short on charisma and direction and script – and in the end the whole business just stops and we realize no one was watching anyway. We're so used to events being portrayed in particular ways that when they actually happen to us, and our life bears no resemblance to expectation, we don't really know how we're supposed to respond. Our lives are unrecognizable to us. Should we still try to be happy, when everything seems so flawed and out of kilter and grey? How are we supposed to be content, when everything on television is so much better?

I believed that Bobby had already found the truth, and that my birth was not recorded in Hunter's Rock, but I had to check for myself. All of the time I'd been driven around by Chip Farling, my childhood had been pulling at me with cold fingers. If my parents had gone somewhere else for my birth, maybe it wasn't that important. Could be they'd gone away for the weekend, a last chance before their family expanded, and had been caught short somewhere far from home. But surely that was the kind of story you tell your child, the kind of anecdote that makes each life unique? I could only assume that it had not been revealed because of the fact that wherever this birth had taken place, it had been of twins. Why this should have made a difference, and why they had done what they had gone on to do, I still had no idea. Perhaps this was the gap that I had unconsciously sculpted my life around. Everyone feels that way some of the time. But I felt it a lot. And maybe I'd finally found out why.

I don't know how long the noise had been going on. Not long, I think. But gradually I realized that I could hear a quiet lapping sound. It seemed very close by, so close that I turned in my seat. There was nothing behind me. When I turned round again I realized I had misjudged the direction, and that it was coming from the far end of the pool. It was a little too dark to see, but it sounded as if water was sloshing quietly into the far end. I sat forward in my chair, surprised. The water in the pool was getting a little deeper: slowly, but noticeably. It was no longer only a few inches deep, but about a foot. It was only then that I realized that there were two people in the pool. Right down at the far end. One was a little taller than the other, and both were at first no more than bulky shadows. They were holding hands as they struggled forward, pushing against the viscous water as it rose. The watery sounds got louder as the pool began to fill more quickly, and the movement of the figures became more vigorous as they tried to come up toward the shallow end, up towards me.

By now the moonlight had caught their features and I knew it was my mother and father. They could have made better progress if they had let go of each other, but they didn't. Even after the water was over their waists, their hands were linked under the surface. I think they saw me. They were looking in my direction, at least. My father's mouth opened and closed, but if he made any sound it never reached me. Their free arms cut down into the heavy water, but made no splashes, and still it got deeper. It made no difference how close they got. The pool did not become more shallow. The water did not stop rising. It did not stop even after it had gone up to their chins, even after it had begun to slop over the edges of the pool and spill like dark mercury around my feet. My mother's eyes were calm until the end: it was my father in whom I saw panic, for the first time in my life, and it was his hand that was the last thing visible, as they almost reached the end, still sinking, but reaching up for me.

When my eyes flew open it was dawn, and Bobby was standing over me, shaking his head.

I sat up, eyes wide, and saw that my pack of cigarettes was no longer in my lap but lying in the six inches of crap at the bottom of the pool. I looked at Bobby, and he winked.

'Must have twitched in your sleep,' he said.

By late morning it had been confirmed. No Ward Hopkins, no Hopkins of any flavour, had ever been born in Hunter's Rock. I talked to a nice young lady behind a desk, who said she'd see if she could find any other information. I couldn't see what else would be helpful, and it soon became apparent that she couldn't either but was trying to help out of a combination of compassion and boredom. I gave her my number and left.

Bobby was standing on the pavement outside, talking on his phone. I looked dumbly up and down the street until he was finished. Even though I'd known it was coming, I felt dispossessed. It was like being sat down and told that you hadn't come out of your mother's tummy after all, but really had been deposited under a bush by a stork. I'd had my tonsils removed in that little hospital, visited it to get two separate sets of stitches in youthful knees. On each occasion I'd believed that I had been revisiting the place where I'd been born.

'Well, my friend,' Bobby said eventually. 'The upstanding men and women of the Dyersburg police department would surely like to know where you are. You'll be gratified to hear that this appears to be out of a concern for your well-being. At the moment.'

'And the house?'

'Extensive damage to living room and hallway, chunk of lower stairway destroyed. But not burned to the ground.'

'So what now?'

'Show me your old house,' he said.

I looked at him. 'Why?'

'Well, honey, because you're big and blond and gorgeous and I want to know *everything* about you.'

'Fuck off,' I suggested, supporting the notion with a weary hand gesture. 'It's a dumb and pointless idea.'

'You got any better suggestions? This doesn't look like a town with limitless entertainment options.'

I took us out along the main street. I couldn't work out whether it was the new or the old stuff that looked most unfamiliar. The most noticeable thing was that the old Jane's Market had been knocked down, replaced by a small Holiday Inn with one of the new-style boxy little signs. I miss the big old googie ones. I really do. I don't understand why rectangles are supposed to be better.

When we were nearly there I drove more slowly, and finally pulled over on the opposite side. It had been ten years since I'd last looked at the house, maybe more. It looked pretty much the same – though it had been repainted in the intervening time and the trees and shrubs around it had changed. A family vehicle of

Far Eastern provenance was parked in the drive, and three bikes were stowed neatly around the side.

After a minute I saw a shape passing behind the front window and then disappearing from sight. Just a nondescript suburban dwelling, but it looked like a gingerbread house in a fairy tale. Its reality was too strong, too compelling, as if overloaded with MSG. I tried to remember exactly when I'd last been inside. It seemed inconceivable that I hadn't wanted to visit again before it passed into someone else's hands. Had I really been so bad at seeing how things might one day be different?

'Are you ready for this?'

I realized that my hands were shaking a little. I turned to him. 'Ready for what?'

'Going inside.'

'I'm not going inside.'

'Yes you are,' he said, patiently.

'Bobby – have you lost your mind? Somebody else lives there now. There's no way I'm going in that house.'

'Listen to me. Couple of years ago my old man died. Didn't matter much to me – we got on like shit. But my mother called, asked me home for the burial. I was busy. Didn't make it. Six months later I realized I was acting kind of weird. Nothing you'd put your finger on. Things were just stressing me out. All the time. Getting anxious when there was nothing specific to make me that way. A panic attack kind of thing, I guess. Holes kept opening in front of me.'

I didn't know what to say. He wasn't looking in my direction, but staring straight out of the windshield.

'In the end some work brought me close to home, so I went to see my mother in Rochford. It's not like she and I were best pals either. But it was good to see her. Maybe "good" isn't the right word. Useful. She looked different. Smaller. And on the way out of town I stopped by the graveyard, stood by the old man's plot for a while. It was a sunny afternoon and there was no one else around. And his ghost, his ghost came right up out of the soil in front of me and said, "Listen, Bobby, chill."'

I stared at him. He laughed quietly. 'Of course not. I didn't feel his presence, or become any more reconciled to the way he'd been. But since then I don't feel so anxious. I think about death sometimes, and I'm more careful in what I do and I'm more open to the idea of settling down one of these years. But the weird thing went away. I found the ground again.' He looked at me. 'Loose ends are the death of people, Ward. You think you're protecting yourself but all you're doing is opening little cracks. You let too many open up at once, the whole thing is going to fall to dust and you'll find yourself like a starving dog wandering the streets in the night. And you, my friend, have got a whole lot of cracks appearing at this time.'

I opened the door and got out of the car.

'If they'll let me.'

'They'll let you,' he said. 'I'll wait for you here.'

I stopped. I guess I thought he'd be coming with me. 'It's your house,' he said. 'And we knock on that door together, whoever opens it is going to think they're going to be starring in the mortuary end of an episode of *Forensic Detectives.*'

I walked up the driveway, and knocked on the door. The porch was tidy and well-swept.

A woman appeared, smiled. 'Mr Hopkins?' she said.

After a beat I got it, and simultaneously cursed and glorified Bobby's name. He'd called ahead, pretended to be me, and laid the groundwork. I wondered what he'd've done if I'd refused.

'That's right,' I said, coming up to speed. 'You're sure you don't mind?'

'Not at all.' She stood aside to usher me in. 'You were lucky to catch me earlier. I'm afraid I have to go out again soon though.'

'Of course,' I said. 'Just a few minutes would be great.'

The woman, who was in middle age and pretty and nice enough to be someone's mother on television, asked if I wanted coffee. I said no but there was some already made and in the end it was easier to accept. While she fetched it I stood in the hallway and looked around. Everything had changed. The woman, whatever her name was (I couldn't ask, as in theory I'd spoken to her earlier), was not unfamiliar with the stenciller's art. In a Pottery Barn kind of way it looked rather better than when we'd lived there.

Then we walked around. The woman didn't need to explain why she accompanied me. I thought it pretty unusual that she would let a man into her house just on the basis of a phone call: a desire to keep half an eye on her belongings was entirely natural. I was soon able to make sufficient comment on the way things had been when she moved in that even this mild guardedness disappeared, and she busied herself with stuff in the background. I wandered through each of the rooms, and then up the stairs. I took a brief look in what had been my parents' room and the spare room, both of which had been largely alien territory to me. Then I girded myself for the final area.

When the door to my old room was open, I swallowed involuntarily. I took a couple of paces in, then stopped. Green walls, brown carpet. A few boxes and some old chairs, a broken fan and most of a child's bike.

I discovered that the woman was standing behind me.

'Haven't changed a thing,' she admitted. 'View's better from the other room, so my daughter sleeps in there even though it's a little smaller. We just store a few things here. I'll see you downstairs.'

With that she disappeared. I stood a few minutes in the room, just turning around, seeing it from different angles. It was maybe twelve feet square, and seemed both very small and bigger than Africa. The space you grew up in is not like normal space. You know it so intimately, have sat and stood and lain down in its every corner. It's where you think many things for the first time, and as a result it stretches like the time before Christmas, as you live there and wait to grow up. It holds you.

'This is my room,' I said, quietly and to myself. Seeing it on the video had been strange. But this was not. The place I'd come from hadn't changed. Not everything in my life had been erased. I shut the door again on the way out, as if to keep something in.

Downstairs the woman was perched against the table in the kitchen. 'Thank you,' I said. 'You've been very kind.'

She shushed this away, and I looked around the kitchen for a moment. The appliances had been updated, but the cabinets were still the same: strong and made of good wood, they'd presumably found no reason to replace them. My father's handiwork lived on.

It was then that I remembered the evening from long ago, eating lasagne with him. A cloth hung on an oven handle, a game of pool that didn't work out. I opened my mouth and then shut it again.

Stepping out of the house was one of the strangest things, the act of leaving that particular inside to return to the outside where I lived now. I was almost surprised to see the big white car on the other side of the street, Bobby still sitting inside, and I noticed how much cars look like huge bugs these days.

I waved to the woman and walked down the path, not quickly, just as you normally would. By the time I was opening the car door the house was shut again behind me, shut and left behind.

Bobby was sitting reading the rental agreement for the car.

'Jesus, these things are boring,' he said. 'I mean, really. They should hire some writer. Get him to spice it up a little.'

'You're a bad man,' I said. 'But thank you.'

He shoved the sheaf of papers back in the glove compartment. 'So I guess we've done with Hunter's Rock.'

'No, I don't think so.'

'What's on your mind?'

'How about they already knew, when we were born, that they were going to do what they did. Maybe, I don't know – maybe they thought they could only support one child or something.'

Bobby looked dubious. 'I know,' I admitted. 'But either way, say they knew they were going to get rid of one of us. But they also knew that one day they were going to die, and that I might do what

214

I'm doing now. I might come home, look around. And I might find out from the hospital that I'd been one of two.'

'So they have you born somewhere else, and in that case all you find out is there's a minor mystery about which particular hospital you arrived in, not that you had a twin they abandoned.'

'That's what I'm thinking.'

'But how come the Agency didn't find a problem when you joined?'

'I was very useful to them at the time. My guess is they skimped on the background checks for expedience, and by then I'm one of the team and who cares?'

Bobby considered it. 'Best we've got. But this is still weird. Your parents went to all that trouble to hide this, why then leave documentary evidence of what they did?'

'Maybe something happened recently that meant they changed their minds about letting me know.'

I realized that the woman might be watching out of the window, so I started the car up and pulled away.

'I'm thinking that maybe we've been looking in the wrong directions. There are three chunks on that video. First one shows a place I could go find. The Halls. Last one tells me something I didn't know. Middle section shows two places. First the house, where I've just been, thanks to you. Nothing there. The other was a bar. I don't recognize it. It's nowhere I've ever been.'

'So?' We were at a junction.

'Bear with me,' I said, and took a left. A turn that would eventually lead us, assuming it was still there, to a bar I used to go to.

Chapter 20

It was never a place you'd go on purpose, unless chance had made it your habitual haunt. I was expecting it to have gone one of two ways: spruced up with an eating room addition and lots of perky waitresses in red-and-white, or bulldozed and under cheap housing where people shouted a lot after dark. In fact, progress seemed to have simply ignored Lazy Ed's altogether: unlike genteel decay, which had settled into it like damp.

The interior was empty and silent. The wood of the bar and the stools looked about as scuffed up as they always had. The pool table was still in place, along with most of the dust, some of it maybe even mine. There were a few additions here and there, high-water marks of progress. The neon MILLER sign had been replaced with one for Bud Lite, and the calendar on the wall showed young ladies closer to their natural state than it had in my day. Natural, at least, in their state of undress, if not in the shape or constitution of their breasts. Somewhere, probably hidden very well, would be a plaque warning pregnant women against drinking – though had such a person been coming here for her kicks the warning would likely be lost on her on account of her being blind or deranged. Women have higher standards. That's why they're a civilizing influence on young men. You have to find somewhere nice to get them drunk.

Bobby leaned back against the pool table, gazing around. 'Same as it ever was?'

'Like I never went away.'

I went up to the bar, feeling nervous. I used to just call out Ed's name. That was twenty years ago, and doing it now would be like going back to school and expecting the teachers to recognize you. The last thing anyone needs is to learn that in the grand scheme of things they were always just 'some kid'.

A man emerged from out the back, wiping his hands on a cloth that could only be making them dirtier. He raised his chin in a greeting that was cordial but of limited enthusiasm. He was about my age, maybe a little older, fat, and already going bald. I love it when I see contemporaries losing their hair. It perks me right up.

'Hi,' I said. 'Was looking for Ed.'

'Found him,' he replied.

'The one I had in mind would be about thirty years older.'

'You mean Lazy. He ain't here.'

'You can't be an Ed junior.' Ed didn't have any kids. He wasn't even married.

'Shit no,' the man said, as if disquieted by the idea. 'Just a co-incidence. I'm the new owner. Have been since Ed retired.'

I tried to hide my disappointment. 'Retired.' I didn't want to seem too pushy.

'Couple years. Still,' the guy said. 'Saved me having to make a new sign.'

'Whole place looks the same, actually,' I ventured.

The man shook his head wearily. 'Don't I know it. When Lazy sold up he made a condition. Said he was selling a business, not his second home. Had to be left this way until he died.'

'And you went for it?'

'I got it very cheap. And Lazy is pretty old.'

'How's he going to know whether you kept the agreement?'

'Still comes in. Most every day. You wait around, chances are you'll see him.' He must have seen me smile, and added: 'One thing though. He may not be quite the way you remember him.'

I started a tab, and went over to where Bobby was sitting. We drank beer and played pool for a while. Bobby won.

We kept the beers coming, and after I'd lost interest in losing any more games Bobby spent an hour practising shots. My dad would have approved of his dedication. We had the bar to ourselves for a long while, and then a few people started to drift in. By the end of the afternoon Bobby and I still constituted about a third of the clientele. I'd lightly quizzed Ed on what time Lazy usually came by, but apparently it was completely unpredictable. I thought about asking for his address, but something told me the guy wouldn't give it up and that the question would make him suspicious. Early evening there was a rush. A whole four people came in at once. None of them was Ed.

Then at seven, something happened.

Bobby and I were playing pool again by then. He wasn't beating me so easily by this point. Somebody had put classic Springsteen on the jukebox and it felt weirdly as if I could have been playing twenty years ago, in the days of hair gel and pushed-up sleeves. I was getting drunk enough to be verging on nostalgic for the 1980s, which is never a good sign.

Out of the corner of my eye I saw the door to the bar open. Still leaning over the table, I watched to see who'd come in. I got just a glimpse. A face, pretty old. Looking right at me. And then whoever it was turned tail and went.

I shouted to Bobby, but he'd already seen. He ran straight across the floor and had crashed out the door before I'd even dropped my cue.

Outside it was dark and a car was on the move and fast. A battered old Ford, spraying gravel as it fishtailed out of the lot. Bobby was swearing fit for competition standard and I quickly saw why: some asshole had blocked us in with a big red truck. He turned, saw me. 'Why'd he run?'

'No idea. You see which way he went?'

'No.' He turned and kicked the nearest truck.

'Get the car started.'

I ran back inside and straight up to the bar. 'Whose is the truck?'

A guy dressed in denim raised his hand.

'Get it the fuck out of the way or we're going to shove it clean off the lot.'

He stared at me a moment, and then got up and went outside.

I turned to Ed. 'That was him, right? Guy who ran?'

'Guess he didn't want to talk to you after all.'

'Well that's a shame,' I said. 'Because it's going to happen regardless. I need to talk with him about old times. I'm feeling so nostalgic I could just shit. So where does he live?'

'I ain't telling you that.'

'Don't fuck with me, Ed.'

The man started to reach under the counter. I pulled my gun out and pointed it at him. 'Don't do that either. It isn't worth it.'

Young Ed put his hands back in view. I was aware of the bar's other patrons watching, and hoped none of them was in the mood for trouble. Folks can get very protective of the people who serve their beer. It's an important bond.

'You the kind of guy who can shoot people?'

I looked at him. 'What do you think?'

There was a long beat, and then Ed sighed. 'Should have known you were trouble.'

'I'm not. I just want to talk.'

'Out on Long Acre,' he said. 'Old trailer by the creek on the other side of the little woods.'

I threw down money for the beers and ran out, nearly knocking down the guy coming back from moving his truck.

Bobby had the car pointed and ready to go. Now that I knew where we were going, it sounded kind of familiar. Long Acre is a seemingly endless road that arcs out from the back of town into the hills. There aren't many houses out that way, and the creek the man had referred to was well out beyond them, the other side of a thick stand of trees.

It took us about ten minutes. It was very dark, and Bobby was driving very fast. I couldn't see any sign of taillights up ahead.

'Maybe he wasn't heading home,' Bobby said.

'He will sooner or later. Slow down. It's not that far now. Plus you're scaring me.'

Soon after that we saw the mirror surface of the creek, silver under the blue-black sky. Bobby braked like somebody hitting a wall and turned off down a barely marked track. At the end you could see the shape of an old trailer sitting in splendid isolation. There was no sign of a car.

'Shit,' I said. 'Okay. Pull around where we can't be seen from the road.'

After about half an hour I started to lose patience. If Lazy had gone some other way to make sure he wasn't being followed, then he still would have been home by now. Bobby agreed, but put a different interpretation on what I'd said.

'No,' I said. 'I knew this guy a long time ago. I'm not rooting through his home.'

'Wasn't suggesting you did it. Come on, Ward. Minute this guy sees you, he takes to his heels. You called right. The bar in the video was to remind you of someone, and this old guy knows something.'

'He could have mistaken me for somebody else.'

'You're probably a little thicker than you were back then, but it's not like you put on a hundred pounds or changed race. He knew it was you. And for someone who's supposed to be old, he put some distance between you pretty fast.'

I hesitated, but not for long. I'd spent a lot of time with Lazy Ed. I'd only been one of many, for sure, and doubtless there had been several generations of underage drinkers since. But I'd been hoping for a more friendly reception.

We got out of the car together and I walked with him to the door of the trailer. Bobby tricked the lock and slipped inside, and a moment later a dim light seeped out through the windows.

I sat on the step and kept watch, wondering if my parents had suspected that one day it would come to something like this. Their son, half-drunk and breaking into the trailer of an old man. I don't like the man I have become, but then I didn't much care for the guy I was before. I wasn't entirely out of line, and it made sense, of a kind: the memory of playing pool with my father long ago, the way Ed had reacted on seeing him back then, was what had made me go to the bar. But it seemed to me, as I watched down the track and listened to Bobby moving about inside, that I heard my father's voice again.

'*I wonder what you've become.*'

Ten minutes later Bobby came back out, holding something.

'What's that?' I stood up, feeling my legs ache.

'Show you inside. You must be cold as fuck.'

Back in the car I flicked on the interior light.

'Well,' Bobby said. 'Lazy Ed is getting through his twilight years with the aid of alcoholic beverages, and has gotten to the stage where he's hiding the empties even from himself. Either that or he's aptly nicknamed, and just can't be fucked to take them outside. It's a zoo in there. I couldn't look through everything. I did, however, come upon this.'

He held out a photograph. I took it and angled it so the light fell on it. 'Found it in a box stowed beside what I assumed must be his bed. The rest was random junk, but this caught my eye.'

The picture showed a group of five teenagers, four boys and a girl, and had been taken in poor light by someone who'd forgotten to say 'cheese'. Only one guy, standing right in the centre, seemed to be aware that he was being immortalized. The others were

221

glimpsed in half-profile, faces mainly in shadow. You couldn't tell where it had been taken, but the clothes and the standard of the print said late 1950s, early 1960s.

'That's him,' I said. 'The guy in the middle.' I felt uncomfortable holding something that was so much of someone else's past and nothing to do with me.

'By "him", you mean this guy Lazy Ed.'

'Yes. But this was taken fifty years ago. He didn't look that preppy when I knew him. By a long shot.'

'Okay.' Bobby pointed at the woman, who was on the left-hand edge of the photo. 'So who's that?'

I looked closer at the figure he was indicating. All I could make out was half a brow, some hair, most of a mouth. A thin face, young, quite pretty. I shrugged. 'You tell me. No one I know.'

'Really?'

'What are you saying, Bobby?'

'I could be wrong and I don't want to steer you.'

I looked again. Peered carefully at the other faces for a while, to refresh my eyes. Then I glanced at the woman again. She still didn't trigger anything.

'It's not my mother, if that's what you're thinking.'

'I'm not. Keep looking.'

I did and finally something caught, and I let it come on. It took a few seconds, and then dropped like a brick. 'Holy *shit*,' I said.

'You see it?'

I kept looking, expecting to become less sure. I didn't. Once I'd seen it, it couldn't be denied. Though a lot of her face was obscured, it was there in the eyes and the slope of the top half of her nose.

'That's Mary,' I said. 'Mary Richards. My parents' neighbour. In Dyersburg.' I opened my mouth to say something more – I'm not sure what – but then shut it again with a snap, sideswiped by a sudden flash of another image.

Bobby didn't notice. 'So what's Ed doing in Montana back then? Or what was she doing here?'

222

'You real set on waiting for this guy tonight?'

'You got another plan?'

'I might have something else to show you,' I said. 'And it's cold and I don't think we're going to see Ed out here this evening. We should head back into town.' My hands were trembling, and my throat felt dry.

'Suits me.'

I got out of the car, went to the front of the trailer and broke back in. I scribbled a note on the back of the photo, apologizing for breaking in, and then propped it up in the middle of a card table. I added my cell number at the bottom, and then I left – taking a moment to reach back through the door and prop a magazine up against its inner surface.

Bobby drove back into town with the headlights off, but we saw no sign of anyone, and when we passed the bar the old Ford was not sitting in the lot. Neither, I realized only later, was the big red truck.

Chapter 21

We checked into the Holiday Inn and I showered and took five as I waited for Bobby. The room was clean and fresh and reassuring. I had a big pot of coffee on hand, delivered by someone in a nice white uniform and an off-the-rack smile, which is usually the best type. I don't have the *Cheers* gene. I'm quite happy with people not knowing my name.

I wished I still had the photograph. I wanted to look at it again, was already halfway to convincing myself it had been a trick of the light. That, and the fact that Mary's dead face was imprinted strongly in my memory. Her body would be lying in a cold drawer in the morgue by now, but nobody would understand what had happened to her. I thought they should know, and running from Dyersburg still rankled with me. I was thinking that a phone call to the Dyersburg PD might point them in the right direction. They'd ask for my name and details, but I could make something up. I'm good at that kind of thing.

I had got as far as reaching for the phone when Bobby knocked on my door. I let the phone be and hauled myself out of the chair.

'You okay?' he said, as he shut the door.

'Been a weird few days, Bobby.'

I opened up the laptop and placed it in the middle of the table. I motioned him to sit back in the other seat, then slipped the DVD-ROM into the slot and loaded up the bar scene from the video.

Loud music. Chaos. The drunken progress of the man holding the camera. The coughing fit, and then a walk round the corner into the area where people were playing pool. A young couple stood with their backs to the camera, and a big man with a beard and his girlfriend were lining up to take their shot.

The camera staggered closer, and the girl with the long hair glanced up. I hit PAUSE on the player software and froze the video on her face. I hit a couple of keys to save a graphic capture of the screen, then booted up Photoshop. I opened up the capture, and this time zoomed in on the woman's face. I grabbed some background, and wiped it over the lower portions of her long hair to remove it. I cloned some skin texture and cut in around her cheeks, making them older and wider, and then picked up some hair and changed the style to one more suitable for an old lady in the year 2002. Did a quick selection, dropped in a steel grey, and then finally added noise over the altered part of the image to mask the difference in grain, followed by a Guassian blur to take the sharp edges away. I zoomed back out again until the picture was half its natural size, and the rough editing was less apparent in the quality of the image.

You had to ignore the fact that part of the scene around the face now looked odd, but it wasn't hard given what had been revealed in the centre. I'd suspected this since Ed's trailer, but seeing it on-screen still made me feel breathless.

'Okay,' Bobby said, very quietly. 'That's her again. Along with your parents.'

'But they only met Mary when they moved to Montana.'

225

'And they said something like: "This Mary woman. Complete newcomer in our lives. Certainly never met *her* before."'

'They acted as if they'd only known each other a couple of years.' My head was spinning. 'And I remember my mother telling me about how she'd just met Mary when she came round with cookies the day they moved in.'

'When actually they'd known each other for over thirty years.' Meanwhile he'd spooled through the clip and frozen the image on the girl sitting cross-legged and weaving on my parents' living-room floor.

I nodded. The way the light caught her nose and cheekbones, you didn't even have to do any editing. It was Mary.

'So what do you think about the Ed guy? Could he be the cameraman?'

'The only time I saw him and my dad in the same room they behaved like strangers.' I'd already described this occasion to Bobby on the way out to the bar. 'But they must have known each other. They all did. For some reason, Mary moves out, possibly not even that long after the time shown in the video. She'd certainly been in Montana a long while before my folks moved out there. In the meantime, my parents and Ed stay here, but not in contact, and the one time I accidentally bring them together, my father lets it happen but neither acknowledges the other.' I thought back to the occasions when I'd met Mary at my folks' house, but all that did was confirm my existing impression – which is that if they'd all known each other before Montana, they went to some trouble for it not to appear that way. I was wondering why they'd all bother to hide this fact from me, and then saw this was muddled and egocentric thinking.

My parents went out there on purpose, I realized. 'They went there because they thought or knew something was going to happen, and that's why the three of them pretended not to know each other.'

'You're stretching just a little bit.'

'Am I? Maybe Mary wasn't killed just because she was in the way.

226

Maybe whoever came out to the house had two jobs, and Mary was one of them.'

Bobby considered, nodded. 'Then, when you turn up back in Hunter's Rock, Ed runs like a jackrabbit.'

'We should have stayed out at his trailer.'

He shook his head. 'He's not going back there in a hurry. By now he'll have called the guy at the bar, and found you know where he lives. Plus you're looking too zonked for any action that might involve chasing people. You left your number. If he goes home, he knows how to get a hold of you. Tomorrow we go back out to the bar and lean on the owner. Find out if the old guy has any known associates or another place he hangs out.'

'Needle in a haystack, in other words.'

'The needle's still there. If it's been placed at random, it could be the very first thing you find.'

'Very deep, Bobby. Let me write that down.'

'Meantime, I'm going on the Web.' He glanced at the cell phone, which was lying on the table. 'And if you're hoping Lazy Ed's going to call, you might want to turn your phone back on.'

While he ran a phone cable out the back of the laptop to the connector on the desk telephone, I watched the screen of the cell. Sure enough, within a few seconds a message indicator lit up.

'Got something?'

I dialled the service and listened. The voice recorded was that of a woman. 'Not him. It's the girl I talked to at the hospital. She said she'd look up some files, let me know if anything looked useful.'

'And did it?'

'She doesn't say,' I said, disconnecting. 'Just for me to give her a call tomorrow.'

'Ward, look at this. You got an email.'

I looked over his shoulder. There was a short message on the screen:

EARN BIG $$$ GUARANTEED!!!

We are a small company offering an EXPANDING service.
Make use of our product to change your world, working
with nothing more than your own dedication. The pure
shall rejoice in there hearts when he seeth our Web site!

Go back for information that could change all our lives!
Start immediately – with a business that's growing fast.
Hundreds are already doing more than they ever thought
possible: Why don't you become one of us?

Don't delay – this offer ends at midnight.

'Look up "junk email" in a dictionary,' I said, 'and they've probably got that printed out in full.'

'But,' Bobby said, 'there's no order form. The sending address looks fake and it mentions a Web site without giving the URL, and then gives a deadline in three hours' time. They're not making it easy for you to get ripped off. Plus look at the two sentences with exclamation marks at the end. The first is odd – some kind of biblical-sounding thing – and the second says "Go back". Go back where?'

I thought a second. 'This has come to me as a result of having already visited some site and having my IP address logged.'

'Sometimes, Ward, it's almost like you've got a fully functioning brain.' He doubleclicked a desktop bookmark, and the browser loaded up. Within a few seconds we had the page in front of us, with just the two words: WE RISE.

But this time they were underlined, and when Bobby moved the cursor over them, it became a pointing hand.

'It's changed into a link,' he said. He clicked on the words and a small dialogue box popped up asking for a password. 'Oh, crap.'

'The Straw Men,' I suggested.

He typed it in. A white page came up with the words UNAU-THORIZED ENTRY at the top. Bobby swore and clicked the back button.

'Show me the email again,' I said. He switched the browser to the background, bringing the email back to the front.

I scanned it quickly. 'Try *there*, as it's spelled in the "rejoice" sentence.'

'Because?'

'It's the only misspelled word in the entire email, and it's in the sentence referring to the Web site.'

He clicked, typed it in. We got unauthorized again. 'It's going to throw us out soon,' he muttered, retracing his steps once more.

'Try it spelt correctly.'

He clicked and typed in 'their'. There was a pause. And then another page came on screen. This was black, with the word WELCOME, in white in the centre.

'Okay,' Bobby said, his voice quiet and constricted. He moved the cursor over WELCOME, and it changed to a pointing hand. I crowded in closer, and he clicked on the word.

There was a pause, and then the screen changed to a forest green, filled with white text.

THE HUMAN MANIFESTO

[image: strawlogo.jpg]

HERE IS THE TRUTH

Some people do not agree with Evolution as a Theory.
This is wrong. We were only told that Evolution was
untrue for so long to STOP US from seeing the real

Truth. But now we have Seen it, and it cannot be hidden again by Politicians or other LIARS.

You think you know the Truth but you don't: You only know LIES.

THE HISTORY OF MANKIND.

In olden times we were all apes. Then one day 5 Million years ago a new line split off to make three new types of apes: the gorillas, the chimpanzees and the 'hominids' – who became us. Anyone who has seen TV programs on how smart chimpanzees are will not find it hard to believe this is TRUE. 2.5 Million years later the first creatures who were true Humanity came into being. They are sometimes referred to as Habilis, although names during this period are open to controversy: This is a dark period in our Evolution, and the scientists use LONG WORDS when they do not know as much as they want us to THINK they know.

By 1 Million years ago we began to see a type called Erectus, so-called because they stood Upright. It is standing Upright that divides us from the apes, and from all other animals. Some of this type became Neanderthals, who were successful for a long time. Over the next few hundred thousand years this type became better at walking, got better tools, and tamed FIRE. Further Evolution then took place in Africa, finishing in Homo Sapiens. Our brain size became bigger, hence our Intelligence, which is unique. The Homo Sapiens supplanted the Neanderthals.

During all of this time, humankind and those who came before us were HUNTER-GATHERERS. We lived in small groups who tied together through Kinship and Co-operation. We fed ourselves with game that we HUNTED and berries and roots that we GATHERED, and then we moved on.

AS YOU SOW SO SHALL YOU WEEP

About fifteen thousand years ago everything started changing. This may sound a long time ago, but not when you think in terms of Millions of years. What happened is we stopped our natural hunting and gathering. Why?

Some people have put this down to growing population, causing a strain on resources, and less freedom to move. Or changes in the weather because the Ice Age had finished, and various other things. I have read all of the so-called Scientific explanations, and no one knows. There were once millions of bisons roaming the plains of America. They were still able to support themselves. They had to move about to find new food, but that is the Natural Way. Humans, who can stand Upright, are DESIGNED for walking long distances. So why did we suddenly stop moving – when we had spent millions of years Evolving to be another way?

The reason is because WE STARTED FARMING. The result was that people started staying in one place, and began living in larger groups up to hundreds and then thousands of people. And once this had started, it could not be stopped. Farming makes more food, but it is a LESS EFFICIENT method of supporting small numbers of people. It only works with big groups. Farming also caused more people to be born, which meant the groups got even bigger. Once you have a bigger population, you cannot give it up and go back to foraging. You are Trapped.

From these changes came towns and cities, which gave rise to even more population growth. These caused LACK OF EQUALITY, and then LEADERS and RELIGION. It also created MORALITY. If you start living in one place for a long time, then you will be seeing the same people tomorrow as you did yesterday. This means that you have to start behaving towards them in a certain way, or they will KILL you. From this people came to believe that they OUGHT to behave in certain ways – even if you do not know the people involved. And for the first time we saw one of mankind's not endearing but most real tendencies, something that makes us different to all other natural species: that of ALTERING THE LAND. Up until then we had lived as part of nature: Since we started farming we have been RAPING the earth and changing it to our own ends.

And yet farming people were actually LESS HEALTHY than foragers. Growing food brought SMALLER returns for the same effort. Hunter-gatherers had MORE LEISURE and WORKED LESS than farmers. They had a better balanced diet than farmers, who relied too much upon root or cereal crops. Farmers were more likely to get infections and epidemics – because everyone was living close together. People did not live as long, and got SICK more.

SO WHY DID THIS WAY OF LIFE SWEEP THROUGH THE

232

WORLD, IN A MERE FEW THOUSAND YEARS? Why, across virtually the entire planet, did our whole Species change its way of living after Millions of years – especially when at first they were WORSE OFF?

THE INHUMAN GENOME

Viruses are very small, but when they are in you they take your body over so it behaves in the way that the Disease wants. Many Viruses make you sick, like colds. Some will kill you, like AIDS. But the cleverest Viruses do not make you sick or kill you – because they want you to be their HOME.

20,000 years ago WE WERE INFECTED. Homo Sapiens brought the virus from Africa, which is why all the Neanderthals died out. They were better adapted to cope with conditions, and with an Ice Age – and yet, within just a few thousand years, they died out.

This Virus made us start living in groups and towns pre-cisely because it would be easier for it to SPREAD AMONGST US. We did not do this because it was better for us. We did it because we were trapped. By the time the Virus had taken hold and we had become its home, our nature had changed and we could not go back.

The Virus has become so much a part of us that the Scientific Establishment will never see it, no matter how clever they think they are.

This is why a Homeland is very important to many people, including the JEWS: If we move then the Virus thinks we are returning to our real way of life and causes trouble for us.

This is why we don't care about people from other countries: They mean nothing to us.

This is why Terrorists and Murderers kill innocent Americans: We mean nothing to them.

This is why our cities are full of Violence: We are forced to live in other people's filth like rats in boxes, which is anathema to us.

This is why things like the Nazi holocaust and Bosnia and Rwanda take place: Different tribes are our Enemies, and if you push us together we will fight.

This is why our leaders are Liars and Fools. Government means stopping us from having our FREEDOM, for the sake of the so-called rights of people we do not know.

This is why people Murder and Kill: Because the only thing that stops us is Morality, which was invented by the Virus.

They are always trying to make us feel like we're the same, and say that we all bleed the same colour, but even that is not true: There are different blood types – because of genetics.

Even at this basic level we are incompatible with each other. Even our blood is not the same.

WHAT CAN WE DO?

We must start the action in the cities, amongst the Blacks. We may not like you – because you are not our type, and we are only brought together because of the

Disease – but you are Victims too. You have been brought from your proper Home and penned into places where there is no hope for Your Kind. You must be the first to rise up. The world will follow.

We are not supposed to live in huge groups. We are not designed to care about people we don't know. We are supposed to be free, not penned in cities and lorded over by people who do not care about us but are only in it for the MONEY. The only way to stop this from destroying us is to KILL the carriers. Politicians will not help, because they thrive in this Evil environment. Like the virus, without 'civilization' they have no host. It is up to us.

Those who Kill will be Free:
Those who do not Kill are Infected.

Cleanse the planet.

Kill the virus.

Guns will make you strong.

I finished reading it a few seconds before Bobby.

'Save it to disk,' I said. 'That's not going to be there tomorrow.'

When Bobby had saved the page, I scrolled back to the top and read through it carefully again. It reminded me of a hundred manias, badly photocopied screeds thrust at passers-by on street corners and skimmed on the way home out of sheer boredom; rants half-overheard in the shadows of bars late at night, voices smudged with alcohol and ignorance and anger. But there was something different about it. I sat back in my chair, and worked out what it was.

'Give him credit,' Bobby said, when he had finished reading it a

235

second time. 'He's been to the library and looked at some books. But it's basically an insanity thing. Right?'

'Yes and no,' I said. 'Terms like "supplanted" don't fit. Or "anathema".'

'Couple clever words don't make it a work of genius. They could have been copied straight out of something.'

'Every single apostrophe is in the right place, Bobby. Plenty of people out there who'd take this as the word of God. Militia guys, for a start. Could even be them behind it.'

He laughed. 'I doubt that. You know what they're like. Grey-haired vets and kids who've seen so many straight-to-videos about 'Nam they half-believe they were there, too. They build a camp in the woods and polish their hardware and fight over the womenfolk.'

'Not all of these people are cavemen. Or stupid.'

'Of course not. But we're talking guys who devour *Soldier of Fortune* cover to cover and buy books telling you how to cook napalm and build man-traps in your backyard. People who took a bath over hoarding supplies for the millennium – and were actually *disappointed* when it all came to nothing and civilization shambled on. They put on fatigues and yack up how the world's gone to shit and the Jews and the Hispanics are to blame, not to mention Capitol Hill and Saddam Hussein. You'd be better off worrying about the blacks in the inner cities, like the guy says. The homeboys are *really* pissed, and some of those fly motherfuckers have whacked someone before they've been laid.'

'It's the same thing. People who've never felt part of any community except the one that's small enough that they know everybody by name.'

'You're making me weep, Ward.'

'Fuck you. You put your trust in a country, love it as much as it tells you to, and then you find out it was just a stroke to keep you quiet and what it really meant was "Anyone can have everything, apart from you guys. When it comes to you, we didn't mean it". It's cultural abuse. How are *you* going to react to that?'

'Okay, Ward. There's genuine sentiment there and the overall IQ probably isn't much lower than in the House of fucking Representatives, and I'll admit that some of them have sometimes got a point. What I sure as hell *don't* believe is that they co-ordinate. Most of these outfits have trouble keeping thirty people pointed in the same direction, never mind agreeing aims and objectives with some other group – much less *groups* – living hundreds or thousands of miles away. Maybe out there in the big bad world. But not here.'

'Before the Internet,' I said.

'There's stuff there,' he admitted. 'Enough manifested psychosis to blow the mind of every therapist in the country. Hate groups, end-of-the-worlders, the illuminati burning effigies of owls in Bohemia Grove – and the face on Mars is a missile base for social control and the nukes are all pointing right at *you*. But I spend my entire time looking at that shit and trust me – any worldwide movement ain't run by these guys. These people hate everybody who isn't them. Put them in a room together and they'd just combust.'

'You can't find every file on every server,' I said. 'You only see what's been left to be found. There could be some whole other Web, using the same computers and the same phone lines and hard disks, full of killers and killing and a plan for the future – and unless you knew where to look, you wouldn't even find the contents page.' Bobby rolled his eyes, irritating me. 'Fucking *listen* to me. *That's what we're like.* Don't you *know* that? Academics created the Net in their spare time so they could trade facts and while away tenure in role-playing *Star Trek*. Next thing you know you can't log on without people spamming you to death and every shoeshine concession has its own domain. Even before that it's wall-to-wall pornography and ordinary men and women sitting in darkened rooms writing each other about how they'd like to dress up like Shirley Temple and be whipped until they bleed. That's what the Net will become – a way of hiding behind anonymity so you can stop pretending you're Mr and Mrs Good Neighbour and be how you really are: so we can stop pretending we give a shit about some global village when our Christmas-card lists are about the size of a small prehistoric tribe and we feel like cutting half of *them*.'

'Nice to see someone so proud of his fellow earthlings. You sound like you're ready to join the cause.' He rubbed his face. 'Ward, this could be just some guy out on his own weird limb.'

'Bullshit. We got here from a bookmark on the computer of a man who shot a few minutes of video in which he referred to "The Straw Men". That man and his wife are dead, along with someone they knew a long time ago. A threat sent to the place shown in the video caused a house and a hotel to be bombed less than two hours later. Christ, even the architecture of The Halls fits in. They're making million-dollar caves for hunter-gatherers.'

'Okay,' Bobby said, holding his hands up. 'I hear what you're saying. So what now?'

'We've found this. What are we supposed to do next? There are no links, no email address, nothing. What's the point of this thing, unless it leads somewhere?'

Bobby turned the laptop towards him and pressed a key combination. The screen changed to a view that revealed the page's naked HTML, the hidden multiplatform Web language used to display the page to whatever kind of operating system tried to access it. He scrolled slowly down through the lines.

Then he stopped. 'Hang on.'

He toggled the view back to normal again, and flipped down to the very end of the document. 'Okay,' he said, nodding his head. 'It's not much, but there's something.' He pointed at the screen. 'You see anything there? Below the text?'

'No. Why?'

'Because there *is* something. A few words, but they've been set to appear exactly the same colour as the background. You're only going to know they're there if you look at the code or print it out.'

'If this strikes some kind of chord, in other words. So what are the words?'

He flipped to HTML again, and selected a short section right at the bottom. Hidden amongst the gibberish was:

<font colour="#339966">The Upright Man</font>

'The Upright Man,' I said. 'Who the hell is that?'

Part 3

History is on our heels,
following us like our shadows, like death.
Marc Augé
Non-places: Introduction to
an Anthropology of Supermodernity

Chapter 22

Sarah didn't remember the first time she thought she'd heard him. A day or two ago, maybe. He was coming slowly, biding his time. He'd come in the night before, she believed, fading away again as soon as he knew that she'd realized something was afoot. She'd wondered if she might be sensing him during the day, too, but back then her head had been clearer and she'd been able to convince herself that she was just being fanciful. Then late one afternoon she heard him above her, and she knew that if he was coming in the daytime then things had to be getting worse.

The psycho had visited a couple of hours before it happened. He had talked for quite a long time. He had just talked and talked and talked. Some of it was about scavenging. Some of it was about a plague. Some of it was about some place called Castenedolo in Italy, which sounded like a place you'd go on holiday and drink nice drinks and maybe have some *food* like spaghetti or salami or steak or squid or soup but obviously wasn't. Instead it was a place where they'd found some guy buried and where he was found proved he was made out of Plasticine or Pliocene and at least two million years old and what did she think of that?

Sarah didn't really think much about it either way. She tried very hard to concentrate on what she was being told but over the last day or so had started to feel very ill for much of the time. She had given up asking for food, and wasn't especially hungry any more. She just made noises, little grunting sounds, when the man stopped talking for long enough that it seemed like he was expecting something of her. In general she thought his methods of instruction, if that was what they were supposed to be, were probably quite effective – and something her teachers at school could benefit from. Half her friends never seemed to learn anything, but regarded school as something halfway between a social club and a catwalk. Boarding them up under a floor and just talking at them *for ever*, she thought, might rearrange their priorities. Could be that all that Spanish vocab would just slip right in. Maybe she'd get Mom to suggest it at the next PTA. But really you had to be given something to eat every now and then or you stopped being able to pay attention.

He waited patiently while she went through a coughing fit that seemed to last about an hour. And then he started talking again. This time it was about Stonehenge and so she listened for a while, because Stonehenge was in England and though they hadn't gone there she knew she liked England. England was cool and it had good bands. But when he started on how Stonehenge was only partly an observatory, and mainly a map of human DNA as it was supposed to be, she allowed her attention to drift.

At the end he gave her some more water. The phase during which she had rejected it hadn't lasted very long. Even if she had wished to keep up the defiance, her body simply wouldn't have allowed it. On the third occasion her mouth had opened without her mind having anything to do with it. The water tasted clean and pure and good. She remembered that once it had tasted different from what she was used to. That had been a long time ago.

'Good girl,' the man had said. 'See – you're not being badly treated. I could have pissed on you then and you'd still have had to drink it. Listen to your *body*. Listen to what's inside.'

'There's nothing inside,' she croaked. And then, for the last time, she had pleaded with him: 'Please. Anything. Even just vegetables. Carrots or cabbage or capers.'

'Still you ask?'

'Please,' she said, her temples feeling as if they were turning to mist. 'I don't feel well and you have to feed me or I'm going to die.'

'You're persistent,' he said. 'It's the one thing that still gives me hope.' He hadn't explicitly denied the request, simply talked about vegetarianism, explaining how it was wrong because human beings had omnivorous dentition and how not eating meat was a result of people spending too much time in their minds, which were infected, and not enough listening to their bodies. Sarah let him drone on. Whatever. Personally, vegetarians bugged her, too, mainly because the ones she knew seemed so superior, like Yasmin Di Planu, who made a big fuss about animal rights the whole time but had the finest collection of shoes in the whole school, the vast majority of them made out of things that had once been able to move about under their own steam and not just because they were strapped around her pretty little feet.

After he'd let her drink this time, he replaced the cover again and went away. During the following two hours Sarah had been completely lucid, which was one of the things that worried her about what had happened next. She knew she had been lucid because she had been thinking about escaping. Not thinking about actually doing it. She seldom imagined that any more, although for a while it had occupied most of her waking thoughts. At first she had pictured suddenly finding the strength to burst up from beneath the floor, like some person who'd been buried too soon and was real pissed at everyone. Then it had been the idea of talking to the man, charming him – she was charming, she knew that; there were boys at school, had been boys, who hung on her every word, not to mention the waiter in the Broadway Deli they'd had one time who came back to the table to check on them, like, *far* more often than had been strictly necessary, and on this occasion, for once, it hadn't been Sian Williams's attention that one of the penis people was trying to catch – or discussing it rationally with him, or finally even just *ordering* him to let her out. Each of these had been tried and proved laughably ineffective. In the end it had been fantasies of her father just coming and finding her. She still thought about this sometimes, but not as often as she once had.

Anyway, then she had heard something coming into the room above her. At first she thought it was the man, but then she realized it could not be. It had far too many feet. These feet had walked round and round the room and crisscrossed back and forth directly over her head. Then they had stopped directly above her. There had been sounds like laughter, high-pitched sometimes, but also deep and ragged. It moved back and forth for a while, making unpleasant noises, like grunting and a strange bark, and bits of its body had thudded and other parts had slid with a kind of heavy rasp. Finally a moan, but it didn't sound like it was coming from just one throat, but from several at once, as if the creature had more than one mouth.

It had been still for a while after that, and then it had gone.

Sarah lay with her eyes wide open. This, she knew, was a bad development. Very bad. That had not been the man, or if it had, then he had changed into something. The thing she had heard was what she had most feared, and now it had come in daylight and was no longer biding its time. There could be no doubt.

It had to have been Nokkon Wud himself.

Chapter 23

Nina left the house early, leaving a note saying she'd call. Zandt spent the morning pacing around the patio. Each morning he woke it was less likely that Sarah Becker was still alive. Knowing this did not open any doors.

He went over the theory he'd presented to Nina, and was unable to find fault with it. He knew it was largely speculation, and understood that he had his own reasons for clinging to the idea. If the man he had killed had been responsible for the abduction of the girls, had snatched them to hand them on to someone he knew would kill them, Zandt believed he would find a way of coming to terms with having killed him. The last two years of solitude had taught Zandt one thing, and taught it well: If you can live with yourself, the opinions of others can be withstood. He was aware that The Upright Man probably thought the same, but that didn't change the fact.

Heavy coffee intake and the view gradually turned his hangover into a generic malaise that he could ignore. The kinks in his neck and back from a night on the couch had gone. The sea could do that for you, even at this distance.

At midday he had spiralled indoors in search of food. Nothing in the fridge. Nothing in the cupboards or the freezer. Zandt didn't think he'd met a woman who didn't even have a small pack of cookies in the house, or some bread in the freezer, ready for toasting. It seemed most women would live on toast, if they had the chance. At a loss, he found himself wandering around the living room, looking at the materials on the bookshelves. There were books on serial crimes, both popular and academic; collections of papers on forensic psychology; reams of photocopied case notes, all in folders, organized by state – an outright illegality. A few novels, none of them recent, and most written by people called Harris and Thompson and Connelly and King. Very little that wasn't concerned with the dark side of human behaviour. It looked familiar, from the afternoons he had spent in the house in 1999, hours during which criminology had been the last thing on his mind. He had made his peace with this a long time ago. Jennifer had never found out, and the affair had affected neither what he felt for her nor the outcome of their marriage.

He took down one of the folders of case notes and absently flicked though it. The first section detailed the activities of a man called Gary Johnson, who had raped and murdered six elderly women in Louisiana in the mid-nineties. A note clipped to the front page recorded that Johnson was currently serving six life sentences in a prison Zandt knew would be a hell on earth: a dungeon full of dangerous men whose small seams of affection were usually reserved for their elderly mothers. It would be a miracle, in fact, if Johnson was still alive. One for the good guys. The next section held information about a case in Florida that, at the time of the most recent entries, had been ongoing. Seven young men missing.

One for the killers. One of many.

He took down another folder.

*   *   *

248

Two hours later he was sitting in the middle of the floor, surrounded by paper, when there was a knock at the door. He lifted his head, confused. It took another few raps before he realized what the sound was.

He opened the door to find a short man with bad hair standing outside. Behind him was a car that had once been gracious.

'Cab,' the man said.

'I didn't order a cab.'

'I know you didn't. The lady ordered it. She said for me to come here, pick you up. Take you. Everything very fast. At all times.'

'What lady?' He felt fuzzy, head full of what he'd been reading. Something within it was pulling at him.

The man grunted impatiently and rooted in his pocket. He pulled out a mangled piece of paper and angled it towards Zandt as he read it. 'Nina is the lady. She say to tell you to hurry. You maybe found something, or she found something, a righteous man – I don't understand that part. But we go now.'

'Where?'

'The airport, man. She said I do this very fast and she give me triple fare, and I need this money so can we leave now, for please?'

'Wait here,' Zandt said. He turned and went back inside. He picked up the phone and dialled Nina's cell phone.

After two rings she answered. There was a lot of background noise, the hectoring, muffled sound of a voice on a public address system.

'What's going on?' he said.

'Are you in the cab?'

Her voice was excited, and for some reason he found this irritating. 'No. What are you doing at LAX?'

'I got a call from the guy I had monitoring the Web. We got a hit on "The Upright Man".'

'It's three words, Nina. It could be an exhibition of Robert Mapplethorpe photographs. And presumably the Feds are already on the case.'

'It wasn't a Fed trace,' she admitted, annoyed. 'I did it independently.'

'Right,' Zandt said. 'Figures.'

'He logged the IP address of the computer that made the search, and hacked out the access line of the call. Come on, John. It's the first time this has come up in two years. I never handed in the note you got. As far as the world at large is concerned, he's still called The Delivery Boy.'

There was an explosion of noise from the handset, as someone bellowed another announcement at the other end.

Zandt waited for it to be over, and then said: 'I told Michael Becker.'

'The hit's not from LA,' Nina snapped.

'Where, then. *Where?*'

'Upstate. Some burg near the border with Oregon. A Holiday Inn.'

'Have you called the local Bureau?'

'The nearest SAC hates me. There's no way he'll send anybody out for me.'

Right, Zandt thought. And in the unlikely event that this turns out to be more than a wild goose chase, you want to be the one making the arrest. Through the door he could see the cab driver still waiting, hopping from foot to foot.

'Too risky, Nina.'

'I'll get some local cops for an escort. What*ever*. Look John, there's a plane leaving in forty minutes. I'm going to be on it, and I bought two tickets. Are you coming or not?'

'No,' he said, and put down the phone.

He went back to the door and told the driver he wasn't going anywhere, giving him enough money to make him go away.

Then he swore, grabbed his coat and a handful of files, and was able to throw himself in front of the cab before it left the driveway. He told himself that he had enough on his conscience without adding Nina to it.

That it was nothing to do with wanting to protect her.

250

Chapter 24

When I woke at nine the next morning, sprawled over the bed as if dropped from a great height, I found Bobby had left a note on the bedside table. It suggested I meet him in the lobby as early as possible. I showered myself into a semblance of humanity and headed down there, shambling along the corridors like a sloth forced to walk on its hind legs, a sloth well past its best. The night's sleep had made me feel different, though not necessarily better. My thoughts were blurred and sluggish, as if full of crushed ice and an unfamiliar alcoholic drink.

The lobby was mainly empty, just some couple standing over by the desk. Soft music was playing in the background. Bobby was sitting in state in the middle of a long couch, reading the local paper.

'Yo,' I mumbled, when I was standing in front of him.

He looked up. 'You look like shit, my friend.'

'And you're as annoyingly spruce as ever. What's the deal? You climb into an egg each night and emerge reborn? Or is it an exercise thing? Do tell. I want to be just like you.'

Outside the sky was cloudless and bright, and it was all I could to do to stop myself from yelping. I limped across the parking lot behind Bobby, shielding my eyes.

'Your phone's on? And juiced?'

'Yes,' I said. 'Though frankly I don't see the point. Either Lazy Ed hasn't been home, in which case we're wasting our time heading out there, or he has and doesn't want to talk.'

'You are beink very negative, Vard,' Bobby observed in a Germanic accent. 'Hand me the keys. I'll drive.'

'I feel negative,' I said. 'Good thing I've got a happy android for company. But if you use that voice again I'm going to knife you.' I tossed the keys to him.

'Stop right there.' This was said clearly and firmly, and it wasn't Bobby who was talking. We looked at each other, and then turned.

Four people were standing behind us. Two were uniformed cops, locals: one was in his late fifties and trim and lean, the other about thirty years old and a good forty inches around the gut. Off to one side stood a man in a long coat. Standing nearest to us, about ten feet away, was a slim woman in a neat suit. Of the group, she looked easily the most intimidating.

'Put your hands on the top of the car,' she said.

Bobby smiled ominously, and left his hands exactly where they were. 'This would be a joke of some kind?'

'Hands on the fucking car,' the younger cop said. He moved his hand closer to his holster, clearly itching to use it. Or at least hold it.

'Which one of you is Ward Hopkins?' the woman asked.

'Both of us,' I said. 'Weird cloning thing.'

The young cop abruptly started walking toward us. I put a hand up at chest height, and he walked straight into it.

'Take it easy,' the woman said.

The deputy didn't say anything, but he stopped coming forward, and just glared at me.

'Okay,' I said, keeping my hand in place but not pushing with it. 'Let's not let this get out of hand. Local PD, I take it?'

'That's correct,' the woman said, flipping identification. 'They are. And I'm a federal agent. So be cool, and let's see some hands being put on that car.'

'I don't think so,' said Bobby, still resolutely underwhelmed. 'Guess what? I'm with the Company.'

The woman blinked. 'You're CIA?' she said.

'That's right, ma'am,' he said, with ironic courtesy and a hick accent. 'All we need is some boys from the navy and we could have us a parade.'

There was an awkward moment. The younger cop turned to his older colleague, who in turn raised an eyebrow at the woman. None of them looked as confident as they had a second before. In the background, the man in the coat shook his head.

I decided to let my arm drop. 'He's CIA. I'm not,' I said, electing, for once, to be helpful. 'Just a member of the general public. Called Ward Hopkins. Why are you looking for me?'

'Wait a minute,' Bobby said. He nodded at the younger cop. 'Let's see you take a few steps back, hotshot.'

'Fuck you,' the cop said, equably.

The woman was still looking at me. 'An Internet search was logged yesterday evening,' she said. 'Somebody looking for "The Upright Man". Traced back to your account, and to this hotel. We're looking for someone by that name.'

'Not for me?'

'Until last night I had no idea you even existed.'

'So why are you looking for The Upright Man?'

'None of your business,' the younger cop said. 'Ma'am, are you going to arrest these assholes or not? I'm really not interested in listening to them otherwise.'

'Have it your own way,' I said. 'You can try to take us in, or you can take a walk. If the former, then, well, you're welcome to try, but really I can't advise it.'

The older cop smiled. 'Are you threatening us, son?'

'No. I'm too gentle for my own good. But Bobby's badly socialized. There's going to be blood all over this parking lot and none of it ours.'

Coat man spoke for the first time.

'Great,' he said, wearily. 'Six hundred miles to talk to a pair of shitheads.'

The woman ignored him. 'The Upright Man has killed at least four young women, maybe more than that. At the moment he has one who may still be alive and we don't have very long to find her.'

Bobby stared at her, his mouth slightly open.

'What?' she said. 'Does this mean something to you?'

'You're about to be scammed, Nina,' coat man said. 'You know what spooks are like.'

Bobby came back to earth enough to close his mouth, but not enough to start a fight. The woman looked at me.

'Tell me,' she said.

'Okay,' I said, 'It could be we need to talk.'

The older cop cleared his throat. 'Ms Baynam, I'm wondering if you really need me and Clyde any more?'

We got a table by the window in the hotel's excuse for a coffee lounge. The room was large enough, and new-looking, but had all the atmosphere of an empty cookie jar. Bobby and I sat close to the table, with the woman the other side. The guy in the coat – who'd finally been introduced, though only as being LAPD – sat a little distance away, making it clear that in an ideal world he'd be in another state entirely. The local law had already zipped off in their cruiser to eat pancakes and swap tales of how they would have beaten us up given the chance.

I took Bobby's sheaf of paper and laid it in front of the woman.

'If you want to know why we were searching for The Upright Man,' I said, 'then this is it. Actually we've been looking for something else. But this is what we found.'

She quickly read through the three sheets of paper. When she got to the end she handed the papers to the other guy.

'So what were you looking for?' she asked.

'A group of people called The Straw Men,' I said. 'Bobby traced a Web site that led to this. Searching for "The Upright Man" was the logical next step. That's all we know.'

'This is agency business?'

'No,' I said. 'It's personal.'

'There was a LINKS button at the bottom of the last sheet,' she said. 'What did that lead to?'

'What button?' I said.

'I found it after you crashed out,' Bobby said, looking sheepish. 'Hidden in a chunk of crashed Java code. Should have spotted it earlier.'

'And where did it go?'

'Serial killers,' he said, and at that the man in the coat looked up. 'Just fan sites. Pages of stuff about guys who kill, laboriously typed up by dweebs without the ambition to become real dangers to society.'

'Could you show me the first page again?' the woman asked.

He shook his head. 'It's gone. I checked back when I was done looking at fuzzy pictures of wackos. File no longer on the server, presumably moved somewhere else.'

'You didn't bookmark the pages it linked to?'

Bobby shrugged. 'I didn't see any reason to. All I had was guys with paranoid delusions and a hard-on for serial killers.'

'It's a leak,' the coat guy said, handing the papers back to the woman. 'Fan sites is right. That's all this is. Somehow The Delivery Boy's real name got out, and some psycho wannabe has set this shit up using his name. An interactive experience for people who want to drool over killer stats, complete with spooky moving site address. The net is full of this shit. Cannibal clubs slung up by fucks who can't earn a five-star badge working at McDonald's.'

I stared at him: 'The Delivery Boy?'

'That's what the press called the man we're looking for.'

'Jesus,' I said. 'You're still *looking* for that guy?'

'And will be until he's dead. Nina, I'm going for a cigarette. Then I suggest we head back to civilization.'

He got up and walked out of the room.

'He means "apprehended",' the woman said, quietly, after he was gone. 'Apprehended is what he meant.'

'Yeah, right,' Bobby said. 'You ask me, that's someone who needs keeping on a very tight lead.'

'What's the deal with these Straw Men?' she said.

'Tell her, Bobby,' I said, standing up.

'Take it very easy,' Bobby said, pointing a finger at me. 'And remember what I just said.'

I left them and walked out into the lobby. I could see the guy in the coat standing a few yards outside the main doors.

'You got a cigarette?'

He looked at me for a long moment, then reached into his pocket. When I was lit, we stood in silence for a while.

'You're that cop, aren't you?' I asked eventually. He didn't reply. 'Right?'

'I was a cop,' he said. 'Not any more.'

'Maybe so. But I was living in San Diego at the time. I read the news. There was one cop in particular, someone who was supposed to be a serial killer hotshot. Didn't catch him, then dropped out of sight. That would be you, I'm thinking.'

'Seems like you remember a lot about the case,' he said. 'Sure you don't have a vested interest? Maybe you're looking to see how many fans you got. Checking you're still a celebrity.'

'You thought I was him, we wouldn't be having this conversation. So don't jerk me around.'

He took a last drag of his cigarette, and then flicked it across the lot. 'So what are you doing?'

'I'm looking for the people who killed my parents,' I said.

He looked at me. 'These The Straw Men you mentioned?'

'I think so. What I don't know is if they're connected to the man you're looking for.'

'They're not,' he said, glaring out across the lot. 'This whole thing is bullshit and a waste of time we don't have.'

'Your friend doesn't seem to think so. Frankly, I don't care. But it seems to me that inside that hotel we've got two people who are connected to law enforcement agencies. Who can get things done. On the other hand, we've got you and me, who are currently connected to dick. We can stand outside and piss into each other's tents, or we can see where this leads and try not to get too much in each other's faces.'

He thought a moment. 'Good enough.'

'So what's your name, dude?'

'John Zandt.'

'Ward Hopkins,' I said, and we shook on it, and walked back into the hotel.

At the door to the restaurant my cell phone went off. I waved Zandt on and ducked back into the lobby.

I paused a second before hitting the connect button, trying to work out the right way to sound to an old guy who was running scared. I couldn't work out how that might be. All I could do was listen to what he had to say. And not shout at him, probably.

I answered the call and listened, but it wasn't him. I had a brief conversation, and then thanked someone. I put my phone away.

When I walked into the restaurant they were all sitting round the table, Zandt more in the loop this time. The woman looked up at me, but it was to Bobby that I spoke.

'Just got a call,' I said.

'Lazy Ed?'

'No. Girl from the hospital.'

'Yeah, and, so?'

'She spent the afternoon yesterday chasing down records.'

'You must have really made an impression.' I didn't reply, so he added: 'You going to tell what she found?'

257

'She traced both my parents back to their hometowns,' I said. 'Neither of which were the ones I had been given to believe.'

My voice was a little cracked. Zandt turned round to look at me.

'I didn't get as far as this bit,' Bobby said. 'But there's a sibling Ward's parents didn't get around to telling him about.'

'I don't think they really told me much at all. Much that was true, anyhow.' I was aware of the woman's eyes still on me; that, and how Hunter's Rock and everything I had thought I'd known now seemed like a favourite story I had been read, time and time again, but of which I could now remember only the title.

'What is it?' the woman asked.

'My mother couldn't have children.'

'Any more?' Bobby said. 'After you?'

'No. Any at all.'

Chapter 25

They came with us out to the bar. Young Ed wasn't fulsome in his greeting, and said only that he hadn't seen the old guy and still had no idea where he might be. He continued to say this even after Zandt had taken him to one side. I couldn't hear what the ex-cop was saying, but Ed's body language was enough to convince me that Zandt's conversational style was compelling.

'Your man is very keen to catch this killer,' I observed to Nina.

She looked away. 'You have no idea.'

Zandt eventually turned from the barman, who quickly slipped back behind the safety of his counter.

'We're wasting our time out here,' Zandt said, as we followed him back out into the parking lot. 'No offence to you guys, but I don't see how an old wino is going to help Nina and me in what we're looking for. Maybe it's relevant to you, but it's not getting us any closer to anything and Sarah is getting closer to death with every minute we waste.'

'So what do you want to do, John?' the woman asked. 'Head back to LA and sit on our butts there instead?'

'Yeah,' he said. 'Actually that's exactly what I want to do. I wasn't just pulling my wire at your house. I think . . .' He shook his head.

She frowned. 'What?'

'I'll tell you on the plane,' he muttered.

'Hey,' I said. 'I'll give you a little privacy.'

I walked away from them to where Bobby was standing, near to our car. 'Think the party's going to break up,' I said.

'So what's our plan?'

'Walk the streets, check the bars and diners and library and places where people hang out. Do it professionally. This isn't New York. There's a limit to how many places he can hide.'

'You knew this guy once. You got *no* clue where he might go?'

'I didn't really know him,' I said, turning to look back at the bar. 'I went in there and drank as a teenager. We passed the time of day and he served me alcohol. That's all.'

I remembered once again the evening my father had come to the bar with me, and the way Ed had given me a beer afterward, and I'd felt a little disloyal. I now realized there could have been some subtext in that night's events, something I'd missed back then. The beer Ed shoved toward me, with rough kindness – it could have just been a generic gesture, but I didn't think so now. Lazy Ed hadn't really been the type. Hadn't he actually been saying, 'Yeah, I know what the guy can be like?' If so, it implied even more strongly that Ed might have been the man running the camera in the first half of the middle section of the video, that he had been the one passed out and used as a candleholder. It also made it even stranger that, confronted with each other over a decade later, they'd given absolutely no indication that they knew each other. Something must have happened in Hunter's Rock, something that broke up a group of friends; but somehow caused three of them to get together again, a thousand miles away, once again pretending to outsiders that there was nothing between them. Nothing old, anyway, nothing in the past.

260

Even to me they'd made that pretence, but now it was looking as if that made perfect sense. If my mother couldn't have children, then who the hell *was* I?

Behind the bar the sky was opaque, making the trees look jagged and cold. It may have been that, or the smell of the pine on the cold air, that took me back so clearly to that night. Smells can do that, more so even than sights and sounds, as if the oldest parts of our mind, the ones that lock us in time and memory, still navigate through traces of scent.

'Hang on a minute,' I said, a faint light coming on in the back of my mind. I shut my eyes, chased the thought down. Something Lazy Ed had been talking about in that year, the kind of project that sounded like the fantasy of a man who wasn't well known for even keeping his bar surfaces clean.

Finally I got it. 'There's somewhere else we could try.'

'Let's do it,' Bobby said.

I looked over to the other two. I could see that in Zandt's head they were already at the departure gate. The woman looked less certain. I made the decision for them. This was a long shot, and not one I had the time or patience to explain to other people.

'Good luck,' I called. Then I got in our car and Bobby and I drove away.

The Lost Pond isn't lost, of course. It's about a mile walk into the forest that stretches north from Hunter's Rock: national land, not much used except by locals and a few hikers. It was a place you'd be taken on trips from school, out into the wilds to learn about bugs and stuff – a bus out to the fringe of the forest, and then a trek among trees through shuffling leaves, pleased to be out of the classroom. The teachers would try to keep everyone's mind on why they were there, but not too assiduously: you could tell from the looseness in their shoulders that they, too, were happy to be free of the usual boundaries. I remember seeing one of them pick up a small rock once, when he thought none of us was looking, and hurl it some distance at a fallen tree. He hit it, and smiled a private smile. That may have been the first time I realized that – contrary to appearances – teachers must be people, too.

When you got older you weren't taken out there any more. Lessons became focused on stuff you could memorize, not experience. But occasionally kids would go out there for the hell of it, and this was when the reason for the name would become apparent. Didn't matter how many times you'd been crocodiled out there with thirty yapping peers, if you tried to find it on your own or with a couple of friends, it never seemed to be where you thought it was. You'd walk into the banks of trees, quietly confident, and within a few hundred yards the track would have disappeared. A small creek ran diagonally away into the small hills, and most people would make it that far. You'd follow the creek until you came to the place where it joined a larger one, and from that point every decision you made would be wrong. Didn't matter how well you thought you remembered the route, how much you all agreed it had to be *this* way; a couple hours later you'd be back in the parking lot, thirsty and dog tired and just glad to be out again while it was still light and without having seen any bears.

Except for me. I went to the trouble, one summer when I didn't have a lot else to do, of learning where the pond was. I would have been fifteen, I think, a couple of years before the night in the bar with my father. I applied scientific method, which I was very impressed with at the time. I methodically worked through all of the route alternatives until I'd found where the pond was – and how to get there. I got very lost a few times, but it wasn't a bad way of spending a few weeks. When you know where you're going, a forest is a nice place to be. It feels safe, and you feel special. The problem was, once I'd successfully made the journey maybe ten times, I realized I'd ruined it for myself. There's no point in a lost pond that isn't lost. It becomes just a pond, and I stopped going. By that time I was getting more interested in knowing about places to go necking, and you couldn't get a girl to go walking in the forest after dark – certainly not in search of some patch of water that you might or might not be able to find. That's not the kind of thing that appeals to most girls. Or I didn't. One or the other.

Bobby and I were walking in single file, following a tributary of the creek. It had been over twenty years, and the environment had twisted and changed. The cover overhead was patchy, and cold shafts of sun came down to throw shadows.

We soon came to another intersection in the creek network, steep banks where it had cut down deep into the earth. I stopped at the top of one of the banks, momentarily unsure. The area didn't look familiar. There was some muttering in the ranks.

'And we're doing this because the guy said that he was *considering* putting up a hunting shelter, about . . . oh, twenty years ago?'

'You can go home now if you want.'

'Without my faithful native tracker?'

After another slow look around, I understood the way the vegetation had changed. One of the trees I had used for a marker had fallen down in the intervening years. Some time ago, too: the remains were moss-covered and rotten. I reoriented myself and headed into the gully.

The sides were steep and slick with leaves, and we were careful on the way down. When I reached the bottom I turned left and took us along the slight incline.

'We're nearly there,' I said, pointing up the way. About two hundred yards ahead, the gully banked steeply to the right. 'I think it's just around that kink.'

Bobby didn't say anything, and I assumed that, like me, he'd become absorbed into the experience. Forests are one of those things that you lose for a while, until you have your own kids and start to appreciate certain things again, see them reborn through a child's eyes – like ice cream and toy cars and squirrels. I spent some time considering if this had something to do with why I liked hotels. Their corridors are like routes between trees, their bars and restaurants like little clearings for assembly and eating. Nests of varying size and prestige, all held within the same structure, a private forest.

The Upright Man's manifesto had gotten into my head more than I'd realized.

'Somebody's watching us,' Bobby said.

'Where?'

'Don't know,' he said, glancing up at the sides of the gully above us. 'But he's up there somewhere.'

'I don't see anyone,' I said, keeping my eyes forward. 'But I'll take your word for it. So what do we do?'

'Keep walking,' Bobby said. 'If it's him, he's either going to wig out or stay put and make a decision on whether to come talk. He sticks his head far enough above the parapet, I'll go after him.'

We covered the last hundred yards quietly, resisting the urge to look up. At the turn in the gully the floor rose sharply, and we scrambled up a couple of feet.

And there, in front of us, was the Lost Pond. Maybe a hundred yards by sixty, steeply banked for the most part, but with a couple of muddy little beaches. A few ducks floated in the middle, and trees overhung much of the shallow water. I walked up to the edge and looked into it. It was like looking in a mirror and seeing myself as I was when I was fifteen.

'You know where the hide was?' Bobby asked.

'All I know is that he was planning one. He mentioned it twice, maybe three times. Not to hunt. Just somewhere to hang. Ed was a bigtime loner.'

'Plus a pervert, maybe?'

'No.' I shook my head. 'No one comes out here to make out. It's kind of spooky at night.'

He looked around, checking out the terrain. 'If I was going to put up a shelter, I'd do it over there.' He pointed at an area of trees and thick brush that extended over the slope on the west side of the pond. 'Prospect- and refuge-wise.'

I led the way round the pond, peering ahead to where Bobby had indicated. Could have been my imagination, but it did look as if an area in the middle was thicker than the rest, as if materials had been gathered and heaped up.

It was then that the first shot rang out. A sharp crack, following a whiz and then a whine.

Bobby yanked me back from the edge of the pond and started running. Another shot swished through the leaves a couple of feet above us. When we were behind the trunks I twisted my head round, trying to see where the shots were coming from.

'What is *with* this guy?'

'Wait,' I said. 'Look over there.'

I pointed at the thicker area of undergrowth. A head was now poking out of the brush – the head of an old man, one who was nowhere near the place the shots were coming from.

'Shit,' Bobby said, a gun now in his hand. Two men in fatigues were running down the side toward the pond. Another man in denim was approaching from the other side.

'That's the guy from the bar last night,' I said. 'The one who boxed us in.'

The men in khaki had reached the opposite side of the pond. The larger of the two dropped to a kneeling position, and fired directly at the stand of trees: measured, unhurried shots. The other was heading fast round the other side of the pond, banking it high to get round the top. Denim man was also shooting.

'Who the fuck are these guys?'

'Bobby – one's heading around toward Ed.'

'I'm on it,' he said. 'Let's have some cover.' He sprinted off. I pulled my gun, stepped out from the side of the tree, and started firing.

The kneeling man executed a neat roll to the side and slipped behind the remains of a large fallen tree. I cut sideways through the trees. I was shooting into cold and slanting light, flickered across my face by the uprights of twisted trees, half my mind on avoiding roots so I didn't go flying. Within ten seconds there was a cry, and the denim man spun around and fell onto his back.

Bobby was ploughing into the undergrowth ahead, firing at the guy coming down the rise, having cut up around in the high ground. The man was ignoring Bobby and me altogether, despite the fact that Bobby was firing at him; he was concentrating on shooting at Lazy Ed's shelter.

I stopped, steadied, and fired.

The first bullet hit him in the shoulder. One from Bobby followed half a second later, and the man was punched backward against a tree. But he kept shooting, and still not at us.

I fired again, twice, getting him plumb in the chest. Bobby had stopped running too now, and three shots of his followed. The man disappeared from sight.

I took a step forward but Bobby flapped a hand back at me, indicating that I should stay where I was. He moved ahead cautiously.

'Ed?' I called. 'Are you okay?'

Suddenly the man in khaki came into view again. He'd slid a little way down the hill, under cover of the undergrowth. As Bobby and I watched, astounded, he pushed himself to his knees, still holding what I now saw was a machine pistol.

Before I could think of moving, the man started firing again. He was dying in front of our eyes, but he had time to put maybe another fifteen shells into the undergrowth. He didn't consider taking us down. It was like we weren't even there.

Then he slumped forward onto his face and was quiet for ever.

Bobby turned on his heel and doubled back, reloading. I ran forward, kicked the dead guy over to check, and shoved my way into the undergrowth.

Right in the middle were the remains of a hide. A loose collection of weathered wood, dry brush, twisted old branches. Unless you were looking for it, you'd probably think it was natural, at most the remains of something from long ago, rather than something a

266

man had put together for shelter because he just liked sitting out in the woods and looking down at a pond. Lying in the middle of it was Lazy Ed.

I knelt beside him and knew that he wouldn't be leaving the forest. You couldn't count the holes. His face was least affected, though one ear was gone and you could see the bone.

'What's going on, Ed?' I said. 'What the fuck is happening? Why is someone killing all of you?'

Ed swivelled his head an inch or so, looked up at me. It was hard to see the man I'd once slightly known, among the wrinkles and burst blood vessels.

'Fuck you,' he rasped, quite clearly. 'You and your fucking family.'

'My family is dead.'

'Good,' he said, and died.

There was nothing to find in the shelter. A few empty cans, a stash of tobacco, a half-full bottle of very cheap tequila. I thought about closing Ed's eyes and then didn't. Instead I turned round and walked back out of the bush.

By the time I reached the pond, and the body of the man in denim, Bobby was heading back down a hillock toward me.

'Got away,' he muttered.

'He looked like he knew what he was doing. You okay?'

'Yeah, except I nearly got lost on the way back.'

'It's a lost pond,' I said. My hands were shaking. 'Jesus.'

'They dealt the play,' he said. 'We weren't looking for this.'

'I know,' I said, overcome with the bizarreness of being back in a childhood environment, this time with a gun. 'But what difference does that make? Someone will always be shooting somebody.'

Bobby squatted down next to the denim man's body and felt through his pockets until he found a wallet. He flipped through it in front of me. There was no driver's licence, no stamps, no receipts, no photos – none of the standard wallet detritus. Nothing except for about forty dollars.

'Did you look at the other dead guy?'

'Only for long enough to make sure he wasn't going to start shooting again,' I said. 'He was wearing a vest, but I'm still impressed at how long he kept going. That guy showed real dedication to his task. Which was nothing to do with us. They could have taken us out easily. They were after Lazy Ed. We were just in the way.'

Bobby nodded. 'There was no identification on him either,' I said. 'At all. I turned back the collar of his sweater, and looked in the back of his pants. No labels. They'd been cut out.'

'It's The Straw Men,' he said. 'They're taking them out one by one.'

'But why? And how did they find us?'

He shrugged. 'The Fed chick did. Maybe they did it the same way. It's their Web page: they'd have immediate notification of any access, without waiting for some hacker to intercept it. Or they could have been on the case before we were, Ward. There's evidence that some sort of cleanup is in operation.'

He looked up at me, looking tired and pissed off with our failure. 'Either way they got the job done. There's nothing left for us here except trouble, and we already got enough of that.'

Without another word we started walking.

Chapter 26

Nina had assumed Zandt would explain to her what was on his mind, but from the moment the other two guys had left, he'd clammed up. When he'd turned up at LAX in the cab, though he hadn't been particularly friendly, he had at least seemed to be present. As soon as they'd established that the men at the Holiday Inn in Hunter's Rock – whatever they might have been up to, and she still had questions about that – were nothing to do with The Upright Man, it was like he'd retreated again. She felt stupid about hauling them upstate, but making a mistake was better than doing nothing. She was very aware of the passage of time, aware of it as acutely as if someone was pulling her skin off her face. In her it bred a desire to talk, to try to do or say something, anything, almost as if they could vocalize a solution into existence. In Zandt it seemed to have the opposite effect. It would not be long, she believed, before he became utterly mute.

The plane was mostly empty and yet he hadn't even sat next to her. He was across the row, studying some old files he'd taken from the house. She called the office in Brentwood, and established that nothing had changed there, while not making it clear that she wasn't exactly just around the corner.

Then she turned back to the window, and stared down at the land passing below as they flew over it back to LA, wondering if they were passing over the very place, the hidden house or cabin, whatever The Upright Man called his own. The knowledge that they might be, that Sarah Becker might be under her somewhere, was impossible to bear. Instead she yanked the in-flight magazine out of the pouch and tried very hard to read it.

Zandt was barely aware he was on a plane, and he wasn't even thinking about Sarah Becker. Instead he was considering four disappearances, spread over the country in a three-year period. There was little to tie them together except that copies of the case files were now on his lap. But if there was some kind of brokering service, the usual rules of serial investigation might no longer apply. If you had a series of disappearances or bodies within a tightly confined geographical area, it was a fair assumption you could limit the search for evidence or corollary events to within that same space. Most killers had their hunting grounds, a few square miles in which they were confident. Some would limit their field of activity to a few blocks, even a couple of streets – especially if preying on sections of society that didn't inspire committed interest from the authorities. Zandt remembered watching footage of the demolishing of the house that had held Jeffrey Dahmer's apartment, the place where young black and Asian men had been dismembered, worshipped, and eaten, in one order or another. Families of the victims watched the event, most mutely, some merely sobbing – but a few demanding an explanation from anyone who would listen, trying to elicit some reason to accept the fact that their children had been taken from them and murdered without anyone seeming to care very much.

Disappearances on opposite sides of the country were seldom

judged against each other, even after the FBI became involved, especially if they took place within a similar time frame. You didn't snatch someone from San Francisco on Tuesday night and then grab another in Miami in the small hours of Thursday morning.

Not, at least, if the same man was involved. Zandt had been looking for disappearances that shared characteristics with those connected with The Upright Man, and that also had taken place in the same years. He was not expecting to find other instances of little keepsakes with a girl's names embroidered on each of them. The Upright Man was clever enough to seek to imply that the LA cases were unconnected with any in other parts of the country.

This was the realization that had been nagging at him when the cab had arrived to take him to LAX: that the sweaters were showy. That they might have little or nothing to do with the killer's pathology, and instead be a way of fencing off a small group of cases by making them appear unrelated to anything else. That The Upright Man might have judged that the police were as likely to be impressed by such a touch as were the audiences for films where chrysalises were left in corpses' throats, or TV series where each week a man caught killers who wore their innermost psychoses on their sleeve. You got a sweater with a name on it, it's one of ours. You haven't, then it isn't, and we're not interested in hearing about it. Our guy's got a pathology. That's what we're looking for. It's one of the few tools we've got, we're sticking by it and can't you see how busy we are already?

Zandt believed it was all too possible that The Upright Man might not have a pathology at all, that he might not be susceptible to profiling. He could be out there doing it, taking victims culled from anywhere in the country. Maybe even anywhere in the world. Just because he wanted to.

The subjects did not constitute a clearly distinguishable group. We covet beauty because beauty makes people recognizable, makes them look famous. Zandt did not consider the long hair to be a reliable indicator either. If he was right in thinking that the sweaters

271

were a false trail, then the length of the girl's hair might simply be a means to an end. There were only two distinguishing features. The first was age. Many young children disappear, and a number of old men and women are battered in their homes. Both unwittingly put themselves in the path of statistics by virtue of their physical weakness. Of the remainder, the majority of women who disappear are in their late teens or early twenties: sufficiently young (and not too old) to have independent lives; women who can be found walking home late at night, who might live alone, who have the youthful confidence to come to the aid of an affable man with his arm in a sling and his face just in shadow in the corner of a parking lot late at night. Women of all ages disappear, but the big spike in the graph came in this range. The Upright Man's known victims, however, along with the missing girls in the files on his lap, had been in their middle teens. Girls who were old enough to present a physical challenge to their abductor, but too young to often be found in the most vulnerable environments. This didn't mean that Zandt could simply batch any girl between the ages of fourteen and sixteen and call them possibles. There were plenty of places all over the country where a girl of that age might well be out on the street at night, plying a trade. If The Upright Man or his procurer had been concerned with age alone, he could have driven a truck to the right part of the right town and loaded it up to standing-room only. Instead he selected not only from a group who were circumstantially less vulnerable than average because of their age, but who also came from social backgrounds that mitigated against easy availability. Elyse LeBlanc's family had been a little less well-off than the others, but still firmly middle class. The rest were verging on wealthy. The Upright Man wasn't just looking for meat. He was looking for what he perceived to be quality.

Zandt sat, staring at the reproduced pictures of the dead girls. His mind seemed to revolve faster and faster, mixing the facts in front of him in with the ones he had internalized two years before. The places, the names, the faces. He tried to see it all as one, removing

272

only his own family and daughter, who he was now convinced had only been chosen as a lesson to him. Zandt had tried removing Karen from the equation before, but had never been able to. An awareness of her disappearance had coloured everything he had thought and done from the moment he and Jennifer found the note outside their door. But now he substituted her with the girls in the new files, trying to sense whether they were connected by anything other than speculation. Trying to reach out from the place where he was headed, where he had lived most of his life, the strange city of dream-makers, of poverty and test screenings and murder and money – to other places, other nights, other hunting grounds. To other cities, other machines, forests of buildings and rivers of concrete where other men and women missed the stars at night and tended small plants on window sills and kept tiny dogs to take for walks along corridors in the endless procession of boxes and intersections and lights; where they rented space in other people's property so they had somewhere to sleep so they could get up and perform profit-related tasks they neither understood nor cared about, simply so they would be given the tokens of exchange they needed in order to rent the space in which they slept and snarled and watched television until finally some of them slipped out of their windows and ran howling down the dark streets, throwing off a numbness handed down from a society that was itself trapped in fracture and betrayal and despair; the lonely insane in a culture turning into a Christmas bauble, gaudy beauty wrapped around an emptiness which was coalescing faster and faster into parking lots and malls and waiting areas and virtual chatrooms – non-places where nobody knew anything about anybody any more.

Abruptly the whirling stopped.

Chapter 27

It was growing dark by the time we got back to the hotel room. There were two messages for Bobby. While he called people back I turned the TV on with the sound muted, watched the local news channel out of a grim interest in seeing how long it took the story to break. The chances were that there would have been hikers in earshot, who would eventually find the bodies. Though there was nothing to tie us to the event, I wanted us out of Hunter's Rock fast.

I walked quickly round the room, packing up my few bits and pieces.

'Christ,' Bobby said, his voice harsh and strange. I turned to see him still on the phone. 'Turn the television on.'

'It is on.'

'Not local shit. CNN or something.'

I flipped through the channels until I found it.

The footage was hand-held and shaky. A big grey building in some urban environment. A school. It had obviously been filmed earlier in the day, because it was still light.

'We got it,' Bobby said into the phone. 'I'll call you back.'

I flipped the mute off, and we listened as the voice-over put the death toll at thirty-two, with many still missing and half the building still unsearched. It was unclear whether the two pupils shot by police had been solely responsible for the atrocity, or whether a third individual had been involved. Rifles and a large home-made incendiary device had been involved.

The camera roved around the devastation, catching glimpses of knots of children and teachers, faces shocked white in the lamp glare. The ambient sound was down in the mix, but you could still hear the sirens and sobbing. A woman staggered past, supported on both sides by paramedics, her face entirely covered in blood.

'Where is this?'

'Evanston, Maine.' Bobby closed his eyes.

The TV cut to live footage. The scene was calmer now, all but a few bystanders held back from the school by incident tape. A man in a tan coat held a microphone, flicker-lit by blue flashing lights. Two additional bodies had been found. Jane Mathews and Frances Lack, both eleven years of age.

Back to earlier footage. Fire trucks, ambulances. Wounded people, both children and adults, lying on the ground, being attended to. Others on the ground with no one holding their hand. People to whom no one could make a difference any more.

'Holy *fuck*,' I said, pointing at the screen. The camera panned along the street opposite the school, at people standing watching the gate to hell that had been opened. Amongst them was a tall blond man with a large shoulder bag, caught from behind. Unusually, he was not craning to get a better view, like everyone around him, but was standing calm and still. The cameraman didn't notice him, and passed on along the line, a slow pan of appalled shock.

'I've seen that guy before,' I said.

A blond man, at The Halls, with a blue shoulder bag.

*　　*　　*

Bobby spent a chunk of the flight on the phone. I overheard him talking to three different people, arranging for tapes to be couriered to Dyersburg airport. Then he sat quiet and stared into his complimentary coffee for a while.

I looked at him. 'They're sure it's just these kids?'

'Their homes are being turned upside down as we speak, but nothing's come up so far. Isn't some global hatred thing this time. This was the handiwork of two well-adjusted young Americans, so far as anyone can tell. The mood in general is not buoyant.'

I could believe this. The atmosphere among the other travellers was subdued, and even the pilot's 'Well, here we are on board' speech had been extremely muted.

'I didn't hear you telling anyone about what happened to us today.'

He laughed harshly. 'Right. "Hey, we just killed a couple guys in the woods, and when we got back to the hotel this friend of mine saw another guy on TV he thinks he recognizes"? This is not high concept, Ward, and you are not exactly remembered fondly. The Agency's cleaned itself up a little, my friend. They'd throw me out even more happily than they did you.'

'They didn't throw me out. I walked.'

'One step ahead of a polygraph subpoena.'

'Whatever,' I snapped. 'Bobby, that was the guy.'

'You said you barely saw him up there. You admitted you didn't see his face.'

'I know. But it was him.'

'I believe you,' he said, and suddenly he looked serious. 'Weird thing, I thought I knew him, too.'

'What? Where from?'

'Don't know. Christ, by the time I saw what you were pointing at he was gone. But there was something familiar about him.'

It was dark by the time we landed. The car I'd left in the airport lot was gone, presumably retrieved by its rental firm. Bobby went to the other desk and got us a new vehicle. All they had was a very

276

large Ford. I fetched it from their lot and swung around to wait by the main exit.

Bobby eventually came out of the terminal with a small box under his arm.

'Cool,' he said tersely, as he climbed in the front. 'Room for the kids and a whole week's shopping. Let's go find us a Publix.'

'Least we can sleep in it if we have to.'

'I'm not even going to think about that.'

'You're getting soft, soldier.'

'Yes I am, and that means I don't have to eat broccoli any more, to paraphrase an esteemed former president.'

'Esteemed by whom?'

'His mother.'

Bobby still had the keys to the room he'd taken at the Sacagawea. After checking that it didn't seem to be occupied by anybody else, he went off to negotiate with the management.

I hunted down a couple of cans of iced tea and then let myself back into the room. It brought to mind long-ago vacations even more strongly than the pool at the motel outside Hunter's Rock. Fifty or more years of people briefly inhabiting the same space, camping out in the middle of a journey. The chair I sat in could once have held someone watching *Gilligan's Island* broadcast for the first time, to whom the tune was not a hot-wired piece of race memory. One day someone else might sit there, in their silicon-enhanced space-clothes sipping a no-sugar, no-caffeine, no-flavour moon drink, and think the same thing of *Friends*: 'Hey – look at all the skinny people. And what was the deal with the *hair?*'

Bobby returned with a massive VCR under his arm.

'Old fool hadn't even noticed I'd left,' he said. 'Though he was sharp enough over a deposit for this piece of archaeology. I think you may actually have to wind it up.'

Once the machine was connected to the room's near-collectible television, Bobby perched on the end of the bed and ripped open the package he'd picked up at the airport. Inside were a couple of

VHS tapes. He quickly checked the labels, and stuck one of them inside the machine.

'This is unedited,' he explained, as he pressed the PLAY button. 'Viewer discretion is advised.'

The cameraman had arrived at the scene of the school bombing very soon after the initial explosion. In most of America's big cities there's a market for freelance news crews, two-person units who roam the city like ownerless dogs. They scan official radio bands and often get to the jumpers and pileups and bullet-scarred bars ahead of the cops, in search of freak-show footage to help the networks and cable channels fulfil their ever-expanding screen-minute quota. Something about the quality of the camerawork suggested this kind of provenance, though I could have been wrong. Confronted with these scenes it's possible my own hands wouldn't have been too steady either. When you see atrocities on television it's easy to forget that – in spite of the impression of verity – the news has already been sanitized for our protection. We watch people standing round mass graves in Bosnia and the rough-and-ready quality of the footage helps us forget that we're not being shown what's inside, or what those dusty fragments mean to the people who are actually *there*, rather than watching safely through a thick piece of glass in a living room on the other side of the world. Even the wall-to-wall coverage of the World Trade Center horror steered clear of showing us what the emergency services saw. We're so used to being edited, so infected with the sleight of hand of the media, that we're more aware of what's been added than of what has been taken away. It doesn't matter how many 'making of' advertumentaries we watch, the latex monster will still scare us in context: and when watching the news we do not question why the pan ended at a particular moment, what was splattered across the frame we did not see. It's soft-core news, set up without the money shot. We're allowed to hear the screams, but at an acceptable and contextualized volume – all the while listening to a voice whose sombre outrage is in itself a kind of reassurance. 'This is wrong,' the voice implicitly tells us. 'This is bad. But it is rare, and it will be made better. This will pass, and in the end it will all be okay.'

This video had no voice-over. No cuts had been made. It said nothing. It merely showed.

The single explosion had ripped the front off of a squat, two-storey municipal building. In doing so it had sent tons of concrete, glass and metal flying out from a central point at very high speeds. These materials had interacted with others of their kind, and also with much softer substances. A great deal of this material had been blown clear to rain down outside. When the cameraman arrived – along with a sound technician whose appalled exclamations were audible at regular intervals – he had simply stumbled through the parking lot in front of the school, taking a curved path through the devastation. Occasionally he had whip-panned across to the out-building to his right, or to the other side of the lot as the police and ambulances began to arrive. But for the most part the camera merely recorded what was in front of its lens.

A girl who was apparently unaware of the fact she had lost an arm, and was running, screaming out someone's name. Parts of bodies, and heads. A young boy whose face was so covered in blood that he looked newborn, wandering through the smoke making a mewling sound. A long stretch of chunks of flesh, like a giant pile of bloody vomit, with a few identifiable features and body parts spread amongst it. Most of an older man, lying on the ground and twitching, all of his facial features burnt away and nothing left except a pink mass where a hole gaped in mute purposelessness. Half of an attractive young woman, her eyes open, nothing below the rib cage except a stump of spine and the hood of the car she had landed on.

Gradually the quality of the background sound began to change, as the most urgent screams died out and the sobbing and shouting climbed in volume to take its place. Slowly a semblance of order began to affect the people in the camera's gaze. Aimless movement was replaced by more directed activity, as society's white blood cells moved in and tried to impose a structure. Some of these men and women moved with purpose: pointing, shouting, bandaging. Others might as well have been victims themselves.

And then we saw him.

By this point the news crew had seen enough of the hardcore, and had gravitated out toward where the parking lot fed into an accessway onto the street. The soundman had been sick twice, the cameraman once. The crowd opposite the entrance to the lot had not yet had time to gather, but incident tape was already going up, fencing the event out of our reality, consigning it to exceptional circumstances.

The man was already there, however, standing more or less where I had spotted him earlier. Tall, with short blond hair, standing with his feet planted solidly on the ground. Looking out over the devastation, gazing up at the plume of smoke generated by a fire that at this point was nowhere near under control. Bobby hit PAUSE.

The man was not smiling. I don't want to give that impression. The picture jumped all over the place, and it was impossible to make out the detail of his face. He was merely watching.

Neither of us said anything. Bobby reached for his iced tea, tried to take a swig from it, realized he hadn't popped the can. He did so; swallowed half of it.

'Okay,' he said quietly. 'The rest is a long shot.' He ejected the tape, unconsciously handling it as if it might be contaminated. He stuck the other tape in the machine and pressed PLAY.

'Got this from one of the technicians in media analysis,' he said. 'It's for internal consumption, a reminder to people in Washington. A marketing tool. Footage of certain things that have happened in the last ten–fifteen years, continually updated.'

The first sequence showed material I recognized quickly, having been exposed to it in short doses for much of the last week. It was the aftermath of the shooting in England. The lighting was harsh, early-morning glare. The camera was rock steady, presumably the work of some well-trained BBC guy. Clumps of people holding each

280

other. Medics clustered around a door from which bodies were carried, some covered in sheets, others merely in blood. A couple of other well-behaved news crews. A ring of policemen around the intersection of two busy roads. There was little shouting or crying. The main sound was of traffic going past: people late for meetings, coming back from the gym, on their way to deliver litres of Diet Coke.

We didn't have to wait for long, but the shot was blurred and inconclusive. A pan across the chain fence, from the inside, showing people gathering outside. Amongst them a tall man, with fair hair. Bobby froze the tape, ran it back and forth. The face was too small, and the pan was too fast.

'It's him,' I said, nonetheless.

Over the next two hours we watched the rest, a tapestry of death stitched with points of light. I lost count after a while, but at least thirty episodes of mass murder were paraded in front of us, until the differences between them – the places, the sounds, the changes in clothing over more than a decade – seemed transparent in the face of the similarities. In most we saw nothing we could point to, but in a few we saw something close enough that we were prepared to add it to the list Bobby began on a piece of hotel stationery:

A food court in Panama City, Florida, 1996. A main street in northern France, 1989. A shopping mall in Dusseldorf, 1994. A school in New Mexico, just last year. An alleyway in a project in New Orleans, back in 1987, where an alleged drug deal gone bad had escalated into a situation that left sixteen people dead and thirty-one wounded.

'It's him,' I said, again and again. 'It's him.'

Eventually the tape stopped, without ceremony. Presumably very few people made it all the way through to the end.

'We need more tape,' Bobby said.

'No we don't,' I said. 'No, we really don't.'

'Yes. Of the ones where he wasn't caught on camera.'

'He probably wasn't there. He won't be the only one. There will be others like him.' I went through to the bathroom and drank about three pints of lukewarm water out of a very small glass.

'Plane crashes,' Bobby said, when I came back. 'Bombings in Northern Ireland, South Africa. Civil wars in the last ten years. Flu epidemics. Someone has to start them. Maybe we've been looking in the wrong places. Maybe it's not fundamentalists for one side or another. Maybe it's people who hate *everybody*.'

I shook my head, but without a great deal of conviction.

Bobby took the tape out of the machine and turned it over in his hands. 'But why just stand there? And what are the chances of him being caught in a camera shot, so many times?'

'It's not chance. It's a signature, supposed to be read by those who know. To say "The Straw Men did this".'

'But we've caught him now.'

'Have we? A blond man, shots too short and long to see properly, and a bunch of unconnected events spread over ten years and half the Western world? You want to call Langley, see if anyone's interested? Or shall we try CNN? We're nobody's idea of Woodward and Bernstein and this just sounds like conspiracy crap until we've got more than glimpses. You could spend all day on a computer and not get half an ID out of any of the images we've seen.'

'What about the Web page? The Manifesto?'

'It's not there any more, Bobby. We could have typed it ourselves.'

'So, what? You're just going to forget about it?'

'No,' I said. I sat on the end of the bed and picked up the hotel phone. 'There's maybe one person who would help. Two, in fact. The pair who hot-dogged it up to Hunter's Rock.'

'Why? They're after a serial killer.'

'And how would you define that term?'

'This is different. Killing a lot of people is not the same.'

'Not usually,' I said. 'But nobody says you can only do one and not the other. This guy is their point man. Organizer, inciter, evangelizer – the man who sets situations up, picks patsies, gets the job done. Terrorism without attribution. Murder for the sake of it. Then he stands and watches people sorting the body parts. You telling me that's not the kind of guy who could be into serial killing too? I think this guy is their killer. I think he's the real Upright Man after all.'

'Ward – you couldn't give the guy a parking ticket on that argument.'

'Maybe not. But we need help. Nina is the only person I can think of. These fucks killed my parents. I don't care what I have to say to get her on side.'

Bobby looked at me, and eventually nodded. 'Make the call.'

Chapter 28

Some of the time it was like being dead. Some of the time it was like being something else, like a fish or a tree or a cloud or a dog, a damn dog. Dogs are manic and preach in the streets but it's better being a damn dog than dead. Most of the time it was like being nothing at all, just a small bundle of sweet nothing floating down a river under a sky in which no birds sang.

Sarah was very ill by now. Very occasionally she would remember where and who she was. Her stomach had ceased to cramp. She had stopped registering its sensations. She believed it was still a part of her, and that she also retained her arms and legs. Sometimes there would be a horrible proof of this, an appalling pain that shot up from her toes all the way through her body. It was like a kind of pins and needles, except that the needles and pins were red-hot and a foot long and someone slid them under her skin and then pushed with all their might and left them there. The pain eventually faded, but Sarah was never present for that part. By the time that happened, she would be back on the river, floating downstream again.

Sometimes people would talk to her as she floated. She heard voices, anyhow. She would hear her friends, her grandmother and sister occasionally, but most often she would hear her mom and dad. Usually they were talking about inconsequential things, as if she was sitting at the table in the living room and doing her homework, and they were just next door and chatting the way you do. You couldn't hear all of what was being said, not usually. It was half-sentences, snatches here and there. 'Charles thinks Jeff's going to fly with this version.' 'Brunch, but this one could be worth it.' 'It's just a third-act thing.' Her mother would say things about her day, where she had been and who she had seen: 'You can do what you like with your face, but you can't hide the back of your hands.' But then her father would say something that had just come into his head, and she would hear all of it, like: 'You know what I'd do if I was famous? Stalk people. I'd find some nobody and just keep popping up in their lives. Who's going to believe them? "Hey, Mr Policeman – Cameron Diaz keeps bothering me." Or . . . "Look, I've got all these letters from Tom Cruise. No, I *have*. He's pestering me. That's his handwriting. It really *is*." You could send someone completely over the edge. Pretty quickly, too.'

Sarah didn't know whether she'd ever heard him say these things in the time before her life had become a drifting thing. She didn't think so. She thought it was something just for her, something to keep her company as she floated. He'd always said words for her, the things that came into his head. Mom didn't always realize they were jokes, and didn't often find them funny. Sarah usually did.

After a while the voices would fade.

At other times she would hear footsteps, and know that it was them come to save her. She would hear them getting closer and closer, until her mouth began to move, ready to say something when the panel was lifted and her father's face appeared. They would stand right above her, their feet shuffling on the boards that covered her body. But they never found her. The footsteps would fade, and then she would be floating again.

Occasionally something would rise up in her body, most often after Nokkon had come. Heaves, which cut across her stomach like a knife dipped in ice, until she felt sure she was going to split in two. There was nothing to come up, not even the water, because her body absorbed that as quickly as it could. Her body had got with the program. Sometimes it talked to her now, ticking her off. It was doing its best to hold steady, but it was really very unhappy with the situation. It couldn't be expected to deal with this. Her body had a voice like Gillian Anderson's. It was very reasonable and spoke in long sentences that it must have thought out very clearly ahead of time. But it wasn't happy, and it had stopped believing that things were going to get better. Sarah listened to what it said, and tried to take an interest, but she didn't think there was anything she could do to help.

Nokkon was her only real friend, and even he didn't come very often any more. Sarah got the feeling he was disappointed in her. He still talked, and gave her water, and told her things, but she sensed it was mainly for his own benefit. He pretended that he was a real person, that when he had been younger he had met people made of hay. That they had found him, or he them. That he had learned from them, and they now learned from him. Nokkon sometimes had those people with him now. That's what he said, anyway, though Sarah couldn't understand why he was bothering to lie. She knew what they were. They were his goblins. They did his bidding and ranged far and wide, watching out for those who were foolish enough to believe themselves lucky, as Sarah once had. They kept tabs on people with microphones and listening bats flying over every house in the world. Some of the goblins were very big, and could stomp hard enough to shake the ground into earthquakes and volcanoes. Others were very, very small and flew through the air and went in through people's pores so they could stir cells around and make black things grow in their lungs and hearts and liver. The big goblins had voices like thunder. The little ones sounded as if they were Welsh. When Sarah coughed she kept her mouth shut so that none of them could fly into her. A few of the goblins were normal sized. They were quite rare. She never saw any of them, but she knew they were there. She banged her head against the wood above her head, trying to make them go away.

Then everyone would fade out and it would get darker again and she would be floating on and on. At first when she'd floated, it had been like lying with her back on the water, borne along on the surface. It had actually been quite nice. But now she seemed to float lower and lower in the water, as if she was sinking. Her ears were already below the surface, and before long it would be her eyes.

When the tip of her nose was under, she knew she wouldn't be floating any more.

Chapter 29

Zandt stood outside a door in Dale Lawns. When his first ring on the buzzer elicited no response, he pressed it again, leaning on it with all of his weight until he saw a figure through the mottled glass in the door's upper portion, coming toward him out of the white light beyond.

Gloria Neiden was dressed in top-to-bottom designer, for an evening at home. Yet from her first words it was evident she was drunk. Not benign, cheerful drunk, or even falling-down drunk. Opaquely drunk. Drunk to be alone.

'Who the hell are you?'

'My name is John Zandt,' he said. 'We met two years ago.'

'I'm afraid I don't recall. I certainly don't remember making any arrangements to renew our acquaintance.' This was delivered well, with only one minor slur.

She started to close the door. Zandt stopped it with his hand.

'I was one of the policemen who worked the disappearance of

Annette Mattison,' he said.

Mrs Neiden blinked, and it was as if the movement caused a grey chemical to spread down through her face, something that imperfectly embalmed it.

'Yes,' she said, folding her arms. 'I remember you now. Good work. All nicely tidied away, right?'

'No. Which is why I'm here now.'

'My daughter is out with friends. And even if she wasn't, I would insist that she didn't speak to you. It has taken us all a long time to try to come to terms with what happened.'

'I'm sure,' Zandt said. 'And has it worked?'

She stared at him, momentarily sobered. 'What do you mean?'

'What I *mean*,' he said, 'is that my daughter also disappeared, and coming to terms with it is never going to happen. I want a very short period of your time, during which you might be able to help me find out who destroyed our lives.'

'Surely you should be talking to the Mattisons, rather than me?'

'I have one question for you. That's all.'

She turned away, this time pushing the door more firmly.

Zandt held it open once again, and spoke without allowing himself to think. 'A question that may stop your husband starting or continuing an affair. That may prevent your daughter from suggesting that it might be better if she doesn't bring her friends home. Which may mean that you're less likely to drive your car into a wall one afternoon because you misjudged a turn or because it just seemed like a good idea.'

Gloria Neiden stared at him. It took a few seconds for her to find a voice.

'Fuck off,' she said, low and hard. 'You have no *right* to speak to me like that. You should have found him. It's not my fault. None of this is my fault.'

'I know,' Zandt said, watching as her face underwent another horrific change, transformed from animal to frightened girl and back to woman, like a putty mask squeezed by a vicious child. 'Nothing that happened was your fault. I know that. Your family knows that. Everybody knows it except you. You can say it, but you don't really believe it. And that's what will kill you.'

They stood like that for a while, one each side of the doorway, both pushing. Then neither was pushing, merely standing.

He called Nina on the way to Santa Monica. She sounded distracted but agreed to meet him in Bel Air. The address was on file.

Michael Becker answered the door, and agreed to come with him without explanation. They left Zoë standing on the doorstep, holding their younger daughter's hand. She did not create a fuss or demand to be told what was going on. Zandt realized it would have been the same if it had been Zoë whom he had asked along, if Michael had been left receding in the rearview mirror of the Beckers' car. The Beckers trusted each other to hold the fort, responsibilities shifting as circumstances dictated. When nothing else makes sense, it is only your relationship to one person, and one person alone, that stands any chance of protecting you against the world. He wished this was a realization he could have had while he was still with Jennifer.

When the car was moving Zandt asked Michael for the address. Zandt told him to drive there, and refused to answer any of Michael's questions. 'You're going to have to see it' was all he would say. 'You're going to have to be there.'

Becker's post-Euclidean understanding of the geometry of LA meant it took nearly forty minutes to get back the other side of the city, but then they were climbing up into the hills and passing houses that got bigger and bigger with every turn, until they were so big that you couldn't even see them from the road.

Finally they came to a cul-de-sac. On either side lay tall security gates. The headlights revealed another car parked discreetly a little way up the road. Nina was leaning against it, her arms firmly folded and one eyebrow raised. Essence of Nina.

'This is it,' Michael said. 'This is where he lives.' He wasn't stupid.

He had begun to make the journey, even if it had yet to reach a fully conscious level. 'What do I say?'

Zandt got out of the car. Nina was more than ready to ask some questions, but he held up a hand and she kept her peace.

'Just get us inside,' he told Michael.

Becker went up to the gatepost and pressed a button. He spoke briefly, and the gates opened within moments.

Then Zandt was walking fast up the path, with Michael and Nina struggling to keep up.

When they reached the house the door was open, and a slim man was standing in the light glow from within. The vastness of the estate stretched out on either side. Zandt grabbed Michael's arm, and shoved him in front as they covered the final yards.

'Hey, Michael,' the man said. 'Who's your friend?'

Zandt stepped out from behind and grabbed Charles Wang by the throat. With his other hand he hit him twice, short-arm punches to the middle of the face.

Nina stared. 'John, what the *hell* are you doing?'

'Shut the door.' Zandt shoved Wang back into the vast foyer of the house. He punched him again, threw him backward to crash into the white marble of the wall. Picked him up and smacked him into a French-style mirror, shattering the top half.

A very young man in a white jacket came running out of a doorway under the staircase which swept around the foyer to the upper floor. He found that Zandt had a gun, and that it was pointing at his face.

'Go back inside, Julio,' Wang said. His voice was steady.

'Yes, Julio,' Zandt said. 'Go somewhere else and be *very quiet*. You pick up the phone, then when I'm finished with this fuck I'm going to hunt you down and pull your fucking head off.'

The boy backed rapidly out of sight.

Zandt turned the gun back on Wang, who half-lay on the floor by the bottom of the mirror, crumpled as if his back was broken.

'Aren't you going to run?' Zandt asked. He kicked him hard, in the side. 'Try to get away?'

'*Stop it,*' Nina shouted. '*Tell me what's going on.*'

Suddenly Wang was in movement, a fluid push up from the floor. Zandt brought the barrel of the gun hammering down into his face, stopping him dead in his tracks. Wang made a short clicking sound in his throat, and dropped back to the ground.

Zandt forced his head up. Wang's eyes stared back at him through blood that began to run down from a cut on his forehead. In them Zandt saw nothing but weakness and guile.

'We fucked up,' Zandt said. 'We looked at level one. We missed level two. We didn't even dream about a level three.'

Wang smiled up at him as if wondering how much he'd cost to buy. Zandt let go of his throat and slapped his face hard. 'Look at *him*,' he shouted. 'Not me. Look at Michael.'

Wang seemed for a moment as if he was going to try to run again, but the jab of the gun in his throat convinced him to stay. He slowly turned his eyes toward Michael Becker.

'We never caught The Upright Man,' Zandt said, 'because we were looking for the person who abducted the girls. The reason why we didn't find the man who *abducted* the girls was that there was no common link, because they were abducted by different men. Today I looked at some other girls, girls who were similar and disappeared at around the same time. In the end I looked at two in particular. Two girls from New York, who couldn't possibly be connected with The Upright Man, because they went missing on the opposite side of the country at exactly the same time as he was working here.'

Wang blinked, tried to turn his eyes away from Becker's face. Zandt shoved the gun deeper into his windpipe, and the eyes swivelled back.

'One girl's father is a development exec for Miramax on the East Coast. The mother of the other girl is halfway up a brokering company who mainly deals with private banks in Switzerland *but* who also – as I established this very afternoon – has a sideline in using the banks' client lists to find sleeping partners for low-budget film production in Europe. But these are New York girls, right? We're looking for West Coast girls. So I called on Gloria Neiden before I called you. I asked her to list every single person she worked with in the year before her best friend's daughter wound up dead. Every partner, half-partner, agent, exec, financier, loser and wannabe. It took a while, because Mrs Neiden is flaky these days and it's a hard thing to ask someone to remember. But eventually a name came up.'

Michael Becker stood a couple of yards behind Zandt, staring into the eyes of a man he had sat in sunny offices with, emailed jokes to, hugged after near-successful runs for the television end-zones. The man who had visited his house a hundred times, who had come to family dinners, who had sat in his daughter's bedroom and chatted to her about what a fine time she'd had in England. Who'd known that talking about England might be a way to hold her attention for long enough for the right moment to arrive to abduct her.

Wang said nothing.

'Charles doesn't kill the girls,' Zandt said. 'He doesn't abduct them either. That would be dangerous. Charles doesn't want real danger. He wants power, and kicks, and a feeling that he moves in myste-rious ways. All Charles does is pass on information. Charles can find special girls, *quality* girls. Charles works on commission, I'm sure, but mainly Charles works for fun.'

'Charles,' Michael said, 'Say something. Tell me this isn't right.'

'Yes. Tell us how much you get per girl,' Zandt said. 'Explain why, when these people could pluck people off the street, it means so much more to them to reach directly into families. To steal from people who are supposed to be your friends. Explain the thrill of that, because we really fucking want to know.'

Without warning he stepped back and stomped viciously on Wang's chest. Then he was back in the man's face, shouting: 'Who takes them? Who does the abducting? Where do they go?'

His eyes still on Michael Becker, Wang licked his lips.

'You think I know their names?'

293

Zandt: 'Describe.'

'If I don't?'

Zandt moved the gun an inch and pulled the trigger. The bullet smashed into the marble just behind Wang's head and ricocheted viciously across the room. Shards of marble and glass sliced across the man's scalp and face. The gun was moved back to his neck.

Wang spoke fast. 'There are three I know of. There were four, but one disappeared two years ago. They all look different – what the hell do you want me to say? You think we meet up and have beers?'

'Describe the one who took Michael's daughter. You must have had contact with him.'

'It was all done by email and phone.'

'Bullshit. Emails can be logged and phones can be tapped. But two guys meeting in a hotel bar someplace, in LA, who's going to pay attention to that?'

Wang licked his lips again. Zandt moved the muzzle of the gun until it was square in the middle of his forehead. Wang watched pressure being applied to the trigger. His lips started to move, but the cop held up his finger.

'Don't just tell me what you think I want to hear,' Zandt said. 'I think you're lying, I'll kill you.'

'He's a tall guy,' he said. 'Blond. Husky,' he said. 'His name is Paul.'

Zandt stood up and wiped the man's sweat off his hand. He took a step back to stand with Nina, leaving Michael facing Wang.

'Is this true?' Becker's voice was barely audible. 'How. How could. *Why?* Why, Charles? I mean . . .' At a loss, standing in a house he would never be able to afford no matter how many studio asses he kissed, he fixed on something trivial but concrete. 'It can't be for the fucking *money.*'

'You're a little man, with little goals,' Wang said bitterly, wiping blood off his lip with the back of his hand. 'Silly girls who've never been fucked. An old maid imagination. You've never touched anything big, and you never will. You'll certainly never touch *her*, not now.' He winked. 'You'll never know what you're missing.'

Zandt was faster. He intercepted Becker, grabbing his shoulders and throwing all of his weight in the other direction. He was heavier than the other man by some margin, but still only just managed to hold him away.

'Didn't happen, Michael,' he said. 'It didn't happen.'

After a moment, the force in Michael seemed to drop away. Zandt still held him firmly, as Becker stared over his shoulder at the man who smiled up at him from the floor.

'We're not going to kill him. Do you understand?' He pulled Becker's face round, so that he could look at him properly. The man's eyes were wide, unseeing. 'I can't promise I can give your daughter back. She may be dead, and if she is then this man is partly to blame. But we are going to leave this house and walk away. That's the only thing I know for sure that I can give you. That you not walk out of here as a murderer.'

Becker's eyes slowly came back into focus. His body went slack for a moment, and then became rigid again. But he took a step back, and let his arms rest down by his sides.

Zandt put his gun away. The three of them looked at the man lying on the floor. 'You're going to have company very soon,' Zandt told him. 'Cop company, fed company. Company with search warrants. Better get the place tidied up.'

Then they left, leaving a pale man staring after them.

Nothing was said until they stood beside the car. Michael looked back up at the house. 'What am I supposed to do?'

Nina started to speak, but Zandt overrode her.

'Nothing. Don't tell the police. Don't tell your wife either. I know you'll want to. But not for the moment. Most of all do not come back up here. What needs to be done will be done.'

'By whom?'

'Get in the car, Michael.'

'I can't let you do that for me.'

'Just get in the car.'

Eventually Becker climbed in and drove away, the car barely

rolling down the road, veering slowly from side to side.

Nina got out her phone and started to dial. Zandt knocked it out of her hand, and it fell to the ground to skitter six feet along the road surface.

'Leave it,' he said.

She glared at him, but let the phone lie where it had fallen. 'So – did you really call the cops?'

'You know I didn't.'

Zandt lit a cigarette and they waited. Ten minutes later they heard the sound that Zandt had been expecting, the muffled report without which he would have walked back into the house and done what was required, regardless of anything Nina did to try to stop him.

And yet, as soon as he heard it, he felt utterly weary and not in the least triumphant. More as if by getting closer to the source of these events all he had done was further compromise himself; as if the smell from what lurked under mankind's surface was now so strong that he would never be able to wash it off.

She turned to look at him. 'So he's dead.'

'All he did was hand the girls higher up the ladder. We could have wasted days interrogating him and all he would have done is fuck us around.'

'Not saying you're wrong. I'm just asking what you're thinking of doing next.'

Zandt shrugged. 'Good,' she said, stooping to pick up her phone. Lights were coming on in porches across the street. 'Because it won't be too long before the cops do get up here. I don't want to be around when they do.'

She strode off toward her car, adding over her shoulder. 'And I have a couple of people who think they might be able to show you where to find a blond man kind of like the one you've just heard described.'

Zandt stared at her. 'What?'

'Hopkins and the other guy. He called just before you did. They have a video showing a man at half of the major-league atrocities of the last decade, including the school in Maine this morning. A guy who Ward also thinks he saw at this place up in the mountains.'

'If you knew this, why didn't you stop me with Wang?'

She looked at him across the roof of the car. 'I didn't want to save him any more than you did.'

Chapter 30

Neither Zandt nor Nina knew that, while Wang had killed himself, he had made a phone call before doing so.

First he had laboriously pulled himself to his feet, hands slipping in the smears of his own blood. He was unable to stand completely straight. He had been beaten up before, had volunteered for the experience on more than one occasion, but this was different. The cop had not been bearing Wang's pleasure in mind, and things were broken.

He stood for a moment, looking in the remains of the mirror under which he had given up his greatest secret. His face was marked and cut. Worse, it looked old. The expensive veneer of diet and exercise, of unguents and self-obsession, had slipped. He looked his age, and in a way that only someone who had done the things he had, kept his secrets as long as he had, could look.

He had never killed. He had seldom even hurt anyone. Not with his own hands. But he had been present at occasions where young men had been left lying in pools of urine and other secretions, barely alive. Where other men like himself had departed in their expensive cars and had been lucky not to end up as accessories to murder. He owned an extensive collection of videotapes in which such events were documented. So extensive, in fact, that it was very unlikely he would be able to find them all, much less destroy them, before the police arrived.

His father would never understand.

Neither, Wang suspected, would the men and women with whom he did more legitimate business – although he knew that some of them had their own secrets, that the inner fire that drove them to fame and success also drove them to darker acts, in which they strove to prove to themselves that they were different and better than everyone else. The adulation of others is never enough. Sooner or later we all need to be able to idolize ourselves, or external regard becomes meaningless. Substances and materials had been obtained, sobbing women paid off, sometimes by Wang himself, who had always been willing to be people's friend. A confidant of those whose desires transcended society's accepted norms. Who wanted to live harder and faster and sweeter. Who could understand that sex with the frightened was different.

It was one of these, a man who had reason to know how helpful Wang could sometimes be, who had brokered a link to some colleagues of his. The representative of this group had been a tall blond man. The man called Paul. This introduction had only taken place after some years, and it was longer still before Wang had come to realize that this man was not quite what he seemed to be, and that he – and the people he represented – had something more than casual pleasure in mind. He'd never been invited to meet them, which had irked him a little. But he had agreed to provide entertainment, to help the procurers find particular luxuries, and the policeman had been right: money had nothing to do with it.

Each has his own road, and experiences two births. For Wang his second nativity had come thirty-five years before, at the age of ten, with a chance glimpse of a naked servant through a window. A spring morning in another country, a sight that had stopped him in his tracks, blindsided him with the sudden awareness of all of the hidden things the world had to show. His father had been in his home office, from which wafted the sound of baroque music, measured and correct, bright and joyous. Wang had stood still for a moment, lost in a few seconds of sweetness. Most people could have experienced this without it changing their lives, but Charles had never been quite the same. From the smallest of acorns, very dark trees sometimes grow.

After that had come deliberate spying, then magazines, and videotapes, trips alone to parts of Hong Kong and then Los Angeles that not everyone knew. Again, for most people these would have been enough, even too much. The sin was not there in the material, or even in wanting it. It was in needing it, needing it before you even knew of its existence – needing it so much that had it not already existed, you would have had to create it. Blaming pornography is like blaming a gun. Neither created itself. Neither is capable of pulling its own trigger. You need a hand. The human mind is this searching hand, its fingers slender enough to find small gaps, and strong enough to pull out what it finds in them. It is similar, too, in that after a time calluses sometimes form, hard-nesses of use that mean that the sense of touch is rendered less acute. Hardnesses that may mean that something hotter or sharper is required to promote the same effect: and there does come a time when you are in blood stepped so far that it stops mattering what you tread in next.

In the last week Wang had experienced only one occasion when the fate of Michael Becker's daughter had crossed his mind. This had been in the context of hoping that Michael got back to work soon, because it looked like the studio really might decide to take a chance on *Dark Shift*. Laughable though Becker was in many regards, he worked hard, and he had ideas. Ideas, moreover, that were acceptable to the common mind. Wang had his own version of the *Dark Shift* treatment, written for his own amusement. It would not have been so acceptable.

None of this would be acceptable. Nothing he had ever done that he had meant or enjoyed. And without those things, there was little left to comprehend, and nothing left to live for. Without the memory and legacy of a spring morning, of a glimpse framed by music and the sound of the water falling in a fountain nearby, there was nothing to him.

By the time Zandt was lighting his cigarette outside, Wang had shuffled into his study. The initial shock was beginning to wear off, and his ribs were in agony. He called a number and warned a friend that someone had come too close to understanding the game they played, had perhaps come to understand it completely.

Then he sat back in his chair. There was no sign of Julio, though it must by now have been obvious that the visitors had gone. For just a moment Wang realized that, for once, it might have been nice to have access to someone whose point was not merely that of disposability. Doubtless the boy would have left the compound over the back fence, to run down the road into some other life. Like a smile from yesterday, he was gone.

Wang unlocked the central drawer of his desk and pulled out his gun. It had custom stocks made of cherry wood.

It was beautiful. There was that, at least.

Chapter 31

At 8.45 the next morning we were waiting in the car just along the street from Auntie's Pantry. It was cold and had been sleeting for two hours, and the sky was full of dark clouds. I had a pack of cigarettes and was smoking them one after another. Bobby had nothing to say on the subject. He was sitting with his gun in his lap and staring straight ahead out of the windshield.

'So what time are they getting up here?'

'No guarantee they'll come at all,' I said.

He shook his head. 'A cop with no badge and a *girl*. Fuck it. We're invincible. Let's invade Iraq.'

'There's no one else, Bobby.'

A nondescript car turned into the top of the street. We watched as it drove past, but the driver was a middle-aged woman and she didn't even glance our way. We were waiting for someone to arrive at an office, and had been since 8.00 a.m. We were hyped and jumping at shadows. Neither of us had slept very well.

'Okay,' Bobby said finally, pointing across the street. 'Weedy dude, red hair. That the man we're looking for?'

We waited until Chip was inside his office, and then got out of the car. I left the doors unlocked. The street was pretty empty. It wasn't the weather for window-shopping, and any real traffic through the town got routed another way.

I swung the door to Farling Realty wide open and walked right in, Bobby just behind me. Chip had disappeared into an office in the back. The big main room had four desks spread around it. Two of these were occupied by well-coiffed women in their forties, wearing boxy little suits, one green, one red. Both looked up expectantly, ready and willing to sell us our dream.

'Looking for Chip,' I said.

One of the women stood up. 'Mr Farling will be right with you,' she twittered. 'Can I get you a cup of coffee in the meantime?'

'I don't think Mr Hopkins will be staying.'

Chip was standing in the doorway to the other office. There was a livid bruise across one cheek and his forehead. 'In fact, I think he'll be leaving very soon.'

'Exactly what we had in mind, Chip. But you're coming with us. We're going up to The Halls, and we need someone to get us in. In your recent capacity as the only realtor working for them, you're in pole position. You can either come with us under your own steam or we can pull you out onto the street by the throat.'

'I don't think so,' he said, an irritating expression on his face.

There was the sound of a bell ringing as the door to the office opened behind us. I turned to see two cops. One was tall and black-haired. The other smaller and fair. The latter spoke.

'Good morning, Mr Hopkins,' he said.

'Do I know you?'

'We've spoken on the phone.'

'I don't recall the circumstances.'

'You called the station. We discussed your parents' deaths.'

Behind me I was aware of the rustle of Bobby's hand, as it moved

303

within his jacket pocket.

'Officer Spurling,' I said.

'He's here at my request,' Chip said. 'I saw you and your friend sitting outside. I've already reported the way you attacked me.'

'I saw it as a minor difference of opinion,' I said. 'Then you had a weird whole-body spasm.'

'I didn't view it that way. And neither do the police.'

'This is bullshit, Ward,' Bobby said.

Chip turned to the two women, who were watching the exchange like a pair of interested cats. 'Doreen? Julia? I wonder if you could go into the back office for a moment.'

'We've come for you, Chip,' I said. 'Nobody else needs to move.'

'Now,' Chip said, staring hard at the women. They got to their feet and trooped past him into the other room. He pulled the door shut behind them.

'It would really be better if you came to the station,' Spurling said. His manner was calm and very reasonable. 'I don't know if you're aware of this, but there has been damage to your parents' house and a hotel fire that seems to bear some relevance. Officer McGregor and I want to help.'

'You see, the thing is,' I said, 'I'm just not sure I believe that.'

'What's the deal with your partner?' Bobby asked Spurling. 'Doesn't say much, does he.'

The second cop gazed back at Bobby, but didn't say a word. That's when I started to get twitchy. Guy looks in Bobby's eyes for long with anything less than respect, he's either stupid or extremely dangerous or both.

'Division of labour,' I said, hoping the situation, such as it was, was salvageable. 'Maybe McGregor here is a dab hand at filing forms.'

'You're an asshole, Hopkins,' Chip said. 'Obviously it's genetic.'

Spurling ignored him. 'Mr Hopkins – are you going to come with me?'

'No,' Bobby said.

Chip smiled. McGregor took out a gun.

'Hey, easy,' I said, now very nervous. Officer Spurling looked even more surprised than I felt. He stared at the weapon in his partner's hand.

'Uh, George . . .' he said. But then McGregor started shooting.

We were on the move the moment Chip's face creased into his smug little grin, but it was still too slow. There was nowhere to run in the office. Hiding wasn't going to cut it.

Bobby's gun was in his hand and firing at McGregor. The cop took bullets in the thigh and chest. But the hits didn't make the sound they should have, and I realized he was wearing Kevlar. The impact was enough to smack him over a chair and onto his back, but he was soon struggling to his feet. Meanwhile Spurling remained stockstill, his mouth open.

I was a foot ahead of McGregor's bullet, having hurled myself to the floor in a roll. I came up behind Doreen's desk and shot back, catching him in the shoulder. Something swished right past my head, and I realized that Chip, too, had a little pistol in his hand. After that I really don't remember too much. I just emptied the gun at whatever came up. You get involved in a gun battle on an open plain, maybe you've got time to consider, to take note of the blow by blow, to think. You spend time thinking in confined quarters with two guys shooting at you, you're never going to complete the thought.

Ten seconds later the shooting stopped. By then I was jammed behind Julia's desk and I had a stinging pain on my cheek and fore-head where something had sliced across it. Not a bullet, I didn't think. Something that got hit and exploded. I was very surprised not to be more badly hurt. The contents of Chip's head were spread across the back wall. McGregor was nowhere to be seen, and the door to the office was hanging open.

Spurling had gotten hit in the leg and fallen over a desk. He was moving but not very fast. His head was still where it should be. I left it that way.

305

Bobby was pressed back against the wall near the door, hand clamped over his arm and blood coursing from between his fingers. I ran over and grabbed him.

We fell out onto the pavement, stumbled across the road, and I opened his door and pushed him in. A passing couple dressed in bright orange ski wear were looking back and forth between us and the shattered realty office windows with their mouths open.

'It's some movie,' one of them said. 'Got to be.'

'I'm okay,' Bobby muttered, as I climbed in the driver's side and started the engine. I jumped on the pedal and sent us hurtling down the street. 'I'm fine.'

'You've been shot, you asshole.'

'Slow *down*.' There was a stop sign right ahead, and traffic to be contended with. I eased off the pedal and by chance managed to squeeze through a gap and into the far lane. 'Where are you going?'

'The hospital, Bobby.'

'We can't go there,' he said. 'Not after that.'

'Spurling will back us up.'

'All he knows is a lot of shooting went down. They both got shot and a civilian wound up dead.'

'He knows that McGregor pushed it. And I can get us out on the highway and find the nearest hospital out of town.'

'Where they'll still have to report it and we'll *still* have shot some cops.'

'Bobby, *you've* been shot. I don't want to have to explain that to you again.'

While I kept us heading west, ducking back and forth between the lines of cars, he gingerly removed his hand from his arm. I glanced across. A fresh glot of blood tipped out, but not as much as I'd expected. Wincing, he pulled the fabric around the hole aside and peered at what lay underneath.

'There's a chunk missing,' he admitted. 'Which is not ideal. But I'll live. And we have a need more urgent than medical support.'

306

'And what's that?'

'Guns,' he said, slumping back in the seat. 'Big fucking guns.'

I left Bobby in the car while I ran across to the store. It was raining hard now, and the clouds were getting darker. Before I swung open the door I took a moment to gather myself. Many retailers like to cultivate the impression that they're selling machines that are only theoretically weapons. You don't want to run into a gun shop looking like you're thinking of using one right this minute.

Inside, a long thin space. A glass counter displaying handguns like jewellery, and behind it racks and racks of rifles on the wall. No customers and no reinforced shield. Just one white-haired fat guy in a dark blue shirt, standing around waiting for business.

'Help you?' The man placed two large hands on the counter. On the wall behind him were two posters showing the faces of well-known Middle Eastern terrorists. 'Wanted Dead' the legend said. 'Or Alive' had been crossed out.

'Want to buy some guns,' I said.

'Only sell frozen yogurt here. Keep meaning to take that damned sign down.'

I laughed heartily. He laughed, too. It was all very cool. We were having a great time.

'So. What kind of thing you looking for?'

'Two rifles with eight hundred rounds, forty clips of soft 45 and I don't care what kind, whatever's cheapest. Two vests, expensive, one large and one medium.'

'Whoa,' he said, still cheerful. 'Planning on starting a war?'

'No. But boy do we have a rodent problem.' His smile faded, and I was suddenly aware that he was looking at my cheek. I put my hand up and wiped it. It came away with a small smear of blood. 'As you can see, it's getting completely out of hand.'

He didn't laugh this time. 'Don't know as I can sell you all that.'

I got out a Gold American Express card and he was soon smiling again. He totalled up the cost of the items by hand, allowing me a

307

discount on the ammunition. If you buy in bulk the unit cost of eight hundred potential deaths is actually very reasonable.

He told me the total and I waved my hand, anxious that he just get on with it. I glanced out the window at Bobby. He had his jacket off and was wrapping a bandage round the wound. I'd picked this up at a veterinary supply store on the way through town, along with safety pins and microgauze. He was wincing a lot. I turned back just in time.

'Don't do that,' I said, pulling out my gun and pointing it at the guy's chest.

He froze, eyes still on me, hand a few inches from the phone. 'Don't tell me. Couple days ago a cop came in here, told you not to sell anything to someone by the name of Ward Hopkins?'

'That's correct.'

'But you're going to do it anyway, right?'

'No, sir. I am not.'

I took a step closer, and raised the gun so it was pointing at his head. I felt exhausted and frightened. He shook his head, and reached for the phone again. 'I ain't selling you nothing.'

The telephone was an old-fashioned model, and made an extraordinary sound when the bullet ripped into it. The man jumped back, very shaken.

'Yes, you are,' I explained. 'Otherwise I'll just shoot you and take what I need and you're in no position to whine because the gun I'm holding was bought from this very establishment. Guess what? This is how they get used.'

The guy stood still for a moment, working out which way to jump. I really, really hoped he'd just do as I asked, because I wasn't going to shoot him and he probably knew it.

Then his eyes flickered. I turned and saw that a young guy was heading toward the store. He was carrying a bag of sandwiches and wearing the same kind of shirt the fat guy was wearing.

I swore, lunged forward, and grabbed as many boxes as I could carry.

'You've been no help at all,' I snapped, and ran out the door, smacking straight into the younger guy and sending him sprawling into a puddle.

I jumped in the car, throwing the boxes of bullets into Bobby's lap. 'Didn't go well.'

'So I see,' Bobby said, watching the fat man as he came out the door holding a large rifle.

I slammed my foot on the pedal and reversed away from the building, as the first shot went high of the car. The younger guy made his feet again and ran into the store, pushing the other guy aside. I hit the brake and skid-turned the vehicle around, and then sent it hurtling back onto the road as a bullet took out one of the back passenger windows.

'Guy in the store had my name on a list.' I took a hard right turn. I wasn't heading anywhere in particular. Just getting us out of the centre of town. 'One question's answered, at least. How The Straw Men managed to get to my folks' house so quickly after I roughed Chip up last time. They didn't have to come at all. They had McGregor already here in town.'

'Adds up.'

'Something else that makes sense: McGregor and Spurling were the cops at the scene of my parents' accident. Except maybe McGregor was a little earlier at the scene.'

'And is now back at Dyersburg PD dripping blood on the floor and chanting our names. We're deeply fucked, Ward – very deeply fucked. What are we going to do?'

There was only one person in town I could think of who might stand a chance of wanting to help me. I said his name.

'Good call,' Bobby nodded, wincing as he settled back into his seat. 'Way things are going, an attorney's going to come in handy.'

According to the card he'd given me after the funeral, Harold Davids's house was right on the other side of town. Unlike the area where my parents had lived, with its hills and twisting streets, the houses here were laid out in a regular grid – albeit a grid with big squares and nice-looking houses sitting in them.

When we pulled up outside we could see that the porch light was on, along with one deeper in the house. There was a car that looked like the one I'd seen Davids in, parked a little way along the street. We sat for a moment, to check we weren't being followed, and then got out.

I rang the doorbell. There was no reply. Of course.

'Shit,' I said. 'Now what?'

'Call him,' Bobby said, watching down the street. I pulled out the cell phone and tried Davids's office number. Then I tried the home number, in case he disregarded the doorbell in the evenings or was deep in some show and hadn't noticed. We could hear at least two handsets ringing on different floors of the house, but after eight rings a machine picked up. The tape gave his work number, but there was no mention of a cell phone.

'We can't just stand here,' I said. 'Neighbourhood like this, someone's going to put in a call to the cops.'

Bobby turned the door handle. It was locked. He reached in his pocket and got out a small tool. I was on the verge of protesting, but didn't. We had nowhere else to go. He had just levered the tool into the lock when suddenly there was the sound of the door being unlocked from the inside. We both jumped.

The door was opened five inches. Harold Davids's face was just visible through the gap.

'Harold,' I said.

'Ward? Is that you?' He opened the door a little wider. He looked as nervous as hell. 'Good Lord,' he said. 'What happened to him?'

'He's been shot,' I said.

'Shot,' he said, carefully. 'By whom?'

'Bad guys,' I said. 'Look, I know this is not what you meant when you said I should call on you. But we're in trouble. And I don't have anyone else left.'

'Ward. I . . .'

'Please,' I said. 'If not for me, then for Dad.'

He looked at me long and hard, then stood aside and let us in.

His house was a good deal smaller than my parents' home, but even just the hallway seemed to contain about three times as much stuff. Prints, local art objects, books on a little oak case that looked like it had been made on purpose. In the background was the measured sound of classical music for solo piano.

'Go straight through,' he said. 'And be careful of the rug. You're dripping blood. Both of you.'

The living-room walls were covered in reproduction paintings, not a single one of which I recognized. The lighting was sparse, just a couple of tall standard lamps throwing shadows. No television, but a small and expensive-looking CD player from which the music was coming. There was an old-looking piano, the top covered in photographs, some framed, others simply propped up. An ornate carpet lay in front of the couch, the edges a little frayed.

'I'll get a towel,' Davids said. He hesitated in the doorway for a moment, and then disappeared.

While he was gone Bobby stood in the middle of the room, holding his arm, making sure that anything that fell out of it went on the floorboards. I looked around the room. Other people's things are so inexplicable. Especially older people. I remembered one time, on a whim, buying my father an old calculator for Christmas. I saw it in an antiques store and thought it looked cool and that he might like it. When he unwrapped it he stared at me, and said thanks in an odd way. I told him I wasn't getting the impression it was the most exciting thing he'd ever received. Without saying another word he took me through to his study, opened a drawer. There, beneath many years' accumulation of pens and paperclips, was an old calculator. It was even the same model. Davids's life was my yard sale: my retro was my father's once-newfangled. You are insulated from those you care about most by decades of durable time, like glass that seems clean but is a foot thick and impossible to break. You think you're right there with them, but when you try to touch, your hand can't even get near.

311

Davids came back in with a cloth that Bobby took and wrapped around his arm. Then Davids sat down in one of the armchairs and looked at the floor. He looked tired and pale, and much older than when I'd seen him before. One of the lamps was just to one side of the chair, etching lines into his forehead and accentuating the planes of his face.

'You're going to have to tell me what's happened, Ward. And I can't guarantee I can do much to help. My field is contracts, not . . . gunfire.'

He pushed his hands through his hair and looked up at me, and that's when a small pale light went on in the back of my head.

I turned, looked at the top of the piano, and then back at Davids. 'You're staring, Ward.'

I opened my mouth to say something, but found nothing there. I closed it again.

'What is it? What have you done?'

His choice of words, which I'm sure was accidental, somehow convinced me. The way they rhymed with 'have become'.

Finally I managed to speak.

'When did you meet my folks, exactly?'

'1995,' he said, promptly. 'The year they arrived.'

'Not before that?'

'No. How could I have done?'

'Maybe run into them at some stage. Somehow. People's paths cross in mysterious ways. Almost like there's something going on that even they don't know about.'

He looked down, back at the floor. 'You're being odd, Ward.'

'How long have you lived in Dyersburg?'

'All my life, as I believe you know.'

'So the name Lazy Ed wouldn't mean anything to you?'

'No.' He didn't look up, but there was no hesitation, no off note in his voice. 'Strange name, if you ask me.'

Bobby was staring at me now.

'Terrible thing,' I said. 'I never even knew his surname. Just knew

312

him as Lazy. Not a great epitaph, but I suppose it doesn't really matter now he's dead.'

'I'm sorry to hear that a friend of yours is dead, Ward, but I really don't understand what you're driving at.'

I took the picture off the piano. It wasn't a group shot. There were only a couple of those, and they were black-and-white, fading mementos of people long dead, frozen stiff in front of a technology they didn't really trust. The one I held was an informal single portrait in colour, taken by some friend long ago, with that washed out and pastel look where the reds retain their fire and the blues stay rich but everything else seemed locked back in a different time, as if the light that reflected off those surfaces was fading, no longer strong enough to reach the present day; as if that era itself was being unmade as fewer and fewer people survived who could remember the feeling of its sun on their face. A young man, in a forest.

'Play the Sodomy one,' I said, looking at a Harold from long ago. 'Put it on Don, big Don man the Don, put it on, Don, put it on.'

'Stop it, Ward.' This time there was a faint quaver in his voice.

Bobby took the photo from me.

'This picture must be from a few years earlier,' I said. 'Harold's younger and thinner than in the video. Hadn't grown his hair yet.'

I turned to Davids. 'You must have been, what – five, six years older than them and Ed, about the same age as Mary. And now you're the only one left. And that's why you didn't answer the door when we rang, and you're not picking up the phone tonight.'

Davids was staring at me. He looked about a hundred years old, and very frightened.

'Oh fuck,' he said, the words coming out as one shuddering breath.

I wanted to grab him, shake him until he talked, until he made me understand what had been going on, until he gave me some means of comprehending my life. But just as he'd shed eighty pounds in the last thirty years, in twenty seconds his face had lost everything I'd previously seen in him, the look you get through a lifetime of telling people where they stand in the eyes of written law. He looked thin, and frail, and even more afraid than I was.

'Tell me,' was all I said.

In the end it was fast and didn't take long.

He told me that a long time ago, there had been five people who were friends.

Chapter 32

Harold and Mary and Ed were born in Hunter's Rock, and grew up together. They'd lived small-town lives and there are worse things than that. Then they happened to meet two young newcomers in a bar and afterwards the five were always hanging around together.

My parents were already married, but soon found they could not have children. Gradually they realized this wasn't the end of the world. They had each other, enjoyed life as friends and lovers. There were many things to do and find: the years would not pass slowly, nor would they never be happy, just because when they closed the door at night it would only ever be the two of them in their cave. They got on with their lives, tried to accept the cards they'd been dealt. A couple of years passed in work and sleep and Friday nights, long games of pool that nobody lost.

Then the world tilted, and they came to realize that passing on genetic material isn't the only way of making your mark on the universe. Suddenly came an era that I suppose I've never really understood. In a flat cultural plain, mountains and gullies appeared, splitting the ground on which people stood. Demonstrations in the streets. Sit-ins on campus, students and faculty pulling together for the first time. Fights in restaurants that wouldn't allow blacks to eat at the same lunch counter. Police firing on citizens, children turning on their parents. Marches. Shouts of nigger-lover, fascist, queer, commie. Ideas hammered into weapons. Long evenings in people's houses getting stoned, talking about what should be done, talking about new ways of being, talking about talking about talking.

They were older than most activists. They had the time and energy to spare – and more perspective than either the teenagers or the angrily oppressed. Beth Hopkins got involved in the unionization of black domestic workers. Harold gave free legal advice to those who couldn't afford it, or to those whose race had always meant they caught the sharp end of the legislative stick. Don Hopkins set up a campaign to prevent whole neighbourhoods being demolished to make way for the beltways that were the first steps toward the post-modern American city, where the undesirables are fenced out of the centre by six-lane rivers of hurtling steel, and inequality is enshrined in the landscape. Mary and Ed were merely followers, but they helped out wherever they could, and whenever Ed was sober. Mary loved Harold, and Ed just wanted some people to hang around. They held down their jobs and worked in their spare time, these older warriors, people who by this stage were over that dread age of thirty and thus able to temper enthusiasm with a sense of what was important: to concentrate on activities that might actually help people, rather than just yield a warm glow inside and the chance to screw some other excitable young thing flushed with the adrenaline of protest.

For two years they waved banners and fists, gave their time and money and heart. A few things changed. Most did not. The status quo has stamina. Loud guitar and free love can only change so much. Gradually the flavour of the times soured, as the same old forces simmered together for another year. It was Harold who first noticed what was going on. He realized that the people coming to him for legal advice, veterans of hot afternoons spent bellowing at the cops, were in worse and worse shape when they showed up at his door. That peaceful resistance was generating more wounds as the months went by, and that the bruises and scars he was seeing were not all the responsibility of the police. That there were factions within the beautiful people, and that these divisions were growing more telling and violent than those between them and the authorities. That there were groups whose aims seemed much more simple and retrograde than progress, whose agenda held no action points, only darkness.

At first the others disagreed. It was just the dream going flat, a trend Don had predicted long before. The natural divisions were resurfacing, that was all: their flames fanned by the frustrated realization that the People's Republic of America was as far away as ever. But then the deaths began. The demonstrations where both cops and students would be found on the ground with glass bottles in their faces. The street fights that bubbled seemingly out of nothing. The rock concerts where a scuffle would break out and bodies and a gun would be found when the crowd scattered. The explosions that took the lives of innocent bystanders without advancing any sane cause by a yard. Some of these events were the work of people who thought they were doing the right thing, that armed struggle was the only way forward. But the worst events were created by people who had a different plan altogether. The people with the guns and the dynamite were more organized than the freedom fighters, and predated both them and their cause. There was a cuckoo in the tie-dyed nest, rubbing its wings and preparing to fly.

Many people backed out at that stage. The Summer of Love was already fading into the Autumn of Jaded Apathy, and drugs had laid many out cold on the slab. Ed wanted out. Mary did, too. They had only really been in it for the excitement, after all, for something to do with their friends. Politics as social life, slogan as fashion accessory. Even Harold wavered. He was a lawyer. His soul yearned for order.

'But Beth and Don,' Harold said, his voice dry and quiet, 'they couldn't leave it alone.'

They asked questions, tracking lines of conflict. They traced the printers of certain hate sheets, and their authors, and found that the bad grammar and hint of madness were often fake. They looked for the friend of a friend of a friend, the one who people thought had maybe been the one who brought the gun to the demo, or who had first broken a bottle, or could broker you an introduction to the people who were *really* doing something, not just talking. They looked, and they started to find.

Eventually the threats began. Two of their friends were found badly beaten, left for dead in the back of a car. Another disappeared one afternoon and was never seen again. Harold found himself without a job, the first sign that these people were a good deal better connected than the students and hippies whose protest they were hijacking.

And in the end my mother was followed one night, and abducted, and driven some distance and held in the car at knifepoint while someone whose face she couldn't see explained that if they didn't stop digging then their next homes would be shallow and for ever and in a forest where nobody walked. She was raped, by four men, before being thrown out of the car on the edge of town, naked and with her hair cut off.

After that my father changed. He hunted them down. For four months he and my mother left the world and everyone in it behind, plunging deeper into darkness until they found the candle shedding light in its centre. The others never knew the details of what went on during this time, only that my parents had changed. They still saw the Hopkinses, but now that they were no longer fighting the good fight there didn't seem as much to hold the group together. Don began to talk about strange things, about some big, loose conspiracy run by people trying to break down our society from within. The other three wouldn't listen, not at first. It sounded too much like the ravings of a couple whose grip on reality was no longer reliable.

318

And then one night the two of them had come into the bar where they all usually met. Mary had been drunk, after an argument with Davids, and didn't even speak to them. My father had taken Harold to one side and talked to him urgently. At first Harold had been reluctant, but in the end the three left together, leaving Mary in the bar with Lazy Ed. These two did the obvious thing and got shit-faced and then went into the woods and slept together. By the Lost Pond, in fact. Harold and Mary had stopped living with each other pretty soon afterwards.

The other three had driven for four hours to a place up in the hills of southern Oregon. They had been armed, and they came upon the place quietly. My mother and father had somewhat lost their perspective by this point, though they might have believed they had found it – that they had learned the harsh lesson that when it comes to the struggle between the people who believed in life, and those who believed in death, the battle had to be fought on the latter's terms.

The camp was in a clearing half a mile off the road, deep in the forest. A cluster of cabins, hand-built and arranged in a circle, the way things used to be. After my mother had looked at each man and confirmed they had been involved in the incident, the three moved quickly, and they shot everyone they found.

There was silence in Harold's living room.

'You went in and shot everyone? *My parents shot people?*'

'Not the women and children,' Davids said. 'And we didn't shoot to kill. But we shot the men. Each of them. In the leg. Or the shoulder. Or the balls. Depending.'

'I don't blame them,' I said. I didn't know whether I meant this or not. I probably did. 'If what you're saying is true, then I don't blame either of them for what they did.'

'Oh it's true,' he said. 'I was there. The last man we found was the one who'd held the knife to your mother's throat. We didn't realize it then, but this wasn't just some group of rednecks off on their own. They had a cause. They've always been around. Your parents found this man sitting alone in his cabin. And your father, the great Don Hopkins, junior realtor, put a gun to his face and shot him dead.'

I tried to see that night, to see my father in that position, and I realized I had never really known him at all. I felt as if information was spilling out of my eyes.

'Then they heard a sound from the other room in the cabin, and Beth went through. The man's wife had left him, or he'd killed her. Either way she'd left their children behind. Twins, barely six months old, wrapped together in a little cot and now orphans. Two little children, exactly what Beth most wanted and couldn't have.' Davids shook his head. 'At least, that's the way they told it. I wasn't there for that part. Perhaps they saw the children first. Maybe Beth found the little ones and your father thought he saw a way to make up for what had been done to her. Maybe they decided that they were allowed one shot to kill.'

'My parents weren't liars,' I said.

'So you knew about all this, did you?'

'They weren't liars,' I repeated, uselessly. 'And this is all crap.'

'What happened to the children?' Bobby asked.

'We brought them back to Hunter's Rock. Don and Beth raised them for a while. But in the end it was decided that they had to be separated. Beth was very, very unhappy about the idea, and so was your father, but the rest of us decided that it simply wasn't safe. The babies weren't the only thing taken from the man's cabin. We found a lot of papers and books. Some were very, very old. There was proof that your parents had been right. There was a conspiracy. The people up in the woods were part of it. Beth and Don thought that they would be able to change the way you were, that environment was more important. It was very big back then, that idea. Not so popular now, of course, not with all this fuss about the human DNA thing and all that. Now everyone thinks that chemicals explain everything.'

320

'The babies were split up,' Bobby said.

'They kept one, and the other was taken far away. The idea was that they might stand more of a chance if they didn't have each other to reinforce the way they were. Or maybe it was a neat little experiment, Ward, cooked up by your father. Nature versus nurture. I didn't ever really understand.'

'Versus *what* nature, Harold? If this is true, and all this happened, why the big fear about the nature of the babies?'

'Well,' he said. 'Because of your genes, of course. Because you were so non-viral. So pure.'

'Jesus Christ,' I shouted, 'You don't *believe* that shit, do you? You don't really think . . .' I stopped, suddenly blindsided. 'Wait a minute. This has to do with the social virus idea?'

'Of course. But how do you know about it?'

'We found The Straw Men's Web site.'

'But how do you even know about them?'

'Dad left a video,' I said. 'I had just found it when you came to the house that time. It had all of you on it, though I didn't realize at first. He left me a note, too. Saying they weren't dead.'

Davids shook his head, and smiled faintly. 'Don,' he said. 'He always planned ahead.' His smile was affectionate, but not only that.

'But if all this happened in Hunter's Rock,' Bobby said, 'how come you all came here?'

'We hung together for a few more years. We had some good nights, but it wasn't the way it had been. After a while I left. I came to Dyersburg. To start again. Mary came out a year later. It didn't work. But she stayed in town. For a long time after that, we were out of contact with the others. Partly it was thought to be for the best. Also, well . . . we'd done some pretty bad things. On the night it had seemed the right thing to do. We got caught up in it, I guess. Frustration that nothing in the world had changed, despite everything we had done, and we were still at the mercy of men like that. But afterwards it wasn't something that any of us really wanted to remember. For Mary and Ed it wasn't so bad. They hadn't actually

321

been there. But they were our friends, and so part of the blame bled off onto them. They knew about it, and kept it a secret with us.'

'My father and Ed bumped into each other once,' I said. 'Long time ago. I was there. They pretended they'd never met each other.'

'Not surprised,' Davids said. 'I don't think your father really trusted Ed to keep quiet. Though he did.'

'Did you know he was dead?'

'Not until you said so,' he said. 'I knew about Mary. I didn't think they'd go back for him. He wasn't even there.'

A car drove past outside, and Davids's head turned like it was on a string. He waited until the sound had disappeared. I'd never seen a man who looked more as if he was expecting bad things to turn up at his door.

'If you guys were supposed to be keeping apart, how come my parents relocated up here?'

'After over twenty years, and nothing happening, nobody coming for us, I guess Don started to feel that it was over. He was sometimes out this way on business, and he visited me a couple of times, and we shot a little pool, got to talking about old times. Before that bad night. The fun we'd had. The period when we felt like we were going to change the world. At first it was strange, and then it was like the other decades hadn't happened. He brought your mother up here for a weekend, and eventually they decided to move. Get the old gang back together. Be young again.'

'So how come they never told me that you'd known each other before?'

'Because . . .' Davids sighed. 'Because The Halls started construction just before they settled here, and Don got to hear about it. He got in touch, pitched to them. He wanted the business. He got it. And after a while he started to think there was something weird going on. After that, he decided we had to go back to pretending. He didn't really grow old, Don. Not like the rest of us. Your mother either, I guess. Most of us, comes a time when you're

322

prepared to let things lie. Not Don. You put a secret in front of him, and he had to know what it was. He had to understand.'

I nodded. This was true. 'So what happened?'

'He started poking around. Trying to find out who was behind the development, what they were up to. He became convinced it was the same people he'd run into years before, in Oregon. Well, not the same guys, but a better connected example of the same kind of people. That they were part of some worldwide movement. Some hidden group, moving behind the scenes.' He shook his head.

'You didn't think so?'

'I don't know what I thought. I just wanted him to leave it alone. Some people put too high a premium on the truth, Ward. Sometimes the truth isn't what you want to know. Sometimes the truth is best left to itself.'

'And they found him out.'

'They realized someone was poking around. Couldn't tie it to him, but there were a very limited number of people it could be. Things started to get harder for Don. Little things. I think they must have someone here in town.'

'They do,' I said. 'He's the man who shot Bobby. He's a policeman.'

'Oh Christ,' Davids said. 'Tell me he's dead.'

'What happened to my parents, Harold? What happened that night?'

'Don decided they had to leave, to disappear. It wasn't a story he could take to anyone. Even if they believed it, he'd have been admitting to murder. But I think he'd also decided that he was going to deal with them for good. I don't know how the hell he thought he was going to do that. The four of us had a combined age of about two hundred and fifty years. But . . . we were going to fake their death, make it look like they were out of the picture. Let The Straw Men think it was over. It was all organized.'

My heart skipped a beat, remembering the note left inside my father's chair, and realizing that he could have closed up UnRealty to make The Straw Men think it was all over, before coming back for them in some way. He'd done it to protect me. It wasn't because he'd distrusted me, and it didn't mean that they were . . .

Davids saw my face, and shook his head.

'They got to them first,' he said. 'Two days before we were going to do it. They were going to drive up to Lake Ely on the Sunday, go boating in the afternoon. Have an accident. Bodies never found. Then on Friday . . . well, you know what happened. They're dead, Ward. I'm sorry. They weren't supposed to be. But they're really dead. And soon, probably tonight, I will be too. And then it will all be over.'

'Fuck that,' Bobby said. 'Fuck that from here to there.' He unwrapped the towel from his arm. It was pretty bloody, but no more came out of the hole in his shirt. 'I'm good to go. Let's get up there and start fucking these people around.'

Davids just shook his head. He looked jumpy. 'We're better off staying here.'

'Sir, with respect, I think not,' Bobby said. 'Last couple days have seen concerted culling of your old crew. If they knew about Lazy Ed, they sure as fuck know about you.'

I was only dimly aware of either of them. I was trying to absorb what I had been told, was trying to realign everything I had thought I'd known about my family. About myself. Davids looked at me.

'It's all true,' he said. 'And I can prove it. Give me a minute, and I can prove it.' He stood up and left the room.

'This is some weird shit,' Bobby said, when Davids was out of earshot. 'You believe any of it?'

'Why not?' I said, though I didn't know what to think. 'It fits, sort of. And why would he lie? He's definitely the guy in the video, so he knew them back then. We know I wasn't born in Hunter's Rock. And I don't see him just making it up on the spot.'

Outside I heard the sound of another car going past, but nothing came of it. I stared at the wall until it began to sparkle in front of my eyes.

'My mother called me, about a week before the accident.'

'Did she hint at any of this?'

324

'I didn't speak to her. She left a message. I didn't get around to calling back. But usually she didn't call. If it was either of them, it was Dad, and generally they waited for me to get in touch.'

'So you think . . .'

'I don't know what to think, Bobby, and it's too late to find out.'

'So now what do we do?'

'I don't know.'

Bobby stood. 'I'm going to see if I can scare up some coffee. This arm is starting to hurt like a motherfucker.'

I listened to the sound of his feet disappearing down the corridor. Some part of me, unbidden and against all the evidence, had apparently been holding out hope that all of this, everything since the phone call from Mary when I was sitting on a porch in Santa Barbara, had been a mistake. Had been wrong. This part had created the dream by the swimming pool, tried to convince me that there was something worth hurrying for, that there might still be people to be saved. Now I knew that wasn't true, that there was room for no final effort. My father had a plan, of course. He always did. But the note I'd found was all that had been left of it.

My phone rang, scaring the hell out of me. The number on the screen wasn't familiar.

'Who's this?'

'Nina Baynam. Are you okay? You sound weird.'

'Kind of. What do you want?' I felt numb, and not in a mood to talk about serial killers or anything else.

'We're in Dyersburg. Where are you?'

'34 North Batten Drive,' I said.

There was a beat before she replied. 'Could you repeat that?' Her voice now sounded odd. 'It sounded like you said 34 North Batten Drive.'

'I did.'

'That's the address of a man called Harold Davids,' she said.

My heart did a hard double-thump. 'How the hell do you know that?'

'Just stay there,' she said. 'Be careful. We're on our way.'

The connection went dead. I turned to the door as I heard Bobby approach, but his face knocked any words out of my mouth.

'Davids isn't here,' he said. 'He's gone.'

'Gone where?'

'Just gone. There's a door out the back.'

I ran to the front window, pulled the curtain aside. Where the big black car had been earlier, there was now a space.

We turned Harold's house upside down. There was nothing to find – nothing that meant anything to us. Just a tidy old house full of tidy old things.

After ten minutes there was a hammering on the door downstairs.

Chapter 33

Nina was still banging the door as I yanked it open. Zandt pushed straight past me and into the house, striding into the ground-floor rooms one after another. I turned to watch him go, my movements slow and vague. I felt like I was asleep, as if one dream had butt-joined into another.

'What's he doing?'

She ignored me. 'Where's Davids?'

'Gone,' I said. Her eyes were wide, with dark circles underneath. She didn't look like she'd slept in days.

'Gone?' she shouted. 'Why on earth did you let him go?' She all but stamped her foot. Bobby emerged from the kitchen.

'We didn't,' he said. 'He just disappeared. What's it to you, anyway? How do you even know he exists?'

She pulled a small pad out of her handbag and opened it, held it up to his face.

'The developers of The Halls are hidden behind about a million

327

dummy corporations,' she said. 'But on the plane I tracked them, and we got close enough. What looks like the trustee company is Antiviral Global Inc., registered in the Cayman Islands. Mr Harold Davids of this address is their designated legal representative in Montana.'

'Fuck,' Bobby said, his face pale. He turned and stalked furiously back into the kitchen.

I stared at Nina. 'You've got it wrong. I've just been talking to him. To Davids. He told me . . . well, he told me a bunch of stuff. He knows about The Halls, yes. Certainly. But from the outside. He's not with them. He's tried to help my parents get *away* from these people.'

'I don't know what he told you,' Nina said. She looked up at the sound of Zandt coming out of the back room. He shook his head at her and hurried up the stairs. 'But I don't think Mr Davids is what he seems.'

'What's Zandt looking for?'

'A body,' she said, simply. 'Hopefully not a dead one.' Her voice was slightly too flat, and I realized that beneath a hard-fought exterior, she was nearly vibrating with tension. The attempted throwaway was not convincing in the least.

'She's not going to be here. Harold is not your killer,' I said. 'He's an old man. He's . . .'

'Nina – you got a number for The Halls?' Bobby was standing in the doorway to the kitchen, holding the house phone.

She glanced into her notebook, flipped a page. 'We have 406-555-1689. But all you get is a recorded message and an interminable menu system. Why?'

Bobby smiled, sort of. He made a facial expression, anyway. 'Harold called that number. It's in his redial list, from twenty minutes ago. While we were in the house.'

'But . . .' I said. For a moment my mouth did nothing but move, without sound, as I tried to frame my objections. 'He looked freaked. You saw him. He was sitting here waiting, knowing they were going

328

to come for him. Like they came for Mary and Ed. You saw him, for Christ's sake. You know how he looked.'

'Sure he looked frightened, Ward. But of us. Of *us*. He thought we knew about him. He thought *we* were going to whack him.'

Zandt came back down into the hallway. 'She's not here.'

Davids had seen me with a knife. He knew we had guns. But I was still at a loss. 'Why would he tell me anything, if he's with them?'

'You'd found out he was part of the Hunter's Rock group. You mentioned a video, a note. You recognized him. He didn't know how much else you knew. You could have been bluffing him. Simplest thing is to tell you the truth most of the way, and then switch it at the end.' He swore briefly but viciously, seeming to take the deception very personally.

Nina's face was a row of question marks. 'Who are the Hunter's Rock group?'

'Later,' I said. 'We've got to find Davids first.'

A cell phone rang. We all reached at once, like strung-out six-shooters. But the call was for Zandt.

'Yeah?' he said.

'Hello, Officer,' said a voice. It was loud enough for us all to hear.

Zandt looked at Nina, talked into the phone. 'Who's that?'

'A friend,' the voice said. 'Though I admit we haven't met yet. Not my fault. You weren't good enough to bring us together.'

Zandt was very, very still. 'Who is this?'

There was a chuckle down the line. 'I thought you'd guess. I'm The Upright Man, John.'

Nina's mouth dropped open.

'Bullshit.'

'Not bullshit. Well done on finding Wang. And for encouraging him to do the right thing. We owe you one. He could have been an embarrassment.'

Zandt's mouth was dry, and clicked when he spoke. 'If you're The Upright Man, prove it.'

Bobby and I stared at him.

'I don't have to prove anything,' the voice said. 'But I'll tell you something to your advantage. If you're not out of that house in about two minutes, you'll be dead. All of you.'

The connection was cut.

'Out of the house,' Zandt said. 'Now.'

By the time we'd reached the street we could hear sirens approaching. A lot of sirens. I unlocked the car and jumped into the driver's seat.

Nina stood her ground. 'I'm an FBI agent. We don't have to go anywhere.'

'Yeah, right,' Bobby said. 'We shot a couple of cops earlier. They're not dead, but we still shot them. You want to stand in the middle of the road with your badge out, be my guest. This isn't HBO, princess. They're going to blow your fucking head off.'

The police had failed to double-up their approach, and we made it to the main drag without incident. I hung a right and put my foot down hard.

Within twenty minutes we were out of town and following the road as it slowly wound upward through the foothills. Nobody asked where I was going. Everyone knew.

Nina explained what had happened back in LA. I told them what Davids had told us. Zandt revealed, not in detail but sufficiently, his background with The Upright Man.

'Shit,' I said.

Bobby frowned. 'But how'd he get your cell phone number?'

'If he's tied in with The Straw Men, that's not going to tax them. They have a serial victim supply chain. They're blowing up things left, right and centre. A cell trace is child's play.'

'Okay – so why call? Why get you out before the cops got there?'

'There's no predicting why he'd do anything. But it wasn't just me he was thinking of. He knew I wasn't alone.'

'Davids told them who was in his house,' I said. 'He turned us in.' I was so bitterly furious that I could barely speak. 'And kind of funny, don't you think, that The Straw Men caught up with my

330

parents two days before they were set to disappear? They planned everything out, had it all in place, and then just before they side-stepped out of danger suddenly there's McGregor setting up the accident that killed them.'

'Davids tipped them off? Why?'

'He knew what The Halls was about right from the start. Then Dad finds out about them, thinks he's got a business opportunity, but finds that's not what it is. Puts Davids in a very difficult position. Say these are the same people, or the same kind of people, that they went up against thirty years ago. Davids said that only the leader was killed outright. The rest presumably survived, could have told someone what happened. The bunch who created The Halls could have found out that Davids was one of the raiding party – could even be why they contracted him as an attorney in the first place.'

'They're that well-connected, why use Davids? They could have hired anyone.'

'Right. But big-shot lawyers are also well-connected. Some of them even have delusions of honesty. The Straw Men can drop Davids off a cliff whenever they choose, and he knows it. "Work for us or it becomes known what you did one night in a forest. Or frankly, we just fucking kill you." What's he going to do? He's old, and afraid, and has everything to lose. He's also good. He's perfect for them.'

'Then your father gets too close, and Davids knows he's in deep trouble if he doesn't let The Straw Men know. So he tells them the Hopkinses are about to fly.'

There was silence in the car for a moment.

'He got them killed,' Nina said, quietly. 'The one man they thought they could really trust.'

'He's a dead man walking,' I said. 'There's no question about that.'

By the time we reached the mountains it had started to rain, cold silver lines against the darkness outside the windows. The river by the side of the road was a torrent. There was no other traffic.

'There's only four of us,' Nina said.

I glanced at her. 'So call for backup.'

'They're not going to scramble choppers on my say so. Most we'd get would be a couple of bored agents in a car in two hours, whose main goal would be proving I was a fuckup.' She looked out of the window for a moment. 'Does anyone here have a cigarette? I thought I might start smoking.'

I reached into my pocket, pulled out the battered pack and put it on the dash.

'I can't advise it,' I said. She returned my smile wanly, but let the cigarettes be.

Fifty minutes after leaving Davids's house, we swept round a long, gradual bend. I'd dropped our speed by now and Bobby was sitting up so he could look at the walls of the hills as they sloped up from the road.

'We're nearly there,' I said.

I saw Nina watching as Bobby and Zandt loaded their guns, then reluctantly check her own weapon. Her fingers were unsteady. Neither man looked the way she probably felt, but I could have told her it was impossible to tell what went on in boys' heads. There isn't a man of our generation who can't quote the 'Well, to tell you the truth, in all the excitement I lost count myself' speech from *Dirty Harry*. We all feel we should be capable of asking punks whether they felt lucky, of being our own portable Clint. And we all believe that someone, somewhere, will look down on us if we don't measure up.

Then Zandt happened to glance at her. He winked, and I saw her realize that it wasn't that after all. The movies might tell you how to behave, but the feeling ran far deeper, went back to the days when nobody wore clothes and everyone had their role and some tended fires and others ran with prey. The only difference lies in how big a group we feel a part of, the distance of our relationship to the people we'd defend to the death. Zandt was as nervous as she was. And so was I.

332

I pulled the car over onto the hard shoulder. 'That's it,' I said. About fifty yards ahead was the small gate.

'Nobody there,' Bobby said. 'Tell me again how the approach works.'

'You go through the gate, drive on grass. Swing round to the left and there's a hidden road, obscured by the trees. It winds up toward the high plain.'

'So there could be someone in the trees, or anywhere up the approach.'

'Pretty much.'

'Let's do it fast, then.'

I nodded. 'Everybody ready?'

'As we'll ever be,' Zandt said. I stepped on the pedal.

The car leaped forward, wheels spinning on the wet road. I sped down the remaining distance and then angled straight at the gate.

'Heads down,' Bobby said. Nina and Zandt complied. Bobby braced himself against the back of the seat and the car door, gun in his hand. A second later the car smashed through the gate, broken slats smacking up off the windshield and sending a spiderweb across Nina's side. The car ploughed into the long grass, started to skid. I struggled with it, brought it round.

I backed off the pedal until I had it again, and then headed for the band of trees, picking up speed. I ran over a hump and saw Nina lift into the air for a moment. She'd barely landed before she was bounced up again. There was a grunt from the back as Zandt suffered the same fate. Bobby seemed to have been clamped to his seat.

There was a lower, harder bump and then suddenly the ground was flat underneath the wheels.

I sped past the trees, wincing. 'You see anyone?'

'No,' Bobby said. 'But don't slow down.'

After a hundred yards the road banked sharply to the right, and then we were heading up the gradient. Bobby was glancing from side to side as I yanked the car round bend after bend, but no shots

333

came. But when he saw Zandt slowly bring his head up, he still reached out a hand to shove it back down. I saw him wince, but his shoulder didn't seem to be a big problem. For the time being.

'So where are they?' I asked.

'Probably all at the top, standing in a line.'

'You're a cheerful fuck. But I'm glad you're here.'

'Some kind of friendship thing, I guess,' Bobby said. 'Though this goes down badly, I'm going to come back and haunt you.'

'You already are,' I said. 'Been trying to get rid of you for years.'

We slid round the last bend, and then the vast gate of The Halls was looming above us up the rise.

'Still no one,' I said, slowing the car down.

'What now?'

'Other side of the gate the road pans left. Couple of large buildings. Entrance stuff, and what looked like storage. There's a high fence all the way across the pasture. The houses are on the other side.'

The other two cautiously raised their heads. 'So?'

'Front gate,' Bobby said. 'No way we're getting over that fence.'

'Entrance is where they're going to be waiting for us.'

'Got no choice.'

The car swept under the stone archway and down toward the clump of wooden buildings. A big light on one of them turned the parking lot a moonish and sickly white. Soon as it was all in vision, I pulled my foot off the pedal again. The car rolled into the centre of the lot and stopped. The lot was completely empty. I turned off the engine, left the keys in the ignition.

'What?' Nina asked.

'No cars. When I was here before it was full of cars.'

Zandt opened his door and got out without waiting for instructions. Bobby swore and emerged the other side, gun ready. The white light made them easy targets, but also showed that there was no one on the roof of the building. Nobody standing waiting. Just two big wooden buildings, and a stretch of fence in between.

Nina and I got cautiously out of the car. Nina's gun looked big and clumsy in her hand.

'That's the way in,' I said, nodding to the building on the right.

They followed me over and gathered either side of the glass doors. Bobby stuck his head out, scoped the inside. 'Nobody behind reception,' he said.

'We going in?'

'I guess so. After you.'

'Hey – thanks for the opportunity.' I leaned forward, pushed one of the doors gently. No alarm went off. Nobody shot at me. I opened the door and stepped in cautiously, the others behind.

The lobby area was silent. The background music was absent, and there was no fire in the grate of the river-rock fireplace. The large painting that had been behind the reception desk was gone. The whole room felt as if it had been mothballed.

'Fuck,' I said. 'They've gone.'

'Bullshit,' Bobby said. 'It's only been an hour. There's no way they had the time to clear out.'

'They had a little longer,' Zandt admitted. 'When we left Wang, it was maybe five or ten minutes before he shot himself. He could have called a warning through.'

'It's still not long. Not to pack up everything.'

'So maybe they were already on their way,' Nina said. 'You kicked the shit out of their realtor. Could be that was message enough, and that would have given them a couple days. Doesn't matter. We're still going to go look at what's out there.'

She started to stride toward the door at the end, the one that would open out into the inner area of The Halls. She looked filled with a kind of wretched fury, a horror that they could have arrived too late, that the phantom she had chased until it was the only light at the end of her tunnel had danced out of reach again.

We were standing still. She evidently didn't care if we came with her. She had to go out there. She had to see.

She didn't hear the shot.

By the time the sound reached our ears she was already falling, thrown awkwardly sideways to crash into one of the low tables. Her mouth opened to cry out, but nothing came. Zandt ran toward her.

I whirled to see a man in the doorway. McGregor. Bobby instead saw a woman behind the reception desk, and a muscle-bound youth emerging from a recessed doorway behind her, a door camouflaged to blend in with the wood panelling.

All three had guns. All were firing them.

The youth died first. His technique was pure television: gun held out sideways, gangbanger style. Bobby had him down with one shot.

I slipped behind one of the pillars and straight out the other side, getting McGregor first in the thigh, then the chest. I still only narrowly avoided taking one to the face, felt the hum as it spun past my head. I dropped to one knee and scooted behind one corner of the reception, praying the woman hadn't seen me. Reloaded, dropping half the bullets.

Zandt knelt down next to Nina, who lay crumpled, her hand fluttering toward the hole in her chest. It was high up, just under the right clavicle. 'Oh, Nina,' he said, oblivious to the cracks and whines in the air above him. She coughed, her face caught between surprise and denial.

'Hurts,' she said.

McGregor was still shooting. The woman behind the desk nearly took Bobby out before I took a breath and stood up, emptying half of my gun into her. Only when she'd slewed backward over the muscle man did I realize it was the woman who'd talked me through the fake entry requirements. I still didn't know her name.

Bobby was standing over McGregor, his boot on the cop's wrist. A gun lay on the floor several feet away.

'Where'd they go?' he asked him. 'And how long ago? Tell me everything you know, or darkness falls.'

'Fuck you,' the cop said.

'Suits me,' Bobby shrugged, and shot him dead.

While Bobby checked the other bodies, making sure nobody was going to wake up and start shooting again, I ran over to Nina. Zandt had her hand pressed firmly over the wound in her chest.

'We're out of here,' I said.

'No,' Nina said. Her voice was surprisingly strong. She tried to haul herself upright.

'Nina, you're fucked up. We have to get you to a hospital.'

She grabbed a table leg with one hand. The other one snatched my wrist. 'Be fast. But go and see.'

I hesitated. Tried to look at Zandt for support, but Nina's eyes held me.

Bobby arrived. 'Oh shit, Nina.'

'I'm staying here and you're going in there,' she said, talking only to Zandt. She looked in pain, but not like she was going to faint. 'Please, John. Make them go. All of you. Please see if she's there. You've got to go see. Then we'll go to the hospital. I promise.'

Zandt waited a beat longer, then leaned over, kissed her quickly on the forehead. He stood up. 'I'm doing as she says.'

I started to reload my gun. 'Bobby, you stay here.' He started to protest, but I kept talking. 'Try to stop the bleeding, and take out anyone you see who isn't us. You're more use to her than either of us.'

Bobby squatted down beside the woman. 'Be careful, man.'

Zandt and I walked fast down to the end doors. 'Whatever happens,' I said, 'we stick together. You got that?'

Zandt nodded, and opened the door. Outside was a path. White light from behind illuminated perhaps fifty yards with clarity, and was enough to suggest the hulks of large houses in the middle distance. None of them showed a light.

We started to run.

337

Chapter 34

'We should have brought a flashlight.'

'Should've brought a lot of things,' I said. 'Bigger guns, other people, some idea of what we're doing.'

We were standing at the first junction in the path. It looked like the main street of some tiny town where nobody had cars. The grass on either side was neatly trimmed. The pasture within the walls of the mountains, an area of only about ten acres, had been sculpted to provide each house with privacy and a gently rolling landscape. It seemed very unlikely there was enough room for a golf course, which meant that even their favoured realtor – the late Chip – had never been allowed inside. To either side of the path, set well back, were two houses. The path stretched out into the darkness ahead, leading via other forks to more dwellings, which couldn't yet be seen.

'You take the one on the left.'

'Did you listen to what I said? We don't split up.'

'Ward, there's how many houses? Nina's in trouble back there.'

'Getting killed isn't going to help her. You want to look in these places, we're doing it together. Which first?'

Zandt walked quickly up the path to the right. As we approached the house, I mentally checked off the features I'd seen on the plans. The house looked like it should be in Oak Park, Chicago, the suburb where many of the early mid-period Wright had been built. It was a beautiful house, and I hated the men behind all this for mis-appropriating Wright's grammar. He had been about life and com-munity, not individuals and death.

Zandt was less taken with the design. 'Where's the fucking door?'

I led him at an angle across the low terrace, to where a court-yard path snaked round to the left of the building under a balcony. A short series of steps delivered us round a corner to a large wooden door. It was ajar.

'Main entrance?'

I nodded. Took a breath, then pushed the door gently open with my foot. Nothing happened.

I nodded to Zandt once more. He went in first.

A short corridor, a little light filtering down from a stained-glass panel in the ceiling, the illumination turned green and cold. At the end, another sheet of detailed glass, screening out the next room.

Carefully we manoeuvred around it, revealing a long, low room. More stained glass, and clerestory windows high up. A fireplace over to the left. Bookshelves, and a seating nook. The shelves were empty. The furniture was in place, but there was no rug on the floor.

We walked very quietly across the room. The house was utterly silent. I held up a hand, pointed; Zandt looked – saw the entrance to another room, partly concealed behind a wooden screen. Nodded, and dropped back beside me. We approached it together, Zandt still glancing behind.

The doorway gave into a kitchen. It was darker, without the high-level windows. Split-level, with a breakfast area down the end. On the table was a single cup, sitting plumb in the centre. The interior was dry and the handle was broken. I opened a cupboard, and then a drawer. Both empty.

'This house has been cleaned out.'

Zandt nodded. 'Maybe. But we're still going to check it.'

We searched the rest of the house.

'There's somebody out there,' Nina said, meanwhile.

Bobby was squatted beside where she lay, braced in one of the big leather chairs. The lobby was in darkness. He'd been of two minds about this, reasoning that the lights had been left on, and that to turn them off would broadcast their presence to anyone else lurking in the compound. It was hard to believe that any such person could have avoided hearing the minute of heavy gunfire, however, and so in the end he'd dug around behind reception and turned them off one by one. It felt safer, though not perfect. The end wall was only partly windowed, and he thought they were safe from view, but he still felt like a sitting duck. The lobby was large, dark, and had three dead people in it.

'I heard something a minute ago,' he admitted. 'Hoped it was them coming back.'

Nina shook her head. 'John will check all the houses. They'll be a little while, even if there's nothing to find. Especially if. And the sound was coming from the front, not back there.'

He nodded. 'Ward will kill me if he finds out I've left you here alone, but I'm going to have to go look.'

'I won't tell if you won't. But don't be long.'

Bobby made sure her gun was loaded, and then dropped back from her to the wall. He scooted along it as low as he could. When he got to the main door he put his head out cautiously. Theirs was still the only car in the lot. There was no sign of anybody else, and he considered just staying put.

But then he heard something again. It wasn't loud, but it was definitely not caused by the elements. It wasn't a rain sound. It was mechanical, a short, isolated *pop*. It sounded like it was coming from

340

over on the other side of the lot, where the second building stood.

'What is it?' Now that he wasn't looking at her, Nina was allowing more of the pain to be in her mind. As a result her head felt very fuzzy, and her voice sounded cracked.

'I don't know,' he said. He turned to check, and saw that Nina was well-hidden in the deepness of the huge chair. Best he could do. 'Keep the pressure on the wound.'

Still keeping low, he pushed the door open. A very cold rush of air pushed past him, ushering in the sound of rain.

The rest of the house was empty. Four bedrooms, den, library, a music room. Empty and cleaned out. Stripped of any identification at all, though it was clear that people had lived there until very recently. No dust. Zandt and I came back down the central staircase, less quietly now, and made our way to the back of the ground floor. There was a second large reception room here, a little less fancy than the one in front. A horizontal band of windows showed half an acre of landscaped yard. I flicked the safety on my gun back on.

'Next house?' It was clear that this one didn't hold anything of interest. I was done with it. I was prepared to help Zandt look for the girl's body, if that's what he wanted, but my own needs were focused on finding a live Straw Man or two. And sitting them down, and getting them to explain a few things. Nothing else could hold my attention. It was already feeling too late.

'I'll take a look out back,' Zandt said. 'Then I guess, yes. Though this isn't looking good.'

He opened the door set in the middle of the window panelling, and disappeared into the rain. I stepped out after him, but stayed at the wall. By now I was increasingly sure that Nina had been right: perhaps this guy Wang had speeded things up, but the evacuation had started right from the moment I had beaten up Chip. I'd fucked up, in other words. Given them warning, and time to get away. I hadn't expected this would be their response. They were bunkered in. They were rich and powerful; this was their land. Why run? But

341

I'd still screwed it up. We hadn't discussed the matter, but I suspected Zandt felt I had, too. There was an increasingly wild look to the man's eyes.

As I listened to the sound of him poking about out there in the darkness, I noticed a long line of wire that lay along the bottom of the wall. It appeared from round the corner, and seemed to be buried in the beds by the wall. Cable, or something. Maybe the much-vaunted ADSL Net access. I was about to take a closer look at it when Zandt made a sudden coughing sound.

I hurried out into the yard. He was standing right in the middle, bolt upright. 'What?'

He didn't say anything. Just pointed.

At first I couldn't make out what he meant, but then I saw that a patch of ground just to the right seemed a little rounded.

I walked over and looked down at it. Licked my lips. 'Tell me that's a pet or something under there.'

Zandt just shook his head, and I realized that he hadn't let his arm drop yet. Instead he was pointing at another spot. At another mound.

'Oh Christ,' I said, my voice catching in my throat. 'Look at this.' Now I was looking for them, I could see that there were other mounds. Three short lines of them. Twelve in total.

Zandt dropped to one knee, pulled at the earth over the nearest mound. The grass slipped out of his fingers, but he got a clump out. Underneath was heavy, wet soil.

I dropped to help him, and we yanked and pulled at the ground. The going was hard and it took a couple of minutes to get down to where suddenly we had something other than soil in our hands and the smell became awful. I started back, but Zandt pulled out two more handfuls before abruptly giving up.

'We need a shovel,' I said.

Zandt shook his head. 'Anything in these holes is dead. Sarah may still be alive somewhere.'

'Come on, man – she's going to be in one of these graves.'

Zandt was already striding back to the house. I followed him, trying to avoid the mounds but realizing I must have stepped on at least one on the way out.

Back inside Zandt strode straight through into the first reception room. 'We're going to have to look again,' he said. 'We missed something.'

'I don't know where,' I said.

'So let's start here.'

We split to opposite sides of the room, overturning bookshelves, pulling furniture out of place. I was quickly convinced that there was nothing there to be found, but Zandt wouldn't be budged from searching every inch.

'This is going to take hours,' I said. 'I don't . . .'

I stopped. Zandt glanced up. 'What?'

I wasn't looking at anything in the room, but staring straight out through the main bank of windows to the front of the house. Zandt stepped over to where I was standing.

'You see that?'

I pointed down to the split in the path, about twenty yards away. There, lying where it forked into the routes to all the different houses, something lay on the ground. It wasn't very large, and at this distance it was impossible to tell what it might be. A small pile of sticks, perhaps.

'I see it,' Zandt said.

'That wasn't there when we came in.'

I flicked my safety off again and we went back out through the front door. I walked slowly down the path; Zandt holding a position back by the door, watching the other houses.

It did look like a pile of sticks. Short curved sticks, very white. Very clean. But I suspected what they were from a couple of yards away. I squatted down beside them, picked one up. Turned to indicate Zandt over.

As he approached, I took over the job of being ready to fire at anyone who might appear. Because someone was here, without

343

question. Someone who knew we were here, too.

After a brief inspection, Zandt said: 'Those are ribs.'

'That's what I figured. Human?'

'Yes.'

'So who put them there?'

'Ward, look.' About five yards up the path was another stick.

I walked forward, bent down to pick it up. 'Girl or boy?'

Zandt took the femur from me. Like the ribs, the leg bone was clean and white, as if some process had recently been used to bring it to museum condition. 'Can't be sure. But somebody not very old. A teenager.'

We stood together, watching either side of the path.

'Someone's leading us somewhere,' I said.

'The question is whether we follow.'

'I don't see we have any choice.'

'But we've already found the house with bodies.'

'A house. The first we looked in. Either that's a cute coincidence – or there's more than one.'

At the next junction there was another bone, just to the left of the path, as if indicating the way to the house on that side. We checked it quickly. This time the graves were spread around the side of the house, and better – or more proudly – concealed. It was only when Zandt realized that the small squares of stone set into the grass would not have formed a useful path, that we realized they were markers.

To one side of the house we found another bone, pointing the way deeper into The Halls. This bone was half of someone's pelvis.

Neither of us was sufficiently expert to tell the sex of the owner right then, though the condition of the bone and the width of the sciatic notch would probably have been enough to tell Nina that it belonged to a young female, of about Sarah Becker's age.

Bobby had stood nearly a full ten minutes in the shadow of their car, waiting. There had been no more sounds since he had left the lobby, and no sign of movement. It didn't make any difference. Something had caused the previous noises, and it seemed unlikely the problem had just gone away. He was remaining stationary merely to see whether that thing would make itself apparent, giving it a chance to present itself without him having to go looking. It was just possible that it was an animal of some kind. A deer, perhaps. Not probable, but possible.

After another couple of minutes he stirred himself. Nina would be worried if he was out here for too long, and he was by now very wet and very cold. His shoulder hurt a great deal. There was no point turning round and going back in. He had to check the other building.

He walked along the line of little posts that had been driven into the tarmac to mark the parking spaces. He was bathed in light during this, but there was no other way of approaching the building. It looked like a large storage unit, without the detailing of the construction on the other side of the lot, and there were no windows that he could see. He walked all the way round the front to the left side, and finally found a door.

A large padlock hung off it, but the padlock was open. He thought about saying Ward's name, to check whether he was in there, but he knew it couldn't be. Ward would have come back through the lobby. This had to be someone else. He nudged the door open, and stepped inside.

He found himself in a short corridor, with walls that only went about two feet above his head before giving way to empty space. Almost like a stable. There was a smell of some kind, though it didn't remind him of horses. Dim light came from somewhere in the building, down at the other end. Ten feet ahead the corridor was intersected by another at right angles.

There were two doors before the intersection, and he opened them both. One held the kind of supplies he would expect for a residential community, along with a long wall of files. The other, smaller room seemed to be a wine cellar. The racks were empty.

345

This didn't bode well. If they had enough time to clear out the Chateau Lafite, they were long gone. Strange to have left any files behind, in which case. He went back and checked that room. Pulled down a file box at random. There were no files in it, only a couple of Zip cartridges, both labelled 'Scottsdale'. He slipped them in his pocket and replaced the box.

He stepped back out into the corridor and edged forward until he came to the crossroads. He stood absolutely still for a moment before stepping out, allowing his mouth to drop open. You heard better that way, picking up the very quietest of sounds – something to do with the eustachian tubes. He didn't hear anything, but he noticed that there was a cable running along the floor in front of his feet. If it controlled the lighting, then he should cut it. It didn't look like part of the general structure, however, but like a more recent addition. He poked his head forward and saw that it ran down the centre of the corridor to his left. He stepped out of the corner, and went to see where it led. He got about two paces before something else utterly took his attention.

This part of the building was indeed arranged as stables. Small, self-contained areas either side of the corridor, divided up into cages about six feet square. Inside the first one, a shape lay on the floor. It looked like a person. A small person.

Bobby dropped to his knee in front of the bars. The shape was a boy, five years old, maybe six. He was naked. His hands and feet were tied with duct tape. It looked as though his mouth had been covered with the same material, but it was difficult to be sure because very little was left of his head. The blood on the straw of the stall was still wet. Taped to the bars was a picture of an attractive young male child, taken somewhere warm. He hadn't been looking at the camera at the time, didn't even look aware that his picture was being taken. It was a picture, Bobby realized, of the boy in his previous life. His name had been Keanu.

Bobby turned from the sight. Used his hands to pull himself along the front of the stall, along to the next. Another boy, a little older

346

this time, but just as dead. Another label on the cage. This time the picture showed the boy smiling into someone's camera, but a little uncertainly. As if someone had stopped him on a street corner on his way home from school, and asked if he minded, and he'd said no, while thinking it was maybe a little weird.

There was a quiet rustling sound, and Bobby's heart nearly stopped. He froze, until he realized it was coming from just the other side of the corridor, a few yards further along.

In this cage was a girl, maybe eight years of age. She, too, was labelled and photographed. Her name had been Ginny Wilkins. She was not quite dead yet, although she had been shot through one eye. The other was dry and flat, but her lower body was moving slightly. Some part of the nervous system still functioned, and would continue to, for a short while.

Bobby knew there were other stalls. At least another two. And he knew that this building would not have been left open by accident. That even when The Halls was in operation it would have been utterly secured against everyone except a select few. But he kept staring at this girl, in her holding tank, this place to which she had been delivered, and then stored, ready for the person within The Halls who had ordered her.

He felt stupid, and small, and sick. He felt ignorant and naïve. He had thought he knew the world's bad things, that he had walked its dark side with the best of them. Having Ward as a friend had helped. He felt Ward looked up to him, respected his wild-side credentials, and this helped Bobby to reconcile himself to getting older, from not walking the wild side any more. As he looked into the cage, unable to stop watching a piece of barely animated meat as it rolled and twisted its last, Bobby realized he had never even scratched the surface of what was possible – that the wars and murders reported in the news were barely more than sports news updates, death for show; that even most of the terrorists he'd interrogated had been dabbling in the shallow end of darkness. They at least wanted people to know what they had done. They were doing it for some god, some ideology, some fallen comrades or ancient grievance. They weren't just doing it for themselves. Bobby realized this made a difference, and also that if we *were* all the same species, there was little hope for us; that nothing we ever did in the daytime would bleach out what some of us were capable of at night. Some aspects of human behaviour were inevitable, but this was surely not. To believe so was to accept that we had no downward limit. Just because we were capable of art didn't mean what lay in front of him could be dismissed as aberration, that we could take what we admired and fence that off as human, dismissing the rest as monstrous. The same hands committed both. Brains didn't undermine the savagery. They made us better at it. As a species we were responsible for all of it, and carried our dark sibling inside.

He heard another sound then, from behind. He didn't look up immediately. Ginny was enough. He was already trying to work out whether he had to shoot her, to put her out of her misery – or out of his misery, perhaps – or whether she would survive the journey back to civilization, and what would be left to save if she did. He didn't think he could face another such decision.

He took too long working it out. It wasn't another child behind him. It was Harold Davids, and he shot Bobby in the back of the head.

Ginny Wilkins's legs were still moving, still slowly thrashing and turning a thousand miles from her home and those who missed her, for several minutes after Robert Nygard was dead.

Zandt was now oblivious to the rain, and had run through the last house without looking in any of the rooms. He was now just following the trail of bones, and he hadn't said anything to me for five minutes.

I hurried after him. The trail was no longer playing with us, proudly showing us what we were amidst, but merely leading us up the centre of the path. A small square, marked out in metacarpals, a patella in its centre. A long snakelike line of vertebrae, laid out at two-foot intervals, in the right order, for all I knew. The Upright Man must have set most of the trail well in advance, only adding the first pile of ribs at the last minute, when he knew we were here to be led. The rest of it had taken time, had been done with care. The killer hadn't gotten us out of Davids's house for our sakes, but for his: he'd already prepared a meeting, and he didn't want his work going to waste. He had, in one way or another, been directing our behaviour for far longer than that.

Finally a pair of clavicles, arranged in an inverted V, with the second femur used to turn it into an arrow. An arrow that pointed up the last fork of the path, to a house thirty yards away.

I caught up with Zandt and grabbed him by the shoulder.

'We're not going in there,' I said.

He ignored me, shrugging off my hand and striding up the path to the steps that led up to the house's terrace.

I grabbed his arm. 'He's going to be waiting for us, John – you know that. He's already killed the girl and he's going to kill us, and then he'll go find the others and kill them too. I know you cared about this girl but I'm not going to let you . . .'

Zandt swung round and smacked me in the face.

I fell heavily backward onto the wet path, more shocked than hurt, and began to wonder if I was missing something. Zandt hadn't even seemed to see me, hadn't looked as if he had any idea who I was.

I slipped and struggled to my feet, and ran after him.

Zandt walked heavily up the steps. Unlike the other houses, this had a door right in the centre of the front elevation. The steps of the terrace led straight to it, as if pouring him down a long, dark funnel. His jaw seemed to want to retreat back into his neck, as if it was only the spasming of his face and skin that was keeping it in place.

There was something lying at the top of the steps.

This time I didn't try to grab hold of him, but walked beside, accompanying him. I was only a step away when Zandt reached the final piece of the trail.

A girl's sweater, now sodden with rain. But neatly folded, and with a name stitched into the front. The sweater was a peach colour. The name was Karen Zandt.

Chapter 35

Something told Nina not to say anything. Not to make a sound when she heard the door to the lobby softly open. Her chest hurt, and the pain was spreading through her body, grinding and clawing through her stomach, down her right arm to where she held the gun. She didn't want to think about what it would have been like had the bullet hit her lower down.

The door swished shut. A couple of footsteps and still nobody said her name. She knew then that Bobby was dead. She couldn't see that part of the room without shoving herself up and turning her head, a movement that would have been both painful and fatally revealing. She tried to sink into the big soft chair. The footsteps continued, along with another sound. A rolling sound. Then something was put on the floor. It was quiet for a moment.

'I know you're here,' somebody said.

Nina's stomach lurched, and she almost said something. Almost confessed. Almost admitted that yes, here she was, as for a while

351

she had been made to do as a child. But that was a long time ago, and now her lips clamped shut and she gripped the gun as tightly as she could. Her hand felt like it wasn't working as well as it should.

'They wouldn't have left Bobby here,' the voice said, 'unless there was someone to look after.'

Footsteps. Exploratory. He didn't know where she was. But she'd be in here, and he'd do what he had been told. He usually had. Though on the outside he looked strong, capable, a leader, in reality he had always followed. He had been guilty and trapped for so long, little else seemed to make sense. Hopkins's father had done that to him. Taken a quiet, reasonable life and turned it into a mess. You couldn't help liking Don, in the old days. You were pulled in the slipstream. You met at his house, drank his beer, wound up with his ideas in your head. Wound up with a life you didn't recognize, and too old to do much about it. Wound up hating the follower in yourself, and knowing who to blame.

'Maybe you're already dead,' he said, 'but I don't think so. Anyway, I have to make sure.'

Nina tried to slip lower, but it hurt. And any move big enough to make a difference would make a noise on the leather.

'Bobby's dead,' the man said. His voice was old, but confident. It left no room for doubt. 'And soon the others will be. We could leave you. But loose ends will be securely tied, and that is my job.'

The footsteps were now replaced by a sliding sound, as the man carefully progressed a few inches at a time, masking the direction of his approach. Nina was so frightened she started to cry, an involuntary response from deep inside and long ago, a response she wasn't even aware of.

She slowly pushed her left arm behind her, bracing it against the side of the seat. She pulled her feet inward, a millimetre at a time. Her hand was shaking, and the nerves within her arm felt as if they were on fire.

'An auspicious night to die,' the man said quietly. His voice was a little closer now. 'This is not the end. Not at all. This is a new

352

beginning. A clean new world that starts with a bang.' He laughed briefly. 'Actually, that's pretty good.'

The sliding sound stopped.

Nina pushed with everything she had. Her body slumped forward out of the chair. She was awkward, locked up, and toppled forward, crashing down onto the glass table in front of her. She knew she'd screwed it up, but she now could see the shadow over to her right.

Davids nodded. 'Ah. There you are.'

She hauled her hand up and pulled the trigger. Once, twice, three times.

There was only one shot in return, and it didn't hit her.

She waited a moment that lasted for ever, waited for the second shot. It didn't come. She pulled a knee forward, pushed herself up, turned.

On the floor six feet away was a body. Now that she was moving, the prospect of further movement seemed almost credible, albeit bathed in a stunning white light of pain.

She planted her feet and tottered forward.

An old man with grey hair lay on the floor. He wasn't yet dead. She stood over him, bent at the waist. Harold Davids looked back up at her.

'You make no difference,' he said, and then was silent.

Nina wasn't listening. She was looking at something that lay near the reception desk. Couldn't quite make out what it was, so took a few steps forward.

It was a small drum. It had cable on it. Cable that had been linked to a set of connectors built into the reception desk, and that then went out the door.

The start of a new world.

She leaned on the desk and looked over, but there was no sign of anything that would act as a trigger. It had to be triggered from somewhere else.

She made it as far as the parking lot before one of her legs gave out, dropping her hard onto the asphalt.

The new pain, along with the splattering of frigid rain bouncing back up into her face, was enough to cut through her confusion. She started to crawl toward the car.

I pulled Zandt back from going in the front door of the house. He was almost impossible to influence by now, but I knew we shouldn't go in the front way. I'd already stopped him from going back to pick up some of the bones, had to pull the man's head into mine and shout Sarah Becker's name, to remind him there might still be someone to find alive. It didn't really matter whether she was dead, not by this stage. She was just someone we had to find. I'd changed my mind by now. We were going into the house. Whatever happened. If the man was there, so much the better, but we had to walk the path to the end.

I pushed Zandt round the side of the house, where we found another door. It was locked. I wished Bobby was with us. He would have been able to open it quietly. I couldn't, so I warned Zandt with a hand sign and then just kicked it open.

We ran in. Nobody was there to meet us. We swarmed left up a half-staircase toward the front of the house, to where someone would have been waiting for us behind the main door. There was no one in the room, just a big old chair with its back to the door, and a fancy bureau in a strange mottled wood. We ran, covering each other, through a layout that was now familiar. Hesitated in the back reception. It was dark and quiet and cold. But not utterly silent.

From above we heard a sound. A thumping sound, muffled and distant.

We headed back around, through the kitchen, toward the central staircase. Upstairs there were four bedrooms, rugs on the floor. Nothing there. Bathrooms. Nothing. Study. Nothing. But still this sound from somewhere.

Back into the first bedroom. The sound was louder here. But now it seemed like it was coming from downstairs. Back into the second bedroom: the sound was quieter in here, but still sounded like it was coming from downstairs. I spun on the spot, gun waving, knowing that any moment someone was due to appear out of the shadows, that no one would have left a trap like this and not want to be there for the springing of it.

Zandt ran back into the first bedroom, dropped to his knees on the floor. 'It's coming from under here.'

'We're on the second floor,' I hissed, but then I heard the sound again and knew he was right.

We pulled the rug aside. Floorboards. A small hatch built into them. Zandt bloodied his fingers levering it up.

Underneath, the face of a girl. Pale, gaunt. Her forehead was livid purple from banging it up against the floor above her, for God knows how long. She was alive.

Sarah blinked. Deep in her mind it felt as if someone had lifted her head, raised it just enough that water was no longer going in her nose. Her mouth moved.

Zandt put his hand down and stroked her face. He said her name again and she nodded, barely able to move her head. Her eyes were red and swollen. Zandt bent close. She tried to speak again, and I could just hear a croaking whisper.

'What's she saying?'

'Watch out for knocking wood.' Zandt bent forward and pressed his forehead against hers, as if he was trying to pour warmth into it. The girl started to cry.

I jammed my hands under the lip of the boards at her neck and pulled. At first they didn't move. 'He's nailed them down,' I said. 'Jesus wept. Help me, Zandt.'

They came up, but slowly and one by one. The girl tried to push, to help, but she was far too weak and if she'd been able to do anything from her position she would have done it long ago.

When the last two splintered off, Zandt reached down, slipped his hands under her back, and lifted her up. He hauled her over his shoulder, and that's when she saw my face and started screaming.

*   *   *

355

Nina had to stand up. She knew she had to stand. She couldn't reach the handle from down here, let alone open it, never mind climb in. She had already noticed, from her very low vantage point, that the cable Davids had been rolling now stretched right the way across the parking lot and into the other building. The building where Bobby presumably lay. And she knew it would go out into the rest of the compound, that this was the final defence and perhaps more than that.

She rested her head on the asphalt again. Her right arm, the arm that had stood her in such good stead all these years, that had done all the things she had asked of it, was now on strike. It was a part of someone else, someone who wasn't on her side and was not listening to what she said. It alternated between feeling like a washing glove full of Jell-o and a claw made of charcoal. This was probably not a good sign.

Nina swallowed twice, raised her head. The ground underneath the car looked dry, drier at any rate than everywhere else. It was possible she could just crawl under there and rest for a while. That's a good idea, her body said, that's a very, very good idea. Even her right arm seemed to come to life at the prospect.

So she rolled onto her right elbow and lunged up with her left hand. The flash of pain spiked her mind clear for a second, and then suddenly she was on her feet. She fumbled at the door with her left hand, couldn't work it, tried with her right – and was amazed that it did what she wanted. The door opened.

She fell forward, tried to pull herself into the driver's seat. Couldn't do it. Pushed herself back onto her feet, grabbed the wheel and stepped up. This time when she fell at least it was on the seat.

She dragged herself more or less upright, pulled the door shut. Scrabbled for the keys.

They weren't there.

'John, listen to me,' I said. 'She's sick. She doesn't know what she's saying.'

Zandt backed down the stairs away from me, his gun steady in front. Sarah was sheltered behind him, her arms looped tightly around his waist, both for protection and to hold herself up. She stumbled, nearly fell. Zandt had to turn to catch her, putting an arm around her shoulders and clamping her body to his. She had stopped screaming now, but only because her voice had dried to a rasp. The noise was still there inside her own head.

I walked slowly down the steps toward them. My hands were held up, and I was talking in a low, calm voice.

'I did not abduct her,' I said. 'I was not *in* Santa Monica at the time. I was in Santa Barbara. I can prove it. I have hotel receipts.'

'It's a half-hour drive.'

'I know, John. I know that. So if I was lying, why would I tell the truth about that part? I could have told you I was in fucking Florida. John, what the hell is going on in your head? You think I'd come up here with you, you think I'd be tracking down these people, if I was *one* of them?'

Zandt reached the bottom of the stairs. Still supporting Sarah, who was still trying to hide behind him, he backed across the wide corridor and toward the front reception room. This time they were going out the front door.

'There's no telling what people will do,' Zandt said. 'Including me. Make a move and I'll blow your head off.'

'It's not me.'

'She says it is. She says you were there in Santa Monica.'

I stopped walking. 'Okay,' I said. 'Okay. Here's what we'll do. I'll stay here. You leave. You get her out, and then you come back for me, and we'll talk.'

'I'll come back for you,' Zandt said. 'But we won't talk.'

Sarah felt herself falling, but the good man held her up again. Nokkon Wud was receding now. He was staying at the foot of the staircase. He was tricking them, she knew. He was making them think they could get away, and then he'd come for them. He didn't

357

have to walk. He could leap up through the roof and into the sky. He could fly over people's houses, he could dive in and kill them from above. He wasn't normal. He wasn't like anyone else.

She tried to say this to the good man, but it was too hard. She tried to tell him to shoot Nokkon now, but she couldn't and he didn't. He just kept carrying her, into the room at the front of the house. Sarah didn't have any choice about where she went. Her legs weren't working. She just had to go where she was taken.

Nina believed he wasn't going to be there. All the time she stumbled across the lot, as she pushed open the door to the lobby, as she navigated through the marooned hulks of oversized armchairs and settees, Nina had half-believed that Davids would have disappeared, that all she would find was an empty space on the floor. It didn't make any difference. She could not start the car without the keys. Either Bobby had taken them or Davids had. She didn't know where Bobby was. She had to find Davids, and she had to start from where he'd fallen.

And that's where he was. Hardly believing it, Nina reached down to go through his pockets. It would be easier to kneel, but she feared that if she did that she'd never get up again. She'd been able to get across the lot and back into the building, but she didn't know how much she had left. She slipped her hand into his jacket.

His hand lashed out and grabbed hers. His mouth opened.

'Mary,' he said.

She stared, terrified, at his face. He pulled her and she fell.

Her knee crashed straight into his face. The neck twisted with a crunch, but she was barely aware of this as her own head smacked into the floor.

She scrabbled at the slippery floor, got no purchase, then realized nothing was pulling at her. She twisted round. Put her hand back in his jacket. He didn't move.

She still had to find the keys. If that was the last thing she ever did, then so be it.

She found them in his right trouser pocket. Found three sets. Took them all. Slid along the floor, keeping as far away from him as possible, until she was by a chair. Maybe the chair she'd been lying in, she thought, though she wasn't sure. That seemed quite a while ago.

Triumphant with possession, it only took her thirty seconds to get to her feet. And then she went back across the lobby, over the body of the dead policeman, through the door, and back out into the lot. Her second wind was ebbing, and she knew it – not because she was hurting more, but because the pain was being occluded from her. Blood loss and shock. Her body was pulling up the draw-bridge. It needed its energy, and she was wasting it.

She got to the car, grateful she hadn't shut the door. Pulled herself across onto a seat that was now soaked with rain.

The second set of keys went into the ignition. She closed the door only then, knowing she wouldn't have to go find Bobby.

The engine caught on the first turn, and she blessed Ford and their wily little car makers. It wasn't like when she was young. Then you had to coax them into life, and as a result you loved them and gave them names. Come rain, come shine, these days the things always started. You didn't have to name them to make them work. All you had to do was know where you were going.

She rested her head on the wheel, just for a second, and felt herself blacking out. Jerked back up, put the car in reverse and kangarooed back ten yards.

Then shoved it into Drive, put her foot right down, and drove straight at the fence.

I kept my word, though I was afraid and confused and didn't want to be left alone in the house. I stayed at the bottom of the stairs, staring at a thick cable running up it, until I heard Zandt's voice from the front room.

'Oh Jesus Christ,' he said, and the girl managed another scream. There was a clunking sound. I ran.

In the front room a single lamp was now on, casting a sallow glow by the window. The girl was scrunched up in the corner, making mewling sounds. Zandt was on his back on the floor, his gun lying yards away. The cop had a very bizarre expression on his face.

Standing over him was a man with a gun. The gun was pointing right at Zandt's head.

'Get away from him,' I shouted, arms straight and my own gun ready. 'Get the fuck away.'

'Or what?' said the man, without even looking. 'Or what?'

'Or I'll blow your fucking head off.'

'You think?' The man finally turned to me. 'Hey, Ward,' he said. 'Long time no see.'

I saw my own face. The world tilted, flipped away.

His hair was longer, and a slightly different colour, dyed a brighter blond. There was something shifted about his features, but nothing more than the impact of being enlivened by a different mind. If you'd seen my face on some days, in some situations, it would have looked the same. Other than that there was no difference. Even our build was exactly similar. I blinked.

'Right,' The Upright Man nodded affably. 'So – you think you can do it now? Kill the only blood relative you ever had?' His finger tightened on the trigger of his gun. 'I'm genuinely interested to know, and don't let the fact you'll be killing John, too, influence your decision in any way.'

He turned his attention back to Zandt. 'Said I'd give her back, sooner or later.' He swung a kick at Zandt's face.

The impact jerked Zandt's head back so viciously that for a moment I thought his neck would be broken. I tried to pull the trigger. But I couldn't.

'You killed one of my co-workers, fuckhead,' The Upright Man continued. 'You put away men better than you. Just so you know, I tried to change Karen. For a long time. It didn't work. So I boiled her. But now I give her back. Did you like the "delivery" outside?'

Zandt rolled his neck, sniffed against the pain. 'I don't care what you call yourself,' he said. His voice was flat. 'I never have. Shoot the fucker, Ward.'

My mouth was open, and the insides were dry. My arms were not trembling, but locked like stone. It was impossible to move my fingers. I felt like I was missing the back of my head, as if I only lived in my eyes.

The Upright Man saw me staring, grinned. 'Weird, huh? We got a lot to talk about,' he said. 'But I know you're going to be a little wigged out, and actually we need to be leaving. As a gesture of good faith to you I'm going to leave one of these two pieces of shit alive. You get to choose one, and whack the other. You done nowhere near enough killing yet, my man. We need to get you up to speed.'

'The FBI is on the way,' I said. My voice sounded vague and quiet and hollow, even to myself.

'Don't think so,' The Upright Man said, confidently. 'They were coming, they'd be with you.'

'Why did you do it? Why did you kill my parents?'

'They weren't your parents, fuckhead. You know that. They killed our father and screwed up our lives. We should have been together, right from the start. Think what we could have done by now. The Straw Men got the money, bro, but we got the blood. We're pure. We're the heart of everything. We're what is true.'

Lying in the corner, Sarah's hands were over her ears and her eyes were screwed shut. She could still hear the man's voice. His hateful, hateful voice, the voice she had heard going on and on, saying thing after thing after thing until she thought it was that which would kill her in the end, not the hunger; that sooner or later he would say something and her head would just split rather than hear any more.

'My advice is you kill John here,' Nokkon was saying. 'He's got nothing left to live for anyhow. And that way you get to keep the girl. She's kind of scuffed up, but hey – we could have some fun.'

Sarah opened her eyes.

'Shoot him, Ward,' the man on the floor said. 'Just shoot him.'

'You're beginning to piss me off, John,' Nokkon said, kicking him again. 'You too, Ward. It's time to move on. My work on this mountain is done. It's time to fly.'

Sarah was confused. The man she'd thought might be her father wasn't, and he was lying on the floor. The other man . . . she didn't know who he was. A mirror man.

Nokkon talked to the mirror man, who wasn't moving. 'Come on, man, let's get this done. Whack the fuck. You know you want to. You've killed before. That's not an accident.'

Nokkon pointed his gun at the head of the man on the floor. He was going to kill him and fly. He'd said as much. And if the man on the floor wasn't her father, then her father might be at home with her mother and sister. But the thing was, their home had a roof. And if the house had a roof then Nokkon could fly through it, and if he'd do all this to her then there was no telling what he'd do to them.

Sarah slid her hands off her ears. They weren't blocking anything anyway.

'It's in your blood,' Nokkon was saying. 'I know you read the Manifesto. You've read it, and you'll know it's true.'

'It's bullshit,' the man called John said. Nokkon's foot lashed out immediately, stomping down on his hand.

'Ward, I'm rescinding my offer,' the devil said, his voice for the first time less than steady. 'You want to kill anyone, it's going to have to be her. This guy's been mine for a long while.'

He lined the gun straight at Zandt's face.

But then his head jerked upright. As if hearing something outside the house.

Sarah didn't even think. She leaped out of the corner.

I saw the girl shoot up from nowhere. Her body wasn't up to it, and the forward thrust was compromised before she was even fully on her feet. But the momentum drove her over Zandt's feet and barrelling straight into The Upright Man. He toppled over backwards, swatting at the girl's bony head, at teeth that were trying to fasten on his face.

One good crack across the eyes and she was falling backward, but the spell on me had been broken.

I fired once, missing him, but then Zandt was on top of him and I couldn't shoot again.

The two men rolled across the floor, kicking, punching. I stood ready to one side, waiting for a clear shot I believed I would take, which I knew I must take at any cost. Then I heard the noise from outside, the sound of a thrashed motor, of a horn being hit again and again. Bobby, thank Christ.

I saw the girl, lying still on the floor, blood flowing out of her nose. I ran to her, knowing this would have been Zandt's choice of priority. I pulled her upright with an arm round her stomach, stumbled toward the front door.

Yanked it open to be bathed in light. I couldn't work out what the fuck and then realized it was the headlights of the car I'd rented from the airport the day before.

I pulled the girl down the steps beside me, wondering what the hell Bobby was playing at but blessing his very soul. Then I realized there was only one person in the car and it wasn't him but the FBI agent and that she looked like death.

I ran round to her window. 'Where's Bobby?'

'Get in,' was all she said. 'Is that her?'

'Yes. Where's Bobby?'

'Where's Zandt?'

'He's inside. Will you tell me where the fuck Bobby is?'

'Bobby's *dead*,' she screamed. 'Davids killed him. I'm sorry, Ward, but get John, please, we've got to go. The whole compound is wired *and we have to go.*'

Cables. All over the place.

I yanked open the back door and pushed the girl in as gently as

I could. Left the door open and sprinted back to the front of the house, shouting out Zandt's name.

Thinking: Bobby's dead.

In the front room there was no one. Zandt's gun wasn't lying on the floor any more. I ran through the house, still shouting, gun out in front, enough of my head still stuck in the world of two minutes ago to be running hot with shame. I hadn't done it, hadn't shot my brother. But I could do it now. I knew I could. I could do it now.

I heard the sound of running from behind and to the side and swerved to pelt into the back reception area. Zandt came hurtling across the room at me. I remembered at the last minute and shouted, 'It's me, John, it's not him, it's me.'

Zandt's face was running with blood. He stopped, gun an inch from my head, trigger already half-pulled.

'Look at the clothes, John, look at my fucking clothes.'

A beat, and then Zandt shoved me aside and tried to run past. I grabbed him round the neck.

'Nina's outside. Bobby's dead. We've got to go.'

Zandt elbowed me in the stomach, knocking me backward. I grabbed him again, yanked his head in tight, screamed at him.

'*The whole place is wired.* We don't go, he's going to get us all. He's going to get Sarah.'

Zandt's rigidity flexed for a split second, and I hauled him into the front room. Pulled him backward across it to the front door, back into the light flooding through it.

Outside Nina was revving the engine, but still Zandt tried to resist, fighting like a bear against the arm looped round his neck. For a second I thought I might have seen a shadow flit across one of the doorways back inside the house, but it was soon gone.

When we were outside Zandt seemed to realize there were other people in the world, seemed for a moment to see a window through which there was something other than the man he had to kill. I shoved him at the car, stooping to pick something up off the ground.

Zandt climbed unwilling into the back, shouting and swearing, banging the back of the seat in front of him with his fists. Nina had slumped sideways, half into the passenger seat. I got in the driver's door and pushed her across, strapped her in.

I found the gas pedal, jammed my foot down as if trying to stand up. The car fishtailed backward on the wet grass and I pulled it round. Nina was banged into her door, and started moaning, rhythmically but quietly.

'Brace Sarah,' I yelled back to Zandt, pulling my seatbelt on, and then we were hurtling back down through The Halls, flashing past all the quiet houses with their treasures.

I thought I could hear bones crunching under the tyres, but that must have been in my mind and I hoped Zandt did not hear it, too. I hoped also that I did not see what I thought I saw, for an instant: the silhouettes of a small group of people standing up on the ridge of the hill surrounding the pasture, looking down on us.

We were going too fast. I couldn't really have seen it. When I glanced back, they were gone.

I aimed at the hole Nina had made on the way in, and almost made it. Boards flew past the windshield. Worse was a bad tearing noise from where the chassis took a hit from one of the posts on the other side, but the car kept on going. It nearly rolled in the left turn out of the lot and I thought everything had been in vain, but I got the wheels down again and took off down the drive, under the gate, and then right into the road out of the mountains. I nearly totalled the vehicle again immediately just around the turn, where Harold Davids had stashed his car, but managed to skid around it.

A series of hairpins, picking up speed, until a final long straight run down toward the stand of trees that shielded the road. I didn't even try to make this turn, knew in advance it wasn't going to happen, and steered instead through the trees, finding gaps large enough to get the car through, aiming us bumping and shuddering out the other side onto the grass. Somewhere between there and the road a flint took out one of the back tyres, and all I could do was try to stop the car rolling as it bounced and skidded down the final slope to smash through the low barricade with a scream of shearing metal.

The car skated across the icy road and clear off the other side into the Gallatin River, running shallow and fast and cold. There was a moment of stillness, in which we realized we were still alive, and then the entire world seemed to explode.

Slumped as I was, bent over and twisted round, all I could see was a new sun of light, bursting out of the mountains like the dawn.

Houma, Louisiana

This is a small motel, and has no room service. I have a small room, out on the end of an arm of equally small rooms stretching out from a dusty office, which is small. The television is old and shit. There is water in the swimming pool, but no one is swimming in it. Least of all me.

Tomorrow morning, early, I will move on. I can remember the name of the town where Bobby's mother lives, and have vague memories of him describing the street where he grew up. I think I might be able to find it. I would like to be able to tell her about her son. What he was like, how good a man he was, and how he died. Perhaps I will even find the graveyard where his father lies buried, and tell him, too. It's the only memorial my friend will ever have.

Ten days ago I sat in a car in Santa Monica and watched as John and Nina walked a girl up to a front door. Sarah was holding one of each of their hands: Nina's left, as her right was in a sling. Sarah was still very pale and weak, but looked a lot better than she had when we got her and Nina to the hospital in Utah. The medic on duty wanted to call the cops. From what he could tell, Sarah had been fed nothing but water laced with lead and a variety of other chemicals, some of them biological agents of a type associated with gene therapy. What was supposed to have been achieved by this, apart from acute poisoning, he wasn't prepared to even speculate. John knew, however, just as he now understood that – had they read the evidence properly – the bodies of The Upright Man's other victims showed similar attempts to create someone like himself through head trauma and sexual violence.

Nina used her badge, preventing the scene from going nation-wide. The doctors checked Sarah and Nina in for a week, but the next morning John and I came and stole them both away. Yes, they still needed treatment. But staying in one place was too much of a risk. Zandt called Michael Becker to let them know he was coming, and then we got in the car and drove.

We headed straight down through Utah, Nevada, and California and then across LA to Santa Monica, Zandt and I taking turns. Though she slept most of the way, I got to know Sarah a little. She was kind, and said I was very different, which helped. In time I believe she'll be okay, and I'll personally lay a bet that next time she's a lady who dines out (probably round about the year 2045, if her father has anything to do with it), she'll be having not a Cobb salad but a burger just the way she wants it.

When they'd reached the step of the Beckers' house, Nina let go of Sarah's hand and rang the doorbell. They looked like a painting for a moment, and then the door opened and there was a flurry of love that I had to look away from. I stared straight out of the wind-shield for a while, remembering the girl's last words to me.

When I looked back Nina was walking toward the car, her head down. Zandt was still with the Beckers. Sarah finally let go of him and went to her parents. Michael Becker shook Zandt's hand and something passed between them, though I don't know what.

368

John stepped back and let the family go back inside. He stood there for a little while, even after the door was closed. And then he walked back up the path and got in the car and we drove away. He is down in Florida at the moment, visiting his ex-wife.

When I saw his reaction to the sweater, I wished I had picked up one of the bones instead. I wasn't thinking clearly – it was an unconscious reaction, a realization that he might want something brought back out of the mountains. I guess a bone would have been better, something that had once genuinely been a part of her. But I think the sweater will give them closure enough. We arranged that we will meet again in a while. We have each other's cell numbers. He appears not to hold against me the fact that I was unable to use my gun in The Halls.

But any such reunion should wait for a while, I think. I hope his priority is meeting back up with Nina, after she has cleared her stuff out of LA. Seeing the two of them standing together on that doorstep, I saw something that I hope they come to understand. They're already together.

For long periods while I'm driving I find myself staring straight ahead. Not seeing what's beyond the glass, just allowing rushing images to run through my head like a strip of film. Sometimes I think about The Straw Men, trying to work out what's true and what's not. I want to believe that what underlies all of this is something more intangible than The Human Manifesto: that the ideas within it are merely a psychotic's way of explaining away the divisions that we seem addicted to. But then it occurs to me that the book many claim as the first novel, Daniel Defoe's *A Journal of the Plague Years*, was written in the aftermath of a disease that swept the whole of Europe, and could have been blamed on the way we live together, cheek by jowl; and that our major forms of entertainment, film and television, both burst into true flower immediately after world wars. I begin to wonder if fictional landscapes and aspirational schemes became important as soon as we started to live together in towns and cities, and if this explains the birth of organized religions at about the same time. The more crowded our way of living, the more interdependent we are, the more important our dreams have become – almost as if all of this is there to bond us together, to help us aspire to something missing, and so to edge us toward a humanity that is more than being merely human. Now the Internet is spanning the globe, knitting everyone tighter still, and I wonder if it can be a coincidence that it does so just as we have listed our genetic code, and are starting to tinker with it. The closer we're brought together, the more we seem to need to understand what we are. I do hope we know what we're doing with our genes, and that when we start to take out the parts that seem like faults, like imperfections, we're not removing the things that make us viable. I hope it is our future, and not our past, that makes the decisions. And I hope that now, when I realize something is missing in my life, I will continue to search for it; even if I know that it may only be a promise, and not really there to be found at all. Otherwise we become men of straw, women of shadow, left standing in empty fields where not even the birds come; waiting for an endless summer, when winter is already here. Given how we live, so far from what was once true, it's bewildering that we cope as well as we do. We dream our dreams to keep us sane, and also to keep us alive. As my father once said, it's not a case of winning, but of believing that there's something there to be won.

Often I think about him, and my mother, two people who are not here any more. Their deaths, like any deaths, are not something that can be made better. You cannot catch death and teach it a lesson, just as you cannot catch unhappiness, or disappointment, and as we have not caught The Upright Man or the group he has come to lead. Perhaps we will someday, perhaps not. Maybe someone like them will always be there. It's impossible to tell right now, just as at the moment I do not know whether the timed destruction of The Halls was merely a wholly successful attempt to destroy all its evidence, or whether the explosion was supposed to

370

trigger the vast pool of molten rock that is gathering force beneath Yellowstone – and so annihilate our culture, and the farms of the Western world, returning us to the way of life that The Straw Men so revere. Returning us, or taking us onwards, into the ruins.

Nina thinks so, from something she heard Davids say: she believes that The Straw Men have convinced themselves that they are the better hunter-gatherers, that their wealth has come from some inner 'purity', rather than fate, that they will prevail in any conditions. I don't know. It's not something I can discuss with anyone now.

The message was delivered to the hotel where I was staying in Los Angeles, the day after Sarah Becker was returned. It was from my brother. I don't know how he found me. An hour later I left the hotel, and I haven't stopped moving since.

The message took the form of a videotape. The first portion had been recorded since I had met him. He was clearly very angry, but had evidently not given up all hope of a *rapprochement*. He filled me in on some of the time we had not shared. His discovery on the streets of San Francisco, a baby boy with nothing to identify him except a name sewn into his sweater. Foster homes, a first murder. A period about which he was vague. His eventual work as a procurer for the rich and sociopathic, his discovery of a link between his employers and his past, his acceptance within a hidden group and first triumph in a McDonald's in a small town in Pennsylvania in 1991. The move into his own experiments in accelerated evolution through violence and abuse, the plan to create a pure bride with whom to create a non-viral strain. A plan he spoke of with an emotion that sounded unpleasantly like love.

The rest of the video is harder to describe. There is something very disturbing about it, and not just because of its subject matter or the implications of its existence. Seeing what looks like myself, in those positions and doing those things, is like having access into a dark dream world, a place where what I believe myself to be is negated, and I become the person I hope I am not. All Bobby and I ever saw were blurred long shots. The Upright Man, or Paul, as I

371

suppose I should call him, had made sure that there was crystal-clear tape of him at every one of those events. Tape taken by himself. Of him standing, smiling, in burning parking lots, of him laying cables and planting bombs, of him in dark rooms with scapegoats in America, England and Europe, giving them guns and plans. Of him squatting naked over the eviscerated bodies of young people known to be missing. Of him eating things.

And thus, of me doing them. Of me at the top of a towering pyramid of guilt, half an hour of evidence.

Even the tape he sent is no use to me. I can't go to anyone with it, and not just because the police of Dyersburg and probably Montana as a whole have joined the list of people I need to avoid. All the tape does is implicate me. There is no record of me having a twin. There's no record of me at all, except what's on the tape and inside my head.

Before she got out of the car in Santa Monica, Sarah Becker leaned across and said something quietly to me.

'You have to do it,' she said. 'Only you can kill Nokkon Wud.'

She's right. I can't do anything except what he wants me to do. I can't do anything except go find him.

In the meantime, as I clock up the miles, keeping on the move, I listen to past voices and think of things that were once done for me, the love that I was given. I don't know the answer to the question of what I've become, and perhaps never will; but I know at least that it is not as bad as it could have been. The note my father left for me, saying they weren't dead, remains true in ways he never intended. They never will be while I am alive. I wish I could have known them better, but like all such wishes its essence is not only that it came too late, but that it would never have been early enough.

The image of them I remember most of all is one I never saw, except through the medium of a television screen. A young couple, both holding pool cues, with their backs to the camera and an arm round each other. And when they turned, how my father grinned, and flipped his finger at the camera, and how my mother stuck her tongue out.

And later, how she danced.